# A DEADLY INHERITANCE

## CHARLOTTE VASSELL

faber

First published in 2025
by Faber & Faber Ltd
The Bindery, 51 Hatton Garden
London EC1N 8HN

Typeset by Typo•glyphix, Burton-on-Trent DE14 3HE
Printed and bound by CPI Group (UK) Ltd, Croydon CR0 4YY

*This book is a work of fiction. Any references to historical events,
real people, or real places are used fictitiously. Other names,
characters, places, and events are products of the author's imagination,
and any resemblance to actual events or places or persons,
living or dead, is entirely coincidental.*

A CIP record for this book
is available from the British Library

ISBN 978–0–571–39044–1

Printed and bound in the UK on FSC® certified paper in line with our continuing
commitment to ethical business practices, sustainability and the environment.
**For further information see faber.co.uk/environmental-policy**

Our authorised representative in the EU for product safety is
Easy Access System Europe, Mustamäe tee 50, 10621 Tallinn, Estonia
gpsr.requests@easproject.com

2 4 6 8 10 9 7 5 3 1

If you prick us, do we not bleed?

*The Merchant of Venice*, William Shakespeare

# Characters

*DI Caius Beauchamp and family*
An Irish-Jamaican detective in the Met, CAIUS is a foodie with a mortal fear of scurvy. He lives in a family-owned flat in North London with his girlfriend Callie where he loves nothing better than curling up with a good book. Feeling duty-bound, Caius joined the Met after the unsolved disappearance of his sister Lydia and is surprised he's still there. He is the son of pragmatic Jamaican-British builder MARCUS BEAUCHAMP and BRIDGET BEAUCHAMP who is from an Irish family but raised in London. Last year, some complicated inheritance tetris meant that Caius's grandfather, the Jamaican son of a second son, inherited a baronetcy from the single worst man Caius had ever come across: Sir Rupert Beauchamp, or rather RUPERT HAMPTON (see below). Caius is working through his feelings over his family's change in fortune.

*Calliope (Callie) Foster*
CALLIE, a semi-posh English rose with a whimsical streak, is a milliner by trade. She recently discovered that she is the illegitimate daughter of her frenemy Harriet's father, the disgraced MP and fast-fashion tycoon Peter Simpson. Unsurprisingly, this caused issues both for Callie's friendship with Harriet, and for Peter's marriage to Harriet's mother Jane. Both have ended acrimoniously. Callie met Caius on the front row of a fringe theatre when an actor threw up on an audience member, who was then discovered to be already deceased. Callie once went on a deeply

misguided date with RUPERT HAMPTON (see below), but thankfully lived to tell the tale and is now blissfully happy with Caius.

## DS Matthew Cheung

MATT is a thoughtful detective and Caius's wingman. He broke up with his girlfriend last August. They are genuine friends and seek out niche craft ales together.

## DC Amy Noakes

AMY is a quick-witted and intuitive detective constable, with a talent for rugby tackling creeps. She lives with her girlfriend Fi and their furbabies.

## Rupert Hampton (previously Sir Rupert Beauchamp)

RUPERT never had a chance. Packed off to boarding school at seven he sustained the expected emotional damage, not that that is an excuse for being a terrible human being. He and Caius first crossed paths when Caius suspected him of murdering his girlfriend Clemmie, whose body Caius found while out jogging one morning. Despite being innocent, Caius has harboured a hatred of him ever since. It has been lately revealed that Rupert is in fact the son of the RT HON. LORD ARTHUR HAMPTON.

## The Rt Hon. Lord Arthur Hampton Member of Parliament for South Rutland

A Tory Cabinet member who keeps an exceedingly low profile, despite his role as political kingmaker. He is the younger brother and heir to the childless 17th Duke of Shropshire who is suffering from colon cancer. He is married to GIDEON STARK-HOWE, known as JEREMY, a charming chartered surveyor who is generally thought to be the more decent of the pair, and much better company. After Hampton's involvement in Caius's most recent case, he has arranged for Caius, Matt and Amy to form a new special unit, which will investigate special crimes he sends their way. In return, Caius can pick a cold case that he wants to solve; any cold case.

# A DEADLY INHERITANCE

# A FRIDAY IN MARCH

# 1

## A Train Carriage

The train billowed steam as it pulled out of Victoria station chuff-chuff-chuffing like a wheezing, ancient and over-pampered lapdog as it went, although by the time it neared Chelsea Bridge it had started to gain a more respectable speed. The train carriage was art deco. The seats, upholstered in a green and mustard chevron-patterned velvet, were like grand armchairs, softly swelling and curling around the passengers who sat in them. A world away from the threadbare moquette and suspiciously sticky plastic horrors of modern public transport. The carpet was a swirling sea of deep emerald – as the train rocked and picked up more speed, the floor looked like seaweed swaying with the tide – and the brocade curtains were an even more bottomless shade of verdancy than the floor. The walls were clad in walnut marquetry – mostly geometric shapes – but above the fine head of a lovely woman, who had been staring out of the window wondering if she'd worn the right pair of shoes, was an intricate scene of an ancient castle perched on a cliff edge.

Calliope Foster, or Callie as she was known to her friends, peered down at her brown leather boots. They were positively Victorian. Tightly laced – constricting almost. The balls of her feet were itching with mild pain and threatening to swell. She wondered if she could take them off discreetly. Their table was covered in a crisp white cloth, so no one would see. No one would be scandalised at the hole on the heel in her left sock that needed darning – it was her last clean pair. If only they hadn't had to run up that escalator. She hadn't planned on doing a hundred-metre dash out of the tube in a pair of boots with four-inch heels that pinched at the best of times. A white-jacketed steward silently appeared at her lover – or rather 'boyfriend' in the less romantic colloquial – Caius's elbow, his presence greeted with politely silent and crease-eye smiles from both passengers, who then duly ignored him as he began laying out all the necessary accoutrements in front of them before pouring them each a cup of English breakfast tea.

Callie looked about the carriage at the three sets of other guests seated at their own tables. At the other end was a middle-aged couple: she was wearing a blue-and-white floral dress – accept-able but very provincial, rather golf-clubby – and he his best tweed jacket. It looked new and, therefore, wrong. A thirtieth-anniversary trip, paid for by the children, was Callie's guess. Next to them was a party Callie could only describe as chronically nostalgic – and that was saying something for a woman in a broad-brimmed felt hat and Victorian-style boots. The group was composed of two young women and a young man. One woman wore a mangy fox-fur stole and the other had victory rolls so crisp that Callie could almost smell the hairspray from the other end of the carriage. The young man wore heavy woollen pleated trousers held up by a pair of bright red braces. He had been wearing a mass-provided but convincing Fair Isle tank top, but the carriage had proven to be too warm for his faux-antiquated constitution and he had removed it. Callie could see that his shirt had a detachable collar, such was his dedication. He'd rolled his sleeves up and was silently filming the two women from across the table as they pulled poses while they drank their tea. She could understand this wholesale aping of the past, to an extent. No one really dressed up any more. Nothing felt special in ill-fitting, unlined polyester, but this felt like a cross between a costume and

6

something psychologically diagnosable. She wondered if they were the sort to forgo the convenience of a modern refrigerator for the sake of their aesthetics. The girl with the fox fur looked up at her and Callie gave her a quick tactfully dismissive smile before looking away. Beside Callie and Caius's table was an elderly lady and her granddaughter. They sat in companionable silence. They both looked suitably remote, with a comfortable, detached ease. They were used to this sort of thing; totally unfazed by it all. Callie saw the granddaughter look up at her grandmother and give her a small smile. The grandmother returned it with a gentle pat on the girl's hand. Callie strained to listen.

'You'll find someone,' the grandmother said.

'Perhaps.' She laughed despite a flash of sadness behind her eyes. The granddaughter had been checking her phone a lot, but Callie saw her turn it off theatrically and put it away with a proud flourish. She took some knitting out of her bag and resumed working on what seemed to Callie to be a baby hat. Now that she was really looking, Callie could see that the grandmother was quite grand, in a respectably understated way. She had that sort of smartness, and yet was somehow also a little dishevelled, which usually suggested family money.

Caius and Callie both took a sip of their tea – a house blend created for that specific train. Callie turned to him and said, 'What are you thinking about?'

'Nostalgia,' Caius replied, knowingly glancing over his shoulder at the three poseurs who had finally stopped filming and were instead busy inspecting the tableware. The girl in fox fur was peering at the underside of her saucer and could be heard by the whole carriage exclaiming: 'Oh, it is Worcester! You have such a good eye for china patterns. Do you think I should start collecting it?'

Callie squeezed Caius's hand. 'You look very handsome today. I don't think I've told you yet.'

'Handsome?' he asked, fishing for an even greater compliment.

'Yes, handsome. You know, dashing, debonaire and so on.' She had been the one to buy his rich olive-green merino jumper, but she couldn't take responsibility for the way he held himself in it.

'Do you mean fuckable?' Caius asked, quietly enough to uphold the sense of decorum that the carriage demanded.

'If you insist.' A flicker of amusement crossed her mouth and she smiled into her teacup. Their relationship was still new enough for this sort of nonsense to be commonplace.

'I'd say that you looked *handsome* too, in both senses of course, but is that a word that can be applied to a woman?'

'I'd rather be handsome than beautiful. You can't turn on the TV without being told by a deodorant company that you're Venus incarnate – but how many women would you call truly handsome?' Callie thought that beauty was fleeting but handsomeness was more about bearing, taste and sense of self. Exactly the type of confidence that Callie could never be accused of lacking.

'Do you want me to take a picture of you?' Caius asked. He wanted to remember how she looked in that dress until he stopped breathing, but he also thought she might want one for obligation's sake.

'Oh God.' Callie sighed. 'Yeah, probably. I bloody hate social media, but I guess this trip is "on brand". It annoys me so much that I have to do this rubbish.'

'Well, to send to um . . .'

'My "father"? Hmm . . .'

'Yes. You know, to show him that you had a nice time. This lovely outing was a present, after all.'

'Oh, I'll just send a thank you card in the post.' Callie was using correspondence etiquette to keep 'father' at bay. 'But I should put one on my stories I guess.'

'You don't have to share it publicly.' Caius was deeply cynical of social media. Privacy felt paramount these days. He had been mentioned in an article in *Tatler* a couple of months ago which charted his family's change in fortunes and had yet to live it down at the station. It wasn't every day that a lower-middle-class mixed-race bloke from Archway finds out he can trace his ancestry back to the Norman Conquest and will one day have to manage a significant country estate with everyone bowing and scraping and calling him Sir Caius. Someone had cut a copy out and sellotaped it to his computer screen. People who were all right with him before looked at him differently now. A sharp elbow to the ribs every time he went to the pub for a birthday or leaving drinks, a joke that he should be buying the whole station a round, everyone doffing imaginary caps at him in the corridor, being referred to as 'little DI Fauntleroy'. Matt and Amy, his team and to Caius's mind the only two decent officers in the building, had had the good sense to rip the piss out of him for half an hour and then never mention it again. Caius took the picture anyway. It would be the new screensaver on his phone.

★   ★   ★

A decadent brunch of eggs Benedict, buttery pastries and delicate bowls of passionfruit parfait, with a couple of sweet and yet bracingly strong Bellinis on the side had been served as the countryside passed by in a bucolic blur. At 2 p.m., the train finally pulled into Bath Spa station. It had been raining, and the gentle smell of petrichor lingered pleasingly on the platform, but not quite strong enough to disguise the overbearing aroma of Cornish pasty wafting from a nearby concession stand. Callie and Caius disembarked after the grandmother and granddaughter. The granddaughter was carrying the old lady's stick as one of the train's porters helped her down. Callie took in her surroundings with a confidence that had been bred into girls like her. She knew people were looking at her, and they could stare if they wanted to. She knew she cut a figure. It was her literal business as a milliner to be dressed so, to advocate for the trade. Her boots and broad-brimmed hat complemented her rich burgundy dress with its almost medieval sleeves. There was a nip in the air; Callie pulled her quilted jacket with its conflicting pattern of cream and black coils around her. Caius, in his cosy merino jumper and Belstaff coat that Callie had nearly had to fight a woman for at a sample sale, became highly aware of the curious looks from other travellers huddled up in black puffer jackets and navy-blue cagoules as they waited for their less flamboyant trains, and was embarrassed by their attention.

Callie decided that her boots fit her fine actually; the swelling had gone down with the three-hour journey so the pair gently meandered through the centre of Bath, taking in the creamy gentility of the town's patched-up Georgian architecture, to the fashion museum in the old Assembly Rooms. Callie took pictures of a piece of lacework she found intriguing, then they walked around the Assembly Rooms holding hands and staring at the ceilings. Callie commented as they went that this was where a bit of *Northanger Abbey* happened. Surprisingly, considering how a whimsical strain of romantic optimism permeated her being, Callie had never read any Austen before last month. She'd only ever watched adaptations. Caius had bought her the collected works, in beautiful clothbound editions for Christmas, and they now sat in pride of place on the bookshelf in their living room. Caius had formally asked her to move in on Valentine's Day after successfully baking a blue cheese soufflé. He was almost happier about the soufflé, but not really. He kept telling her that though. They had cohabited blissfully for over six weeks now and, bar a couple of moments around cleaning – they hired a woman in the end – March was thus far enchanted.

As they left the Assembly Rooms, Caius spotted, and was nosy enough to listen to, the granddaughter from their carriage pacing outside the entrance on a phone call. The old woman hobbled out of the building calling her name and she turned quickly, hurrying towards the entrance. The granddaughter steadied her by the elbow and gently led her over to a nearby bench. The heavens opened.

Caius checked the time on his watch after opening his umbrella. 'If we're quick about it we could go see the Pump Rooms before we have to board the train.'

'Lovely. Let's do that,' Callie said, taking his hand and looking up at him adoringly.

Callie leaned into him and further under the umbrella. They looked cinematic as they kissed in the pouring rain, until Callie pulled away and sneezed. 'I think I've got a cold coming on.'

\* \* \*

Only the wife returned from the golf-clubby couple in the corner. Their steward had been visibly confused. Callie saw him talking hurriedly to the wife, but the wife seemed to reassure him that everything was fine. Callie assumed that they'd had a fight, and he was staying to cool off in Bath. Deliciously dramatic. It was Caius who had first noticed the man's absence:

Callie had been too distracted by the vintage trio again. She couldn't place their energy. They were in quite lively spirits after a shopping spree – they'd handed the poor stewards a vast number of bags from Bath's many vintage shops when they reboarded the train – and were now filming themselves eating their starters. From where she was sitting Callie had seen the man playing footsie with both girls. She wasn't judging them, but she wanted to know what their relationship was. A throuple, maybe? Then she felt bad for trying to define strangers like that. It wasn't her business, after all.

Caius had popped to the loo between the pork and braised leek terrine and the Dover sole à la Meunière, leaving Callie alone at their table. The old lady was also alone. Her granddaughter had disappeared about five minutes before, looking agitated. Callie could feel her looking at her. Never one to ignore such things, Callie turned and amiably smiled to her.

'Good evening,' Callie said.

'Good evening,' the old lady said, looking her up and down. 'What a delightful hat.'

'Thank you—' Callie began, before being interrupted.

'My eldest granddaughter likes to dress up, a little too much if anything. My Rosie is more restrained, but she'd look lovely in a hat like that.'

'Thank you.'

'Who is it by? I doubt it's from a department store, it fits you too well.'

'I made it.' Callie saw the old lady's eyes light up and she instantly regretted telling her. 'I'm a milliner actually.'

'May I have your card? I may go to Ascot this year if my friend Daphne is up to it. She hasn't been well recently but it's important to have something to look forward to.'

'Of course,' Callie said, fishing out her card case – a sweet little leather wallet that Caius had also bought her for Christmas – from her handbag and handing one to the lady. She didn't really need the business, if anything she wanted to be less successful and more selective of her clients, but she didn't want to be rude.

'Oh, I thought I recognised you,' the old lady said, reading the card. 'I read about your father in the papers, and then about your boyfriend's family. I thought he looked familiar earlier, but I couldn't place him. I take it your father's stepped down.'

'Yes. Enjoy your evening . . .' Callie gave a weak smile and became intensely interested in her glass of wine as Caius returned to the table and they all resumed courteously ignoring each other's party – and yet failing to. The steward returned with their next course and the train chuff-chuffed back to London.

'I keep dreaming that someone's broken into the house,' the grandmother said to her granddaughter as she sat back down at their table. 'You won't be out too late will you tomorrow? One worries.'

'Don't worry,' said the granddaughter, putting her phone back in her handbag. 'I shan't be back that late.'

SUNDAY

# 2

## Marigold House, Barnes

Rosie woke up with a start. She was alone, naked and sticky. She found her phone: it was gone 3 a.m. Rosie read her messages, and struggled to remember the day that had led to this. The Boat Race was over. Oxford won. An appalling quantity of chilled rosé had been consumed. Rosie had nearly passed out in the pub loos. It had had bright pink wallpaper – a kitschy and repetitive landscape with a lady in a bonnet, a coy deer at her elbow, all under an apple tree like an old china pattern. Something proper and traditional to look at when having a not-so-tactical vomit. The deer looked like it was going to leap away in disgust as Rosie had slowly got up from her position clutching the toilet bowl. Her friend Lucia had called an Uber and Tristan, an acquaintance who had long hoped to be more than that, had seen her home safely.

She must have fallen asleep. She pulled her pyjamas out from under her pillow and put them on. Rosie felt like something had died in her mouth. Something had died in her soul too but she was going to pretend for now that that hadn't happened. She desperately needed a glass of water. Rosie crept down the staircase barefoot – finding her slippers was too much effort – and into the large entrance hall. It was cold and the air smelled damp. It had been raining out. She could hear the pitter-patter of yet more rain through the open front door. Shit. Rosie quietly closed the door so she wouldn't wake her grandmother, took a quick look around the entrance hall. There were no missing paintings or vases. She went to the kitchen and took out a glass from a cupboard, not bothering to turn on the light as she went. Rosie turned to go towards the sink but stopped abruptly. She'd stood on something sharp.

'Fuck,' she shouted, the shock of pain forcing her to hop as she moved over to one of the chairs around the kitchen table in the dark – treading her other foot in something sticky as she went. Rosie held up her injured foot, followed the soreness to its cause and pushed the offending shard of glass out between her thumb and forefinger and put it on the kitchen table. Rosie, even in her quarter-cut state, realised she should turn the light on to avoid further injury – although how a load of broken glass had ended up on the floor she had no idea. Had she already been in here when she came home? Had she dropped a glass and then gone to bed without dealing with it? That wasn't like her but then again everything after the third bottle of wine appearing on the table was an uncharacteristic blur. Her grandmother would definitely not have broken something and left it. Even at her age she'd have got a broom out. Rosie put her foot down on the floor. Well, she meant to. She looked down and instead of the black and white tiles she was expecting, she saw thick crimson blood beginning to congeal into a blackened sludge under the body she'd inadvertently stepped on.

# 3

## Frithsden Old Hall, Hertfordshire

Caius drove his battered Volvo, affectionately known as Sven, through the winding country lane. He pulled onto a grass verge – Callie's passenger side window pressed into a hawthorn that had yet to bloom – so a dusty old blue Range Rover could squeeze past. Caius carried on up the lane and turned right through a pair of monumental wrought-iron gates, past a little red-brick gatehouse with a dormant rose growing around the front door that the gardener and his wife lived in and down a long gravel path before pulling up in front of Frithsden Old Hall, his family's new house. Well, their old manor. This was not a three-bed terrace with a loft conversion. It was a Jacobean manor with priest holes and a bloody history. The sight of it gave Caius a fight-or-flight impulse that refused to be quelled by familiarity; by family.

Nearly every Sunday was like this now. Callie said she didn't mind it. In fact, every time they came to visit, she proclaimed loudly at how much cleaner the air felt and delighted in roaming the gardens, taking in tremendous gulps of particulate-free air. Caius opened the door for Callie. She climbed out, passing him a carrot cake that she'd baked yesterday once her train ride-induced hangover had subsided. She'd had red wine with dinner. It didn't suit her temperament any more.

'This is still so bizarre.' He gave her back the cake tin.

Callie squeezed his arm. 'There are worse things to inherit than however many acres and a house with a library. You could have had a congenital heart defect.'

'When you put it like that.' A doe was grazing in the nearby parkland. 'But I liked how things were. I like my little flat. I like my little life. With you.'

'You say that as if I'm going somewhere.' Callie turned and looked at the grounds, there was a ha-ha out there somewhere, and was amused by the idea of it. 'You never know, you might like what's to come.'

Caius nodded. His grandfather's inheritance had stranded him in uncharted territory, but at least he had Callie and while she didn't have a map, this whole world wasn't totally unknown to her. He knew there were dragons though. Lurking just out of sight.

'Shall we?' she asked, looking up at him as she cradled the cake tin.

'Yeah,' Caius said, kissing her on the forehead before heading into the house. 'My parents are going to love you.'

'I know.' Callie stopped in front of a seascape. She hadn't given much thought to before. 'Is that the one? The Turner?' she asked, taking in the confected light as it hit the surface of the sea. She could almost smell the Margate brine.

'It is.'

'Wow.'

'Yeah.' Caius felt funny about the painting. It was beautiful, but still. There was a running debate about what to do with the painting amongst the 'new' Beauchamps. Turner himself had wanted his work to belong to the nation when he died and Caius thought they should gift it to the Tate, but his father wanted to keep such a valuable asset. His grandfather, who had inherited the painting and so was the only one who could do anything about it, wavered between both. The fate of a daubed canvas didn't seem too important to him at this stage of his life.

'I'll take this through to the kitchen,' Callie said, weaving her way into the working bowels of the house. Caius started to follow her until he heard a familiar voice behind him.

'Caius, is that you?' his mother asked, appearing from another door.

'Hi, Mum,' Caius said, hugging her. His parents had taken the Eurotunnel home the day before after signing the paperwork finalising the sale of their house in France. The responsibilities of Frithsden Old Hall being too much for his grandfather, Caius's father Marcus had little real choice in the matter. They'd sent the furniture they cared to keep home in a removal van the week before, which was now being stored in an outbuilding, and had moved into Frithsden with Caius's grandfather, who refused to stay any longer in the nursing home he had been in. He wanted to live out the rest of his days here on his ancestral land. Marcus had hired a carer to come in and help with him, as well as keeping on the old order's housekeeping and gardening staff. His wife had told him firmly that she could not be expected to dust a house like that and they should probably hire extra parlour maids or whatever they're called nowadays too.

'Where's your new girlfriend?'

'In the kitchen with the cake she baked yesterday.'

'That's nice,' Bridget said. She raised her eyebrows at him.

'She's trying to impress you,' Caius said. Callie had gone as far as baking a practice one the week before. Not that she would admit that that was what it was. After all the hoo-ha with her birth father – and her mother's lies throughout her childhood about not knowing who he was – she was perhaps hoping to gain another, more agreeable set.

'I don't need impressing.'

21

'Yes, you do.' Bridget had never been mean to any of his girl-friends, as such. They had all known how she had felt about them though.

'Pickney.' Caius's father appeared and slapped him on the back. They looked very much alike. Same stature, same bearing, same watchfulness. 'Don't mind your mother, she's vexed with her cousin and taking it out on everyone.'

'Eileen said I had "notions" yesterday.'

'How dare she. What did you say?' Caius asked.

'That I've got a husband who looks ten years younger than he is and all she's had for the last ten years is an urn on her mantle-piece. And he hated her when he was alive. I can't blame him. The series of strokes must have been a relief.' Bridget said all this with an aloofness that half implied she didn't register the lack of mercy in what she had said.

'Mum! Jesus!'

'Don't swear!'

Marcus was used to her and blithely changed the subject. 'Where's your new bird then?' Caius gave him a weary look. 'What?'

'You can't say "bird" any more,' Bridget said.

'Why not?' Marcus asked.

'It's not appropriate,' Bridget said.

'Not since 1997 at least,' Caius said, shaking his head. 'New Labour banned it.'

'All right then, where's the female you've been chirpsing?'

This was not much of an improvement. 'In the kitchen.'

'Pops is in there,' Marcus said, making towards the door. Caius senior was a little cantankerous these days. He'd always had a sharpness to him, but old age, creaking joints and impending heart failure had given him an even pricklier edge.

'We'd better check on them,' Bridget said, following her husband.

'Oh no, it's all right, he's sweet on her.' Caius strolled after them slowly. 'He likes Callie a lot more than he likes me. He always asks to speak to her when I ring in case she's got any good gossip for him.'

The three of them went into the kitchen to find Callie filling a teapot with hot water from a recently boiled kettle. 'Apparently, they're getting divorced.'

'Anyone could see that a mile off,' Caius's grandfather said in his warm Jamaican lilt from the kitchen table as the three of them filed into the room. He turned to look at them and smiled. 'I fancied a cup of tea.'

'Hello, I'm—' Callie began before being interrupted.

'Gorgeous,' said Bridget enthusiastically.

Callie wasn't sure what to do with such effusiveness. She was uncharacteristically still, choosing eventually to hold aloft her creation. 'I brought a cake.'

*　　*　　*

They'd had lunch. Roast pork, mashed potatoes with so much butter that Caius wondered if his cholesterol would recover and sautéed red cabbage – made for them by the cook who, despite only working for the family for a few days a month, had whipped up two weeks' worth of home-cooked food, frozen it all and had even left a little goody bag for Caius to take home. Caius and Marcus were sitting in the library, discussing the renovation of the almhouses on the estate.

'I don't know when, but I'll fit it in somewhere,' Caius said.

'You can't keep your job,' Marcus said. He slouched back into an ancient chesterfield armchair. Marcus had a beer and Caius a glass of orange juice. He had to drive back. 'I know I've said it already and you keep saying no, but you need to quit the police soon.'

'Why?' Caius asked. He hoped his mother was being kind to Callie. Bridget had insisted on going on a walk with her around the gardens. She seemed to like her, but you never knew with Bridget. He was worrying about what horrors were unfurling amongst the topiary and not paying enough attention to his father.

'I can't run this estate alone,' Marcus said loudly, trying to grab his daydreaming son's attention. 'It's a bigger job than when I had my own building firm. I'm sixty-four, Caius. I'm too old.'

'Dad, look . . . I can't really devote much time to this.' He gestured at the library. 'You should hire more people.'

'I will, when I can,' he said firmly enough for Caius to revert into feeling like a teenager. Marcus had retained the farm workers from the previous regime. He was quite happy to admit he knew bugger all about sheep and wasn't keen to learn. 'The inheritance tax was a killer.'

'Look, I've already agreed to take over the meetings for the almshouses,' Caius said. Caius's father had surveyed their new fiefdom and had tasked Caius with supervising the renovation of the estate's almshouses built in the eighteenth century for the 'deserving' poor. Caius was reluctant to do it, but Marcus didn't really hear the word 'no'.

'We . . . you have different responsibilities now. Would I like to sell this money pit and sit on a beach? I would, but it would break your grandfather's heart. He's just got what always should've been his. We have to carry it on for his sake alone. We, and I mean "we", are going to make this place work. There's money to be made here and there are people's livelihoods at stake. The old Beauchamps buried their heads and weren't using the money from their London property portfolio to properly look after this place. God knows what that kid was spending it on.' Marcus shook his head and took a sip of his drink. He assumed it was coke after what Caius had told him. 'Look, I spoke to that Lord Arthur fellow on the phone. I know you think he's a wrong 'un. I'd be foolish to dismiss your judgement. I know something went down, and I know the house was part of it, but I don't want to know the particulars beyond what you've told me already. We need friends – in the loosest way – like that now, and he's been quite helpful with discussing the practicalities. He's given me lots of advice about government grants . . . There's a whole orchard scheme . . .'

'Dad, no. Arthur Hampton can't be trusted. More than that, he's dangerous,' Caius said, frustrated that they were treading the same ground over and over again. 'Dad, I need you to trust me.'

'All I'm saying is that he had a lot of advice. He's invited me for a drink actually at his club. Apparently, they have dress requirements but he said you'd be able to advise me. I think we can make this estate earn good money, if we—'

'This estate . . .' Caius interrupted, but floundered for the words to express his disquiet. 'Our ancestors weren't good people. Exploiting the local peasantry. I'm pretty sure they were slave owners. They made so much money from the Empire.'

'Of course they were terrible people. No one who could afford to build a house like this was a good person. But we can be better. We can use our new-found position to do some good. Like the almshouses for example. You—'

'How's Pop's health? He looks frailer every time I see him.'

'He says he wants to go home.' Marcus reluctantly accepted that Caius still wasn't ready to listen, yet.

'To Notting Hill?'

'Jamaica.'

'Why? He's never been back.'

'He's being very firm about it. I guess it's his last chance. I've booked tickets for me and him for late next week. BA. Business Class. We're fancy now.'

★ ★ ★

Back at their flat, Caius and Callie changed into their 'home clothes' – Caius into a pair of trackies and a hoodie and Callie into a floaty white cotton nightdress and a silk kimono she'd found at a car boot sale – and were cuddled on the sofa.

'Did I make a good impression?' Callie asked, looking up at Caius from her position sprawled across his lap. 'Did your mum like me?'

'I . . . Yeah . . . but honestly, who knows,' Caius said. The doorbell rang, Callie disentangled herself from him and he got up to answer it, returning a few moments later with their Chinese. 'Sorry, that was a dickish thing to say. My mum . . . I think my mum, like all mums I guess, is a bit odd. More than odd. She's unaware that she can be a bit savage.'

'I feel really good right now.'

'No, shit. Shit. I kind of meant to say that it doesn't matter what she thinks.'

'So she doesn't like me?'

'No! Yes! Yes, I think my mum likes you.' Caius stood there in the middle of the living room holding the white plastic bag aloft in surrender. 'Sweet and sour chicken balls?'

'Sure.' Callie felt a bit deflated. She thought she'd been a hit.

Caius took the bag of takeaway over to the table ready to be decanted. His phone buzzed.

*Mum*
*19.34*
*What a delightful girl Callie is. Such lovely manners and*
*so elegant. Very pretty. That cake was fantastic. Much nicer*
*than the last girl. Your dad says that you've started to*
*sound plummy since you met Callie by the way. I told him*
*to shut it and that he should get rid of his glottal stop too*

Caius read all but the last three sentences aloud to Callie, who, relieved at the positive verdict, joined him at the table for a feast of beef in black bean sauce, salt and pepper chips, egg fried rice and the aforementioned sweet and sour chicken balls.

*You*
*19.35*
*I don't know why she's with me (crying face emoji)*

*Mum*
*19.35*
*Me neither!*

# MONDAY

# 4

## Hammersmith Police Station

'Hampton?' Caius had asked. He'd hoped Hampton was on the other end of the line and that he wasn't lucid dreaming about the man.

'It's been a while, hasn't it?' Arthur Hampton said. His call had woken Caius up at precisely 6.30 a.m. 'I've got a case for you.'

'Fuck off, you prick, it's early,' Callie murmured, thankfully not loud enough for Hampton to have possibly heard, before rolling over and burying her head deep into her pillow. She was pure evil in the morning until she'd had a cup of tea and a piece of toast.

'Right,' was all Caius could muster.

'There's some background you need to be aware of, which I don't think your colleagues will have got to yet. I'll have one of my people send the material over. Details of the handover to follow. We must have dinner soon. You can tell me all about whatever "case célèbre" you want in exchange for this one over a nice Beaujolais.'

And that was it. DI Caius Beauchamp had then received a call from some minion of Hampton's informing him that his team were to take over a multiple murder in Barnes. That was how Caius, DS Matt Cheung and DC Amy Noakes now found themselves escorted into an empty room in Hammersmith station at 10.00 a.m. Officially the trio were a Special Crimes Unit based out of Camden and Islington, recently formed by the Home Office as a trial looking into improving modern policing methods.

They were to be assigned to some of London's more challenging cases. In reality, what had happened was Caius had shaken hands with Arthur Hampton – Right Honourable Member of Parliament for South Rutland, duke-in-waiting and scheming enigma with an air of medieval subterfuge – last September and come to a gentlemen's agreement that made Caius morally uncomfortable: Caius would look into any cases that Hampton wanted and in return he could pick another case that took his fancy. Less *quid pro quo* and more *mortem pro morte*. This was the first case that had been sent Caius's way since the agreement. Caius had had his sights on the case he wanted in return for a month – he'd been doing his research and the case may be his lucky break – but had waited patiently for the opportunity to earn it. If he was right it might tell him something more about what happened to his sister. It had nearly been fifteen years since she disappeared.

'What do we know so far?' Amy asked. She cast Matt a sideways glance. They were uneasy with the whole special unit thing, but both of them felt loyal to Caius. Well, loyal enough to see where it would take them for six months, and definitely only until things got weirder than they could comfortably deal with.

'I only know the headline,' Caius said, leaning against the desk and straightening his tie. 'Double murder in Barnes.'

'Yikes,' Amy said.

'What's the angle?' Matt asked.

'How do you mean?' Caius said. He knew what he meant, but the whole situation still felt grubby enough that he needed to feign some sort of distance between himself and the slimy labyrinth of quasi-corruption that had led them to the case. He didn't fancy himself as much of a Theseus.

'Why's Hampton interested? Family friend?' Matt clarified.

'I don't know yet. He said we'd talk soon.'

'At his club again?'

'Probably,' Caius said.

A brisk knock at the door and in walked DI Faisal Riaz, who had been in charge of the case for just over a day. He was a genial man in his forties, with the unfortunate habit of smiling from only one half of his mouth, making him look like he was being more sarcastic than he was capable of.

'You must be the guys from the special unit,' he said.

'For our sins,' Caius said, shaking his hand and introducing himself and the others.

'Cool, let me take you to the incident room and show you where we've got to,' he said, gesturing for them all to follow him. 'Not very far I'm afraid.'

* * *

'The first victim to be found had been stabbed to death. It was bloody. He didn't go down without a fight,' Faisal said, pointing to the crime scene photos that had already been put up in the incident room. 'None of the neighbours claim to have heard the altercation, but the house has a large garden.'

'The victim was wearing a balaclava,' said Caius.

'Burglar,' Matt and Amy said in unison.

'Caught in the act?' asked Caius.

'Well, the front door was wide open, I'll explain more in a moment.' Faisal continued. 'They fought and he's killed.'

'Who found him?' asked Caius, wondering whether they were also the murderer. Kills the burglar and feigns shock at finding him.

'Rosalind Krige found both bodies. Known as Rosie. She's the granddaughter of Mona Frogmorton: the second victim, the murdered homeowner. Rosie returned home at 23.17 on Saturday night from a day at the pub with her friends. We have the Uber receipt so we can be that precise. We also have two witnesses: Tristan Sowerby, an acquaintance who she'd spent the evening with – who saw her directly to the front door – and her Uber driver, a man named Steve James. We're yet to interview either of them. This is when we get less certain of events. According to Rosie, she goes to her room and falls asleep. She wakes up at about 3.30 a.m. and goes down for a glass of water. The front door is wide open, so she shuts it assuming she left it that way when she came home in a state, although she thinks she definitely locked up. Rosie then goes into the kitchen and cuts her foot on a piece of broken glass on the floor, alerting her to the presence of the first body. She rings 999 at 3.37 a.m. The responder keeps her on the line as she goes upstairs to her grandmother's room, only to find that she's dead too, apparently smothered with her own pillow. Rosie was breathalysed at the scene and was officially plastered. So far, her version of events sort of stacks but can't be proven either way.'

'Anything taken?'

'No. Nothing. Rosie walked through the house for us and didn't notice anything was gone. There's a not insignificant silver collection in the house that's untouched. Some of those pieces were easily pocketable. There was cash in a drawer in the entrance hall that was left. No missing passports and no missing laptops. Nothing obvious. Might be worth asking Rosie again when she's in a better state. Something small like jewellery could've been taken and she might not have noticed.'

'Where did the glass come from?' asked Amy.

'A broken windowpane just above the door handle in the

kitchen.' Faisal pointed to a picture of the back door. 'Classic burglary.'

'So is that how you think the first victim got in?' Matt asked.

'It seems that way.' Faisal swayed on the spot. 'However, there were no fingerprints on the door beyond the old woman's. According to Rosie she used to go out every evening to feed the hedgehogs. Forensics are still going over everything but they have found quite a few prints at the scene.'

'What about the front door then?' Caius asked.

'Exactly,' Faisal said, waving his arms to emphasise the oddness of Rosie's version of events. 'We currently have two theories. The most obvious perhaps: two or even more people break in. They smother the old woman before they start doing over the place, wearing gloves of course. They turn on each other quickly and one is killed. The second burglar flees through the front door rather than the back and accidentally leaves it open. Where this sits with Rosie's return is dependent on the post-mortems, but it would explain the door if Rosie is telling the truth that she'd shut it and they broke in after she'd gone to bed.'

'What's your second theory?' Caius asked, though the first solution seemed elegant enough.

'It's a bit silly, but not impossible. Rosie finds the burglar and kills him, opens the front door and cuts her foot all as a cover, all so she could murder her grandmother for her inheritance while suggesting the involvement of another assailant.'

'Both solutions are money motivated. Burglars quarrel, or an inheritance,' Caius said. It was usually something base like that.

'That's what we've been thinking too. We were planning to apply for a warrant to see Mona's will and see whether that's plausible or not, but Rosie just doesn't seem like the type. She works for a charity.'

'There are some absolute bastards who work in places like that though,' Amy said, folding her arms. She'd read a news article recently about western aid workers who'd committed unspeakable crimes against children in the developing world. 'It's called the halo effect. You stop seeing them properly because you think they must be a saint.'

Faisal tried to hide that he'd taken umbrage with Amy's school ma'am tone. 'Normally I'd agree with you, but I just can't see it. It's already so rare for a woman to kill, especially someone who's not their abusive partner.'

Amy couldn't argue with that.

'Do we know the identity of the burglar?' Caius asked.

'We don't. Unsurprisingly, he wasn't carrying his driver's licence on him,' Faisal said, shrugging. 'This is what we know. Caucasian. 5'9. About forty. Sturdy build but not overweight. Dressed in black with the requisite balaclava and gloves. Kitchen knife through the back of his chest – there was a fair bit of slash-ing involved. He fought back. A bloody knife that matched a gap in the knife block was next to the body, suggesting it wasn't premeditated. Definitely killed in the kitchen. It's worth noting that there's a set of bloody footprints running through the house that match Rosie's version of events. We also had a medic confirm that she had actually trodden on the piece of glass which was retrieved from the kitchen table.'

Caius nodded. 'What were your next steps going to be?'

'How do you mean?' Faisal asked, leaning forward nervously.

'I'm just curious about what your tactics might have been. Maybe we could learn from you.' Caius wanted to get this case over with quickly and didn't want to tread over the same ground. Anything to lessen his dealings with Hampton.

'Identifying our burglar is . . . was our first priority. See if we can find him on our databases. No one takes up burglary as a mid-life crisis hobby. Someone has come across him before. Forensics are searching for evidence still. A public appeal if they don't throw anything useful up. Reinterviewing Rosie. Speaking to her mother Josephine Krige. Uniform started canvassing the neighbours a couple of hours ago, we're asking everyone with a doorbell camera on the streets around to give us the footage, and we were about to begin speaking to Rosie's mates she was out with in case she was acting out of character that evening. Tristan – who showed her home – Lucia and Harry. Oh, and the Uber driver.'

'Great,' Caius said.

'Was that right? I defer to you: you're the special unit.'

'That's exactly what I would do too.'

Faisal looked relieved. He felt put on the spot having Caius's team there. 'Oh, and there's one more thing. Silly really, but there was a business card on the old lady's nightstand too. We're grasping with that last one, but worth a shot.'

'A business card?' Caius asked.

'Yeah, for some posh woman who makes hats.'

Caius nodded slowly, then stood up to take a closer look at the picture of Mona on the whiteboard. He'd only given her half a glance before.

'We'll send the crime scene photos over to you guys ASAP, and we've obviously recorded the interview with Rosie. We're expecting the post-mortem results through soon, but if I've forgotten anything you can just give us a call.'

'Thanks, Faisal,' Matt said. Caius was ignoring them all and staring intently at Mona's photo still.

'Yes, thanks,' Caius replied a few moments too late.

# 5

## Marigold House

Caius, Matt and Amy nodded to the uniformed officer guarding the gate to Marigold House, home of the late Mona Frogmorton, and ducked under the police cordon. The gate was made of scrolling metal strips. It was there more for decoration than security. There was another larger, more robust-looking wooden gate to the side that allowed access to a thin gravel drive leading up to a little building that would have been the stables when the house was originally built. It was a large Edwardian villa with a garden in the front whose heritage roses needed regular professional attention and a larger tree-shrouded lawn in the back.

'Amy,' Caius said, as they watched a forensics team crawl along the grass looking for the tiniest piece of evidence. The small path they were working on led to the back garden and ultimately the kitchen door with a broken pane of glass above the handle that they'd spent a big chunk of yesterday investigating. 'Forensics permitting, do you want to have a shifty around the back? See if you think there's another way someone could have got into the building. Find out if you can get into that old coach house.'

'I'll look out for a hedgehog or two while I'm at it,' Amy said. She slyly shot Matt a look. Caius had been uncharacteristically quiet in the short ride from the station to the house. He'd barely glanced up from his phone in the last half an hour.

'All right, amigo.' Matt glanced about, making sure that no one was around to overhear. 'What's the connection to you?'

'Mona Frogmorton was at the table next to me and Callie on

that fancy train ride we took on Friday. I texted Callie in the car and she said the old woman had liked her hat, so she gave her a business card. It's that simple.'

'Are you sure that's it. She's not her cousin or something? Or yours?'

'For fuck's sake, Matt.'

'Sorry.' Matt wasn't actually sorry. There had been tension building between Caius and the others over the last six months as they got on with their usual line of domestic violence cases and gang stabbings. It had started small, but then it began to build and build as they waited and waited. They'd braced themselves for Arthur Hampton's return all winter, only for Christmas to come and go without a whisper from the man, bar a tasteful Christmas card of his ancestral pile sent to Caius's flat cheerfully wishing him 'Merry Christmas and a Happy New Year'. 'I was joking.'

'It's all right.' Caius knew he wasn't joking, but actually he was glad someone had finally said something to relieve the pressure by a pascal or two. A little pin to his side wasn't the worse thing as long as he didn't pop. He'd been trying to keep things sunny, trying not to let the stress of everything going on with his family and the estate bleed over into his work, but he'd realised early on that he had to be in a bit of a shitty mood somewhere, and as much as he liked Matt and Amy, he didn't love them. He'd rather be grumpy and overwhelmed with them than with Callie. His dad's continued insistence that he needed to quit his job – he'd texted him about it after their cosy library chat – had left him so distracted last night that Callie had to ask him whether he was listening three times during one conversation. He suspected his dad was right. 'Things have started to change a bit, haven't they.'

'Yeah.'

'I'm sorry. This is all my fault.' Caius looked at Matt.

'No, it isn't. Not really.'

'It's a Monday, but do you want to go for a swift one later?' Caius didn't think a crime scene was the right place to talk about his personal life, but he could manage to tell Matt how quickly a whole new set of crushing expectations and duties had fallen upon him in a quiet corner of a pub after a pint or two. 'Well, as long as Hampton doesn't call.'

'Yeah, sure.'

'I swear that we just happened to be sitting near Mona Frogmorton. There's nothing else going on there.' That he knew of, yet.

'OK.' Matt nodded. Caius was many things – and apparently would one day become many other things again, a baronet amongst them – but he definitely wasn't a liar.

'I wonder if Hampton has an alert on our names or something and that's what he meant when he said there's more background to the case.' Caius thought it was unlikely that the presence of Callie's business card was the cause of all this. 'Although all that would have happened if Faisal and his team had continued their investigation, is Callie would have told them exactly what I just told you and that would have been that.'

Matt nodded. 'We'll find out soon enough.'

Caius shifted his weight around. 'I did, however, overhear Rosie the granddaughter having a private conversation on her phone in Bath. She looked a bit distressed, that's why I took an interest. I'm a nosy bastard. I suppose you have to be to do this job.'

'Yeah, I love a good bit of gossip.'

'I'd stepped outside of the Assembly Rooms and I could see that she was put out. She was arguing with someone.'

'Hmm.' Matt looked around the garden. 'Rosie lives with her

nan. That's going to be, what, one of three things: one, they're close and it's a lovely, multigenerational solution to the housing crisis; two, she's broke and it's a convenient, tolerable enough solution; or thirdly, she wants something.'

'As there's a question over Mona's estate then we will eventually need to speak to Josephine, her daughter. She's likely to be the main beneficiary.'

'Did Mona and Rosie seem close when you saw them together?'

'Yes. Rosie took quite a lot of care with helping her move about.' Caius turned to look at the house. Now that he was closer, he thought it needed a lick of paint and the windows weren't double-glazed. If the house was modernised it would be worth millions. Large rooms with generous proportions, lots of light and the sort of garden that feels like a public park to your average Londoner. You could probably see the river from the upstairs rooms, and Barnes Village with its duck pond, artisanal bakeries and gastropubs was a five-minute walk away.

Caius and Matt headed up the front steps. The front door was painted an austere and respectable glossy black with a gleaming brass knocker that had been recently polished, as had the brass letterbox and door handle.

'The infamous front door,' Matt said, taking a good look at it before checking the lock. It had one of those Yale locks that if the catch wasn't up, which it appeared not to be, then all you had to do to shut the door was pull it to. 'The mechanism looks fine and no one's taken a crowbar to the door itself.'

'Do you think she left it open?' Caius wondered out loud. 'It's really not impossible. I guess it depends on how drunk she was and how careless she is. My mate Jake did it twice in one term when we shared a house in uni. He was doing a lot of ket that year, but he also lost his house keys once a week.'

'What would the alternative be?' Matt asked.

'Unless either woman was a sleepwalker, then someone else opened it after Rosie came home. Our second burglar fleeing the scene. If you were already in the house, having come through the back door, you wouldn't need a key to open it. We need to find out if anyone else has a key. I imagine that Josephine has one. The house is pretty big and, judging by this entrance hall, dusted fairly regularly. Do they have a cleaner or even a housekeeper? They might have a copy.' Caius looked around. There was a cast-iron umbrella stand with three enormous and ancient-looking golf umbrellas in it near the door. There was a mirror with a carved gilt frame on the wall opposite the staircase, a grandfather clock that began chiming for midday, and a large round table with a tall, empty blue-and-white vase on it. A few oil paintings were dotted on the walls: one of a horse, a couple of landscapes. Caius thought it was all very sedate, if not a bit old-fashioned. 'Mona was the sort of woman who makes sure her house is polished, everything is well looked after, but she didn't care to buy more contemporary furnishings or make expensive improvements like getting new sash windows. That all speaks to someone well-to-do, but with a miserly streak.'

'Put on an extra jumper rather than turn the heating on.'

'Exactly the type.'

'My dad's like that. It's mildly amusing in September but bloody annoying in December. He likes to see how long he can last without turning the heating on. My mum has programmed the boiler to come on when he's not at home.'

★ ★ ★

Caius and Matt were standing over Mona's bed. They'd followed Rosie's gruesome trail up the stairs – the bloodstains faded with each step until they were no longer perceivable – and to a substantial four poster death bed with carvings of animals on the headboard. The bloodstains faded with each step she took until they were no longer perceivable next to where Mona's body had been found. It was a homely room. There was a large dark wood wardrobe and a dressing table with a silver-backed hairbrush and a half-empty pot of Pond's cold cream on it. It was decorated with off-white wallpaper covered in dainty rose buds. The curtains matched and Caius suspected the bedding had too. The pillow that Faisal thought she'd been smothered with, as well as the other bedding, had been removed by forensics. Callie's business card was gone too.

If Callie were here, she would have described the room as 'Laura Ashley core' – everything anyone ever did now appeared to be a 'core' something. Callie had begun renting out her flat in Acton once she'd moved in with him, and had picked something similar for one wall in her old living room. She'd wanted to do a little refresh to see if she could get more money for the place. It had worked; there'd been a bidding war between renters with the victor offering to pay six months' rent in advance. Or rather, Caius had done a tiny bit of redecorating and London's inhuman rental market did the rest.

'What's that smell?' Matt asked as he opened a drawer to find nothing but socks.

'I think it's lily of the valley. My nan used to like it. I used to buy her the talcum powder and hand cream from Crabtree & Evelyn every year for her birthday,' Caius said, staring at the bare mattress.

'It's very generation specific.'

43

'It's the opposite of Lynx Africa body spray,' Caius said, moving over to the bedside table as he put on a pair of gloves. He opened a drawer and found it mostly empty, apart from a book of stamps and a pile of notepaper with Mona's name and address printed on the top. Caius picked up a sheet. Mona was a woman who took life's details seriously – why else would she have personalised notepaper?

They left Mona's bedroom and trundled down the hallway to Rosie's. It was decorated in much the same way as the rest of the house, with solid furniture and floral touches, but it was clear a much younger woman inhabited it. On her dressing table was a whole apothecary's worth of bottles. There were perfumes and lipsticks and all of the paraphernalia of the delightful that Caius was unable to accurately name. A floaty floral dress was strewn over the back of a chair, and a pile of 'going out' shoes and leather boots were spilling out of the wardrobe. There was a scented candle on the mantelpiece and a novel with a pink neon cover about an impossibly sad young woman self-destructing in a meaningful way on the bedside table. It was as expected. Caius opened the wardrobe and glanced at the things hanging in it. He noticed a couple of ball gowns hanging up as well as a section of smart clothes from Hobbs and LK Bennett that must be for work. There were a couple of handbags on the shelf at the top. He took one down, a beaded going-out bag, and opened it, finding a receipt for two old fashioneds from an overpriced underground cocktail bar in Clapham that used to be a public toilet from the previous month, a lip oil, and an empty half-bottle of Smirnoff vodka.

'Pre-drinking?' Caius asked, holding up the bottle for Matt to see. 'It looks like the bag she uses when she goes out?'

'London's expensive even when you're crashing with family.'

'Unless she downed it before she was breathalysed to make

her look feeble.' Caius didn't think that was totally impossible. 'Anything weird over there?'

'Not weird weird. There's just a lot more wool than I was anticipating,' Matt said, pushing a clear plastic tub full of yarn back under the bed. Rosie, it seemed, had a knitting problem. Caius was looking at him funnily. 'Look, I just don't like women who knit. There's something about them.'

'Rosie was knitting on the train.'

'Exactly. That was a fancy trip right, with gourmet food and picturesque scenery and what does she do instead? She knits,' Matt said, looking under the other side of the bed and finding a large clear plastic box containing art supplies. Tubes and tubes of oil paint, watercolours and even charcoal. 'She's crafty.'

★   ★   ★

Amy had returned from the garden and joined Caius and Matt in the kitchen. They huddled into the middle of the room, keen not to disturb forensics who were busy with the damaged back door.

'The only way into the property is through either of the front gates. I had a quick chat with forensics, and they've not found anything yet to say that anyone was out there that night, but that doesn't mean they weren't,' Amy said, staring out the window at the house that backed onto Mona's.

'None of the neighbours saw anything?' Matt asked.

'No one's come forward yet,' Caius said, taking out his phone and quickly scanning through his emails. 'Uniform's investigations are still ongoing though. Faisal has emailed the pictures through already,' Caius added, opening the files. They huddled round the screen. 'He was right. The amount of blood means the burglar was definitely killed here. Stabbed in the back of his ribcage, but the body was found under the kitchen table facing upwards. He'd been rolled over.'

'The killer wanted to be sure he was dead,' Matt said, as Caius tilted the phone, orientating the photo in the space.

'I'll get Barry to have a look at these pictures. He's a savant with blood splatter patterns,' Caius said, looking up from his phone. 'We need those autopsies. Hammersmith are going to do them as they've already taken charge of the bodies, but I'll get Barry to have a glance.'

'I got into the garage stables thingy, by the way,' Amy said, nodding at a set of keys on a hook beside the fridge. 'It was locked up, although the key was hanging up in the middle of the crime scene. Totally empty apart from a lawn mower, some gardening shears and a few tins of old fence paint.'

'OK.' Caius flicked through a couple more photos of the body. This time the angle changed so that more of the man's facial features could be seen.

'Shit,' Caius cursed. He'd seen the man before.

'What?' Matt asked.

'He's the steward from the train to Bath.'

# 6

## The Police Station

Caius had come off the phone with the train people half an hour ago and they still hadn't sent through the list of staff from Friday's trip to Bath. He refreshed his inbox again. Still nothing. Matt appeared at his shoulder with a mug of peppermint tea. He thought Caius might pop a blood vessel soon if he didn't stop holding his breath.

Caius closed his eyes and put his head on the table. 'I miss the days when I did fun stuff and no one died. I go for a jog. There's a body. I go to the theatre. There's a body. I'm scared to go play five-a-side in case I get someone killed. I turned my mate Errol down last month. He played for Chelsea Under-11s and everything.'

'I'm sure it's just a coincidence, mate,' Matt said, hoping it was but not especially confident. 'We all brush past death all the time without realising it. Someone I sat next to on the tube last week could've died. I wouldn't know. They could've got out the station and immediately been hit by a bus. "Phwack". No more. Choked on their lunch. Had a random brain aneurism and just dropped dead in the supermarket. Splat, right next to the fish counter.'

'It's starting to feel personal is all I'm saying.'

'Yeah, I get that. Look, perhaps the way to look at this is that you were lucky enough to have been there. Lucky enough to have seen these people before they died in order to solve their murders.'

'Optimism is a disease.'

'So's chronic stress, buddy. Drink the peppermint tea. Not everything is about you.'

'That's it. Keep it coming. More of that, please,' Caius said. He took a sip of his tea. 'One of you needs to speak to Callie. She did a lot of people watching that day.'

'I'll do it,' Amy said, piping up. She'd been busy texting her girlfriend while Caius and Matt were having their long-due emotional moment over a herbal tea. 'Fi wanted me to ask Callie whether her hat-making classes have space still.'

'That reminds me. Callie's been getting at me to invite you all – the lovely Fi included – to dinner sometime soon. She unpacked a dinner service last week and she's itching to use it.'

'We'd be delighted,' Amy said.

'I don't have anything better to do,' Matt said. He'd broken up with his girlfriend just over six months ago and hadn't quite managed to find something/someone else to fill up his time just yet. He was working on it.

Caius put his mug down. 'Amy, can you also speak to uniform? Faisal said they were canvassing the neighbours for camera footage. Hammersmith have to be done by now, surely.'

'Sure,' Amy said.

Caius picked up his tea and took it with him as he called Callie from the corridor.

'What do you think the timeline is here?' Amy asked Matt pointedly.

'Well, the murders occurred—' he began.

'No, with Caius.'

'How do you mean?'

'This,' she said, gesturing around the incident room, 'isn't going to be forever. It can't.'

'I know, but I'm going to see him out to the end.'

'I give him two years.'

'Three, tops,' Matt said, wobbling his head as he weighed everything up.

'This special unit is bollocks. We can't sit around here doing our regular job for most of the year and then do a favour for Arthur Hampton's nefarious third cousin twice removed when a body turns up somewhere where it shouldn't.'

'Just get to the end of the year.'

'And then what, Matt?'

'Study for your exams. You'll pass easily. You need to prove yourself on the job for a little bit longer. Then you'll get a promotion and a transfer. You'll gloss over the last year when anyone asks and instead tell them all about how you single-handedly took down the Finsbury Flasher outside of a primary school when he was about to emotionally scar a load of seven-year-olds.'

'And you?'

'I don't know.'

Amy looked at Matt. She hadn't been able to work out how he was feeling. She decided to change the subject. She'd been candid and he'd responded accordingly. Amy was here if he cared to reciprocate. 'I heard Caius muttering about someone called Turner into his phone last week. He sounded proper stressed. I think he was talking to his dad.'

'He was probably talking about a Turner painting. They own one now.'

'The cloud guy?'

'Yeah, him.'

'Shit. How much is that worth?'

'Millions.'

Amy shook her head as she found Faisal's number. She called him and he confirmed with a little bit of a tone that uniform's efforts had not thrown up a witness and they were still chasing doorbell camera footage.

Caius came back into the incident room and put the empty mug down on his desk. He checked his email again. 'The train company have finally come back with the staff list.' He opened the attached document and scrolled through it, scanning the accompanying pictures.

'What?' Matt asked, as Caius grumbled exasperated vowel sounds into the ether.

'He's not there. The steward isn't there,' Caius said.

'But you saw him. It's the same guy, right?'

'I'm adamant.' Caius leaned back in his desk chair and swivelled round. If he ignored the fact that he'd been there three days before with both victims, then he was beginning to enjoy himself. Enjoy wasn't quite the right word, relished the challenge perhaps, or the distraction of the puzzle. 'There are a few possibilities here: first of which is that I'm imagining this guy – which isn't impossible, but I should get checked out for a brain tumour.' Caius looked up at Matt and Amy, relieved to see that they found the idea of him having cancer unlikely, but also slightly amusing.

'Or John Doe was working there but the information you've been sent is wrong somehow,' Amy said, wondering how possible that could be. 'Is there a long waiting list for MRI scans at the moment?'

'Of course there is, the NHS is on the verge of collapse, but never mind, our Caius can go private now,' Matt said.

'Go private and miss the opportunity to have my scan cancelled three times because of a strike? Not likely,' Caius said.

Amy smiled. This was bittersweet after her and Matt's conversation. 'John Doe might have been there because someone called in sick, and he covered last minute. The information may not have filtered through to whoever sent the list over. That's not implausible.'

'I'll go back to them to double-check the list is correct,' Caius said, squinting at his inbox. 'Amy, run every employee through the system to see if they've got a record. Then send out the least gory picture of the steward to the usual internal suspects. If he was a career burglar, then someone knows him.'

'All right.'

'Matt, mein Liebling, I've got the transcripts of the 999 call and Faisal's interview with Rosie. We'll listen together. Get her in. We need to speak to her ourselves.' Caius chewed on one of his beloved Muji fineliners. 'I wonder if she changes her story at all.'

'Kein Problem.'

# 7

## The Old Vicarage, Lower Snoddington, Gloucestershire

Josephine Krige (née Frogmorton) was holding a ceramic mixing bowl as the radio played in the kitchen. She'd decided that the best way to deal with her mother's violent demise was to bake a Victoria sponge. She was the sort of woman who displaced her feelings with activities, often baking, but also volunteering in the community. She'd tell you about it too. Josephine volunteered with the Brownies on a Tuesday evening; she was Snowy Owl. She was Chairwoman of the Lower Snoddington Women's Society and on the fundraising committee of St Mark's (C of E). The roof of St Mark's was forever in peril – even with the committee's Herculean efforts. They didn't mind this.

A tear landed on the edge of the bowl and Josephine quickly wiped it away with a green-and-white gingham tea towel. The doorbell rang. She turned off the radio, a cream-coloured Roberts retro style that Richard, her dear late husband, had bought her for her birthday three years ago, after much insinuation on her part. Josephine opened the door to find her neighbour Theresa on the doorstep with what threatened to be a home-cooked meal. Theresa's property was a substantially smaller, and not terribly smart, cottage a few doors down. In Josephine's opinion Theresa was, for the most part, well-intentioned but poor at the execution of such sentiments. She'd been dreading her visit. It was a small village, and Josephine had known that as soon as she had told Deborah, the vicar's gossipy wife, what had happened then all and sundry would know her business. She couldn't bear that she was now a conversational topic down at the village shop.

'Hello, Jos,' Theresa said, with an apologetic grimace on her face. 'I just heard the terrible news from Deborah when I was in the Co-op.'

Theresa had a West Country accent, which always annoyed Josephine despite her having lived in Gloucestershire for the better part of thirty years. Theresa always sounded earnest. Yes, that was it. Josephine couldn't bear people without artifice. She also couldn't bear being called Jos by people she hadn't given her express permission to do so. The shortened form of her name was reserved for a few select old school friends.

'Would you like to come in?' Josephine asked, giving her a slow, sad smile. She was too polite not to offer.

'Oh no, I can't stop. Sorry.' Despite having gone to the trouble of making a lasagne, Theresa didn't quite fancy coming in and hearing of Josephine's raw grief just yet. 'I've got to take Millie to the vet.'

'Of course.' Josephine nodded. Millie was Theresa's yappy Jack Russell. Josephine wanted to kick the little shit every time she saw it.

'I made you a lasagna,' Theresa said, handing over the clingfilm-covered dish.

'That's so kind of you.' Josephine took it from her, holding it aloft almost. The bottom was still warm.

'It's the least I can do.' Theresa nodded. Yes, the lasagna had been the perfect thing, the neighbourly thing to do. 'It's vegetarian. I replaced the mince with green lentils.'

'Gosh, how thoughtful of you.'

'How's Rosie?' Theresa asked. Rosie was the nicer of Josephine's girls. Sienna was exceedingly pretty and such a go-getter – according to Josephine, who rarely drew breath when talking about her eldest – but it was Rosie who always asked you how you were when you bumped into her in the village. Although Theresa hadn't seen Rosie about much over the last couple of years since Richard died. Nor Sienna or William, really. Only Josephine walking briskly to the village hall with an agenda or a bag of ingredients for the Brownies' cooking badge under her arm.

'Dreadful.'

'Is the poor lamb home?'

'No, she's staying with a friend in London. She's too important a witness to leave. All I want right now is for her to be here, but who can argue with the Met?'

'It's just awful.'

'Yes.'

Theresa nodded. 'Your girls will be such a comfort over the next few weeks.'

'Yes.'

'I'm so very sorry I can't stop for more of a chat.' Theresa had run out of sympathetic things to say to Josephine, who was looking at her far too expectantly. 'Millie isn't eating.'

'Poor Millie.' Josephine nodded along. 'But still, it's very kind of you to bring this round.'

They said their goodbyes and Josephine shut the front door. Josephine contorted her face into a grimace. She held the lasagna at arm's length as she walked back into the kitchen and returned to her cake batter, giving it one final firm stir before splitting the mixture equally into two separate tins. Josephine put the cake tins in the pre-heated oven and set a timer. She then picked up the lasagna, scraped it straight into the bin and set the empty dish in the sink, ready to scrub the burnt 'béchamel' off the side. No wonder Millie wouldn't eat. If Theresa thought this was acceptable food for humans, then what was she feeding the poor bloody dog?

# 8

## The Police Station

Matt looked down at his notepad and Caius looked down at his. They'd decided to be a little old-fashioned when listening to the recordings of Rosie's 999 call and her interview by drawing a line down the page, writing down the facts and comparing the two.

'Any discrepancies?' Caius asked as he leaned back in his chair and took a swig of the dregs of his placebic peppermint tea. It had made him feel calmer.

'Nope, you?' Matt asked, looking back down at his notepad and physically cross-referencing the timelines with his biro.

Caius shook his head. 'The 999 call sounded pretty frantic. She's emotionally all over the place. She wasn't lying.'

'And pretending to be hammered is hard to do convincingly. When I've come across it before, people over-egg it and miss the fact that your brain isn't just being a bit slow, it isn't putting connections together at all like it would normally.'

'There was definitely slurring.'

'Yeah, it sounds genuine. Either she didn't kill the guy or she should be on the stage.'

'They breathalysed her at the scene: she'd had more than one Aperol spritz for sure.' Caius sped back through the recording and replayed the moments up to finding Mona dead.

Granny? [a floorboard creaks as Rosie moves across the room] Granny! Why are you under your pillow? Granny? Granny?

Granny? Oh God. Oh my God! She's cold.
She's dead. Oh my God, Granny's dead.

'The first responder asks her if she's alone in the house which was what prompted her to go to her grandmother's bedroom in the first place. Before that she was freaking out and going in circles about the first body and having stepped in a pool of blood,' Caius said.

'Understandably so,' Matt said.

'Can you imagine the squelch as all that blood coagulates?'

'No, and nor do I want to.'

'If Rosie *had* killed her grandmother then she would've called after going to "wake her up". It's too hard to fake discovering a body.'

'And I doubt she'd have trodden in the blood barefoot if she killed the steward.'

'It's a pretty gross thing to do if you can avoid it.' Caius looked down at the notepad one last time. 'Neither of us thinks she did it?'

'Right. But . . .'

'But that doesn't mean we're right. I am wrong all the sodding time.' Caius liked playing devil's advocate. 'All right then, why would she do it?'

'Money,' Matt said, shrugging at the obvious answer. 'But we don't know what Mona's assets were and how they are going to be inherited yet.'

'We can assume she owned that house. That must be worth a couple of million at least. If Mona was murdered for an inheritance, then Rosie wouldn't be the only potential beneficiary. What about her mum? Other family members?' Caius looked at his watch. He was expecting Rosie to arrive within the next ten minutes. 'The steward.'

'Yeah, the steward/burglar.'

'Why would Rosie kill him?'

'He broke in. Self-defence?'

'That's logical. She comes into the kitchen and is surprised by him.'

'Not impossible, but I doubt Rosie would win that fight. He wasn't a small bloke.'

'Was he invited? Are the steward and Mona connected beyond dying in the same house on the same evening?'

'The train ride, duh.'

'It can't be a coincidence that they were both in the same carriage.' And for that matter, him and Callie too. 'He's definitely a burglar, right? There's not something else going on here?'

'He had a fucking balaclava. No one with a balaclava on them has good intentions,' Matt said, closing his notebook. Caius saw that the front desk was calling him. Rosie must have arrived. He got up. 'It has to have something to do with that trip to Bath.'

⋆   ⋆   ⋆

Caius discreetly took in Rosie's form. Not in a creepy way, though he was worried he looked like he was, but rather to establish whether she could've stabbed the steward to death. Rosie was of a fairly average height and slim build. The steward was 5'9. From the photos Caius thought he looked more like a wiry old chicken who ran ultra marathons than a plump male model gym buff, but he looked strong. Hard to imagine Rosie could overpower him. Caius introduced Matt and himself to Rosie and her solicitor and explained that they were a special unit taking over the case. They stated their names for the tape. They trod all the same ground that Faisal had, in case Rosie started contradicting herself, but she stuck to her story. The hazy bits, where she had already admitted that she was a little too worse for wear, stayed hazy.

'You said you came home in an Uber with your friend Tristan Sowerby and that he walked you to the front door,' Matt said as Caius sat back in his chair watching her. 'And you didn't notice anything amiss at that point?'

'No, but like I said, I wasn't paying my full attention.' Rosie glanced at her solicitor, a serene-looking man with a shiny forehead and a blank face of pure unreadable pleasantry. Rosie hadn't brought legal representation when Faisal had interviewed her. She glanced down at her hands, avoiding eye contact.

'Do you usually leave doors open like that?' Caius didn't think she was lying. She seemed embarrassed more than anything.

'No, I'm pretty cautious by nature.'

Caius watched her intently. Trying to decide if he thought the prim, pretty girl who helped her aged granny off trains and knitted baby clothes was the same one who'd gone on a massive bender and left her front door wide open. Cautious people don't drink like that. 'You weren't at home that day?'

'I was out with friends. We were in the pub from 11 a.m.' Rosie's brow was creased. She was struggling between being unable to make eye contact and being unable to break it. She had cried twice in the early part of the interview and she was now clutching a tissue tightly in her hand.

'Who do you mean by "we"?'

'My friend Lucia, she invited me, and her friends Harry and Tristan.' Rosie released the tissue. Not wanting to leave the ragged soggy thing on the table she quickly shuffled it into her pocket. 'Lucia and her friends went to Cambridge. They booked a table at a pub on the river. They make a day of it every year.'

'Do you usually drink that much?'

'No. I just got um . . . got swept up in the atmosphere.'

'The atmosphere?'

'Yes well, everyone gets so excited. Rowers like to drink, not like rugby players, but still. Drinking games and things.' Caius looked at her expectantly. 'Lucia and her friends make a huge thing of the Boat Race every year. It's a blowout. I was just joining in with the spirit of it, I suppose.'

'And one of these friends is Tristan, who shared an Uber with you?'

'Yes.' Rosie blushed.

'And he was with you until when?'

'He walked me up to the door, said goodbye and then I went in. He wasn't there for very long at all. And look, yes I'd had a drink but I'm sure, so very sure that I shut the door behind me. It's very unlike me. I'm a very careful person.'

'Right,' Caius said, nodding along. Rosie was almost pleading with him. Something about the slight whine to her voice put him on edge. 'And you went in alone? Tristan didn't pop in for a night cap?'

'Oh no. Granny's quite strict about that sort of thing. Different generations . . .' Rosie began fiddling with her necklace.

'Are you sure that you went straight to your room once you got home?'

'Yes, I went straight to bed.'

'You didn't stop to get yourself a glass of water or a piece of toast? Put the telly on for a bit?'

'No.' Rosie looked up at him, blushing as she did so, and away from her ruined manicure. A complex mixture of grief and embarrassment played out across her face.

'What was your relationship like with your granny?' Matt asked.

'We lived together,' Rosie said quietly. Grief was winning over embarrassment now. 'Obviously, she was more than that to me. I just . . .'

'Would you describe yourselves as close?'

'Yes, of course. Very close.'

'But did you spend much quality time together?' Matt was curious as to whether Rosie's living arrangement was borne out of necessity or affection.

'Yes. We ate breakfast and dinner together nearly every day.'

'Did you share any hobbies? Go on holiday?' Caius chipped in, desperate to know whether them all being on the same train was a coincidence or not. 'Take any day trips?'

'I took her to Bath on Friday. I'd won the tickets in a raffle. We went on an old steam train.'

'Where did you win the tickets?'

'At a sort of work thing.' Rosie furrowed her brow. 'I work in the legal department of an environmental conservation charity and my boss is fairly well connected. He gets invited to the odd fundraiser.' Rosie looked flushed and slightly pained.

'And he took you with him?' Caius fought every impulse to not raise an eyebrow.

'Yes, Felix did. We work together but we also sort of move in the same circle, I guess. He's friends with my brother-in-law.'

'Felix what?'

'Felix Drake,' Rosie said, almost throwing his name away. She watched Matt make a note of his name. 'We're just friends.'

'And he's your boss,' Caius said, tailing off.

'Yes. He's very bright, very driven. He's built the British Society for Rewilding from the ground up. I really admire him. As a colleague.'

'Right. This ticket you won?'

'I bought a single raffle ticket and won the train trip. Felix was a bit miffed he'd bought a handful of the things but then he says he's unlucky. You go to these fundraisers and feel obliged to bid. Granny said I should always make a small donation. It's the right thing to do. They're fundraisers, after all. She'd put a little money in my account whenever I went to one.' Rosie stifled a sob. 'Granny was a very kind woman.'

Caius nodded and sympathetically paused for a moment to allow her to regain her composure. 'What was the charity?'

'I can't quite remember. It was a cancer one though.'

'When was the fundraiser?'

'Last November I think. Hang on.' Rosie pulled out her phone, and scrolled through her calendar. 'Colon Cancer UK. Sixteenth of November at the Dartford Hotel. I thought a trip to Bath would be the sort of thing she would like, she gave me the money for the ticket, after all.'

'Did Bath mean anything particular to your grandmother? Did the place have any special meaning?'

'I don't think so. She's never mentioned the place before.'

'If you don't mind me asking, detectives, what's the pertinence of this Bath trip?' asked Rosie's solicitor sharply, his shiny pleasantness slipping away.

'I was there. I was sat at the table next to you,' Caius said, turning to Rosie. He felt that full disclosure was best. 'And the man who was found murdered in your kitchen was one of the stewards on board. He looked after our tables.'

'Oh my God. Really?' Rosie appeared shocked by this news.

Caius took out the picture from the crime scene. 'Are you sure you don't recognise him?'

'I don't. I mustn't have been paying attention,' Rosie said, her brow furrowed. 'I was a bit distracted.'

'By your knitting?'

'Um, yes.' Rosie kept trying not to look at the picture, but a morbid curiosity that Caius couldn't quite understand gripped her and she glanced at it before recoiling in horror and pushing the picture back towards Caius and Matt. A nice girl like her wouldn't want to look normally. After a moment she quietly said, 'Who can remember what their waiter looked like?'

'Yes,' Caius said, reflecting on how the steward's white jacket and service role would have made him invisible to most.

'Rosie,' Matt began, taking over the interview. 'Can you tell us about your family?'

'Sure.' She bit her lip. 'Granny is on Mummy's side. My late father's parents were South African. They're all dead now. Mummy stayed at home while Daddy worked in the City. He died three years ago, heart attack. There's my elder sister Sienna, me and then my little brother William. William lives in Toronto. Sienna lives nearby.'

'Oh,' Caius said, making a note of Sienna's proximity.

'She's forever trying to get me to babysit for her,' Rosie said, feeling obligated to try and lift the mood. She failed but continued to nervously chatter. 'She calls, a lot. I'm ever so busy so I can't help her out as much as she would like.'

'Is William over in Canada right now?' Matt made a note to check that.

'Yes, I last saw him at Christmas. He stayed with Granny and I.'

'And Sienna lives nearby. Where?' Caius asked, taking over again.

'In Wandsworth with her husband Charlie. They've just had their fourth baby.'

'And what do Sienna and Charlie do?'

'Sisi, well Sisi runs her own company. She's just launched a feminine meditation app called *Freya* that Charlie helps run.' Rosie paused, searching for the correct phrase and facial expression. 'It's all very exciting,' she said a little too enthusiastically, betraying her true apathy.

'Is it very exciting?' Caius asked, failing to hide his scepticism.

'She says so. I have to admit, I downloaded it to be supportive, but I've not been on it. I'm not one for all that woowoo stuff. I just like to "get on with it" as Granny would say. Sienna has some eccentric ideas. Sound baths, energies and alignments. That sort of thing. She used to drive Granny to distraction with some of her notions.'

'What does Charlie do?' Matt quickly glanced at Caius who was trying to work out what a 'sound bath' was.

'He works in tech. He's very clever.'

'So, he's what? A programmer?'

'No, I think he's more on the management side of it. Although I think he used to be a coder at one point perhaps. I'm not sure. Data, maybe?' Rosie smiled as she tried to lower everyone's expectations of her understanding. 'It's all too clever for me. I zone out when he starts talking about advisory boards and start-up investment costs.'

'I see,' Caius said, watching Rosie closely to see if her vagueness was genuine.

Rosie giggled nervously.

'What do you think of your brother-in-law?' Caius wasn't sure it was pertinent to the case; he was just being nosy now.

'Umm . . . well Charlie . . .' Caius could see that Rosie was trying to contain her dislike.

'Yeah?'

'He's all right.' She furrowed her brow; her real feelings were going to poke out even if she tried to hide them. 'In our family we don't have that weird uncle, you know what I mean, we have Charlie and Sienna. He'll often say something about freeloaders on benefits. He's a self-made man and very driven. I don't think he understands that not everyone is capable of what he is.'

Rosie looked at her solicitor. She knew they were fishing around her family and no longer asking about that horrid night. She shifted about in her seat; she felt wrong for being so candid about Sienna and Charlie even if she wasn't fond of them.

Caius changed direction. 'Do you know what your grandmother did the day she died?'

'I think she was in the garden in the morning, but I went out for practically the whole day so I'm afraid I don't know.'

'Did your grandmother have any enemies? You'd be surprised of the outcomes of neighbourly fights over hedges.'

'Not that I know of.' Rosie took a deep breath as she tried to grasp the idea of her sweet little granny having a mortal enemy. 'We barely ever see the neighbours. One side is flats and they're mostly empty anyway. Investments, apparently. And the other side I think split their time between here and the US so we rarely catch sight of them. I don't know the people at the back. We can't see them through the trees.'

'Did your grandmother hire a cleaner?'

'Yes, Zofia. She's Polish, I think. Comes in the week. I don't really have much to do with her. I'm always at work when she comes so I've never actually met Zofia. Granny has an address book. It'll all be in there.'

'Does the cleaner have a key?'

'No, I think Granny lets her in.'

'Who does have keys?'

'Me, obviously.' Rosie paused for a moment. 'My mum and my sister. That's it I think.'

'Who were your grandmother's friends?'

'Her best friend is a lady called Daphne. My late grandfather and Daphne's husband had been stationed together somewhere and both families were close. Daphne is my mother's godmother. We used to see her a couple of times a year. She lives on the coast so Granny would go and stay with her for the sea air and Daphne would come up for a week or two in the spring. She was keen on tennis and they would go to Wimbledon. She's very sweet. We always go and see a play when she's visiting. A farce or something. Maybe a Shakespeare. Usually, a concert too. Cadogan or Wigmore Hall. I always go with them. You don't want a taxi driver taking advantage.' Rosie took a breath. 'Oh God. I'm going to have to call her. She's had to go in a home recently. Her memory has started to go, quite rapidly, and she couldn't live on her own any more. Most days she doesn't know where she is. Granny was so upset.'

'Did your grandmother have any hobbies?' Caius couldn't believe a woman like Mona wasn't arranging flowers at the parish church every week.

'She volunteered at the primary school nearby helping children who were slow with their reading, and she was a member of the local library's book club. Granny came with me to the Barnes Baby Bank sometimes too. When there was a fundraiser, you know. We do a couple a year in the church hall. Tea and cakes, bring and buy, a tombola. She took charge of the white elephants. Me and Granny are always volunteering. Mum too, I suppose. Sienna is too busy for that sort of thing – she has her own projects instead. Granny always talked about "doing our duty".'

'What's the Barnes Baby Bank?' Matt asked.

'It's a charity where people donate things for babies and small children. We distribute them to local mothers in need. It's mostly clothes, but also nappies and formula, prams and toys. I knit a lot of cardigans and baby blankets for them, as well as volunteering.'

'Do you know who your grandmother's solicitor was?'

'My firm represents the family's interest,' said the solicitor interjecting, handing Caius his card. 'David Miller, our senior partner, will be in touch.'

'Thanks.' Caius read the card. Miller & Miller. Established 1874. 'Rosie, I just want to confirm again whether you recognise the man who you found in the kitchen from before?'

'No. I know you said he was working on the train but I really can't be certain. Sorry.'

'I heard you in Bath getting quite upset with someone on the phone.'

Rosie blinked. 'It was probably an automated thing . . . I hate how hard it is to get through to a person these days.'

Caius looked pointedly at the solicitor and then back at Rosie. 'You were ringing your bank while you were out on a daytrip?'

'No . . . umm.' She fiddled with her necklace again. 'I remember now, it was just Felix.'

'Your boss?'

'Yes, he had a question about a contract I'd been working on. He works so hard. I don't think he realised I was off that day. I got a tiny bit peeved with him for calling.'

'I see.' Caius didn't quite believe her. 'What do you think your grandmother's arrangements are?'

'Her money?' Rosie looked a little disgusted at the baseness of the question.

'Yes.'

'It'll be split between us all, I think. I don't know the particulars. It's Granny's to do with as she liked,' Rosie said firmly. Caius looked at her pointedly and she swallowed hard.

★ ★ ★

Amy had filed a warrant request to see Mona's will and had started to write up the timeline on the whiteboard in the incident room. She was staring at the board while eating a bar of Dairy Milk when Caius and Matt came back.

'You've had a delivery,' Amy said, looking pointedly at a box sat on Caius's desk. She worried that it had some sort of Pandora's curse lurking at the bottom of it. She couldn't bear being left with nothing but hope. Naked hope was foolish.

Caius opened the small cardboard box and in it found a dog-eared pastel-pink-coloured biography called *The Stratford Sisters* – he checked the front of the book and it was published in the 1980s – and a heavy cream envelope. Caius opened the envelope, noting the headed notepaper and thinking he should probably get his dad to invest in some. He'd check with Callie, but it appeared to be the done thing.

Dear Caius,

Dine with me tomorrow night at 7.00 p.m. at the usual place.

A

'Do we get to see you in your James Bond get-up again?' Matt asked, watching Caius as he cautiously put the note back in the envelope.

'Yeah.'

'I still need to get myself a tuxedo, you know, just in case,' Amy said, acknowledging to herself that the only time she'd need one is if she were getting married.

Caius put the letter in his pocket and picked up the book again, scanning the blurb. This must be what Hampton had meant when he said there was additional context to the case. Caius put the book in his backpack and started tapping his fingers on the desk as he tried to predict how dinner at Hampton's club would go.

'I spoke to the people at the train company,' Amy said loudly, hoping to jolt Caius out of whatever well-heeled introspection he was lost in. 'They're summoning all the staff from that carriage to the headquarters so we can speak to them tomorrow morning.'

'Brilliant,' Caius said, absentmindedly, acknowledging Amy's administrative prowess.

'What did you think of Rosie?' Matt asked.

'I don't think she killed anyone,' Caius said, snapping out of it.

'Me neither,' Matt said. Rosie had seemed too artless.

'She lied about the phone call. Perhaps it wasn't her boss? The sister who always wants a free babysitter? She knew something about how the estate was going to be split too. She was rather sniffy about that question.' Caius hoped for her sake that that lie wasn't going to come round and bite her on the arse. She'd seemed like a nice girl until that point. He was going to let the lie play out a little while longer. 'We'll know soon enough what's going on with Mona's estate.'

'What did you think of the family dynamic?' Amy asked. She'd watched the interview from behind the two-way mirror.

'She thinks her sister is a vain, fluffy-headed idiot, and her brother-in-law is a rich but questionable bit of rough. At least, that was my observation. Bristled at the talk of money, tries to rise above anything that vulgar, and does an inhuman amount of charity work. She's a holier-than-thou snob.'

'The sister, Sienna, and her husband live in Wandsworth. That's only about fifteen minutes by car in the dead of night,' Matt said, getting up Google Maps on his phone to check the distance. 'They sound loaded.'

'Doesn't mean they are though. They could be up to their eyeballs in debt. Mortgages, school fees, business loans,' Amy said.

'They could very well be,' Caius said, printing out the pictures of the staff from the train. 'I'm always astounded at the fees people pay so their kids don't have to go to the school round the corner. Amy, could you check out the sister's app? You're more likely to understand the "nuances" than me or Matt.'

'I'm already on it. Sienna Worthing is basically a life coach with a very pretty Instagram grid and a little meditation app attached. A lot of it is quasi-spiritual stuff, you know, manifestation and astrology and crystals. It seems pretty slick though, considering the initial hippy vibe. It's also ultra feminine. She talks about womanhood and having children a lot in her bio.' Amy flashed them her phone with the app open. It was grey and soft pink. 'She's followed by quite a few minor celebrities. It seems she had a baby boy two months ago, but before that she was running these expensive wellness retreats in the countryside every other week.'

'That sounds like something for people who don't have real problems.' Caius Blu-Tacked the images of the train's staff to the whiteboard. Something wasn't right there but it wasn't jumping out at him straight away.

'It's a bit culty.'

'Culty?' Matt asked.

'Yeah, a very aesthetically driven, nice, white lady cult. Everyone at the retreats have good teeth, a sizable disposable income and dodgy beliefs about modern medicine.'

'Is she a creepy cult leader?' Caius asked.

'Probably just deluded,' Amy said.

Caius sat back down and spun around in his office chair as he took that in. He thought it was unlikely that Mona's family dynamics had any real bearing on the case. What they needed was to find out about the burglar and his accomplices but at least they could say they'd looked at it.

'Do you think the case is linked to the Colon Cancer charity auction?' Matt asked. He had a quick look at the Colon Cancer UK's website. It was legitimate. It had a well-attended programme of sponsored 5Ks in parks and a minor royal as a patron.

'I doubt it.' Caius was curious about those sorts of functions. He wondered if he'd ever be invited to something similar. Caius found the environmental charity that Rosie worked for. He opened the 'About Us' page and looked at a picture of Felix, Rosie's boss. Felix looked like the sort to be invited to ballrooms. His eyes twinkled. His nose was on the characterful side of patrician which just stopped him from being *too* handsome. He wondered if Rosie and Felix were more than friends, but then he remembered her blushing over Tristan. 'The charity Rosie works for is interesting. The founder Felix went on a walk with a friend through the English countryside, there were no bees, Felix didn't like that, his friend said you should do something about that, so he is. That simple. Imagine being so confident of your place in the world that you see a monumental ecological problem and go yeah, I'll rent an office and tackle that. As far as

I can tell he doesn't have a degree in ecology, biology or even agriculture. How is that possible?'

'Spectacular arrogance and inherited wealth is how,' Matt said, peering over Caius's shoulder at the page. 'At least he's having a crack at it, I suppose. Better than sitting at home and whingeing.'

'Does anyone regulate environment charities? I don't like dashing amateurs. Everything should be left to the professionals who have letters after their names and who plod on doing the job. I wouldn't want my appendix taken out by an enthusiast with a scalpel they bought on Amazon.' Caius closed the tab. He looked at the time on his watch. 'Time, ladies and gentlemen. Pub?'

'I'm off to netball practice tonight,' Amy said.

'New team?' Matt asked. This was the first time she'd mentioned netball in a while. Amy had left her previous team a few months earlier. All they knew was that there was some sort of out of court settlement last year, which had caused a mutiny between Amy and a couple of her friends who had quit the team after their annual general meeting in January in protest.

'New league.'

'Fair enough.' Caius could sense that Matt was looking at him with suppressed amusement. Neither of them had yet to work out what had really happened at Amy's last team, but they had come up with increasingly wild theories, the latest one involving a rabies scare.

'Hopefully this league will be more civilised,' Amy said, waving goodbye as she headed for the lift.

'Pub?' Matt asked.

'Pub,' Caius said.

# 9

## The Red Lion Public House

The Red Lion was close enough to the police station to be convenient, but not so close that they were likely to bump into any of their colleagues. It had a large greenhouse-like extension at the back overlooking a beer garden they enjoyed in warmer weather. Often it had the football on and, depending on whether the landlord was paying the subscription fee, sometimes the cricket played in the summer. They had chosen a quiet spot where they couldn't be overheard. They were on their second pints, and two packets of crisps – one sweet chilli and the other mature cheddar and caramelised red onion – had been meticulously opened until the packets were laid flat and placed in the middle of the table. It was tipping it down. The sound of raindrops hitting the conservatory roof was soothing. The pub had a passable selection of proper beer. Matt had a pint of Jolly Yeoman (a surprisingly zesty IPA) from a brewery in Hackney that neither of them had heard of. This was unusual as East London craft breweries were one of the few socially acceptable fetishes, other than Arsenal and niche trainer brands, that they felt they'd been permitted. They both peered at the label on the can – there was a very muscular, shirtless man with a very tight grip around the handle of a scythe standing in a wheat field in the centre and the outside of the label was surrounded by a garland of wildflowers – before Matt poured it into his glass.

'I had my offer accepted this morning on a shared ownership flat in Clapton. Just off Murder Mile,' Matt said, putting his pint down. 'Just got to get all the mortgage stuff sorted.'

'Wahey, congrats, mate.' Caius raised his drink. 'You'll be wearing those weird toe shoes before we know it.'

'I cannot wait to move.' Matt lived in a flat in Morden with a guy he'd found on a house share website five years ago. They got on all right, which really meant they ignored each other most of the time other than pleasantries in the kitchen, but Stewart's extensive Warhammer collection had started to spill out of his room and into the communal living space. 'Talking about houses . . .'

'Yeah, well . . .'

'It's one hell of a house.'

'One hell of a legacy to keep going.' Caius sat back on the leather banquette and played with the label on his beer bottle, pulling the edges away as he prepared to tell his one friend who he thought would get how he felt. 'All of a sudden I've gone from thinking my surname was a living relic of the crimes of a plantation owner and everything true about my family history beyond the imperfect measure of my skin colour was lost to the mists of time, to being able to trace my family directly back to the Norman Conquest. I think we have a claim to the French throne. I don't know who I am any more.'

'You're still half Irish.'

'Harbouring a recessive redhead gene has been my only constant.'

'I guess the Rupert connection doesn't help?'

'No. I'm there every weekend and all I can think about is that bastard's smug, punchable face. I've been near the lake. I need to exorcise that demon. My mum might actually be up for having the priest round.' Caius was going to text her about it later. It wasn't the worst idea.

'How's your dad taking it?'

'Unsurprisingly Dad intends to step up and be lord of the manor. He gets bored really easily. Despite his protestations he's loving it. My mum is chuffed because she gets to swan about the grounds.' Caius pushed down thoughts of what had happened at the pond. 'I need to build happy memories there and try to forget about last summer. Callie thinks we should throw a party.'

Matt nodded. 'How's Callie? I've not seen her since we lost that pub quiz a few weeks ago.' They were sure the team who came first had been googling the answers in the loo. Why else would their knowledge span the breadths from the Punic Wars and organic chemistry to the early noughties output of Simon Cowell's pop factory?

'All right. A bit stressed. She's busy teaching an evening class at a community centre. She's gearing up for what she calls "the remnants of the season". All those Victorian events that women wear hats to, plus summer weddings.'

'Weddings?' Matt gave him an expectant look.

'You're as bad as my mother.' Caius helped himself to a couple of chilli crisps. 'They met this weekend. It went surprisingly well.'

'Callie's pretty damn charming. I don't think she's the sort of person people take umbrage with.'

'Yeah.' Caius smiled smugly to himself. 'How's your love life? Sorry it's been a while since I asked. I figured you'd tell me what you wanted me to know but I'm one beer down and feel like asking.'

'There's this girl who I've got a casual thing going with, but it's not serious yet.'

'The barmaid from the pub quiz?'

'How did you know?'

'I'm a detective, and she was very clearly flirting with you.'

'Yumi slipped me her number when she gave me a free packet of artisanal roasted peanuts.'

Two women sat down at a table at the other end of the conservatory from them.

'Once and for all, do you think Amy bit someone at netball or did someone bite Amy?'

'I can't call it either way.'

'Me neither.'

# 10

## Caius and Callie's Flat, Tufnell Park

Caius was propped up on the sofa reluctantly rereading the blurb of the book Hampton had sent him. It wasn't apparent why he had been sent it. The TV was on in the background – a news report about severe flooding near Bristol – and Callie was making dinner in the kitchen. It was her turn. She had been sewing silk flowers onto wide-brimmed straw hats for most of the day and her fingers still felt a little sore as she chopped up a lemon. She'd stopped off at the supermarket to buy a large chicken. She was trying to keep her cold at bay and fancied making a hearty, nourishing soup with the leftovers. The bird was roasting in the oven, smothered in garlic, butter and slices of lemon. Callie placed two teacups and a teapot containing a magic potion made with hot water, lemon, ginger, honey and a generous dash of turmeric on the coffee table in front of Caius and sat next to him.

'I'll come in tomorrow to speak to Amy then.' Callie was intrigued by the baby-pink cover of the book that Caius was holding apprehensively. That wasn't the shade of novel he usually read. He was prone to reading serious books with paintings on the cover. 'What have you got there?'

'It's for work,' he said, showing her the cover. 'The government-minister-who-shall-not-be-named sent it over as background for this case.'

'The Stratfords! My goodness. They were wild.' Callie snuggled into him. He smelled good. Well, just about – she was losing her sense of smell.

'You know who they are?' Caius asked, putting the tome down next to the teapot on the table.

'I know a bit about them.' Callie looked again at the cover. It looked familiar – she'd probably read it on an adolescent trip to her grandmother's when her mother got too much. She would moodily languish in the conservatory eating as many biscuits as she damn well wanted and read whatever books were lying about the house. 'My granny was a little obsessed with them. I read Anne Stratford novels aloud to her while she was in the hospice. That family was scandalous. Well, one of them was an out and out Nazi, so more than scandalous. Repulsive but fascinating nonetheless.'

'Nazis? That's all I bloody need right now.' Caius took his phone out and began to search for the Stratford sisters. 'Do they have a Wikipedia page? This book is nearly five hundred pages long.'

'You don't need Wikipedia. You live with me.'

'Go on then,' Caius said, putting his phone down, reaching an arm around her and stroking her hair.

'The Stratford girls were these three aristo sisters.'

'Right.' Caius opened the middle of the book and looked at the grainy black-and-white photographs as Callie talked.

'And between them they span the great political ideological landscape of the twentieth century. Isca was a communist and attempted to defect to the Soviet Union in 1946 but was talked out of it by their mother. She ended up leaving Blighty and moving to New York where she became a journalist and literary critic. Anne, the famous author, wrote snarky society novels. My gran was a huge fan. Lots of people getting married too young and having affairs with the wrong people and saying witty, withering putdowns. Very arch. Anne had an affair with the Argentinian ambassador and then after the war moved to Paris to write biographies of renaissance figures. And finally, Artemisia who married Sir Wulfric Fowley in Berlin; you know, the leader of the Union of English Fascists. Hitler came to their wedding. Anne shopped Artemisia to the authorities as an active fascist during the war and Artemisia was sent to Pentonville for the whole thing and lived on gruel and spite. They never spoke again. Actually, there was a fourth younger sister, but she quietly got married and no one pays much attention to her. Oh, and they were Winston Churchill's cousins somehow.'

'I thought you said you only knew a bit about them,' Caius said.

'That's not five hundred pages' worth, is it?' Callie leaned forward and poured them each a cup of hot lemon.

'I guess not,' Caius said, picking up the book again. He ran his finger along the edge. 'This page has a corner turned over.'

He opened the page to find a paragraph neatly highlighted in fluorescent yellow pen. He read it aloud to Callie who was slowly sipping her magic potion, cupping her hands around the cup with a devotional reverence.

Artemisia's second marriage to Sir Wulfric Fowley occurred on 17 May 1936 in Berlin. In attendance were many prominent members of the National Socialist Party including Himmler, Speer and even Hitler himself who had befriended the beautiful socialite the previous year on one of her frequent trips to Berlin. Hitler and Artemisia had been seen on multiple occasions having tea in some of Berlin's smartest hotels. The marriage came as a shock to much of London society. Artemisia's divorce from her first husband had been finalised but three months before. For those in the know, however, their marriage was no surprise. They had carried out their affair in the darkest corners of London's smartest and yet lenient clubs who, by this point, were very accustomed to the antics of the Bright Young Things. By then Sir Wulfric had already broken clean away from his Conservative roots. The week before the wedding his 'purple shirt' movement had caused much alarm in the East End by marching through predominantly Jewish areas.

Caius saw through the paper that another paragraph on the next page had also been highlighted. He turned the page and read that aloud too.

The previous year there had been a rumour circulating that Mary, the youngest Stratford daughter, was desperately in love with Sir Wulfric, who she had met while staying in Berlin with Artemisia to improve her German. Mary, it seems, had also been a favourite of Hitler's, who was keen to be seen about Berlin with her. She was shyer and less confident than Artemisia but to many observers more beautiful. Tall, like the rest of the Stratford girls with deep blue eyes and a quiet sense of mischief. It was rumoured that the Führer had given her a pair of diamond earrings as a gift. Lord Snitterfield, evidently more protective of his youngest child than the others, whisked Mary away to his estate in the Warwickshire countryside and out of danger.

'I told you they were wild,' Callie said.
'Wild indeed,' he said, reflecting on the passage. Caius flicked to the index and searched through 'B', desperately hoping there

wasn't a Beauchamp mentioned. He did not find one. 'What a charming family.'

'Perversely I should say that they were charming,' Callie said. The timer on the oven went off and Callie left Caius on the sofa trying to ascertain how the hell it was pertinent to the deaths of Mona Frogmorton and the unnamed steward-turned-burglar as she took the chicken out to rest.

Caius looked up at the television and saw a report about Islamophobia on the news. Johnny Bull, an MP that Caius liked to ignore, had been at it again. Bull had made a comment to a journalist that English had almost been eradicated as a spoken language in Leicester, and contrary to the facts, was defending his words on Twitter with worse and worse rhetoric. Caius looked at his face. He looked so ordinary. You'd pass him on the street and merely think 'he's probably an estate agent'.

'Who are the British going to be in forty years? Will they still speak English? Will they look like us? Will we be strangers in our own land? Will this become Englistan?'

Caius turned the television off.

TUESDAY

# 11

The Albion Historic Railway
Company Headquarters, Victoria

Caius was in the boardroom addressing the staff who had worked in 'his' carriage. He felt self-conscious. They all were looking at him curiously. They had known him as a punter, sat in his chair gobbling and quaffing whatever they put in front of him and now they knew he was a dour plod, a bog-standard policeman. He didn't like it when his two separate realities left their compartments. The train company's offices were in a town house round the back of Victoria station and away from the bustle. It was a smart red-brick building with iron railings and steep stone steps to the front door. The Albion Historic Railway took up only the top few floors. The basement and ground floor were occupied by a nannying agency. The offices were painted in what Callie had recently referred to as 'heritage' colours. Deep and reverential, almost medieval feeling, and the offices themselves had something 'old boy' about them. Fat brown leather chairs and precisely the right amount of worn-out Persian rugs. The staff based in the office comprised a small marketing team, a scowling woman called Lara who oversaw staffing, a finance bloke who blended into the background and the CEO: a nervous man called Justin who kept rubbing his hands together. Caius and Matt had already spoken to Lara and she had repeated with a firmness that bordered on aggy that the list she'd sent over was indeed the staff who were present on the day. Lara had also given the contact details of the other two parties who'd been sat in their carriage.

'We believe that a recent murder victim was working in the carriage with you that day. Advance warning – we will be showing you a photograph of the deceased's face from the crime scene,' Caius said, looking at the five staff members in front of him. Normally he wouldn't have been this blunt about the steward's violent death, but he wanted to shock them into giving something away. Three of them he recognised from the trip – another steward who he'd seen serving the golf-clubby couple and the time-jump trio, a porter who had helped Mona out of the train, and the wine waiter who judiciously kept topping their glasses so that they didn't do much the next day – all of whom looked understandably alarmed. Of the other two staff members, one sat with his arms folded, clearly perplexed by the whole situation, and the other was trying their hardest to not look like anything. 'We'd appreciate it if you keep your recollections of the day to yourself. We don't want things to get muddled.'

Caius and Matt then proceeded to interview the three staff members that Caius had initially recognised one by one. The train company had made the marketing team vacate their office for the purpose and sent them all to a busy coffee shop in Victoria station to think of ways to sell fancy train rides to aspirational commuters who already spent a good portion of their lives on trains as it was. The interviews had all been short, and Caius hadn't felt the need to show them the picture of the dead steward. All three agreed that the deceased burglar had indeed been working that shift, that they'd never worked with him before and didn't have any complaints on the day. No one had noticed anything unusual about him. He'd said that his name was Phil and that he was covering temporarily. They'd all said that Karl, the younger lad who'd been sat with them attempting to appear blank in the boardroom earlier, had called in sick last minute and Phil had been his replacement. Vincenzo, a fastidious young Italian man who was the other steward in their carriage, mentioned the fact that the husband of the couple in the corner didn't catch the return train which he thought was odd.

Then they interviewed the chef, who had sat cross-armed and perplexed earlier.

'That Phil came to a nasty end then?' asked the chef, a middle-aged man called Mark who hailed from Yorkshire via Wiltons. 'I didn't like him.'

'Why not?' Matt asked.

'I saw him looking at the passenger manifest for a bit too long with his phone out.'

'The passenger manifest?' Caius asked.

'It's a list of guests. It has allergies and the like. Vegetarians. Even vegans,' he said with mild disgust. 'Contact details et cetera. There's a copy kept in my kitchen. I came back from my break when we were in Bath, and I saw him taking a picture of it on his phone. I asked him what he was up to, and he said that he was just checking the allergies for the dinner service. Clearly a lie. I said it were people's personal details and that he wasn't to take pictures. He left me well alone after that. I meant to mention it to Lara and tell her not to have him back, but I forgot. Never mind.'

* * *

Caius had Lara join him for the last interview. Karl was squirming in his seat. Caius had purposely left him to last, leaving him in the boardroom with Lara to make sure he didn't do a runner.

'All right, Karl,' Caius said, doing his best paternalistic 'I'm not upset just disappointed' face at the youth. 'Do you want to tell us what happened?'

'It's my fault,' he blurted. 'Phil said he'd pay me double what the shift was worth if I didn't go in. He's my dad's cousin.'

'Oh, Karl,' Lara said, utterly shocked at his lack of professionalism.

'I called up Chef on the day and said I was ill after eating some bad prawns and that Lara had approved Phil to cover me. I'm so sorry, Lara.' He initially looked relieved at having told the truth but now the consequences were creeping up to him. He looked at Lara ashamedly. 'You're going to fire me, aren't you?'

'Yes,' Lara said. Caius could see her filing the paperwork in her head.

'What's Phil's whole name?' Matt asked.

'Philip Campbell.'

'And has he been in trouble before?'

'He got done for burglary when he was young, but Dad said he'd gone straight. He'd been working in hotels for years and years. He'd recommended a training course when I was thinking of going into hospitality. I didn't think he was up to anything dodgy. I thought maybe he wanted to try something new. Maybe he wanted a change from the hotel. I really needed the money. I bet my last month's wages on the Liverpool match and my mum was furious with me. She won't lend me money any more.'

'Who's his next of kin?'

'My dad, I guess.'

Caius took down Karl's father's number and then Lara escorted Karl out of the building.

'I sort of feel sorry for him,' Matt said. It was just the two of them now.

'Naivety ceases to be an acceptable excuse beyond twenty-one,' Caius said. Karl should've known better. He was twenty-two.

'Hey, at least you don't have a brain tumour.'

'Hurrah.' Caius looked out of the window of the marketing office. He could see Victoria a quarter of a mile away. 'Philip Campbell paid his cousin's son to take his place so he could find a mark.'

'A luxury train ride is not a bad hunting ground.'

'He stole the contact details of the passengers in the carriage and settled on Mona.'

'Makes sense. An elderly woman.'

'She was clearly the frailest out of everyone in our carriage and you have to assume that anyone on one of those trains has spare cash to burn. The tickets are nearly £500 each.'

'Wow.'

'I didn't buy them, Callie's dad did.'

'I was going to say.' Matt paused, he'd been feeling a bit weird about Caius flashing the cash but it was Callie's dad who had more money than sense after all. 'Is that still weird between them?'

'Yeah, Callie is keeping him at arm's length and I am avoiding him entirely.'

'Makes sense. We ended his career.'

'We merely facilitated its inevitable demise.' Caius took his phone out, quickly scanning his email.

'Five hundred pounds each, fuck. That's a lot for Bath and back. You could fly to New York for that,' Matt said.

'I know. It was nice though. Peter's trying to shower Callie with gifts in lieu of thirty years' worth of an honest relationship. He's sent so many bunches of flowers. Keeps trying to take her to Nobu. He's asked her to go to Ascot with him this year – something that Harriet used to make a big deal out of.'

Lara came back into the room, apologising profusely for the data breach, followed by Justin the CEO who begged Caius not to close them down. Caius, who said he was no expert in data protection by any means, told him that he was duty-bound to report it to the correct team. Caius and Matt left.

'I wonder who Phil was working with?' Matt asked, getting into the car.

'That's the question,' Caius said.

# 12

## The Police Station

Amy placed a petite, pale pink cool bag on Caius's desk. She turned and looked at the suit bag hanging on the door of a cupboard behind it and shook her head. Amy had just returned from taking Callie's statement about her brief interaction with Mona on the train. She'd been very frank, as Caius had told her to be, and people-watcher extraordinaire that she was, had also given Amy a colourful description of her observations of her fellow passengers, including a rundown on the vintage throuple's footsie antics, and the golf husband in the ill-fitting jacket not making the return journey.

'You forgot your lunch,' Amy said. Caius, who had been deep in thought staring at the incident board, looked up at her. 'Wifey brought it in for you.'

'You didn't call her that to her face, did you?' Caius asked, alarmed. It wasn't that he didn't want to marry Callie one day. He did, very much so. In his most idle moments, he was daydreaming about what their wedding would be like. But he wasn't prepared to be publicly exposed as a totally hopeless romantic. He looked up at Amy. It was no good. She knew he'd planned their life together in his head and smirked back at him.

'No I didn't, I don't want to scare Callie off. Fi would never forgive me.' Fi, Amy's paediatric nurse girlfriend, was a little twee in that sapphic way and had decided that she wanted to be friends with the milliner who had such a good eye for hemlines and general whimsical ephemera. 'You should buy Callie some flowers though. I showed her the picture of the dead steward and good news, I guess, she positively identified him too, so you haven't had a stroke.'

'Do I want Callie to associate flowers with corpses?'

'Maybe not.'

'Here you are, darling, forget about all the blood.'

'Get her some fancy shower gel. A bit of Jo Malone or something. She can metaphorically wash the image away in the shower.'

For a fleeting moment Caius thought Amy was a genius but then he saw her lip begin to curl. 'You are so mean to me. I'm your gaffer not the other way around. You're precocious.'

'I do it for your own good. Just buy the poor girl some flowers.' Amy sat down at her desk. 'I got Philip Campbell's record up after you called from the train company. He did a stint in 1996 for three burglaries in Manchester. He was working with a guy called Louis Dixon. Dixon died last month. Nothing recent for Philip, not even a parking ticket. A model of prison reform. I've got an address in Cricklewood.'

Matt entered the incident room with a box of physical evidence that Faisal had had sent over from Hammersmith. He put it on an empty table to the side of the room. 'Have those autopsies come through?'

'Not yet,' Caius said, checking his emails. 'I'll chase Hammersmith. Both autopsies were supposed to be happening today.'

'Officially a burglary gone wrong then?' Matt said.

'Yeah.' Caius got the record up that Amy had found earlier and quickly read it. 'Looks like we may be able to get rid of Hampton quicker than we thought.'

'Well, the burglary explains what happened to Mona. Kill the old lady before doing over the place. Callous and totally unnecessary but logical,' Amy began, taking an apple out of Caius's drawer. He'd become the team's unofficial fruiterer. 'Burglary explains why Philip was there, but it doesn't explain what happened to him.'

'Does it explain what happened to Mona?' Matt asked, peering over Caius's shoulder. He'd worked on plenty of burglaries in his early years at the Met and very few of them resulted in murder. 'Did he use violence previously?'

'No, the houses were always empty,' Caius said, wondering who Philip had teamed up with as his old accomplice Louis Dixon was dead. This accomplice was now the prime suspect.

'I'll get in touch with Greater Manchester Police and see if anyone who worked on the Altrincham cases remembers him or Dixon,' Amy said.

'I'll put a warrant request in to search his address,' Caius said, looking at the time. 'If I'm quick we may catch a judge before they go for lunch.'

'Submit it and just tell Hampton. One of his minions will make sure it's sorted quickly,' Matt said, patting his stomach. 'Lunch? Pizza?'

'Caius's wifey brought him a little packed lunch in,' Amy said, pointing at it and the special little bag it had come in. Caius scowled back at her.

'Did you sneak off to a registry office or have I missed something here?' Matt asked.

'Callie brought my lunch in with her this morning and Amy is relentlessly teasing me about it,' Caius said.

'Oh, so just the usual then. I was worried my invite had gone astray, and I'd have to never speak to you again,' Matt said.

# 13

## Fulham Mortuary

'Mr Campbell?' Amy asked the stony-faced man in the waiting room.

'Yes,' he said, standing up.

Amy shook his hand. 'Thank you for coming so quickly.'

'Not at all.'

Amy led him down the corridor and into the mortuary. An assistant was waiting to show them the body.

'Mr Campbell, could you please confirm whether or not this is your cousin Philip Campbell.'

'That's my cousin,' he said, stepping back.

★   ★   ★

'Would you like another cup of tea?' Amy asked. The colour had begun to return to his cheeks.

'No, thank you.'

Amy had taken him through to a side room to recover from the sight of his bloodless, mottled relation.

'I just . . . I can't believe it. We all thought he was on the straight and narrow. He was round our house last week for Sunday lunch. My poor aunt. I can only imagine what this would've done to her. He broke into a house, you say, and there was an altercation?'

'Yes. It appears so. Did he have any close friends we could speak to?'

'I don't really know. I saw him a few times a year. Christmas.

Easter. The odd barbeque in the summer. We weren't in each other's pockets. He'd had a girlfriend a few years ago. Nice girl, but she broke it off when she realised he wasn't as serious about it all as she was.'

Amy nodded.

'Whatever he was trying to nick, I hope it was worth it. Got himself killed and Karl fired.'

\* \* \*

'Detective Constable,' the medical examiner on duty said, following Amy down a corridor as she was gleefully about to leave the building. 'The two autopsies from your case are next up.'

'Thanks,' Amy said, turning to briefly smile at them before disappearing through the double doors. She didn't want to linger. She hated it there. Bodies in drawers. The clinical smell. The finality of it. The terrible reminder that we are all just a sack of organs with a consciousness that thinks we're better than that.

# 14

## Cricklewood

Caius and Matt were loitering in the hall of Philip Campbell's building as a team of forensic scientists from Hammersmith swept through his flat. It was small – what is euphemistically referred to now as a studio apartment rather than a bedsit. Nothing ostentatious about it. Nothing to suggest a crime spree had taken place. Campbell's mobile phone had been left on the kitchen surface and had been bagged up. An IT specialist would go through it to find any communication between him and an accomplice.

'Did he have a car?' Caius asked, noticing a letter on the side that looked like it contained insurance information. He opened it. 'A Vauxhall Corsa.'

'I'll get uniform to locate it,' Matt said, making a note of the reg.

Amy was ringing. 'All right, Amy?' Caius asked.

'Yeah. Philip Campbell's autopsy has just happened. They're doing Mona now. Cause of death is no surprise. They'll send through the full report tomorrow, apparently.'

'Great, did they say anything about the timings?'

'No, sorry. Just a brisk call from a very harried medical examiner.'

'All right, cheers. I think we're going to be here a while. Can you get the other passengers from the train, Josephine Krige and all of Rosie's friends she was out with that night in tomorrow? I just want to cross them off the list.'

'No problem,' she said before hanging up.

Caius's personal phone started to vibrate. He picked it up. The number was withheld.

'Hello,' Caius said.

'Terribly sorry. I can't do dinner tonight. I'll swing by yours just after 7 p.m.,' Arthur Hampton said.

'Trouble at the Treasury?' Caius asked, this having been the euphemistic excuse given last time they were supposed to meet and Hampton bailed.

'No, the MoD for a change.'

'All right.' Although, it wasn't all right. He didn't really want Hampton in his flat. He wasn't sure how Hampton had got his address. Hampton hung up.

'Trouble at the Royal Mint?' Matt asked.

'Trouble in my flat,' Caius said. He'd need to ring Callie and give her a heads-up. She wasn't keen on ever seeing Hampton in the flesh again lest hers crawled away. Caius also needed to vacuum.

'Did you see the think piece Hampton wrote in *The Economist* last week?' Matt asked. He'd still got a Google Alert set up for him. He didn't want to mention it before in case he Beetlejuiced it and made him appear, but seeing that Hampton had now made his much-vaunted appearance he felt free to mention it.

'No, what did he say?'

'A lot but also nothing. The thing that surprised me was that he said the government has failed us.'

'But he's in government.' Caius thought he probably was the government. He would speed through it before tonight. Caius still couldn't work out exactly what Hampton's modus operandi was. It wasn't as if Hampton was without power. He sat in the room where the decisions were made. The PM was supposed to be his pet. There must be some wrangling going on behind the scenes that the general public weren't privy to.

'Exactly. I guess to the uninitiated he appears to be on the fringes of it. I'll send you a link.'

'Cheers.'

'Excuse me, sir,' said a member of forensics coming into the hallway.

'Call me Caius.'

'Well, Caius, we've just found a wodge of cash hidden inside a cushion. Looks to be a couple of grand in used £20 notes.'

# 15

## Lucia's Flat, Putney

Rosie had been dreading calling her granny's best friend. She'd been putting it off all morning. She was tempted to get her mother to do it instead but that would mean speaking to her and she didn't quite feel up to that.

'Hello, may I please speak to Mrs Daphne Winter?' Rosie asked the receptionist of the facility Daphne was now living in.

'Of course,' said the receptionist. 'Mrs Winter is having a good day today. She's been very talkative.'

Rosie waited for Daphne to come to the phone as she sprawled across Lucia's sofa with a daytime TV quiz show playing in the background. She couldn't watch a drama; nothing with a plot or feelings, people to care about, no allegories, nothing profound. Rosie just wanted noise and facts children should know.

'Mrs Winter speaking,' came the steady, measured reply.

'Daphne, it's Rosie, Mona's granddaughter. I'm afraid I have some terrible news. Granny was killed a few days ago, in a botched burglary.'

'Poor Mona. Oh dear. Oh Mona! Killed!' Silence as Daphne Winter composed herself. 'How dreadful.'

'It was dreadful, Daphne. I can't explain how awful it was to find her.'

'Oh, my dear. Is there anything I can do?'

'No, no I'll be all right. I'll push through. I'm staying at a friend's for a little while.'

'Very sensible. Best not to be alone in times like these.'

Rosie paused in reflective silence as she remembered the last time Daphne had come to visit them before her memory started to fail. They'd gone to see *The Merchant of Venice* at the National Theatre. Daphne had sent her off with a fifty-pound note to get them all a tub of ice cream in the interval and had insisted she keep the change to get herself something nice. She was about to share the memory with Daphne when the old lady said her name and asked who was speaking. Rosie claimed to have called the wrong number. She realised now that a 'good day' for Daphne now was sustaining a few minutes' worth of considered conversation.

*   *   *

Four years ago, Rosie had done a law conversion course at the same professional college where Lucia had been studying for the bar. A student bar, actually, was where they had met. It was a networking event arranged by the college. Rosie, sweet Rosie with her habit of opening her eyes too wide if she found something displeasing, had ended up hiding in the toilet from a rather intense young man on her course who had a monumental crush on her. In his head he'd already named their children and bought a commutable detached house in Hertfordshire. He'd tried a bit too hard to impress Rosie with his intellect, arguing against every single thing she said. He'd have said the sky was red if he'd had the chance. He couldn't see that Rosie wasn't interested and, worse than that, couldn't stand him. She'd fled to the loo to get away. Lucia had seen it all happen from over his shoulder as she barely sipped a glass of cheap Pinot Noir and had followed Rosie. Lucia found her leaning against the sink, scrolling through her phone. Lucia had said, 'Bloody hell, he's a bit much,' and Rosie rolled her eyes and said, 'Tell me about it.' Theirs was one of those beautiful lifelong friendships forged in a mere moment in the ladies' loos. Lucia had popped her head out to see if the coast was clear and the two of them escaped to a nicer pub down the road with leafy-green painted woodwork and tasteful botanical prints, while Rosie's admirer was queueing at the other bar for another watery beer, wondering how much longer she was going to be in the bogs. Rosie and Lucia shared a bottle of rosé and found out that they both liked painting, Yorkshire puddings and Taylor Swift. They had been inseparable ever since.

Lucia thought that Rosie had a specifically English sort of charm, a dainty prettiness that her name suggested, but any awareness of it had been squashed out of her by not wanting to stand out too much. She was good too. Like a little fairy doll. All sweet and soft and pink. Bloody nice, unless she was pushed, at which point a defiant streak of righteous anger appeared. She gleefully chatted to strangers on the bus. She gaily baked cakes for charity coffee mornings at work. She merrily helped parents get their prams up flights of stairs on the tube. She remembered everyone's birthday. She volunteered once a week at a local baby bank. She lived with her elderly grandmother and cheerfully did all the cooking. Lucia liked Rosie because she wasn't like that. Lucia would automatically lean into any 'unpleasant' feeling, whereas Rosie's first instinct was to flee from it, confronting it only if it failed to resolve itself. Blunt and exceedingly direct about everything she chose to succeed in, Lucia didn't have it in her to think too much about other people because she was too busy trying to defend their inalienable rights as a collective than to be drowned in the personal; the individual.

Rosie had made toad-in-the-hole for dinner. Lucia was welcomed into her flat by the smell of a colossal Yorkshire pudding rising in the oven.

'Oh, Rosie, you didn't have to,' Lucia said, coming into the living room. She was glad she had though. She was knackered. The case she was working on was particularly thorny. A mother and newborn left behind in a warzone because the Home Office said the British-born parent didn't meet the income criteria to bring the mother over.

'I want to keep busy.'

'Understandable.' Lucia put her backpack down beside the table.

'Food is real. It's grounding, as Sienna would say.' Rosie rolled her eyes.

'Have you spoken to her?' Lucia tried to say this without prejudice. She wasn't fond of Sienna. She'd barely spoken to the woman apart from at Rosie's recent birthday dinner, but Lucia had caught her looking at her sideways when she snorted loudly at Sienna's silly idea that you couldn't be happy as a woman unless you'd given birth vaginally.

'Yeah, she called earlier. I'm going to go round tomorrow. Have a cuddle with the baby and then take the girls to the swings. All of the unpleasantness between her and Granny over the last couple of years will be finally buried with her.' Rosie had seen much less of Sienna while her sister and her granny were not talking, and had almost missed Sienna, despite her tendency towards a cloying sort of selfish manipulation that always made Rosie feel a little queasy. And yes, Sienna did spout nonsense about feminine energy, but Rosie just zoned out, or if Sienna was persistent told her that she wouldn't talk about feminism or politics with her. Yes, Sienna was amusing for a bit, if you stuck to talk of throwing parties or holidays or the children. Rosie adored her nieces and nephews. In truth, if it wasn't for them, she'd have stopped bothering by now. 'She keeps trying to rope me in to shit.'

'"No" is a complete sentence.' Lucia took her laptop out of her bag and started to charge it. She needed to draft an email to Amnesty International.

Rosie resumed her spot on the sofa and picked up her knitting.

'Is that for the baby bank?' Lucia asked.

'Oh no, this is for Sienna's little one. It's a little set. I saw the pattern online and I couldn't help myself. I've already done the hat.' Rosie picked up the ball of soft woad-coloured wool. 'This is real wool from British sheep and hand-dyed in Shropshire. I wouldn't use anything but acrylic for the baby bank. I'm not sure the women who use it would appreciate the difference. I'm making a little cardigan with matching booties to go with the pointy little hat that looks like it's meant for a gnome. I can't believe she has four children. Who has that many these days?'

A timer on Rosie's phone went off and she took the toad-in-the-hole out of the oven and drained the peas that were boiling on the hob into a colander in the sink.

'I quite like coming home to a housewife,' Lucia said.

'I think I'd make quite a good housewife actually.'

'Bit of a waste of your degree and your legal training, right?' Lucia opened the fridge and took out a Diet Coke. 'You'd end up like one of Betty Friedan's subjects taking all afternoon to clean out the fridge with a toothbrush because you have nothing else to do and chugging Xanax to get you through the boredom of it all.'

'Isn't that preferable to working all hours and being perpetually single? Not just single, alone? Can a string of sad one-night stands sustain your soul?' Rosie looked at Lucia rather blankly.

'Uh-huh.' Lucia loved her career. She wasn't interested in breeding. Never had been. She wasn't in a relationship but she was definitely not alone. Rosie was staying in her flat for starters. 'Friends, Rosie. Friends.'

'Yeah, I suppose.' Rosie shrugged and continued her thought. 'I probably should take Xanax to get me through the boredom of always being around people and yet still being constantly alone. The lack of a silence and peace found in a true purpose.'

'You sound like your sister.'

'Do I? Oh God.' Rosie shook her head.

'You sound susceptible.' Lucia squinted at Rosie. 'You're either trying to tell me you're pregnant or joining a commune.' Lucia had both a fulfilling purpose in life and enough of the conversation.

'What?' Rosie laughed. 'No, God no. Just mulling over the trauma of modern womanhood. You can't have it all. So why pretend.'

'OK.'

'Maybe I've been watching too many videos about people moving to the countryside and living off grid. They bake their own bread and can the tomatoes they grew in the summer.'

'Do they keep chickens?'

'Always.'

'That's how they get you, with the chickens.'

'They're so fluffy though.'

'Yeah, but the fluffiness won't stop acres of tedium because you're living like it's the nineteenth century. What about botulism?' The smell of the toad-in-the-hole was as close to intoxicating as British food got and Lucia's stomach rumbled loudly. She took out two glasses from the cabinet, filled them with water and placed them on the table, hoping this would rouse Rosie from her homestead fantasy. It didn't, so Lucia resorted to noisily laying the cutlery out. Rosie sprang to her feet after Lucia practically threw a fork down and started serving dinner. 'What gorgeous flowers,' Lucia said. She'd only just noticed the bouquet on the dining room table.

'Work sent them.'

'Work?'

'Yeah.'

'Or are they from your rather sexy boss Felix?'

'Work.'

'Have you still got a crush on him?'

'No.'

'Good, because I heard from a little bird that Tristan has intentions towards you.' Lucia went to pick up the card that came with them from the table where Rosie had left it, but Rosie swooped in while holding a full gravy boat and grabbed it without spilling a drop. Rosie put the small card in her pocket. 'Harry was messaging me for the goss and I said I'd ask.'

'Look at the gravy I made,' said Rosie, putting the boat down firmly on the table and heading back into the kitchen. 'I bloody love gravy.'

'Me too,' said Lucia, perplexed. She wondered if she had overstepped a boundary when she went to pick the card up.

'But not as much as I love toad-in-the-hole,' Rosie said, appearing with their plates. 'I've already given Tristan my number but he hasn't messaged me.'

'God, men are rubbish.'

# 16

## Caius and Callie's Flat

'Is he staying for dinner?' Callie asked, smelling the bunch of roses that Caius had returned home with for her. They weren't scented but then she couldn't have everything. She had a vase filled with water waiting and wanted to start arranging them but was now worried she was going to have to make a three-course dinner appear from nowhere.

'I don't know, he said "swing by". That isn't definitive.'

'I'll cook something informal and aim for it to be ready at 8.30 p. m. That way he can stay if he wants to, but he won't interrupt our dinner. Half of having good manners is making things easy for the other party.' She took a pair of scissors out of the miscellaneous drawer filled with ketchup packets and plastic sporks and cut the flowers out of their wrapping. Then she began cutting down their stalks and arranging them in the vase in the middle of the dining room table. 'I'll be here when he arrives, I'll say "Hello, lovely to see you" as if he didn't use me as a test subject to see if the self-control of his rapist son had improved, and then I'll pop out to the Co-op for some milk or something. You should offer him a proper drink. There's that brandy from the distillery near your parents' old place in France. That'll do. He'll like the story around it.'

Caius, who after a long day had not taken in everything she had just said, asked, 'What's informal food? Oven chips?'

'Cottage pie!' Callie said from the fridge, relieved to see a pack of minced beef and a couple of carrots that had yet to go slimy.

'You can feed twelve thousand people with one. It wouldn't be too much of an imposition if he actually did stay.'

'Jesus fucking Christ.'

'Go and vacuum.' Callie said it forcefully enough that Caius thought she meant it more generally and that despite the cleaner she was still doing too much housework and him not enough.

★ ★ ★

The carpet was spotless, not a dust bunny in sight. Caius tipped the reeds in the diffuser upside down, releasing the smell of vanilla and peach blossom into the room, and sat down on the sofa. He'd never really given much thought to how his flat smelled, he was an open window and an Air Wick plug-in sort of chap, but Callie had a whole philosophy of scent that he was now a reluctant devotee of. He clicked on the link Matt had sent and started reading Hampton's think piece in *The Economist*. He referred to, in Caius's mind at least, some of the most pressing crises: housing, benefits and climate. Honourable mentions to inequality: structural, wage, racial, gender. Mass extinction event. Societal collapse. War. There was a lot of gloom, but just enough hope in the form of a potential green revolution, one that wasn't described fully enough to convince Caius of anything. He was surprised to see the words 'traditional' and 'hierarchy' mentioned as frequently as they were. Caius went onto Twitter. He'd deleted the app a while ago, but logged in periodically on a browser and searched the quoted tweets from when *The Economist* shared it. No one seemed fully convinced but they were all delighted that someone of Hampton's assumed political convictions was taking the country's, the world's, problems seriously.

★　★　★

Callie said a polite hello to Arthur Hampton and asked after his charming husband Jeremy. She had liked Jeremy when she'd met him last year when she'd been invited to a dinner party at their house. She couldn't avoid the subject of bloody Rupert so eventually she asked after him too. He'd been spending a lot of time in the country, apparently. Callie didn't want to know, but she knew that pretending that Hampton's son wasn't a cretin would 'win favour', or at least smooth things over for Caius. Hampton had commented on how lovely the flat looked and she graciously took the credit before tactfully popping out to the shop for milk. Hampton had made a joke asking her to find out how much a pint of semi-skimmed cost in case he was asked by a journalist trying to accuse him of being out of touch. Hampton then noted that the irony was his family had a sizable herd of Friesians and all he really needed to know about the price of milk was that it was far too low, and the supermarkets were all a bunch of thieves paying the farmers so little that it was nearly impossible to carry on.

'Brandy?' Caius asked, as Arthur Hampton made himself comfortable in one of the plump armchairs that Callie had brought with her when she moved in.

'Yes, please,' Hampton said, sinking into the chair. He'd clearly had a long day.

'It's from this tiny little place near where my parents were living in France. They've sold up now.' Caius poured them both a glass. He didn't want to share a drink with Hampton but this odd, forced civility was better than being sent to the Tower of London or whatever theatrical horrors the man was capable of. Not that Caius needed to imagine the horrors, he'd smelled the stench of rotting human flesh on a hot day in Islington last year. There was no theatre to a two-week-old corpse in an unseasonably hot June.

'How delightful,' Hampton said, taking the glass from him. 'The French are so good at preserving their traditions. Much better than us. Did you know it was Hitler who did for the artisanal British farmhouse cheese?'

'No, I didn't,' Caius said, sitting down in the opposite armchair.

'Between rationing and the industrialisation of the process in order to maximise food production a lot of heritage was lost.'

'Rather that than the Holocaust though.' Caius stared into his drink. He couldn't help himself. He'd not managed to filter that one out. He was more like his mother than he cared to admit. Caius looked up at Hampton who had taken his comment in much better humour than he feared. 'My dad said he'd spoken to you.'

'Yes, I spoke to your father. I wanted to make sure that your family settled into Frithsden. I'm not sure old Sir Edgar kept on top of things.' Hampton took a sip of the brandy. He seemed to approve of it. 'He's very switched on, as one might say. As if he were a light bulb.'

'Dad gets bored very quickly. He has to have a project on the go.'

'Well, your father is in the right job now then.' Hampton put emphasis on the word 'father', letting Caius know that it was the more suitable noun. 'It never ends. How's your grandfather?'

'Creaking on.'

'And how are things with Peter?' Caius could tell he was fishing for info on his one-time opponent.

'Awkward.' Caius didn't want to give him more than one word. 'How's your brother's health?'

'Still terminal.' Hampton's lip twitched. He hadn't known that Caius was aware of his brother's situation, but then he could hardly say he was surprised. Hampton put his brandy down on a side table next to the armchair where he already had placed his phone.

'I'm so sorry.' Abi, a rising political journalist and Caius's friend from university, had given him the heads-up over His Grace's condition when Caius first met Hampton last year. His cancer diagnosis had been the driver behind Hampton changing the law so he could formally declare Rupert, his biological son, as his heir.

Hampton didn't care to reflect on the moment. 'I'm sure you're wondering why I put you on this case.'

'I am. Although I think I read between the highlighted lines.'

'Indeed.' Hampton's phone lit up and he glanced at it quickly. He put it down, shaking his head. 'The Hon. Mary Stratford was whisked back from Germany by her parents when it was realised she was in the family way. She spent the pregnancy on their country estate and the baby, a little girl, was adopted by a Mr and Mrs Barker. They were connected to the family solicitor and very discreet. The child was well provided for. While Lord and Lady Snitterfield did a good job of brushing the whole business under the carpet, all it would take is one interested journalist, or in fact anyone intent on finding a new angle to the whole Stratford sisters industrial complex, to realise that as well as the fortune inherited by her mother Mona Frogmorton (née Barker) Josephine Krige received a small sum of £120,000 in 1992 from the estate of Mary Stratford. Mona was the adopted baby. Mary Stratford's will confirms it. The tabloids would have a field day. Have you seen pictures of the Stratford sisters? They don't look much different from the Krige girls.'

'Why have us investigate?'

'Consider the company the Stratfords kept, consider the timings. If the father had been "respectable" then Lord Snitterfield would have forced the marriage. Those were the rumours flying around Eaton Square back in the day. I will say that my mother, who was never wrong about such things, was certain that there was great *shame* about the identity of the father. My mother knew all about your grandfather's branch of the Beauchamps too, for that matter. She had an excellent ear for gossip.'

'I'm sorry, are you trying to say that Mona was the daughter of . . .' Caius began.

'Perhaps, but I think that "perhaps" is a large enough one that we get this whole thing over and done with as quickly as possible. We don't want to excite those of that particular "political persuasion". Lord knows they keep slithering out of the woodwork and it's not just illiterate skinhead thugs any more, there are some quite respectable people.'

'They aren't respectable then, are they. Fuck.' Caius was embarrassed that he swore but Hampton didn't care for such middle-class niceties.

'Well, quite influential people then.'

'Like Johnny Bull? I saw him on TV last night. I take it that's the kind of person you mean. I can't believe the way he behaves. He was toeing the party line until quite recently. I hadn't heard of him until six months ago and then bang. He's everywhere, spouting awful things about any and every minority group he can until he finds something that sticks and turns into a media frenzy. And it's not just on Twitter. I got yelled at on the tube last week by a drunk who didn't like that I had on my back a very smart coat and on my arm a very white girlfriend. Do you know what he said?'

'That there's only one race and it's the human one?'

'That he'd vote for Bull as PM if he could. God forbid.'

Hampton did not respond beyond finishing his brandy.

'Another one?' Caius felt obliged to ask. He took a moment to calm down. He didn't want the neighbours – his parents' tenants – to hear.

'I can't stop much longer, I'm afraid. Delightful though. Very fruity.'

'As it stands the case very much looks like a burglary gone wrong. Not a fascist in sight.'

'All very normal then. Well, normal for your line of work.'

'We're just waiting for the full autopsies, then we're speaking to Josephine and Sienna Krige, and confirming Rosie Krige's statement just to say we have done it. Our focus now is trying to locate Philip Campbell's accomplice. They seem very likely to be the murderer.'

'I daresay it'll all be wrapped up nice and quickly but do keep me abreast of any interesting developments.' Hampton put an emphasis on the word 'interesting' that made Caius pause. He wondered what else was actually at play here.

'Sure.' Caius hadn't intended to bring this up, but the brandy had loosened him. 'That article in *Tatler* . . .'

'Yes, sorry. That was me. Rather saccharine, but then again you are exactly the type of thing they're excited by. Modern, but reassuringly old-fashioned at the same time. They'll be trying to get you for a cover I daresay. At least a spread with pictures of you at Frithsden.'

'Hmmm.' Caius couldn't think of anything worse.

'We had to get our version of events all square in the public consciousness once I formally designated Rupert as my heir. Your family inevitably had to come along for the ride, given how entwined we all are now. I do think the picture they used of young Calliope "rumoured to be in connection with you" – what a euphemism – was delightful. Jeremy chose that one; he said it was the most handsome. He has a very good eye for that sort of thing.'

'Very handsome,' Caius said. He couldn't but wonder at the timing of this investigation. 'I read your *Economist* piece. That's a big boy publication.'

'And what did you think?'

'It was hard to disagree with what you said because you didn't say much. Just named things. All the country's problems were laid out clearly. It felt like common sense but . . .'

'But what?'

'You didn't offer any concrete solutions. No policies, no change to the system at all. Your tone was meant to distance yourself from the circus that is Downing Street. "I'm not like the other politicians in government. I'm clever and write in *The Economist*. I care about the little people and the big problems."'

'Well observed.' Hampton smiled to himself. 'Nothing concrete, indeed.'

'You're gently setting out your stall, aren't you?'

'No comment,' Hampton said, but the twinkle in his eye contradicted him.

'I bet that's why the nutters like Johnny Bull have started thrashing about. You're all sharks and can smell blood in the water. How long has the PM got before a vote of no confidence and your name on a ballot paper for leader? You're the heritage candidate. You're painfully English, painfully reassuring. You're in with a chance. Well, at least that was what last week's *Cutter* seemed to think.'

They heard the front door open. Callie had returned from the shop with four pints of whole milk and a box of disgustingly sweet cereal that should really be classed as pudding – she'd been loitering in the aisle for so long being eyed up by the security guard as she did so that she felt obligated to purchase some – just as the timer on the cottage pie went off.

Caius got up to check the cottage pie but it didn't quite look done so he left it in the oven.

'Would you like to join us?' Callie said, taking the milk out of her canvas tote bag – it was from a local indie bookshop that they frequented in a self-satisfactory manner – and putting it in the fridge. Hampton, as keenly astute as he was, smiled to himself when he saw two full cartons in there already. It was a shame that Rupert was still in such a state when he met her. Callie would've been good for him. They had looked well together.

'I can't, unfortunately. Jeremy has got me on a rabbit food diet. Lots of salads with seeds on top. He's the one with high cholesterol not I, but apparently I need to be on it too for "emotional support". Whatever that is.'

'We're having cottage pie. Callie made it from scratch,' Caius said.

'Oh no, I really can't. He'd smell the mashed potatoes on me.' Hampton briskly shook Caius's hand, complimented Callie and bade them both a good evening before leaving.

'How was it?' Callie asked, boiling the kettle.

'Same as usual.' Caius leaned against the kitchen work surface. 'He looked tired.'

'It seems the PM's on his last legs.'

'How are you suddenly this up to date on politics?'

'My friend Abi from uni has just started writing a column about Westminster goings-on for *The Cutter*, and I've subscribed to show support. The reporting's good and you know paying for proper journalism keeps a democracy healthy. Besides, it's funny. They have silly cartoons.'

'No need to justify your magazine consumption to me,' Callie said, wondering why Caius had taken on a slightly defensive tone. The girl must be pretty. Never mind. She didn't live with him. 'I can't say I'm surprised that the PM's deeply unpopular after what he's done to the nurses, the doctors, the trains, the environment and the economy, and then there's his silly wife stealing loo roll from Buckingham Palace for a laugh. It doesn't feel like the grown-ups are in charge any more.'

'The fact that the Palace had to issue a statement on the Queen's behalf . . . How is that acceptable?'

'Stealing a loo roll is one thing, it's vaguely funny, I guess, but putting it up on eBay after one too many Chablis then denying it, only for screenshots to escape a WhatsApp group is bonkers.'

'Are you much of a royalist?' The subject had never come up before. Caius never really thought about the monarchy.

'I don't know. Maybe. They do a lot of charity work which sets a good example. Doing one's duty and all that. You?'

'They fill a vacuum. A touch of mystical pageantry. Would I rather have a president? I hate when people try to justify them by the amount of money they bring in through tourism. I don't think economics should be used to define the national spirit. Whatever that spirit is.'

'It's gin.'

'Gin?'

'It includes Pimm's too.'

'Yes, gin is definitely the national spirit.' Caius laughed. 'I guess my problem is that the continued reverential, borderline mystical, presence of the royals props up the rump of a medieval system that few benefit from.'

'Oh to be one of those few.' Callie side-eyed him before changing the subject. 'How do you think bogrollgate got out?'

'Our brandy-swilling friend, no doubt. Your dad said the PM does what Hampton tells him and has done so since school. Hampton knows when to sacrifice a pawn.'

'We're pawns now, aren't we?'

'Yep. At least we can retreat to the country when we are inevitably publicly shamed, like a disgraced Tudor courtier. Frithsden doesn't have a moat or even battlements, but I think we'd survive.' Caius was joking, but his fall from grace did now feel inevitable. The kettle boiled and Caius poured the water into a waiting pan filled with broccoli. 'Do I need to take the cottage pie out?'

'Oh no, it's got at least another five minutes to go.' Callie took out her phone and checked. 'Seven actually. The real timer is on my phone. I set the oven to go off ten minutes early. I thought it might hurry him along.'

'You sexy, Machiavellian genius.'

'I didn't want Hampton lingering. He'd give me indigestion.'

# WEDNESDAY

## 17

## The Police Station

'Mona was a Nazi love child? Hitler's her dad?' Matt said. He had never expected to say those words.

'No. No. No. I don't believe Hampton,' Amy said. She was sure something else had to be at play here. That was too weird a reason for Hampton to be involved even if it was true. 'What does Hampton get out of this?'

'I'm not sure. I think it's something to do with stemming a tide of neo-fascist hate but that feels a little altruistically abstract for a grubby realist like him,' Caius said, leaning back in his chair. He had also been thinking this question over. 'I think for now we need to take it at face value until we find something to change our minds. I might give Abi a call. On the bright side, this whole Nazi love-child thing could be worse! Hampton could have put us on a case that would take down the government. That was always a possibility.'

'If Hitler did have living descendants it would be a huge deal. Imagine how all the racist weirdos that keep popping up would react. Sienna and Rosie would be treated like Aryan princesses. There would be a freaky little cult around them. They'd have to go into hiding,' Matt said, rubbing his eyes. 'Did Mona know? Do the family know that about themselves?'

'I have no idea,' Caius said, eating a spoonful of his breakfast. Callie had made overnight oats. She had to get to her workroom early that day to prepare for three back-to-back client consultations that morning. Normally they'd eat breakfast together, and she couldn't bear the idea of him being sad on the bus eating an inferior supermarket croissant.

Caius swivelled around on his chair for a moment before standing straight up. 'Could you imagine living with that though? The guilt must eat you up.'

'Well, it's not like they did those awful things,' Amy said.

'Yes, but is evil intrinsic? Are some people just evil? Is it genetic?' Matt asked.

'Evil's human. I think anyone is capable of evil in the right circumstances. What is Australia or any of the other settler colonies if not a British Lebensraum?' What was Frithsden Old Hall? Caius asked himself. He opened his inbox and saw that uniform from Hammersmith had found Philip Campbell's car parked near Mona's house and towed it away for forensic examination. He forwarded the email. 'Matt, can you deal with the car.'

'Sure,' Matt said. He was disappointed that their discussion on the nature of evil was over. Last night he'd had to contend with a lecture from Stewart on the best way to paint texture onto Warhammer figurines while Matt tried to quietly cook his dinner and had hoped for something more stimulating that morning. He picked up a pile of correspondence they had taken from Philip Campbell's flat yesterday and started opening a letter.

Amy's desk phone rang. 'DC Noakes. Yes, I did. Hang on one moment, I'll put you on speakerphone so my DI can hear.' She pressed the button.

'Hi there, I'm DCI Daniel Mason. I worked on the Philip Campbell case twenty-three years ago.'

They exchanged pleasantries as the three of them huddled around Amy's desk and the Mancunian regaled them with the tale of Philip Campbell's illustrious early career.

'Dixon was the driving force behind it. Campbell was a nice kid who fell in with the wrong crowd. Not a natural thief, but clever.'

'Tell me about the MO?' Caius asked.

'Campbell used his job behind the bar of a posh golf club to find marks. Before that Dixon had been choosing houses in the Greater Manchester area fairly randomly – he'd follow the classic bins left out too long, must be on holiday logic – but once he gets friendly with Campbell that changes. Campbell starts listening in to the conversations at the swanky golf club in Altrincham, makes a note of who's going on holiday and when. Then he and Dixon would break in when they went away. My DI at the time realised that there was always a set of golf clubs by the door and then went from there.'

'Same MO as here. Campbell took over a steward shift from his cousin's kid on a luxury train ride and scoped out marks among the guests present. Did Campbell and Dixon ever use violence?' Caius asked.

'No, but they never came across anyone. Like I said, they only burgled empty houses. He wasn't known to be down the pub scrapping either though. Didn't seem to have that sort of temperament if I remember.'

'Did they have any other known accomplices?' Amy asked.

'No. It was just the two of them. Dixon was in and out for years. Died recently, it appears, during his latest stay at Her Majesty's pleasure at Buckley Prison. Shame Campbell ended up like this. I hadn't heard anything of him since he'd got out. He'd turned straight. I think Campbell was part of an initiative run by a charity that helps young offenders to get work after their stint.'

'Thanks, Daniel. You've been really helpful,' Caius said. The call ended and he turned to Matt and Amy. 'Now that I think about it, during dinner I overheard Rosie saying that she was going to be out all of Saturday and wouldn't be back until late,' he added, trying to remember what he'd heard when he came back to the table. 'Campbell was there too; he was serving us.'

'Campbell thinks he can risk breaking in if it's just the old lady,' Matt said, picking up another letter from the pile. The first one was just a summary of council tax spending for that borough.

'Big house in Barnes: he thought she'd probably not hear what's going on downstairs,' Amy said.

'Why now?' Caius asked, pacing around the incident room. 'Like DCI Mason said, Campbell had gone clean. He hadn't even got a parking ticket since coming out. Two thousand pounds hidden in a cushion on his sofa – he's active again.'

Matt held up a letter. 'It's a P45. He was let go from the Dartford Hotel earlier this month.'

'Why does the Dartford Hotel sound familiar?' Amy asked.

'It's where the charity gala thing was held where Rosie won the tickets,' Caius said, taking his phone out and googling the hotel. He scrolled through, finding a picture of the Grand Ballroom. Gilt ceilings and Corinthian columns. A sprung floor. A tremendous portrait of Queen Victoria. Waiters waltzing round tables.

# 18

## The Dartford Hotel

Caius stood in a quiet corner of the ballroom as porters moved large round tables around and into place. The ones that had already been set down were furnished with burgundy table-cloths, and a group of quick-footed Romanian women chatted quietly as they laid silver and glassware out with precision.

'I'm a little short on time,' said Simon, the hotel's assistant manager, checking his watch. He started moving quickly. Caius followed him down an empty corridor that led past the bar and into a service staircase. 'Is this private enough?'

'Yes, this is fine.' Caius waited as a chef walked past them to a lower level. 'I have some questions about a member of staff that worked here until recently.'

'Philip Campbell?'

'What did he do here?' Caius noted that he hadn't needed to say his name.

'He was our head waiter. He oversaw the service side of things in our restaurant and any large functions we were hosting.'

'Did he work on the Colon Cancer UK charity auction on 16 November?'

'Let me check.' Simon pulled out his phone, taking a few moments to scroll through looking for the right schedule. 'Yes, he worked that event.'

'Why did he leave the hotel?'

'He got drunk at the end of a shift and punched a sous chef.' Caius nodded.

'No charges were pressed, but of course we had to let him go nonetheless.'

'Was this out of character?'

'Very. He was known to be quite a sociable man, shall we say, but never anything like this. We cannot accept violence in the workplace even if it was a drunken one-off.'

'And his character in general?'

'Philip was well liked, always punctual. Incredibly professional. We've never had a problem with him in the twenty years he worked here.'

Caius remembered what DCI Mason had said about a charity initiative. 'I understand that Philip had been through some sort of programme post-prison.'

'Yes, a number of our staff have. The owner of the hotel is also a patron of the charity and likes to hire young people with convictions. Prison isn't the punishment; it's how the world treats you after you get out, how people look at you. I should know, I went down for GBH nineteen years ago.'

'And look at you now,' said Caius, smiling at him.

Simon led Caius back down the corridor and past the ballroom where a small army was now laying down cutlery. Simon noticed Caius's attention wander. 'We have a dinner for a group of scientists tonight. Some physics prize.'

'Do you host a lot of events like that?'

'Oh yes, a lot of charity fundraisers and things. A couple a week. Lots of weddings on the weekends too.' They arrived at the entrance. 'What's happened?' he asked quietly. 'I texted him last week, as a friend, and he didn't respond.'

'I'm sorry to say that he's dead. I can't comment any further at this time.' Simon understood. Caius shook his hand before stepping outside and into the rain-speckled grey of early spring. A black cab sped through a puddle-filled pothole, drenching him.

## 19

## The Police Station

'Caius, put your gross feet away. Rosie's friends have all arrived,' Matt said, taking the still-damp socks from the radiator and chucking them at him. 'Janet at the front desk is being snippy because Hampton sent your package to the station.'

'She called me little DI Fauntleroy again, didn't she?'

'Yeah.'

★   ★   ★

Harry performatively stated his full name for the tape, enunciating all the consonants with glee. He was a trainee at a firm of solicitors dealing mostly with criminal law – thrilling crimes but not enough pay – and was thinking of switching, before being pushed, to something more lucrative, maybe go internal for a multinational. Still criminals, but with better suits.

'Harry, can you tell me about the day you spent with Rosie?' Amy asked.

'We all met at the pub at 11 a.m. Had a late brunch. I had a cooked breakfast, including black pudding, if you're interested?'

Amy wasn't. 'And then what?'

'Then we watched the Boat Race. We lost. Unfortunately, but hardly unsurprisingly. Oxford have been recruiting ginormous ringers from American colleges and putting them on made-up post-grad courses. Then we kept drinking until it was late.'

'And you saw Rosie leave?'

'No, but I saw her just before. Lucia was escorting her out to an

Uber and Tristan trailed behind.' Harry smirked. 'I went back into the pub and drank myself to oblivion. Lucia had to unceremoniously scrape me off the floor and sent me home in my own carriage not too long after if my Uber receipts are correct.'

'What sort of state was Rosie in?'

'Blotto. Lucia had scraped her off the floor also. We'll have to start calling Lu the cleaner. She'd hate that.'

'And what was Rosie like that day? Different from normal?'

'No. Pretty much the same as she always is. I don't know her too well. She's Lucia's friend who comes along every now and then. Lucia, Tristan and I all were at Cambridge together. Tristan is a bit obsessed with her. He pretends he isn't but it's clear. Rosie is nice enough. My cousin went to the same school as her, so we know quite a few of the same crowd. She's prettier than she realises which is always a nice quality for a girl to have. You can have a good conversation with her, and she wouldn't be the sort to sleep with your brother behind your back and go on dates with him to mid-chain pizza restaurants.'

'Right.' Amy wondered what was going on in Harry's personal life to make not sleeping with his brother an essential characteristic of Rosie's personality. 'I'm sorry, pizza restaurants?'

Harry sighed. 'I didn't want to talk about this.'

'You brought it up.'

Harry widened his eyes in his best affectation of a puppy dog. 'My mum saw my girlfriend Cate cheating on me with my brother in Pizza Express in Guildford the day of the race.' He sighed and looked at her in a particularly pained way that made Amy recoil.

'Right.' Amy wished she hadn't asked. 'And what did you talk about with Rosie this time?'

'The usual things: restaurants we'd been to recently, holidays, nothing too deep.' Harry paused, smirked to himself and carried on. 'We both briefly mentioned our work. Not for long though. Don't want to bore everyone on race day.'

'And what did she say about her work?'

'She works for some sort of back-to-nature project. She'd been working on a land acquisition that had turned out to be more complex than initially thought. Her boss keeps buying random patches of countryside and fencing them in, leaving them alone. It's some sort of radical rewilding concept. Letting nature sort itself out. No humans to ruin things.'

'Did she mention her family at all?'

'She said she'd just been to Bath for the day with her grandmother. It was very pleasant and so on, lots of rain, delicious food, but other than that, no. Lucia isn't a fan of how her sister talks to her though. I know that.'

'Her sister?'

'Yes, Lucia said the sister tried to get Rosie to move in with her and her ever-expanding family to "save money" when Rosie decided to take her low-paying charity job over a proper training contract. Harry leant in towards Amy. He loved to gossip. Lucia thought she wanted to take advantage of Rosie and get hours and hours of free babysitting in lieu of rent. That's why she lives with her grandmother. I think I once heard Rosie say to Lu that the granny saw through the family's bullshit. "Bullshit" wasn't the word she used but that was the general idea.'

★   ★   ★

Lucia finished telling Matt how she had met Rosie. She stared at Matt. Matt stared back. Lucia's feelings about Rosie were very clear: she needed to be protected. Lucia kept everything plain.

There wasn't any verbosity to her speech – it veered towards the blunt if anything – but it was a passionate defence of her friend's character.

'Rosie is a good person,' Lucia said firmly.

'A good person?' Matt asked, wondering what Lucia's aim was here. It was, however, clear that she wasn't going to just answer his questions, she was going to make an argument.

'Yes. The absolute best.'

'What do you mean?' Matt asked. He didn't care for vague blanket sentiments on morality.

'I am giving you an account of her character up front before you start asking me whether or not I think my best friend is capable of murdering not one but two people, including her beloved elderly relative who she lives with and borderline cares for. I mean, I know her family is a bit complicated, but she's the straightforward one.'

'Complicated?'

'Well, yeah, her sister is . . .'

'Do you think she's capable of murder?'

'Sienna?'

'I meant Rosie but do you think Sienna is capable of it too?'

'Rosie, of course not. It would never cross her mind as a possible course of action.' Lucia stopped, stared into the mid-distance, took a large breath and resumed her staring at Matt. 'I have met genuine war criminals. I've met murderers. Human traffickers. Genocidal warlords. Rosie is built to be a vicar's wife. She's meant to organise charity bazaars and save church roofs.'

'And Sienna?'

'I don't know her well enough to comment.' Matt could see that this wasn't quite true.

'The thing is, Lucia, that question wasn't why we got you in today. We just want to double-check Rosie's alibi, but your defence which is more of an offence, suggests to me that you have thought that perhaps your friend is capable of murder? That indeed you think this is murder and not just a botched burglary.'

'No. That's not what I'm saying.'

'What are you really saying?' Matt was the one to break her gaze this time as he looked down at his notepad. 'Was Rosie out of sorts on Saturday?'

'No. She was her usual cheerful self. Nothing out of the ordinary whatsoever.'

'Is it usual for Rosie to drink so much that you have to help her into an Uber home?'

'No. She's usually a bit more controlled than that, but who doesn't have one too many every now and then? Look, normally Rosie will split a bottle of wine with me at mine, but she's not a sambuca shots and dancing on the tables sort. She was lit that night. We're allowed to have one too many and get a bit messy. We're British, for God's sake. If you take that right away from us, we'll have nothing left.'

'What changed?'

'She was upset that she's single. That's all. We've all been there.'

'How drunk was Rosie then?'

'She threw up in the loo twenty minutes before I put her in an Uber with Tristan, who was going to make sure she got home safely. That's the state she was in. I should've got her to stay at mine instead. It's not far from the pub.'

'Why didn't you?' Matt was just being nosy now.

'I was chatting to a guy at the bar and wanted to keep my options open,' Lucia said, very matter-of-fact, although tinged with pink embarrassment.

Matt nodded, his face immobile. Of course, Lucia for her bluntness still felt guilty about sex. 'What's Rosie's relationship with her family like?'

'She rings her mother once every two weeks for fifteen minutes. The same time on a Saturday morning like clockwork. She isn't close with her sister.' Lucia looked at the clock on the wall.

'Despite their proximity.'

'Probably because of it.'

'What do you mean?'

Lucia's animosity towards Sienna bubbled up again. She obviously had strong feelings towards her that she was failing to keep hidden. Lucia sighed. 'Sienna is a little . . . overbearing. Quite a personality. Holistic this, organic that. She fancies herself as some sort of earth mother. She gives birth every two years to give her life meaning. I don't want to gossip but there's something about Sienna and Charlie that I don't like. It's almost an animal repulsion. They have this energy. I'm sure you'll speak to them. Someone like *you* will understand.' She looked pointedly at Matt. 'Rosie had to put a hard boundary in with Sienna that they weren't to talk about politics or anything like that. There was one comment too many that made Rosie feel a bit uncomfortable. A lot of "scroungers receiving crazy money in benefits" and "immigrants abusing the NHS", those sorts of things. I've only met Charlie once, but he is intense. If they didn't have children I think Rosie, and Mona, would've kept more of a distance than they already did. Sienna tends to get her way with Josephine too, sometimes to Rosie's detriment. It makes things difficult for the whole family.'

'Any examples you can give?'

Lucia was sure that Rosie wouldn't ever bring 'the will' up as she considered the unpleasantness over with, but Lucia couldn't help but feel that it may in fact be pertinent to the characters of the others involved. Lucia also felt morally, if not legally, obligated to mention it. It didn't show Rosie in a poor light, after all.

'There had been an argument over a deposit for Sienna's house. Josephine inherited a chunk from some distant relative many years ago. She bought a property somewhere in West London. Chiswick, I think. As you can imagine it had become quite valuable over the years. It was supposed to be for all of her children to live in rent-free when they graduated – naturally they'd want to live and work in London for a little while at least – but Josephine rented it out in the interim. It meant she didn't have to work. When the girls moved on to wherever they were going to permanently settle, Josephine was going to start renting it out again. There's six years between the girls, William smartly went abroad straight after graduating, so Sienna was living there without Rosie for a few years, but by the time Rosie started her law conversion course in London it turned out that Josephine had just sold the place for a packet. She gave all the proceeds to Sienna, who used the money as the deposit on her marital home in Wandsworth. It was a wreck when they bought it. Squatters, the works. Sienna started out on social media recording the renovation. This left Rosie with nothing but an offer to move in with her grandmother who was so appalled that her daughter had reneged on her promise that she left everything to Rosie. She's been living there for well over five years now.'

'Really?' Matt tried to not look as if Lucia had given Rosie a very good motive for murder. 'Mona changed her will in Rosie's favour?'

'Yes, but there had been a detente in recent months.'

'How so?'

'Rosie had to go to lunch with her sister and grandmother to patch it up. Sienna's swelling brood of blue-eyed cherubic children swayed Mona to write her back in.'

'Is that what Rosie said?'

'Rosie said that Sienna claimed she'd thought Josephine was going to help Rosie buy somewhere with an equal deposit – which it turns out she didn't have. Rosie didn't buy it but the grandmother was getting on and was feeling sentimental despite her better judgement.'

'So the will's been changed and everyone's on friendly terms?'

'Rosie, her sister and grandmother are all on good terms now. Rosie sometimes refers to Sienna as "the leopard" when she's on her second glass of Whispering Angel, but she's going to pop in and see her nieces and nephews this week so . . .'

'"The leopard"?'

'She hasn't changed her spots.' Lucia shrugged. 'Look, Rosie isn't interested in money. She doesn't have expensive habits. She doesn't want to live like that. She wants to make a difference in the world.'

'Did Rosie like living with her grandmother?' Matt asked, changing tack before Lucia could make another speech about her friend's impeccable virtue.

'I don't think she'd have chosen to live with her if she could've afforded to avoid a house share. I don't think Mona was a hot chocolate and cuddles sort of grandmother but out of all of the family she appreciated Rosie most. She understood what sort of person Rosie is. She was at Rosie's birthday dinner and seemed proud of her. In fact, I think Mona paid for the dinner.'

'Not her mum?'

'No. I'm sure of it actually, because Mona had a say in the venue. She didn't want anything too "exotic", so we went to this classic British place on Clapham Rise. They had game on the menu. I found shot in mine.'

'Who else was at Rosie's birthday dinner?' Matt asked, curious about how the family's dynamic played out in public.

'Sienna and Charlie were there. It was after they had all made up. I sat at the other end of the table with a couple of Rosie's friends from Warwick uni. A girl from her office – Maddy, I think. She'd invited someone else from work, but they didn't show.'

'Her boss Felix?'

'Yeah, they're friendly.' Lucia straightened up at the mention of Felix's name. 'Not friendly enough to turn up to her birthday though. I've met Felix a couple of times. He's quite smooth, shall we say. All talk and no trousers, as my granny would've said.'

★ ★ ★

'How long have you known Rosie, Tristan?' Caius asked the would-be Romeo. Rosie had blushed as she mentioned him when giving her statement. Caius thought chivalry was dead and that if he'd walked a drunken Rosie to her front door then he wanted something.

'A couple of years, I suppose. She's a friend of Lu's. We first met at one of Lu's birthdays. She usually hosts a dinner party in her flat. Lucia, Harry and I are friends from Cambridge. Sometimes other friends tag along. Rosie is one of those other friends.'

'Walk me through your Saturday.'

'Sent a few emails in the morning after I'd been out on the water.'

'Out on the water?' Caius interjected.

'Yes, I row. Not competitively. Just a jaunt on the Thames

every Saturday. I'm a member of a boat club in Putney. More of a social thing than anything else. I rowed for my college. I was neither good nor dedicated enough for the Cambridge crew, but I keep my oar in, so to speak. It's good cardio and lord knows we all have to "keep fit".' Tristan raised his eyebrows at the phrase. 'A couple of chaps from the boat club were there at the pub too – one of the guys, Rupert, chatted up Lu actually. I spent quite a while with them, propping up the bar.'

'Do you watch the Boat Race every year then?' Caius had to hope that there was more than one Oxbridge-educated Rupert who rowed out there.

'Of course. We always have a good time. It's one of my favourite days of the year. We met up at the pub. Had brunch. Poached eggs. You look like you work out, you know how it is. Got to get my lean protein in after an outing.'

'Yeah.' Caius wondered why Tristan was trying to flatter him but then Caius was ten years older than him, scowling, and well, not white enough to make him comfortable.

'We watched the start, it's just outside the pub, and then the rest on the television. Ordered more food and more drinks. The day passed in good company. Next thing you know midnight is creeping upon us. Lu was putting Rosie in an Uber and I thought I should jump in too. She said before that she lives in Barnes so not too far from my place.'

'Where do you live?'

'On the border of Barnes and Putney. I live with my parents. Trying to save up so I can do my own thing.'

'Do continue.'

'I jumped in the taxi. Rosie was a little worse for wear, so I thought I'd do the gentlemanly thing and make sure she got home all right.'

'And ask her out?'

'Well, yes.'

'Why then?'

'I'm sorry?'

'Why did you ask her that day? Because she was drunk?' Caius thought he was pushing it here but he couldn't help himself. Mention of 'Rupert', any Rupert, made him suspect the worst.

'No, of course not. I'm not the sort to try and take advantage.' Tristan had assumed he was merely here to confirm Rosie's account of her evening, not to be treated like a sex pest.

'Right.'

'Lucia said she was bummed out over still being single. I'd had a few too so I decided it was now or never. We exchanged numbers when I walked her to the door, but that was it. I just wanted to make sure she got home safe. You don't know who's out there,' Tristan said, staring down at the table. 'Or even in your own home, I suppose.'

'The door,' Caius began. He felt he had a good measure of Tristan now. He seemed affable, reliable even. Solid. The right sort of fellow to know – always doggedly bright and merry, agreeable to a fault. 'Did you see Rosie close it?'

'No, but I turned around at the bottom of the garden path and it was definitely shut. I heard it thud as it closed. It's a heavy Victorian thing. The porch light was on. That's how I can be certain.'

'Did you see anything suspicious while you were there?'

'No,' Tristan said unconvincingly.

'Are you sure? Anything, no matter how inconsequential, would be helpful.'

'I thought I saw something move in the living room, but I assumed it was a cat. But, like I said, I'd had a few. If I'd have thought it was dangerous I'd have helped. I was in the University Officers' Training Corps in uni. I'm not Bruce Lee but I might have been able to do something.'

'Can you describe what you saw in the living room?'

'Honestly, it was just something fluttering in my peripheral. But I don't think I was sober enough to be sure.'

'Did you see anything else?'

'How do you mean?' Tristan tensed up.

'Anyone acting suspiciously near the house. Watching it? Anyone loitering or acting strange?'

'Another taxi pulled up on the road. A black cab.'

'Right. Who got out? Where did they go?'

'I wasn't paying attention.'

'Right.' Caius wasn't quite able to place Tristan's energy. Perhaps he was just a bit overwhelmed. Caius sat back in his chair and watched him. Tristan shifted around uncomfortably. 'Are you sure?'

'Um, are we finished?'

'No.' Caius had spooked him. 'What is it?'

'Sorry what?'

'You look uncomfortable, Tristan.'

'This is uncomfortable. I umm nearly bumped into a murderer.'

Caius let it drop, for now. 'Did you get back in your Uber?'

'No, I walked home for the last bit. He'd gone while I walked Rosie to her door. I meant to rebook him. You know Uber. It's only about twenty minutes from my parents' gaff so I walked it. I stopped off at a corner shop and bought a packet of Monster Munch and a Twix.'

'Did anyone see you get home?' Caius saw him bristle slightly. 'I have to ask.'

'My parents are away so it's just me at the house.'

'How did Rosie seem that day?' Caius asked, smiling at Tristan. Trying to make him feel at ease again.

'Like she normally does, if a bit drunk.' Tristan shook his head and turned back to Caius, looking a little wounded as he did so. 'Rosie's a lovely girl and she hasn't hurt anyone.'

★   ★   ★

'What did we all think of Rosie's friends?' Matt asked as Caius walked into the incident room. They'd been waiting for him to escort Tristan out before they began their analysis.

'Harry's a knob,' Amy said, swivelling around in her chair.

'There's not really a nicer way of saying that, is there?' Caius said, sitting down at his desk and taking an orange out of his drawer. They'd all watched each other's interviews from behind the two-way mirror.

'He's a box ticked,' Matt said.

Caius started to peel an orange. It was juicier than he anticipated so he took out a tissue from the box he kept in his drawer and peeled the orange over it. He didn't want to catch Callie's cold and he'd rather eat fruit than take a vitamin C tablet. 'Tristan seemed like a "solid chap". Massive crush on Rosie. He saw something move in the living room but dismissed it as a cat. Mona didn't have a cat.'

'How drunk was he?' Matt asked, taking a swig from his water bottle. 'If he did see someone then they'd have been in the house with Rosie for a while too, but they didn't attack her.'

'Well, Tristan said he'd had a few. There was something off with him. I can't say what though. Apparently, another taxi dropped someone else off in the street at about the same time.

He was funny on the details, but all he might have actually seen was a car's headlights as the taxi did a U-turn.'

'Drunks are the worst witnesses,' Amy said. She was teetotal and just couldn't fathom why anyone would bother going to the expense or the effort to get drunk when it left you so vulnerable. Not that she victim-blamed. Of course not.

'Both Tristan and Lucia have put Rosie on a bit of a pedestal, which makes me think she is either a saint or . . .' Caius said.

'Manipulative?' Amy asked.

'But they're all lawyers,' Matt said, tapping his fingers on the desk. 'There was a guy I went to high school with who in hindsight may have been a sociopath. There was an inherent lack of empathy there that he couldn't always hide. He's a lawyer now. Makes big money working for an oil company. My point is, if Rosie was like that then she would've got a high-paying, high-status job, not trying to save the whales or whatever it is she does.'

'I think Rosie is sincere.' Caius nodded. He understood where Amy was coming from. It was always good to be sceptical of people who looked too good to be true, but he agreed with Matt. 'I think if anyone would be able to sniff out an arch manipulator it would be a group of lawyers. They can probably smell a psychopathic pheromone.'

'Did you catch what Lucia was insinuating about Sienna and Charlie?' Matt asked.

'Yeah,' Caius said, giving Matt the look. 'Something to bear in mind.'

'The autopsies have come back,' Amy said, checking her emails. 'Nothing shocking. Philip's death is estimated to have occurred between 9 p.m. and 11 p.m.'

'Right. And Mona's?'

'Mona's death was estimated to have occurred between 10 p.m. and 12 a.m.'

'All right, so there's a good hour of crossover there.'

## 20

'You have one new message.'

'Hi, Rosie, it's Tristan. I just wanted to call to say how sorry I am for your loss. Umm . . . I . . . Goodbye, Rosie.'

★   ★   ★

*Lucia*
*12.09*
*Just got out of the police station. I know I've said it before Rosie, but you are more than welcome to stay with me for as long as you need to x*

*Rosie*
*12.18*
*Thanks Lucia! You really are the sweetest! I don't know when I'll be able to go back to the house but I've decided that I'm heading back to work. I need to do something. I can't watch another daytime talk show or my head will explode x*

*Lucia*
*12.26*
*It's good to keep busy. I'll sort dinner tonight x*

★   ★   ★

*The Gang (Group)*
*Harry*
*12.45*
*Did anyone else have fun with the boys in blue? I had a girl actually. Could tell she fancied me*

*Tristan*
*12.47*
*Mate . . .*

*Lucia*
*12.47*
*Harry ffs. Rosie's grandmother was murdered . . . Be a better person . . .*

★   ★   ★

*Harry*
*12.53*
*Hey Rosie, it's Harry. Just wanted to say how sorry I am for your loss! Do let me know if there's anything I can do*

*Rosie*
*12.59*
*Thanks Harry. That's so kind of you x*

# 21

## Sienna's House, Wandsworth Town

Rosie rang the doorbell. She was carrying a paper gift bag – the best one she could get from the card shop in Wandsworth shopping centre – that had a picture on it of a chubby giraffe, the gangliest of creatures. Inside the bag were the knitted things for baby Cosmo. She noticed that she was holding her breath. Rosie blew all the air out of her lungs before taking in a huge gulp of air in an aggressive attempt at calmness. She hoped Sienna was home alone. She could cope if it was just Sienna. There was a chance she'd adhere to the no-politics rule if it was just her. Rosie would just try to focus on the children and if it got a little much she'd make her excuses. Rosie had only been to Sienna's house once since the detente, when she accompanied her grandmother two weeks previously. She'd spent the last six months going out to coffee shops with Sienna instead. She'd been worried that she'd get roped into Sienna's schemes if she met her on her home turf. When she had visited with Granny, Charlie had been fussing around them both, making a big show of being on paternity leave and doing the washing-up. He couldn't help telling Rosie exactly what he really thought though over the soap suds while Granny had popped to the loo: that he was too good for domesticity, too brilliant to be scrubbing pans, too manly for women's work.

Rosie had just stopped off at Waitrose and picked up a few things for lunch: a selection of plant-based tapas-style bits, some pre-made salads made with ancient grains, and organic grapes. Rosie knew that Sienna had a girl for that sort of thing but she couldn't bear to turn up to see a newborn without bringing a meal. She marched along Sienna's road, the food heavy in her backpack. She hadn't brought an umbrella with her, not that it would've done much good with the wind howling as it was. The sky looked violet. Rosie put the bag containing Cosmo's gift inside her raincoat, hugging it close to her as she dashed down the road. The rain came and Rosie discovered after walking through a deceptively deep puddle that there was a hole in the sole of one of her boots. She finally reached Sienna's front door and was about to knock.

'Hello, Rosie,' said Sienna's nanny, opening it wide as Rosie's fist floated in mid-air. 'So lovely to see you again.'

'Hi, um . . .' Rosie couldn't remember the girl's name.

'Grace,' she said, taking the gift bag from Rosie.

'Yes, sorry.' Rosie took her coat off and hung it on the coat stand. 'I think all this rain has made my brain soggy.'

'What terrible weather we've been having. Just dreadful. All these floods.'

'I know. Did you see that footage of that DLR station underwater?'

'We are living through the end times,' Grace said, looking Rosie up and down. 'I love your jumper.'

'Thanks, I knitted it myself.'

'Where did you get the pattern from?'

'An old book of my grandmother's from the 1980s.' Rosie started to feel self-conscious.

'Oh really? Which one?' Grace leaned in a little too closely. 'I've started knitting too.'

'I can't remember.' As overly pleasant as Grace was she was here to see her sister not her nanny even if Rosie did think that Grace was a damn sight nicer, if not a little syrupy, than Sienna could be. 'Is Sienna here?'

'Yes, but I was sent to intercept you.' Grace frowned. She looked like she wanted to laugh, but it would be painful if she did. 'She's just filming some content in the kitchen.'

'What about?'

'Nutritionally balanced recipes to feed growing children.'

'Don't you do all that though?'

Grace didn't say anything.

A peel of tinkling laughter came through the closed kitchen door. Rosie knew that was what Sienna sounded like when she was trying to charm. The door swung open.

'Hello, darling. Come meet my guys,' Sienna said, beckoning Rosie into the kitchen and gently patting her on the shoulder repetitively as one would an old family dog. Baby Cosmo was strapped to her by a leopard-print cloth sling that looked great with her outfit. You wouldn't have known she'd given birth in the last two months. 'Guys, this is my baby sister Rosie. I was telling everyone earlier about Granny,' she said, looking Rosie in the eye in an almost painful manner before turning back to the two men in the kitchen. 'I was saying how important it is that we support each other. Poor Rosie has really been through it.'

Rosie nodded. She finally had a chance to look at the two men. One was holding a boom and the other was stood behind a camera. Both of them wore black T-shirts with their company name on and were looking at Rosie in the sympathetic way you do when someone has lost a relative. They were all a little too calm. Rosie assumed that Sienna hadn't told them that Granny had been murdered by a burglar but had passed away in her sleep. They were also both young, handsome and somewhat puppyish. Sienna was enjoying playing with them. Rosie watched as they shot another take, reflecting that Sienna's

Instagram was turning out to be an exceptionally well-produced, one-woman maternity propaganda machine.

'I think that's a wrap,' the first man said to Sienna. 'I'll start editing it all this afternoon and send the videos over tomorrow for you to review.'

'You utter star,' Sienna said. The two of them started packing up. Grace had clearly been instructed to disappear, lest her presence detract from Sienna's feminine prowess.

Rosie looked around the kitchen and saw on the island a zoo's worth of animal-shaped biscuits. 'These are so cute.'

'Try one.'

Rosie took a bite out of an elephant. It was oaty, there was a bit of cinnamon going on and maybe banana, but it was rather cardboardy.

'Low sugar for the little ones. I put extra flaxseed in to increase the fibre count, omega-3 and extra polyunsaturated fats. I bake them in batches and freeze them. Saves on waste. It pays to be frugal.' Sienna gestured around the kitchen extension which included a whole new basement level that had been dug out – Charlie jokingly referred to it as his bunker – that her tech husband had paid for with a bonus he'd awarded himself. At least her mother hadn't paid for it.

'That's so clever.' Rosie nodded vigorously. She composed herself before she looked too ridiculous in her fawning. Sienna often elicited that response from her, but it was easier to overdo it than atone for perceived apathy.

'I know,' Sienna said, watching the film crew pack up. 'I think I should write a little cookbook on the subject. Aim it at those struggling. Like your baby bank. Proper childhood nutrition is so important, and I think I could really make a difference. What do you think?'

'That's an idea, isn't it?' Rosie didn't think it was a good idea though – Sienna wasn't a qualified nutritionist for a start – but she wasn't going to contradict her. The families that went to the baby bank she volunteered at were nothing if not resourceful. The baby bank had initially started out as a place that handed out donated clothing but now they had supplies of formula, nappy cream, shampoo, moses baskets. If you needed it to look after your infant, then they had a box of them ready to hand out. Those families didn't need Sienna patronising them about the omega-3 content of a teaspoon of chia seeds, they needed a functioning society. Rosie wasn't going to mention this though. The no-politics talk boundary was there for her to respect too.

'Bye, guys. Lovely to see you both,' Sienna called to the camera crew as they showed themselves out. The door clicked behind them, and Grace reappeared from nowhere it seemed. Sienna took Cosmo out of his sling.

'Do you want me to take him?' Grace asked as Sienna went to hand the baby over.

'Oh, I'd love a cuddle,' Rosie said, taking him instead, nuzzling the top of his head. 'He's got that new baby smell.'

'That's how they get you,' Sienna said. She sat down on the slouchy sofa in the kitchen extension. 'I'm so tired. The girls are at pre-prep and Atticus is napping but he's going to blow any moment. Plus, this little boob monster won't leave me alone.'

'I can only imagine how tough it is,' Rosie said, sitting opposite her and rocking Cosmo in her arms.

'I don't want to discourage you. You'd make a lovely mother.'

'Ha ha, well.' Rosie didn't want to have this conversation again. Sienna had dropped into conversation recently about her friend Johnny being single. Sienna liked to think of Rosie as a doll sometimes.

'It's just that my friend—' Sienna's eyebrows rose in expectation.

'I brought you something,' Rosie interrupted. She wondered where the gift bag had got to, but before she knew it Grace had appeared holding it. She passed it to Rosie who passed it to Sienna.

'Oh my goodness, these are so unbelievably adorable,' Sienna said, holding up the booties.

'I knitted them using wool from this amazing company I found online. It's two women in a cottage in Shropshire doing it all by hand. The spinning, the dying, all the other steps.' Rosie left out that they were married to each other.

'No, I love it. This colour is gorgeous.'

'It's an all-natural dye. This colour is made from foraged woad. Like Boudicca or something.'

'Shut up, I love it. Send me their name. Do they have socials? You are so clever.'

Rosie knew that Sienna was partially thrilled because she could make content out of it, but she took the compliment.

Sienna was watching Grace as she started putting the cardboard animal biscuits into plastic lunch boxes to freeze them.

'No, Grace, put them in the glass containers,' Sienna called, turning back to Rosie to roll her eyes at her nanny's incompetence.

'Sure,' Grace said, catching Rosie's eye.

'Poor, Rosie . . . So terrible to find Granny like that. You've become so close recently.' Sienna put her hand on Rosie's knee and gave it a reassuring squeeze. 'Tea?'

'Yes, please.'

Grace went and filled the kettle up.

'Granny made you executor, didn't she. Poor, Rosie. If I can help in any way . . .'

'You've rather got your hands full already,' Rosie said, trying to brush Sienna off. She didn't want to talk about money with family. Not again. The whole nasty business over the house deposit was stressful enough the first time around. She didn't want a second round over the will. Her grandmother had thought it was crude to discuss such matters, and Rosie had inherited her distaste.

'Yes, but it's not fair you having to take responsibility for all that on top of what you've been through. I'm honestly happy to help.'

'That's all right. I am technically a solicitor.'

'Oh gosh yes. I forget about that.' Thwarted, Sienna gave a little laugh. 'What sort of tea would you like?'

'Normal.'

'English breakfast for Rosie and I'll have a rooibos,' Sienna called to Grace. She turned back to Rosie and affected a casual shrug. 'Do you know who Granny left her jewellery to?'

'No, I've not seen the will yet.'

'I'll come with you to the solicitors when you go. You remember that she promised me those lovely diamond earrings she has. The chandelier drop ones? I am the eldest granddaughter—' Sienna was interrupted by Grace dropping a mug. It was one of those purposefully ugly handmade ones that Rosie hated being given. They were impossible to grip. 'Do take care, Grace.'

'Sorry,' Grace said, a little too cheerfully.

'I've done a bit of a sort out.' Sienna pointed at a couple of paper bags near the door that Rosie hadn't noticed before. 'I've got some things for you. Matrescence is such an interesting life stage. I've got things that I love but can't bear to wear any more and well, I'm sure you'd look lovely in them.'

'Thank you. That's so kind of you.' Rosie picked up one of the bags and peeked inside, trying to hide her delight. Sienna spent

147

silly money on her wardrobe considering brands gave her stuff for free. One of the perks of maintaining this relationship was Sienna's cast-offs.

'Cosmo's latch is terrible. Apparently, he's not tongue-tied. How's your love life? I'm a withered old married lady. I need to live vicariously through you.'

Rosie failed to react.

'Rosie? Your love life? I want the gossip. Earth to Rosie.'

'It's complicated as per . . .' Rosie blushed as she tried to regain her composure. 'I was asked out by a friend of a friend just before I found . . . well.' Rosie remembered the feeling of congealed blood between her toes.

'What's his name?' Sienna asked, dancing around the dead bodies concealed by Rosie's euphemistic 'well'.

Rosie froze as the tangy smell of iron came back to her. Her heart had starting racing as the colour drained out of her cheeks.

'Rosie, what's gotten into you today?' Sienna waved at her. 'What's his name?'

'Tristan.' Rosie tried not to remember the night he asked her out, tried not to remember the blood all over the kitchen floor, tried not to remember her grandmother's cold hand. She took a deep breath as Sienna prattled on.

'Solid name. Arthurian. Show me a picture.'

Rosie obeyed, scrolling down her follower list until she found him, and held her phone up for Sienna.

'Oh, he's cute. Yes, I approve.'

Rosie focused on his face, pushing down the horrid memories as she stared at the picture of him on holiday with his parents. 'Tristan is an old friend of Lucia's.'

'Oh Lucia.' Sienna's enthusiasm fell away. 'Are you still friends with her?'

'Yes.'

'I really don't like her. She's not our sort.'

'What do you mean?'

'She's very . . . North London.' Sienna gave Rosie a pointed look that she didn't understand.

'And not shire enough for you? Not everyone had a lovely upbringing in a pretty little village like us, Sisi. Someone had to grow up in Stanmore.' Rosie stared at Sienna, waiting for her to interrupt and explain more of what she meant. Charlie was a normie after all, albeit a very rich one.

'Tell me more about this Gawain then?' Sienna asked, ignoring Rosie's previous statement.

'Tristan is also a lawyer. Works at one of the big city firms. He's living with his parents in Sheen or around there somewhere. Oh and he rows.'

'Big and strong. Well paid. Sounds like a catch. What's his surname?'

'Sowerby.'

Sienna didn't object to it. 'Rosalind Sowerby. It could be worse. When's the date?'

'He hasn't set one up yet. He walked me to the door the night I . . . I found Granny, so obviously with, you know – I think he's just giving me space.'

'Well, I'm glad you're over your silly little crush on Felix. Not that you'd admit to it. He wouldn't have been good for you. Felix is rather a weak man. He has no conviction. If you were after one of our friends then go after Johnny. He's the one with a really bright future.'

Cosmo began to grumble and Sienna lifted her top and unlatched her nursing bra, again. She took him from Rosie.

'I love it when they're this small,' Sienna said, stroking

Cosmo's head. 'How is working with Felix? I couldn't handle seeing him every day.'

'Good. I like it at the charity.'

'Yes, I guess he can be a sweetie when he wants to be. I'm so glad Charlie put you on to that job. It seems to really suit you. We watched his bit in that nature doc. Felix does talk so well and he's rather grown into his nose. Felix used to have such a thing for me back in the day, you know. I chose Charlie over him, of course,' Sienna said off-handedly. 'I'd love if Felix found someone. He and Charlie have been close for so long, but I have to admit I'm a bit sick of having him around so much. Charlie feels indebted to him, you see. Felix helped him out so much in the early days. He's always popping round asking about the company's finances when Charlie just wants to relax in the lovely home that I've created for him. I've tried to set Felix up with so many gorgeous girls at dinner parties here, although nothing ever seems to happen. I do sometimes think that Felix still holds a little torch . . . I think he's a teeny bit obsessed with me.'

'Well . . . actually. Felix . . .' Rosie began, but then thought better of it. She knew Felix's feelings over Sienna. He thought she was silly and vain. He thought she was a sycophant of Johnny's. He could barely stand her. Kept encouraging Rosie to go no contact with her; kept saying she was in denial.

'Don't tell me you've got feelings for him? Rosie, no! What about this Tristan guy?'

Rosie blushed but shook her head. 'No, we work together. It would be highly unprofessional.'

'Good. Charlie's worried that he's a bit inconsistent. He thought he'd grow out of it, but alas.'

'Inconsistent? What, with girls?'

'With everything. But yeah, Charlie says he dicks around. I bet he's lovely to work with though. Charmers can get away with so much.'

Rosie looked out of the window and watched a blue tit land on a cherry tree in the garden. 'He does have a bit of a temper sometimes. He can get quite frustrated when things take longer than he wants, but you can't rush a land acquisition.'

'I suppose that's to be expected with men like him?'

'How do you mean?'

'Hypermasculine.'

'I don't know if I'd call Felix "hypermasculine".' Rosie wasn't exactly sure what Sienna meant by the term.

'I would. He's a man's man. Testosterone. Loves the outdoors and getting things done. Doesn't take no for an answer. That's the only thing he has in common with Charlie any more.'

'Right.'

'Charlie's exactly the same.'

Rosie followed the bird with her eyes as it flew away. 'Charlie has a temper too?'

'Oh yes. It's extremely easy to stay on the right side of him though. I just have to trust him to be himself. Charlie knows what he wants. He's a planner. Has a ten-year plan that he's following very closely.'

Rosie didn't fancy talking about Charlie for much longer. 'Will Cosmo be your last?'

'Never say never.'

Grace brought their tea over, placing it on a small side table. 'I'm going to collect the girls.'

'Yes, you rather ought to,' Sienna said to Grace. She was obviously displeased with the girl.

'I'll do it,' Rosie said, standing up. She'd sensed an exit looming and she was going to take it. 'I'm sure you have so many other things for Grace to do.'

'Oh would you?' Sienna asked, smiling up at Rosie. 'There's an awful lot of washing to sort, isn't there, Grace?'

'I'll take them to the park on the way back.'

'Wonderful idea. I'll just call ahead to the school and say that you'll be the one to collect them. You'll have to give the password to their teacher at the gate. Their school has such tight security. It's a marvellous system. The password's "Valkyrie".'

# 22

## The Police Station

Matt had taken Caius's bottle of extra virgin olive oil – or EVOO as Caius had seriously started referring to it – from his desk drawer and into the break room.

'Excuse me,' Caius said, pointedly putting his forkful of left-over cottage pie down.

'Healthy oils.'

'You're excused.'

Matt sprinkled some oil over the bone-dry supermarket salad he'd picked up from the shop to go with a chicken thigh from the hot food section.

'Do you want some balsamic too, mon ami?'

'Amigo, did you even need to ask?' Matt nipped back into the incident room for the vinegar.

Amy came into the break room with a lunch box filled with pasta. 'I'm carb-loading for krav maga tonight, before you ask.'

'How's that going?'

'I might go back to judo instead.'

'It didn't grab me,' Caius said, before returning silently to his reheated cottage pie. He'd been to a couple of taster sessions with Amy, but he hadn't got on with it and gone back to his runs and squats in his garden. He picked up his phone and started scrolling through *The Guardian* app.

'Mona's dad . . . It can't be,' Matt said, returning with the bottle of balsamic. He didn't like to talk work over lunch but the others seemed to be only concerned with talk about their evening plans and he had nothing to look forward to but shutting out the sound of Stewart's goblin army cresting a papier mâché hill. 'The whole love-child thing has been spinning round my head all morning.'

'I really fucking hope it's not Hitler,' Caius said, pushing a pea around his plate. 'I don't want to deal with skinheads.'

'Talking about skinheads,' Amy said, twisting a piece of tagliatelle around her fork. 'I followed Charlie on Twitter. He shared a picture of himself from his student days and guess who's got his arm around him . . .' She took her phone out and showed them the picture in question.

'Johnny Bull,' Caius said, peering at his surprisingly fresh face.

'They know each other?' Matt asked, wincing. He'd just bitten into an underripe cherry tomato.

'I don't know how well,' Amy said.

'That feels icky,' Caius said. He'd just been reading about how the PM had refused to condemn Bull's latest comments. 'It's a burglary gone wrong. We need to find Philip Campbell's accomplice. But, Amy, just to be sure, do a little snooping on everyone's social pages.'

★   ★   ★

'I dropped her off fine. She seemed in a bit of a state. I was worried she was going to puke in the back for a bit, but we arrived without incident,' said Steve, the middle-aged Uber driver who had picked up Rosie and Tristan.

'What about the guy she was with?' Caius asked.

'Kept his hands to himself, thankfully. I don't like things like that going on in the back of my car. I only Uber on the weekends to pick up a bit extra cash, not that it even pays that much. It's not my profession.'

'Was he acting strangely? Anything off about him?'

'No, not that I can say.'

'What about her?'

'Oh, she was hammered, but I think she was turning it on a bit. Doing a damsel in distress thing. A lot of "thank you so much for making sure I get home safe". You could tell they fancied each other.'

'What happened when you arrived at the destination?'

'He got out and opened the door for her. I only remember because it's unusual for young men to be polite like that nowadays. Then he helped her through the gate and so on.'

'Was that the last you saw of them?'

'Yeah, I got another booking right after.'

'Did you overhear anything they said to each other?'

'Not much. I wasn't paying attention.'

'What did you hear?'

'Something about Pizza Express.'

'Did you see anyone else around that night?'

'Nope. Not a soul about.'

* * *

Amy had gone through everyone's online presences. Philip Campbell had a Facebook page but that was it, and it was set to private. They needed to gain access. Then Amy searched through Rosie's socials, again all private, before looking at her charity's website. There were a lot of pictures of deer wandering through woodland clearings and temperate rainforests. Amy read through a report on their five-year plan and all of the various sites they intended to acquire and their goal for creating more woodland. She could understand how Rosie ended up there – they were creating pockets of Eden. Amy looked up Rosie's and then her friends' LinkedIn pages (degrees, internships, Duke of Edinburgh badges, volunteering) and their social media pages which were unfortunately private – all very prosaic. Amy turned her attention to Josephine and a quick search of her name threw up her failed attempt at becoming a local Lib Dem counsellor three years prior but very little else.

Amy then started scrolling through Sienna's Instagram account – the task she'd been building up to. She surrendered herself to it. There were a lot of family photos of impossibly gorgeous picnics in the countryside. All wicker hampers and gingham and hand-made sausage rolls sprinkled with nigella seeds. Pictures of the children running through meadows taken so that their features were blurred – Sienna had made a heartfelt video about respecting their privacy. Elegant dinner tables with superbly clashing plates, pastel gingham tablecloths, bijou vases of flowers that didn't get in the way of 'enlightening conversations' and napkin ring holders that somehow pulled everything, all that eclectic chaos, together into art. Sienna had made a whole series of curated cookery videos called 'wholesome kitchen restocks' where she turned leftover Sunday dinners into pies and batch baked loaves so she didn't have to buy store-bought bread with all its nasty additives. Amy believed that Sienna was enjoying herself. It was fun, beyond the average time-pressed person for sure, but there was a cheekiness, a flirtatiousness to it. She couldn't shake the feeling that she'd just witnessed something uncanny though. Very occasionally, there was a slight touch of scolding to the videos. 'If I can do this then so should all other women too.' It jarred. And nothing had challenged her initial observation that there was something a bit culty about Sienna; there were a few too many mentions of motherhood and the 'sacred feminine'.

Amy opened up Sienna's meditation/life coaching app, *Freya*. It was smooth, very pink and had even more gingham. It was not that Sienna's social media wasn't flawlessly executed, but it had a certain sort of authenticity. It was just homespun enough to feel real. The app, Amy thought, had Sienna's tech entrepreneur husband Charlie's marks all over it. It felt too accomplished, too opaque, to be all Sienna's creation. Amy sent a link over to Fi asking what she thought of Sienna – she was a connoisseur of cottagecore. Fi instantly sent over a one-word reply: 'ick'.

★  ★  ★

Matt had taken Mona's pocket diary that had been on her bedside table when she died out of evidence and was busy transcribing her last week onto a whiteboard. He was trying to work out who her closest friends were, who she might have spoken to if she was concerned for her safety. He finished writing the last calendar entry onto the board and stepped back to read it.

Monday:
Dentist

Tuesday:
Book Club
The Great Big Wool Shop – 12.49

Wednesday:
2 – 10 a.m.

Thursday:
Marks & Spencer Food Hall – 11.09

Friday:
Bath with R

Saturday:

There were also a couple of recent receipts taken into evidence from the bottom of her sturdy handbag that Matt used to populate Mona's last week with specific timings. She'd probably popped to the wool shop for Rosie. He'd called both the library and the school and spoken to the librarian who ran the book club and the teacher whose class Mona volunteered in, but neither of them had noticed anything off with her. Matt had also taken Mona's address book out of evidence. He flicked through to 'Z' and found an entry for 'Zofia (cleaner)'.

'Hello, can I speak to Zofia, please?' Matt asked.

'Speaking.'

'Hi, Zofia, my name is DS Matthew Cheung, from the Met Police.'

'Oh, you are ringing about Mrs Frogmorton? I heard yesterday. How terrible.'

'Yes, I take it she employed you as her cleaner?'

'Yes. For the last five years. It's very sad news. Such a nice lady.'

'What were your duties?'

'I do a thorough clean of the bathroom and kitchen. Vacuum everywhere. A lot of polishing. Mrs Frogmorton was keen on polishing. She has a lot of wooden furniture. I even have to polish the banister. It takes quite a while. I'm there for four hours in total. It's a large house.'

'While you were working for her did you notice who her friends were?'

'I don't really know much about her personal life. Mrs Frogmorton was not very chatty. She lets me get on with the job. She does sometimes have another nice lady come to stay for a week at a time though. I would always give one of her guest rooms a good deep clean before she came and put on the nicest bed linen.'

'Do you know the lady's name?'

'Sorry, no.' Zofia paused. 'How did Mrs Frogmorton die? Her granddaughter called the agency and said not to come because there had been a burglary and Mrs Frogmorton had been killed. I can't believe it. Was it fast?'

'I can't comment.'

'Daphne!' Zofia said with force.

'Daphne?'

'Her old friend. That is her name. Like in the story. Turns into a tree.'

'When did she see Daphne last?'

'A while ago now.' Zofia went silent for a moment. 'Although, Mrs Frogmorton was on the phone to her when I was polishing on the landing a couple of months ago.'

'Did you overhear what they said?'

'Not really. Something about not liking the boyfriend?'

'Whose boyfriend?'

'I don't know. I was trying hard not to listen. It would be rude of me. I just remembered that phrase. Mrs Frogmorton was too old for a boyfriend. I thought it was funny. I guess she meant her granddaughter's.'

Matt thanked Zofia and ended the call.

'Did she mean Tristan?' Amy asked Matt.

'No.' Matt scratched his nose. 'Rosie and Tristan's romance is brand new and I doubt Rosie would have told her old-fashioned grandmother about it until things had got serious, let alone referred to him as her boyfriend. I know she knits but I doubt she's lost her head over him.'

'What do you mean "she knits"?' Caius asked. This was the second time Matt had mentioned the knitting thing.

'Young women who knit are a type. They stay at home rather than go out in the evening unless it's to dinner with other knitters maybe. They like whitewashed coffee shops round the corner and practise making the perfect cinnamon buns at home. They wear berets and scour charity shops for grandma tat. They yearn after the guy at the office who's having an affair with the hot receptionist.'

'What have you watched?' Amy asked. She felt like he was describing a bad rom-com that played in the middle of the day.

'I dunno.' Matt shrugged. 'C'mon, you know the girl I'm talking about. Impossibly nice because they take all their bad feelings, strangle them with yarn and turn it into a little cardigan with squirrel buttons. They're so wrapped up in their wool they don't have to see what's in front of them. Knit one, purl one, drop one, die alone.'

'Who hurt you, and what was she knitting at the time?' Amy asked.

'Rosie *is* impossibly nice. She's probably just knitting booties for the charity she volunteers at,' Caius said, dismissing Matt's weird idea.

'I don't know.' Amy had latched onto the idea of strangling someone with a ball of wool and then she wondered if you could stab someone to death with a pair of knitting needles. She decided that knitting needles were too blunt to cause much damage without a considerable amount of force. 'She could be a prepper,' Amy said absentmindedly.

'Huh?' asked Caius.

'You know, nutters who "prepare" for societal collapse by hoarding tins, learning how to use bows and arrows and growing their own fruit to barter instead of having their wife sell themselves. That kind of stuff.'

'And what, knitting is a survival skill?' Caius asked.

'Something like that. I caught the end of some show about a man from Peterborough who's built a fallout shelter at the bottom of his garden. It was late and I was flicking through terrestrial.'

'Right,' Caius said, wondering how they'd found themselves here. 'What if Zofia has slightly misremembered the conversation and actually Mona had said she didn't like the "husband". That makes more sense. She had a falling out with Josephine and Sienna over the house deposit. Mona might have thought Charlie was the one putting pressure on Josephine to give them the money?'

Caius's desk phone rang. 'The other passengers from the train carriage have arrived. Matt, you take one set and I'll take the other.'

*   *   *

'Thank you for coming in today, Mr and Mrs Cook,' Caius said to the middle-aged couple in front of him. The wife had a wrinkled nose like someone had pissed in her cup of tea.

'That's all right,' she said briskly.

'You both were in the same carriage as this lady and her granddaughter.' He showed them a photo of the pair they'd taken from Mona's house. 'She was murdered that weekend. We're just trying to gather information around her last days.'

161

Mrs Cook looked down at the picture and spoke for both of them. 'Yes, I remember the old lady.'

'Right. Was she acting oddly?'

'No.'

'How about the granddaughter?'

'No.'

'Did you notice any of the staff acting suspiciously?'

'No.'

'Do you recognise this man?' Caius showed her a picture of Philip Campbell.

'The waiter.'

'Yes.' Caius looked expectant, finally a piece of information. 'Did you see him interact with either the elderly lady or her granddaughter?'

'No.'

'Did you see him interact with anyone else? Another member of staff perhaps?'

'No.'

'Did you take any pictures of the day?'

'No.'

Caius turned to the silent husband, desperate for anything. 'Mr Cook, why weren't you on the return journey?'

'I took too long in the loo and Tracey got on without me.'

'I told you there would be consequences if you didn't start having Bran Flakes. I was not holding a whole fancy train up because you have an appalling diet. Not again, Gerald. Not again. He sneaks out for fry-ups, detective.' She turned to look at her husband. 'Your heart is going to explode next time you get con-stipation and I'll be glad of it.'

Caius ignored her outburst, but wished he could have told Callie about it. 'How did you come by the tickets?'

'I won them in a contest in the paper,' Gerald piped up but was glared back into silence by his wife.

★   ★   ★

'Oh my God, so the old lady was murdered?' Lauren asked. She was wearing the battered fox-fur stole that Callie had mercilessly described.

'Yes, Mona Frogmorton was murdered.' Matt was dreading this. 'I'd just like to ask you a few questions about your experience of the train ride to and from Bath.'

'This is so cool.'

'Sorry?'

'Oh, I am just a big Dorothy L. Sayers fan. I love Lord Peter Wimsey. They're my comfort reads. The whole murder on a train thing. It's a vibe. Sorry. You're being very serious and I'm being silly.'

'Right.' Matt, who had read one of those as a teenager, nodded. Caius was basically that now. He'd gone from chipper North Londoner who grew up with school friends who lived on an estate to having an estate. 'Did you notice anything about Mona?'

'Not especially. To be honest, we were fascinated with the couple sat next to them. The hot mixed-race guy and the stunning woman in the hat. Me and Lisa were trying to build the courage up to ask her where she got it from, but she looked a bit posh so we backed out. They had pricey knitwear. And the sleeve on her dress. Divine.'

'Right.' Matt slid Philip's picture in front of her. He wasn't going to tell Caius this. His ego didn't need it. 'Did you see this man?'

'I don't think so.'

'Are you sure? He was a steward in your carriage.'

'Sorry. Don't recognise him.'

'Did you take any pictures or footage of the day?'

'Of course. I'm waiting for Lisa and Dan to come back from holiday in Spain before we post anything.'

'Could you send all of it over.'

'Imagine if we captured the killer on film when we were making one of our silly little videos.'

'Imagine that.'

'I mean, I say silly, but we have 300K followers combined across all platforms. We were invited by the train company as part of an influencer initiative. I can afford to work part-time in a vintage boutique and not as a dental hygienist now.' She squirmed at the memory of other people's dirty mouths.

★　★　★

Amy had spent the last hour looking at Charlie Worthing, Sienna's husband. Charlie didn't do much social media. The picture he'd shared with him and Jonny Bull had been the first thing he'd posted in weeks. His company did though. There were a lot of blog posts about growth projections that Amy didn't feel smart enough to understand. She looked through the available records and investment literature. Nothing looked obviously dodgy. He had started the company at his kitchen table in Dalston with a friend who after investing had left the business at an early stage. No further details of this friend were to be found on the website. Charlie had probably shafted him. She'd be pissed off if she were that friend. Amy wondered if this was part of the myth-making process. The singular genius. The man of action. The hero's journey. This wasn't Charlie's first attempt at glory. He'd founded another start-up the year before, a political polling company aimed specifically at gathering the opinions of those under thirty-five, that ultimately failed due to that demographic's gaping apathy and the inability and unwillingness of traditional political parties' to take advantage of it. In the process he discovered that he couldn't afford to rent a whole office but he also couldn't rent just a desk so he set out subletting empty office space to other start-ups. The company talked about itself as the future of tech. But Amy wasn't sure what tech they'd developed beyond an online booking system. The company was now about to IPO. It was being touted as a potential unicorn and had already attracted considerable investment from overseas regimes with dubious human rights records but impeccable investment histories. Charlie was already rich, but he was about to become immorally so. Filthy rich. She'd worked out the timeline of his marriage based off Sienna's anniversary posts and theirs had been a whirlwind romance. Met, married and pregnant all within a year. She'd also listened to him talk about what running a start-up was like on a podcast aptly called *The Man, the Mythos*.

'This Charlie guy is slick,' Amy said as the episode wound down and an advert for a psychology book called *How to Do Your Busy-ness* played.

'Sleezy slick?' Caius asked.

'No, he comes across as quite earnest actually. Blunt, but you can hear he's chuffed to be interviewed, he's taking it all very seriously, although there's an edge there. I wouldn't want to get on the wrong side of him. Could be menacing. I feel like I've come across men like him before. I dunno. I might be reading too much into it. Listen to this.' Amy decoupled her headphones and skipped back to the last question of the interview.

Interviewer:
What next for Charlie Worthing? When this IPO happens what will you do?

Charlie Worthing:
I don't anticipate much changing with the IPO. I'll still be CEO. They'd have to kill me to keep me away from the boardroom. [They all laugh.]

Amy paused the podcast. 'He meant that.'
'Yep,' Caius said, nodding. 'He'd have bullied me at school.'
Amy clicked play.

Charlie Worthing:
One thing I hope to do is pay forward a bit of my good fortune to feisty, growing, challenger businesses. I recently became an advisor to a small Hackney brewery committed to preserving traditional brewing methods. Our heritage is under threat and we need to do absolutely bloody everything we can to protect it. It's unacceptable for our way of life to be destroyed.

Interviewer:
[Laughs nervously] Traditional brewing methods?

For example, they gather their Kentish
hop harvest by hand. I am always on
the lookout for burgeoning businesses
that might benefit even slightly from my
expertise.

'He hit "burgeoning" a little hard there. Wants us to know he knows big words?' Caius asked, wondering how in the space of six months he'd started looking down on people with a similar accent to him for having a large vocabulary. 'Or am I being a snob?'

'No, I think he's patronising,' Amy said, pausing it again. 'He sort of laughed a bit when talking about diversity earlier. He went through the motions and said the right thing but you could hear he didn't really believe it.' She clicked play.

Interviewer:
What's the name of the brewery?

Charlie Worthing:
The brewery is called Squires. Other beer
is available, but I don't rate it as
highly.

Amy paused the podcast. 'He's pretty hot, well, you know, if you like men.'

Caius looked up the brewery. 'Matt,' he yelled across the room. Matt took his headphones out. 'Didn't you have a pint of Jolly Yeoman at the pub the other day?'

'Yeah, it was all right that,' Matt said, nodding along. 'Surprisingly zesty.'

Amy got up from her desk and peered over Caius's shoulder as he scrolled through the corporate governance page. 'What a cliché.'

'Well, what else do men our age have to make ourselves feel different from the other lager-swilling, footie-playing louts? It's that or rock climbing.'

'He does that too,' Amy said, noting that he had the arms to prove it on his photo on the brewery's website.

Caius kept scrolling, stopping at a familiar face. 'Felix, Rosie's boss . . .'

'The floppy-haired naturalist?' Matt asked.

'Yeah, he's also on the board.' Caius clicked on the 'History' page. 'It's his family's brewery. That's how he can afford to buy random fields in Devon and give it to the butterflies.'

'Ah, so you were right, he's a proper gentleman amateur then,' Matt said.

'Charlie's a bit mockney, isn't he?' Caius said. There was a guy in halls that had sounded like that. He talked about the ends he grew up in South London when in reality he'd gone to a private school in Wimbledon. He'd been mortified when his very pleasant mother with a swishy blonde bob collected him at the end of the year and told Caius's mum all about their summer plans sailing around the Aegean.

'Makes him sound authentic or something,' Matt said. He'd seen a video recently saying that you should never invest in a business by someone who had a nice childhood. They don't have trauma. They have nothing to prove. Everyone loves a self-made man.

'What's his background?' Caius asked.

'Hang on,' Amy said, opening up Google. 'He went to Edinburgh university, as did Felix Drake and Johnny Bull.' Amy googled 'Charlie Worthing + school' and found nothing until she clicked on a newsletter from a Croydon comprehensive claiming him as one of their own.

'My bad.' Caius stopped for a moment and wondered who he was really talking about. 'Maybe Mona didn't like him because she thought he was "common" or something.'

'Not impossible,' Matt said. They all fell silent.

Caius turned to look at his email. 'Forensics found six different sets of fingerprints in the house so far. One set they've identified as Mona's – they're all over the house. Philip didn't leave any, apparently. Rosie's are also obviously everywhere. Then there are four more sets.'

'Safe to assume that one set is Zofia the cleaner's,' Amy said.

'I'll get her in,' Matt said, scanning the same report. 'They've run all the fingerprints through their database of known offenders but no matches.'

'Who are the other three?' Caius asked, looking up at the schedule of Mona's last week that Matt had put on the board. 'None of those diary entries suggest a planned visit from someone. Mona is the sort of woman who would've noted that down.'

'Hammersmith's forensics team have very helpfully put the locations they were found on a map of the house's layout so you can trace their journey,' Matt said, pressing print on the fingerprint maps.

'Let's have "fun" with that tomorrow,' Caius said.

'They've also sent through the results from the pillow Mona was smothered with and the knife used to kill Philip. There are three of the six sets of prints on each thing. Mona's prints were on the pillow and two of the unknown sets,' Matt said, going to the printer.

'Mona sleeps on the pillow, Zofia changed the bedding, and the killer,' Caius said, taking a sheet from Matt. It was for a set of fingerprints that were only found in the living room. He Blu-Tacked it to a spare whiteboard. 'Spectacularly careless of the murderer. It wasn't premeditated. Makes me think it isn't Philip's mystery accomplice. There were no fingerprints on the back door. Most burglars know to wear gloves. It's thieving 101.'

'They could've been a newbie? What about his cousin Karl?' Matt began Blu-Tacking the rest of the fingerprint maps.

'He seemed genuinely shocked to find out that Philip was dead,' Caius said, remembering the quivering mass of twenty-two-year-old child.

'The knife had Mona's and Rosie's prints on it as well as the killer's,' Amy said, looking at the fingerprint maps on the board.

'Well, Rosie wasn't there for Philip's death. We know that she was in the pub during the window in which it occurred. Her prints had to be there before,' Matt said, standing in front of the whiteboard. 'Lucia said she did all the cooking.'

'We will have to assume for now that the third set of mystery prints still belong to Philip's accomplice,' Caius said. He wasn't convinced but they hadn't found anything contrary to the notion yet.

# 23

## Lucia's Flat

Lucia couldn't be bothered to cook, but she knew that she probably should appear with something appropriately hearty to comfort her guest after last night's spectacular toad-in-the-hole. She'd had a long day at work, in and out of meetings with Amnesty International, so she collected a feast from the Japanese place round the corner. She put the final sharing box of sushi down on the table. Lucia had been craving salmon and avocado rolls all day.

'Rosie,' she called to her new flatmate. 'I've brought dinner back with me.'

'That's so kind of you,' Rosie said, appearing from Lucia's guest room. She was wearing her old uni hockey team hoodie that said 'Rozza' on the back and a pair of navy-blue Canterbury jogging bottoms. Her eyes looked pink. She'd clearly been crying.

'I picked up a crazy amount of food. There's sushi, gyoza and pumpkin korokke. I bought a couple of miso soups too. It's so good for you.'

'I love sushi,' Rosie said, taking a wodge of tissue out from where she had shoved it down her sleeve.

'Well, you've had one hell of a week and deserve a nice treat.'

Rosie nodded. The infernal damnation had yet to cease. 'The police are going to speak to my mum tomorrow. She just called to complain. Thank God I managed to shake her off in under five minutes.'

'Are you all right?' Lucia asked, picking out two clean glasses from the cabinet and bringing them to the table before sitting down. She'd picked up two bottles of Pocari Sweat too.

'Yeah,' Rosie said, breaking her chopsticks into two.

'How was everything with Sienna?'

'Fine.'

'Really?'

'Yeah. I held the baby, picked up the girls from school, got a swag bag of her old clothes, but she's just texted me asking me to a dinner party.'

'What's so bad about being invited to a dinner party?' Lucia sat down and picked up a box of prawn maki. 'I mean, other than it being Sienna's dinner party.'

'It's this week.'

'Oh.'

'It's way too soon.' Rosie hovered over a salmon and avocado roll but then put her chopsticks down again. 'I'm not being funny, am I? I told Sienna that I wasn't sure I felt up to social-ising like that with everything going on and she told me that Granny would've wanted us to keep going and get back to normal.'

'Rosie,' Lucia said, staring at her poor friend who looked like she was going to cry into her miso soup. 'You're not being funny. Not at all. You're being generous. I suppose, well perhaps Sienna hasn't processed everything that's going on and is in denial.'

'That sounds possible.'

'You can say no to her. You can chuck a swear word in if you fancied too.' Lucia took a bite out of her maki. It took everything she had not to say what she thought of Sienna. 'This sushi is so good.'

'Can I?'

'Yeah. Of course you can.'

'I know she's my sister, but sometimes I just don't like her as a person. You don't like her, do you?'

'No, I think there's something off . . .' Lucia had been building up to this conversation. She didn't want to lose her friend over it.

Rosie's phone buzzed.

'Is it Tristan?' Lucia looked up expectantly. She was simultaneously rooting for them but also dreaded being caught in the middle if it went wrong.

'No.' Rosie turned vibrate off. 'Just an email from a shop.'

'I take it he hasn't asked you out?'

'No. He left a message saying sorry for my loss.'

Lucia nodded. 'He's a really respectful guy.'

'I think I messed up?'

'How?' Lucia asked, looking at Rosie sidewards. 'Tristan won't be put off by speaking to the police for twenty minutes, if that's what you're worried about.'

'I don't know.' Rosie blushed as her phone lit up again. She flipped it over so she couldn't see the screen. 'Are there any more pumpkin korokke?'

'Help yourself.' Lucia slid her the box across the table.

# 24

## Caius and Callie's Flat

Caius was sprawled on the sofa reading one of Anne Stratford's novels. Callie had a couple knocking about and her copy of *Romance in Frigid Temperatures* had a well-cracked spine, so he figured she'd read it a few times for good reason. He was three chapters in and it was so acerbic, so acid-doused. It was the literary equivalent of licking a well-spoken lemon. It was refreshingly unsentimental in its observations of the hopelessly romantic and terminally naive heroine and her louche friends. The doorbell rang. Had Callie forgotten her keys again? Caius checked his watch. It was too early for Callie; her evening class wasn't over yet. He got up from the sofa and opened the door.

'Alan, mate. Come in,' Caius said, gesturing for his old DCI to enter the warmth. It had started to drizzle. Caius was surprised. Alan, a deadpan Cockney of the old order, had refused all previous invitations to come this far north. They usually saw each other once a year for a swift pint in a pub of Alan's choosing. Alan wasn't the sort of person to turn up uninvited. Caius wondered what had brought him to Dartmouth Park. 'It's bloody good to see you.'

'I know,' Alan said as he shuffled through the door, taking his heavy coat and flat cap off and leaving them in the hallway. He lugged a backpack into the living space.

'Tea?' Caius called as he filled the kettle. He missed working with the old guy. No one affectionately told him to fuck off in quite the same way. Amy was closest.

'Three sugars, ta.'

'Alan! You're diabetic.'

'Don't you bloody start too. I can just about tolerate Susie doing it, but she's the love of my life and you're just some prat I used to work with.' Alan sat down in an armchair and made himself comfortable.

'How is Susie? I can't imagine she's enjoying your retirement.' Alan looked thin. He'd been a big man, but now he seemed lost in the armchair. He was threatening to disappear into the upholstery.

'She's fine. She's got an allotment to get away from me.'

'I'd love an allotment,' Caius said, then realised he didn't need one now that his family owned actual farmland. The kettle boiled and Caius poured the hot water into two mugs – the most presentable ones they had. He'd chucked out the ones with chips and the novelty ones from childhood Easter eggs when Callie moved in and brought her collection of carefully curated, lead-painted, mismatched charity shop finds with her.

'I heard you socked your old DS.' Alan raised his eyebrows expectantly. He wanted to hear all the gory details from the champ himself.

Caius turned and looked at him, frowning. He didn't like to be reminded of that incident. His old DS had used a racial slur after incorrectly assuming Caius was some sort of indeterminate Mediterranean. It was the only time he had lost his temper like that.

'Can't say I blame you. Always thought he was a slimy toad. Back in my day that was how you settled "workplace disputes". None of this namby-pamby HR nonsense. Janet at the front desk told me. We do the odd pub quiz together; we're not bad actually. I do the sport. She does music. Susie does history and Janet's bloke Neil knows all the weird ones. Anyway, Janet keeps me up to date with all the juiciest station gossip.'

'Did she also tell you that she calls me "little DI Fauntleroy"?'

'She did. I can't believe you turned out to be a posho.'

'Me neither. None of us had any idea. My grandad had just buried it.' Caius stirred the milk in and added the sugars to Alan's mug – making a big display of doing what he was asked to do against his better judgement – before joining him. 'What brings you to North London this fine spring evening?'

'I'm dying.'

'Jesus, Alan.'

'Colon cancer. Too much inactivity, bacon and beer and not enough fibre, apparently.' Alan calmly took a sip of his tea and pushed on. 'I need your help. There's a case that's plagued me for the last twenty-five-odd years and you're the only one I trust to solve it. I'm too old now. I haven't got the legs to traipse over London, but if you needed a little moral support then I guess I could come along. You know, for old time's sake. Me standing behind you, making sure you don't fuck it up.'

'If I can help I will. What's the case?' Caius could see that he was desperate to see this case closed.

'That Hampstead Heath murder in the summer . . . Clemmie O'Hara, Hottie on the Heath, society girl found dead under a bush. Misadventure? You got too close to something, didn't you. Don't worry I won't tell a soul.'

'Pretty much.'

'Was it the Beauchamp boy that did it?' Alan looked at him, narrowing his eyes as he waited for a response. 'The other Beauchamp boy, that is.'

'Don't worry, he isn't my cousin.' Caius noticed that he pronounced 'Beauchamp' correctly. 'Only indirectly responsible, although he is definitely guilty of at least one other crime.'

'I thought it might have been something like that again. It's an old cold case.'

'Which one, Alan? Another cover-up? Is it connected to Rupert? Because if it is we'd need to tread extremely lightly.'

Alan handed him a large file.

Caius opened it, stopping at the victim's name. 'I thought it was an accident of some kind?'

'That's what they said to hush it up. I was the DI on the case. I was based out in West London then. I knew they were going to make it disappear when they suddenly stopped the autopsy from happening, so I quietly made a copy of the paperwork and hid it in my loft before everything vanished for good.'

'They?' Caius began, flicking through the papers.

'I don't know who. The establishment? She was very well connected.'

'What are the main facts?' Caius asked as he looked at the crime scene photos.

'Alethea Beauchamp, the victim, had left her husband that day. She had moved into a mews house near Sloane Square that she inherited from a bachelor great-uncle. Alethea's head was bashed in with a cast-iron skillet from the stove. They hit her in the saw first and then once more on the temple. The poor thing didn't die straight away. The attack was rage-filled. Angry. Smashed her in the face. She'd been beautiful and the killer clearly hated that. Forensics reckoned this happened close to midnight. The child was asleep upstairs. Couldn't have been much more than four years old. Too young to remember any-thing. Slept through the whole thing. There was an open bottle of wine, and one full glass on the other side of the table. In front of her was a glass of Perrier. Only her prints on the glasses. So we can assume it was premeditated. She drank from her water, but the other person didn't touch their wine. No sign of forced entry. None of the neighbours saw or heard a thing. No fingerprints from the attacker. The body was found early the next morning by her mother's help. Poor woman.'

'Who did you suspect?'

'The husband, naturally.'

'Naturally.'

'There were divorce papers on the table from her solicitors. They got pretty bloody. Problem is, the husband had a cast-iron alibi. He spent the whole evening in a gentlemen's club in Mayfair (not the dirty kind, one of the fancy ones) with friends. He arrived at around 7 p.m. for dinner, they stayed in the bar afterwards and he was paralytic by 11 p.m. A couple of staff members carried him up to one of the members' bedrooms where he passed out. They woke him up at 10 a.m. the next morning with a full English breakfast and copy of *The Telegraph*. He was in no fit state to have gone across town and committed murder.'

'He couldn't have pretended he was drunker than he was and sneaked out?'

'Would've had to have gone past security and they all swore blind that he didn't.'

'Why would Alethea pour a glass of wine for the man she was divorcing? She'd moved out. I doubt it was amicable.'

'Exactly! The problem is that the investigation was shut down before we could establish whether anyone else had a motive for the murder. We didn't even get to formally interview the friends the husband was with. The case was spirited away before we could get the two of them down the station. We didn't even get to speak to a single friend of hers. Like I said, "they" even stopped the bloody autopsy from happening.' Alan took a swig of his tea. 'Is it too early to ask for something stronger?'

'Not in this house,' Caius said as he got up and fetched two glasses for brandy.

'I got a phone call from some old boy telling me that the case wasn't being investigated any more and that £20,000 had been deposited into my bank account from an untraceable account in the British Virgin Islands, as a courtesy for the inconvenience. They then added that if I tried to tell anyone then they had "proof" that I was bent and had been taking bribes. That was a lot of money in the early nineties. So, I did what any sensible family man would do, paid off my mortgage and pretended it never happened.'

'Until now.' Caius wasn't sure that was what he would've done but it felt hard to judge Alan in the state he was in.

'Until now. The bastard,' Alan said, shaking his head. 'I was in the waiting room at the hospital, and I saw them, the two friends who'd informally alibied the husband. Older of course, but I recognised them. One of them had lost all his hair – he looked chemo bald. It felt like a sign and when I heard from Janet about the O'Hara case, that you'd cracked a couple of cold cases recently and were in a new special unit. I thought I'd try my luck before it runs out entirely.'

'Alan.' Caius wanted to touch his hand but couldn't. 'I'll do my best. Knowing the characters involved, I'll have to keep it totally off the books. I won't let my team know until I really have to.'

'You're a good kid, Caius.' Alan got up from his chair, looking relieved. It was more than the weight of the folder he'd shed. 'I best be off. I don't like the air this far north of the Thames.'

'There's a miasma.'

'You and your bloody big words. Call me a cab to the tube, you git.'

Caius did as he was told. Five minutes later, he saw Alan off at the door, watching him shuffle through the drizzle and into a minicab. He sat down in the armchair and stared at the outside of the folder Alan had left when the doorbell rang. Caius opened the door to a group of Jehovah's Witnesses with leaflets. 'Sorry, we're Catholics,' Caius said before shutting the door.

He flicked through the papers before hiding them at the bottom of the laundry basket. He didn't want to leave gory pictures about the place – it disrupted the vibe – and that was the best place he thought to hide them. He was also a little worried that Hampton might show up uninvited. He was definitely the sort of man to feel at liberty to flick through a random folder in someone else's house. Caius started chopping onions and potatoes before frying them in a large pan. Five minutes later Caius heard Callie's keys in the door.

'Hello, darling girl,' Caius said as Callie came into the room and put a large plastic box stuffed with feathers that she'd been using in her class on the dining room table. He was cracking eggs into a bowl. 'I think I'll go to confession tomorrow.'

'I mean, what we did last night wasn't a big sin. Just a little one and I don't think God cares about those *that* much.'

Caius laughed, but Callie could see a mortal fear creeping behind his eyes.

'You're serious.'

'Yeah.' He stirred the onions and potatoes into the eggs before frying the mixture.

'I've not been since I was seventeen and my grandmother made me. She died a few weeks later and I've never been back.' Callie opened the fridge and took out a bag of salad leaves. 'I'll come with you.'

'You don't have to,' he said, putting his arm around her.

'Well, it's a comfort, isn't it? Getting it out. Acknowledging your faults and wanting to be better.' Callie buried her head into his chest. 'I'll light a candle for her.'

'Yeah.' Caius said, kissing her on the top of her head.

'Talking about wanting to be better, my father called as I was on my way back. He's insisting that he see me on Friday. He sounded off.' Callie pulled away to put the salad leaves in a colander and washed them, setting the colander down to drain in the sink. It said pre-washed on the bag, but she didn't trust it.

'You'd better go,' Caius slid the omelette out of the pan and onto a plate before flipping it back into the pan. 'We had a lot of eggs that needed using so I've made Spanish omelette for dinner.'

'Yummy.' Callie got out the extra virgin olive oil, balsamic vinegar and the tub of Maldon sea salt from the cupboard.

'Don't do any laundry this week. It's my turn,' Caius said, pressing the omelette with a spatula. 'You've been doing more of the housework than me and that's not fair.'

'Where did I find you? Heaven?'

'No, on the front row of a fringe theatre.'

'Oh yeah.'

Caius flipped the omelette one last time before sliding it out onto a plate. 'There's a nature documentary that I want to watch tonight.'

'A nature documentary?' Callie raised an eyebrow.

'Not that type of nature. Birds and stuff.'

'And the bees?'

'No, like squirrels.'

'And beavers?'

The recipe Caius used said to let it rest for ten minutes but he was too hungry for that. Callie dressed a green salad while Caius cut the omelette into slices. They sat down on the sofa with their dinner – Callie still found this novel; she was never allowed to do this as a child. Caius opened the *BBC iPlayer* app on the television and found the programme. David Attenborough's voice calmly swept through the speakers. The opening credits played and they watched an orca hunt down a seal pup, teaching the pod's young how to drown their prey.

★　★　★

'I always thought British Wildlife was boring,' Callie said, eating a bowl of Greek yoghurt with honey and flaked almonds. They'd been transfixed by the first episode. 'But that little bee was magical.'

'Do you mind if we just watch a bit of the last episode? It's the one with the experts. There's an interview I need to see.'

'Yeah, sure.'

```
Felix Drake:
Our work at the British Society for
Rewilding is revolutionary. We are at
the forefront of the rewilding movement
in Britain. We're putting nature back
in charge of the natural world. We
acquired our first site in Devon in 2016.
The soil was basically dead. The amount
of synthetic fertiliser needed to grow
anything was crazy. There was little life
there. There were no insects so there
were no birds. It was devoid of song.
We've created our own slice of heaven. We
need to find our connection to the land
```

again. This soil is in our blood. We need
to protect it.

[Cut to a before shot of an empty muddy
field. Cut to an after shot showing a
meadow filled with wildflowers. Flashes of
red, yellow, orange and blue dot the lush
green of swishy long grass. Bees dashing
from flower to flower. A shy doe pops her
head out of a thicket. Young oak trees
are sprouting on the edge of the meadow.]

'I'd wear wellies for him,' Callie said, sighing. 'I'd wear any-
thing he wanted.'
'Hey!'
'He's not as handsome as you.'
'All right then.'

# THURSDAY

## 25

## The Police Station

Caius finished trawling through Philip's messages. IT had been able to access everything on his phone. There wasn't half as much as he had expected. Caius had come in early to get a head start but was done before 8.30 a.m. There was indeed a message from the week before from Simon, the hotel manager, asking if he was all right and apologising in a personal capacity for Philip's dismissal, asking to catch up and offering a good reference. Philip never responded. There was also another set of messages from his cousin about Sunday lunch, and a message from poor Karl telling him where and when to be to take over his shift on the train. But other than that, there wasn't much else. There were no outgoing or incoming calls between Friday and Saturday. Caius opened up his Facebook messenger app and saw that the last message was from a woman called Tasha Dixon-Jones inviting him to her brother's funeral. Caius checked the date. It was the same day that Philip had been fired. It was the trigger for getting drunk, punching a sous chef and losing his job. The only recent picture was the one Philip had taken of the train's passenger list. Caius got up and moved around the room. What was missing of course was a message to a fellow ne'er-do-well setting up the details of Sunday evening's bloody escapade.

At 9 a.m. Matt bounded into the room.

'Hola.'

'Buongiorno.'

'Philip didn't have an accomplice.'

'What?'

'There's no communication to suggest so.' Caius stared out of the window.

'Really?' Matt turned his computer on without taking his jacket off and opened his emails. He read through a report that had just landed. 'Forensics don't have anything to suggest that anyone else had been in Philip's car recently. No prints, no hair, nothing.'

Amy swung through the incident room doors.

'Philip picked the wrong house,' Caius said, staring into the mid-distance as he processed the fact that their working theory had been proved false.

'Good morning to you too,' Amy said, taking her coat off. 'I saw Barry when I was getting in the lift. He seemed very excited even for him. Something about working his magic. Anywho, he said that Matt should put the kettle on.'

'He did not say that,' Matt said, aggressively taking a sip out of the reusable cup that he'd brought his morning coffee in.

★ ★ ★

'Barry, my favourite wizard,' Caius said when his favourite forensic medical examiner entered the room. 'I hear you've done some magic.'

'We prefer the term "mage",' Barry said, placing a clock inside an evidence bag on Caius's desk.

'What have you got for me, Bazza?' Caius asked.

'I'm chuffed with myself,' Barry said, staring at the clock. 'I noticed on the picture you sent over, Caius, that the blood splatter pattern suggested that the attack had a slashing upward motion and that the clock on the wall was likely in the splash zone. So, if I'm right, which I now know I am . . .'

'Of course you are,' Caius chimed in.

'The blood hit the clock which is open-faced. It hit the hands, so if we look at where the splatter pattern is interrupted—'

'Then Philip died at 9.17 p.m. exactly,' Matt said, peering over Barry's shoulder.

'Et voilà,' Barry said, unfolding his hands triumphantly. 'I checked the report from the scene and the clock was showing the correct time. I'll get this written up for you.'

'Barry, tu es super,' Caius said.

'I know.' Barry picked up the clock and set off.

'So, Philip died at 9.17 p.m.,' Amy said.

'Yes,' Matt said, going back to his desk and finding Mona's file.

'Mona's death was estimated to have occurred between 10 p.m. and 12 a.m.,' Caius said, regretting telling Hampton that it was a burglary gone wrong. 'Philip didn't kill Mona. He was already dead.'

'It was Philip's accomplice?' Amy asked.

'But we don't have any evidence that they exist. There are no messages or calls to arrange the theft. There's no evidence anyone else was in the car. Philip's spiral towards rock bottom began because his teenage best friend who he used to burgle with died. He lost his job which he had to live for because he didn't really do much else.' Caius started pacing around the incident room, trying to come up with a new scenario. 'We assumed that Mona was killed first, then the burglars fought and Philip was killed. The other burglar then fled after Rosie returned, leaving the door open, but with this new information we could assume that another person who wasn't Philip's accomplice kills Philip discreetly, searches through the house for something for an hour or so at least then goes upstairs, either interrogates Mona or accidentally wakes her, and then smothers her. That doesn't sound impossible, but most people would scramble as quick as they could from a murder scene.'

'Rosie comes home drunk. They realise she's in a state and not a threat. They wait for her to amble up the stairs and go to bed and exit through the front door, so they don't go back through the kitchen and risk leaving a hair or something.' Matt wasn't sure either. 'There are no fingerprints on the back because burglars know to wear gloves and they also know not to contaminate a crime scene.'

'There could be two killers. With these timings, someone kills Philip, they flee. Rosie then stumbles across the scene when she comes home and takes the opportunity to kill her grandmother so she can inherit her chunk of the house and whatever and blame it on this burglar. Rosie could have killed Mona,' Amy said, holding her hands out. 'Look, I don't trust people who work in charities. No one is that nice.'

'Are you projecting or just that cynical?' Matt asked.

'A bit of both,' Amy said, staring him down. 'You think she's off because she knits so I don't know why you're being uppity.'

Caius stared at them both for a moment before carrying on. 'We need to look at the family properly this time. Josephine is coming in anyway. A disputed will may be enough of a motive for Rosie, Josephine or Sienna to kill Mona. Let's keep this to ourselves and let everyone else think that Philip was the killer.'

'Sure,' Amy said.

'I need a cup of tea,' Caius said.

'It's Amy's turn,' Matt said.

'Make your own,' Amy said.

★ ★ ★

'Listen, troops,' Caius began, standing up and putting his hands behind his back. He affected an old-fashioned BBC accent. He'd just finished his brew. He'd made it himself. 'This case may have looked like a burglary gone wrong and we thought we'd knocked it for six, but we now know it's just not cricket. We need to cover our bases and currently the lingering question of Mona's estate are making me nervous. We don't want to find ourselves with a sticky wicket. We have Mrs Josephine Krige arriving here at the station at eleven hundred hours sharp. Private Noakes. Question her. Mona had money and a history of strained relations with her daughter and granddaughter Sienna. It could be why she was killed.'

'Yes, sir,' Amy said, saluting him.

'Josephine won't realise she's a potential murder suspect,' Caius said, pacing up the incident room.

'I won't give the game away, sir. I shall ply her with our finest digestive biscuit ration and cups of tea to keep her sweet.'

'That's a cunning plan, private.' Caius turned to Matt who wasn't sure what was going on but decided to play along. 'Lieutenant Cheung.'

'Sir, yes sir,' Matt said.

'Private Noakes's warrant request to see the will has been granted. I've spoken to the secretary of Mr Miller, Mona's solicitor, and he is expecting you at 11.45, shipshape and Bristol fashion. Their offices are located off Cheapside.'

'I shall get to the bottom of the changed will, sir.'

'I myself will make the arduous trek all the way to Wandsworth and shall informally interview potential enemy combatant, Sienna Worthing. Dismissed.' Caius sat back down again and opened the lunch bag that Callie had prepared for him that morning. He'd not had it in him this morning to sort anything out before he left, instead saying that he'd get a meal deal. Callie, who could think of nothing more miserable than a soggy pre-made sandwich, had quickly packed a lunch bag with the last of the chicken soup and a Gruyère-topped roll from the bakery on the high street. She'd also put in a little grated carrot salad with a honey and mustard dressing, an apple, a banana and a flaxseed oaty bar she'd concocted. She'd also added a little love note to the bag that he was too embarrassed to open in front of the others. He'd eat his lunch in his police car later and moon over the note at the same time. In short, their shared love language was lunch. He zipped it up again. 'I keep thinking about Lucia.'

'She clearly thought Sienna held some "objectionable views",' Matt said.

'Look, I've said it already: Sienna's giving cult. Who knows what she could be involved in. She's asking her followers to bow down to her womb while selling them sound baths,' Amy said.

'Do you ever wonder what it would be like to be an accountant?' Caius asked.

'All the time,' Matt said.

'Cup of tea?' Amy asked, knowing full well that Matt and Caius would both decline as they needed to leave soon. Amy was still upholding her anti-trolley dolly stance and would only make them begrudgingly or offer to make one at an inopportune moment.

'No thanks,' Caius predictably said.

'Yes please, I'll take one with me,' Matt said. He'd got wise to Amy. Matt handed her his reusable cup.

As she had kindly offered Amy was now duty-bound to make him one. She wondered if she should make it poorly so he wouldn't take another from her, but weaponised incompetence was probably a step too far in her avoidance of traditional female roles/career traps. It was too masculine a tactic.

'Matt,' Caius said, looking over to him. 'See if Mr Miller, the partner, knows anything about the family more generally too. The solicitor who came with Rosie said that their firm represents the "family's interests" so he may know a little gossipy titbit. He'll probably keep schtum, but you never know.'

'You know me and gossip.'

# 26

## The Police Station

Amy had strategically put a box of tissues next to Josephine's elbow as she sat down opposite her. She had turned up without a lawyer. Amy wondered whether this lack of presence from the family's firm meant that Josephine had indeed been written out of the will. Amy asked her all the standard questions about her mother, letting her divulge childhood memories of teddy bears' picnics and walks along Cornish beaches in the summer holidays, but now she was going to gently work out whether Josephine had the opportunity and motive to murder her mother and an interloping burglar.

'When was the last time you were inside your mother's house?'

Josephine frowned at the supermarket own-brand digestive biscuit in front of her. 'Two and a half years ago.'

'And were you alone on the evening the murder occurred?'

'Most of it.' Josephine furrowed her brow. 'I did pop into the local pub at about 7.30 p.m. for a swift gin and tonic with one of my friends from the save the roof committee but I was home alone by 9 p.m.' Amy made a note to check how long it would take to drive from Lower Snoddington to Barnes. 'I can give you her number if you want to check?'

'Yes please, Josephine. We've heard that you and your mother had had a bit of a falling out in recent years,' Amy said slowly and calmly. She tried to make the idea of 'falling out' seem trivial so Josephine would talk about it.

'Oh that.' Josephine predictably brushed it away with the wave of her hand.

Amy raised an eyebrow expectantly, sitting in silence until Josephine was forced to continue.

'There was a minor quarrel over what I do with my own money.' Josephine opened her handbag and took out a tube of hand cream. She began applying it vigorously. The cloyingly sweet floral smell took over the room. 'My mother took it quite far considering it's my property and my children. She wrote me out of the will. It's almost funny really, like a Victorian hysteric addicted to smelling salts.'

'I'm sorry, but would you mind expanding on that?'

Josephine rolled her eyes. 'I owned a property, a terrace in Chiswick, that I sold to help Sienna get a foot on the property ladder. There was a misunderstanding as to what I had promised Rosie. I was always going to help her out too, of course I was. The thing is . . . Sienna is a, well, a precious soul. She was premature so she always needed a little more attention. She needs helping in a way that William and Rosie never will. William is out in the world doing his thing and Rosie is much the same. Sienna, bless her, has her head in the clouds. Rosie, for her sweet demeanour, is a tenacious pit bull. I love her. I do, and she does so much good with her work and whatnot, but Sienna is the sensitive one. I love both my girls, but Rosie will always land on her feet. Yes, that girl could survive a nuclear bomb unscathed.'

'Like a cockroach?'

'I'm sorry.'

'You just likened your daughter to a cockroach,' Amy said, smiling if only out of shock of Josephine's favouritism.

'Did I?'

'What do you think of Charlie?'

'Why are you asking that?'

'Standard line of questioning.'

'He's not in any financial trouble, is he?'

'Not that I'm aware.' Amy made a note that that was the conclusion Josephine had naturally come to.

'Charlie's fine, I suppose. I do wish Sienna had picked someone a little more our speed though.'

'Your speed?'

'Yes. Everyone loves a self-made man until he uses the wrong fork.'

'And what about Sienna's work?'

'Bless her. So sweet to call it work. I always thought she'd be the one off doing a law course. She seems happy. The children are delightful.'

'Do you know much about Sienna and Charlie's friends?'

'Why?'

'We're just trying to get a full picture.'

'Why aren't you chasing after this wretched burglar instead?'

'I can assure you that we are exploring every avenue open to us.' Amy smiled her best meek apology smile before leaning in and saying quietly, 'I was just wondering whether the burglars were targeting the families of people with influence.'

'Ah I see. Yes.' Amy had calculated correctly that Josephine would enjoy a little name-dropping. 'Well, Sienna went to boarding school with a few girls from notable families. I'm not totally sure who she's still in touch with. Charlie, for his very normal upbringing, has some interesting friends. He lived with Johnny Bull at university, not that I approve of him, and that chap Felix who started the charity that Rosie works for. I understand Felix has been good to Rosie. He employed her when no one else would, after all.'

★ ★ ★

196

*Matt*
*10.02*
*Amy!!! Did you leave the teabag in on purpose???*

*Amy*
*10.04*
*\*Divorced Dad Energy\**
*(Rainbow cat GIPHY)*

★   ★   ★

## Miller & Miller Solicitors, the City

Matt was shown into a wood-panelled office. The room felt heavy. The curtains were a bulky green velvet and the furniture was unchanged for a hundred years. Rows and rows of leather-bound law books lined the bookshelves that ran along one side of the room. Portraits of whiskered men who all looked the same hung around the rest of the room, staring down at their descendant going about the family business. Sat behind a sturdy wooden desk built like a ship's prow was a small grey-haired man with a neat moustache. David Miller, senior managing partner, stood up and shook Matt's hand. He had the same chin as Rosie's shiny-foreheaded solicitor.

'Detective Sergeant Cheung,' he said, relaxing his grip. 'Do take a seat.'

'Thank you,' Matt said, sitting down on a chair with sloped curving arms. A church bell loudly chimed and Matt instinctively looked out of the window to see that the building was practically on top of the ancient church next door. A plate-glass skyscraper then loomed over both buildings.

'Tea?'

'No, thank you.'

'I believe you're here to talk about Mrs Mona Frogmorton, née Barker.'

'I am, yes.' Matt presented him with the warrant for her will.

Mr Miller read it briefly before taking out a paper folder from his desk and handing it to Matt. 'My assistant will send a digital copy to your superior officer.'

'Thank you,' Matt said, taking the will out of the folder and scanning quickly through it while the solicitor watched him. 'Is there not a more recent version?'

'No. I believe my assistant was in the process of scheduling an appointment for her over the coming weeks. Although the appointment may have been about any number of her concerns.'

'Like what exactly?'

'Her share portfolio. Her property. All manner of potential reasons.' He leaned towards Matt. 'Mrs Frogmorton was a very particular woman who had us deal with all her business. We were her trusted advisors. We've looked after her since she was a child. My long-dead great-great-uncle in fact was the first one to deal with her back in the 1930s.'

'When she was a child?'

'Yes, a distant family member had made certain financial provisions for her education, which we handled. I'm not entirely sure of the circumstances, it was well before my time.' He laughed. 'But that will all be in the public domain on the probate registry.'

'Yes.'

'Miss Rosalind Krige is the executor. She'll be coming next week to view the will.'

# 27

## Sienna's House

Caius knocked on the imposing black front door of Sienna Worthing's house, a double-fronted red-brick house with bay windows and white slatted wooden blinds. The small front garden was populated with dormant lavender and Caius could tell that the black and white tiles on the path leading up to the porch were new but designed to look like an original feature. None were cracked like you'd expect one-hundred-odd-year-old tiles to be. Like her grandmother, Sienna evidently liked her brass door knocker polished on a regular basis. The door opened and a harassed-looking young woman stared at him.

'DI Caius Beauchamp, I'm here to speak to Mrs Sienna Worthing. May I come in?' he asked, showing her his warrant card. Amy had sent him Sienna's socials so he knew it wasn't her. Sienna preferred cashmere lounge sets post-partum rather than this woman's ordinary leggings, T-shirt and wonky-looking cardigan.

'Yes, come this way,' said the young woman. Caius couldn't help but notice that she had the faintest smell of warm Parmesan cheese clinging to her which he could only assume meant she had just been thrown up on by the latest addition to the Worthing household. She showed Caius into the living room and gestured for him to take a seat on the plush olive-green sofa. 'Mrs Worthing will be down in a moment. She's just breastfeeding,' said the nanny before she turned and left, leaving a tantalising scent trail of curdled milk behind her as she went.

Caius looked about the room. It was immaculate. He couldn't imagine that any young children lived here. He had to assume they weren't allowed in it. His Jamaican grandmother had forbidden anyone from entering her 'good room' and had put plastic covers over the sofa. That was the only explanation for how impeccable it was. Not a dust mote, not a cushion out of place, not a stray Lego brick. Then again, the Worthings could afford to hire help. It had been recently decorated – hints of fresh paint still hung in the air – and was filled with houseplants, rattan baskets holding pure wool woven blankets, and shapely lamps. There were inbuilt bookcases in the alcoves. There were a few modern history titles dispersed in between tasteful curated tchotchkes. The art on the walls was a mixture between abstract paintings and architectural prints. He noticed that the infamous edition of *Tatler* he had been mentioned in was on the coffee table. Sienna was just the sort of person to read the magazine, but it wasn't the latest edition and he couldn't help but think it had been placed there on purpose. Sienna was telling him she knew who he was. The nanny's cheesiness had been replaced by a warm, spicy smell that Caius realised was coming from a terracotta pomegranate on the side table. Caius looked again at the bookshelf and realised that the titles weren't just modern history, they were all about the Second World War. Sienna wafted into the room suddenly and, flustered, Caius picked up the scented terracotta pomegranate.

'The top notes are bitter orange and bergamot,' she said cheerfully, taking it from Caius, placing it back and then sitting opposite him on the other sofa. She was so jaunty and reassuring that Caius had forgotten why he was there for a moment. 'It's delicious, isn't it? A friend brought one back from a recent jolly to Italy. I was supposed to go too, but I was far too pregnant to travel.'

'I understand that congratulations are in order.'

'Yes, thank you. Cosmo is our fourth.'

'You must have your hands full.'

'I do. Do you have children, detective?'

'No,' Caius said, before adding a hopeful, 'not yet.'

'It's the greatest joy. Motherhood really is my calling.'

Caius smiled at her before looking down at his knees. He held his breath as he tried to think how to segue into his reason for visiting. He needn't have bothered.

'Thank you for coming here to check on me.' Sienna had started weeping. 'Gosh, I'm so sorry. I told myself I wasn't going to cry when you came. I shall blame it on the hormone dips. I cried this morning when my toast came out more charred than I like it.'

'Not at all, Mrs Worthing.' Caius felt that she was the sort of woman who enjoyed the distance her married name placed between them. 'It's totally natural to feel like that when you've lost a relative in such a way.'

'It's such a shock. Such a shock. A burglary gone wrong. What is London coming to? I can't understand how anyone could hurt Granny. She was such a sweetie. So considerate of others and so kind. I can only assume that they were some vicious maniac who shouldn't have been allowed here in the first place.'

'When was the last time you saw your grandmother?' Caius asked. He understood what Lucia had meant. He really wanted to ask her where she was the night her grandmother died but he thought she would need to work up to the idea. He wasn't sure she would take kindly to the faintest hint of her being a suspect.

'Two weeks before she died. She came to see Cosmo for the first time. I don't like visitors for a few weeks after I've given birth, but I made an exception for her and Rosie. I'm so glad I did. If only I'd known she'd only get to see him once.'

'I am so sorry, Mrs Worthing.'

'No, it's quite all right.' She took a tissue from the box on the table. It also had a rattan cover.

'Were you close with your grandmother?'

'In truth, not as much as I would like. Especially in recent years. There was a misunderstanding between Granny and Mummy that unfortunately I got pulled into. Silly Mummy. All her fault really. Terrible at communication.'

'And Rosie?'

'Oh poor Rosie. Poor thing finding that whole mess.' Sienna, clutching the tissue to her breast let it fall to her lap. 'Rosie is Granny's favourite. She looks just like her when she was younger. It was very kind of Granny to have Rosie stay with her. I offered too but I believe Granny is a little more Rosie's speed. She's a little country mouse. And the commute was easier from there.'

Caius could have sworn that Sienna put far too much emphasis on the first syllable of 'country'. 'Commuting time makes such a difference in London, doesn't it?'

'Oh, so much!'

'Where does your husband commute to?'

'Wandsworth Town to Waterloo and then he hops onto the Waterloo and City line. His office is near Liverpool Street. That's why we moved here.' Sienna placed her hand on a magazine on the coffee table. 'It's so convenient when the trains run properly. This government has let us all down. The whole country is falling to pieces. Nothing works. We need someone to take charge and make the trains run on time.'

'What's your relationship with your mother like?'

'My mother? Detective, are you my therapist?'

'I'm not qualified for that.' Caius paused and stared at a vase on the mantlepiece for a moment. He was confused – he almost thought she was flirting with him. 'You've touched on the fight your mother had with your grandmother and Rosie already.'

'Yes. It was deeply unpleasant. I found the whole thing very stressful. Especially as we had the house to deal with too. When we bought it the place was a wreck, you wouldn't believe the work we've had to do. New roof. Repointing. Plastering. The floors. We had a basement dug in. The house was a steal for the area because it was so ramshackle.'

'Right.' Caius nodded. He'd ask his dad but he knew that such renovations would've been costly. 'Was your husband close with your grandmother?'

'Charlie? Not especially. He tried of course, he's like that, but she could occasionally be prickly.'

'I listened to a podcast he did recently.'

'*The Man, the Mythos*?'

'Yes.'

'He's such a good talker, isn't he?'

'He's really something.'

'I'm so proud of him.'

'To build a property company out of nothing is really impressive.'

'You should know,' Sienna said, a little pointedly. 'Charlie actually works in tech. He has one sort of property company that's listing, but his other enterprises are all based in Old Street at Silicon Roundabout. He has multiple start-ups on the go.'

'Other companies?'

'Yes, *Freya*, my app for starters. Your girlfriend should try it, here.' Sienna picked a business card up off the coffee table and handed it to him. It was soft pink with a QR code on the back. It had been conveniently laid out next to the *Tatler*. 'One month's free membership.'

Caius put the business card in his pocket to be polite, but it was going in the bin. 'Tell me, the brewery he's on the board of. I love a craft beer. How did that come about?'

'Oh that's Felix. He inherited it when he turned twenty-one.'

'Felix?'

'He's an old friend of Charlie's from university. He was Charlie's first backer actually. Felix has an eye for talent if nothing else. Had Charlie join the advisory board last year. Those boys really support each other.' Sienna rolled her eyes.

'Is that the same Felix who Rosie works for?' She was clearly not enamoured of Felix.

'Yes. He's fighting the good fight in his own special way.'

Caius tried not to linger on the history books on the shelves too long. Sienna was watching him intently. He took a deep breath. 'I hate to ask, Mrs Worthing, but where were you on Saturday?'

'I totally understand. You have to ask such questions so you can catch the monster that did this.'

'Yes.' Caius didn't want to ask again. He wondered what her grasp of the situation was. She didn't seem to like answering simple direct questions. 'And where were you?'

'I was here.'

'Alone?'

'With my husband and children. Charlie had taken Atticus to his little friend's pirate-themed birthday party that day, while I took my twin girls to their ballet class. I put the baby in a sling. He loves it. He can hear my heartbeat. We all went shopping in the afternoon. The children enjoy the fruit and vegetable stalls at the farmers' market on Northcote Road. Then we came home and made our own pizzas. I've got a sourdough starter on the go that we use. We put a nature documentary on for the children.

Then they went to bed. Charlie and I stayed up a little longer and then I went up. Cosmo wants feeding every two hours so I try to get as much sleep whenever I can. Poor Charlie works terribly hard, so he had a few emails to send. But he was there next to me by ten. I was writing in my gratitude journal after a feed; you see, I make a note of the time to see if it affects my mood.'

Caius regretted not specifying 'Saturday evening'. 'All right then,' he said, standing up and moving towards the door. He thanked her for her time and congratulated her again on the new baby. 'Goodness. You must be the busiest woman in Wandsworth.'

'Oh, well. I do have help. Grace is a marvel. It's so important to get that support. I do run my own business too. I don't have a village; you know, people close by that I can consistently rely on, so we have to pay for it. It's such a shame. This capitalist modernity was supposed to free us from overbearing small-town life, but it's all I want. I want to be surrounded by my broader family; people who know me, who look like me and look out for me. We don't value motherhood any more than we value our precious traditions, our very way of life. What have we if that perishes? A neo-liberal hellscape, that's what's left. A barren wasteland.'

'OK.'

'Don't you agree?'

'Sure.'

'But I do feel like Grace really is part of our family now.' Sienna said the last part loudly as if she were performing it.

At the second mention of her name, the young nanny appeared from down the hallway from what Caius assumed was the kitchen with a snuffling scrunched-up ball swathed in a crisp white babygrow. Sienna took Cosmo from her. She kissed him on the top of his little wrinkled head and held him tenderly to her chest.

'I love it when they smell all milky.'

Caius nodded.

'Four down, four to go,' said Grace.

Caius, bemused by the statement, looked up at Grace. She gave Caius a knowing flash, a look of subversive sarcasm. He hadn't really looked at her properly before. She was young, but lacked naivety. She was wearing a different jumper now, another baggy hand-knitted effort that didn't quite sit right on her, but no longer smelled of rancid Parmesan.

'My husband says he wants eight children,' said Sienna, step-ping almost in front of Grace. She started laughing, a tinkling of irreverence and an eye roll letting Caius know he shouldn't pay attention to the silly girl.

'If you go for eleven you could field a football team in the winter and a cricket team in the summer,' Caius said, ushering himself out the door. He felt uncomfortable and it wasn't just the strained dynamic between employer and employee, but something else.

'I shan't put the idea in his head,' said Sienna as Grace shut the door, not quite quick enough for Caius not to see the look Sienna shot at the girl.

★   ★   ★

Callie, who had her hair piled up in a messy bun on top of her head, opened the door to her studio.

'I was just across the river, and I thought I'd respond to the note you left in my lunch bag in person,' Caius said.

'Did you now,' Callie said, closing the door behind him.

★ ★ ★

Caius was straightening his tie in the mirror in Callie's showroom.

'Guess who popped in an hour or so ago.'

'Who?'

'My old man. Still wants to see me tomorrow but he couldn't wait. It didn't go brilliantly. Jane wants my studio as part of the divorce settlement,' Callie said, sitting on top of the workbench as she put her lilac lambswool jumper back on.

'God, that's petty,' Caius said, stepping back into the workroom and standing in front of her, taking in how cute she looked with pink flushed cheeks. 'And very clearly an attack on you.'

'I expected no less from Jane,' Callie said, shrugging and then readjusting Caius's tie for him. 'He feels a bit funny about you still.'

'That's not surprising.'

'I assured him that you didn't set out to get him.' Callie picked up a lip balm off the table and applied some. 'Peter wants to go for lunch next week. I guess he has a lot of free time since he stepped down from his constituency.'

'Are you going to go?'

'Maybe.' Callie tipped her head from side to side as if she were a scale weighing up the possibility of her sitting down for a weekly cappuccino with the man who didn't tell her he was her father for thirty years. 'Bloody Jane.'

'Look,' Caius said, leaning into her, pulling her into his chest. 'This is just a building; we can always get you another workroom. You're the important one not this space.'

'I know. It's just that I've been weirdly comforted by the fact that he bought this place for me. He wanted to support me even though . . .'

It was the least he could do, Caius thought, but didn't want to say out loud. 'Let's do something fun tomorrow evening. We could go to the cinema maybe? See if there's an arty film on at the Curzon that we may or may not understand. I should be trying harder to keep my French up. We could go to dinner beforehand.'

'That would be lovely.' Callie looked at him and smiled to herself. 'Amy's nice,' she said quietly, taking a white mug with speckled green flecks of paint from the cupboard and putting a bag of Earl Grey tea in it.

'Most of the time.' He looked at her. He hated it when his work collided hard with his life. His real life, not the seemingly unending grind of human misery that he called his profession. He tried not to think about what his father had said, but if he was going to quit his job it would be for Callie and not for the estate.

The kettle boiled and Callie poured the water into the mug. She put the kettle down and came back over to Caius, winding her arms around his waist before pulling back and gently poking him on the nose. 'Boop.'

'Boop.' He did it back to her. If he'd been watching two strangers doing this he would have vomited. 'I've got to get back. I'll actually eat my lunch while I'm stuck at a traffic light somewhere.'

'I love you,' Callie said, kissing him goodbye.

'And I love you,' he said.

'Don't forget we're having supper with Dotty and Georgie tonight.'

'How could I?'

'You like them really.'

'Do I?'

'No. But you're going to come to like them.'

# 28

## The Police Station

Amy had popped to Greggs after she'd finished with Josephine. She'd been craving a vegan sausage roll all week and with Caius gone she could eat all the flaky pastry she wanted in peace. Although she had noticed that he'd begun to mellow about food recently. He still ate 'well'. Lots of dubious green things smooshed up but the anxiety around it had started to drop off. It was a welcome change. Callie was bloody good for him. As much as she and Matt had taken the piss out of Caius and his clean-eating drive last summer, she had seen a friend of Fi's start out talking about food as either good or bad, with this benefit or that, to progress on to safe and unsafe. Fi, using her stern nurse's voice, had talked her into seeing a therapist. Despite her misgivings about eating 'clean' Amy had bought a fruit salad rather than an iced bun so she must have thought that Caius's grumbles about ultra-processed food were probably right. To be scared of a need; to be fed with a slow poison. That was dramatic – too dramatic for Amy. Something was going to get her as it would everyone, so why run yourself into the ground thinking about micros and macros, antioxidants and calories. Eat real food and move. But then Amy's family were strap on a pair of boots and go for a six-hour walk – strategically stopping off at the pub on the way – sort of people. They just got on with it and stopped breathing when they did, refusing to think too much about it in the interim.

Amy crumpled up the Greggs paper bag and chucked it into the bin in the break room. The ball of paper hit the rim and fell straight in. It annoyed her that there was no one else there to see it.

Matt came into the break room carrying a Greggs paper bag.

'While the cat's away, the mice eat steak bakes,' Matt said, sitting down next to Amy. He too had bought a small fruit salad which he pulled from his coat pocket and put on the table.

'Caius has got into our heads,' Amy said, picking up her pot of kiwi, melon and strawberry and waving at it.

'It's all his talk about scurvy.'

★ ★ ★

Matt and Amy were poring over Mona's will when Caius walked in with three Greggs bags. 'A Greggs just opened on the high street and I thought everyone looked like they deserved an iced bun today.'

'Mon ami!' Matt said, taking the bun from him. 'Bitte.'

'Thank you,' Amy said gratefully, taking the sticky treat from him. She peered into the bag and took the cherry from the top and popped it into her mouth.

'I've had confirmation that William was definitely not in the country,' Matt said.

'Great, Will Krige is no longer a suspect even though we practically forgot about him.' Amy rubbed his name off the whiteboard. After the realisation that Philip may not have had an accomplice after all, she'd moved the Krige clan over to the suspect board.

'How was the solicitors?' Caius asked, coming over to Matt.

'Well! Mona hadn't updated her will. Josephine and Sienna are still disinherited,' Matt said, handing Caius the folder he'd received from David Miller before taking a bite of his bun. 'She's left £100K in cash savings to William. The rest of the estate, including the house, stocks and shares, and savings to Rosie. Rosie is about to become rather rich.'

'That's not what Lucia said,' Amy said between bites of her bun. 'Which really means that's not what Rosie has been telling people. Perhaps she didn't know the will hadn't been changed yet.'

Caius took the will from Matt and started reading it. 'Rosie is executor of the will and the sole beneficiary. Ah voilà, un bon motif pour le meurtre.'

'The government website is saying that probate is taking a minimum of twelve weeks at the moment, so Sienna won't know for a while unless Rosie tells her,' Amy said, having googled it quickly.

'Let's keep that under our hats for a little while too,' Caius said, putting the will down. 'How was Josephine?'

'She basically called Rosie a cockroach.'

'What?' Matt asked.

'She said she'd survive a nuclear explosion and that she was much tougher than you think she is.'

'Was that just Josephine being pissed off with her over falling out with Mona?' Caius asked.

'I don't know. She confirmed that Charlie is friends with Johnny Bull though.'

'I can't stand that awful man,' Caius said, logging in to his computer and briefly scanning his emails. 'Rosie. Rosie. Rosie. I hate to say it but you're both right. I'm starting to think she's a bit dodgy.'

'I told you. I bloody told you. She knits.' Matt held his arms out in vindication.

'I called it first. I said she worked in a charity so she had to be bad.'

'Quit squabbling, toddlers,' Caius said.

'What was Sienna like?' Amy asked.

'She scared me.'

'Scared you?' Matt asked.

'Yeah, I don't know. She was very friendly. At one point I thought she was flirting with me, and then the next felt like she was trying to recruit me for some back-to-basics crusade.'

'Yuck,' Matt said.

'Very yuck. She was . . . Oh, I don't know.' Caius searched for the words. 'Stepford Wifey?'

'She's a wannabe cult leader,' Amy said, again.

'Sienna has four children and the house was immaculate, she was immaculate. There was a scented pottery pomegranate on a dustless coffee table and not a single teddy bear to be seen. I don't know. It felt like a performance. I'd just expect there to be a trace amount of chaos with that many children. She did have a nanny there, a girl called Grace who was a bit off. We can probably assume they have a cleaner as well. For someone who's married to a tech entrepreneur, Sienna made a comment about capitalism being a shitty system to live under. Kept talking about traditional ways of living. Maybe she was just a bit too upper middle, but it put my heckles up.'

'Have you seen your girlfriend?' Matt said. He thought that Caius was adjusting quite nicely to those heights.

Caius looked at him – he wanted to hit back, but Matt wasn't wrong. 'She fawned over me a little bit and it was weird. She had that *Tatler* there.'

'Ah, so she's just a garden variety snob then,' Matt said.

'Maybe? There were a lot of history books on Second World War which isn't that weird. This country likes that war, we were the goodies for once, but I can't shake it. A lot of the things she was saying, if taken at face value were fine, but I think she was alluding to Mussolini. But the thing is, she kept smiling at me. People don't smile at me while making those sorts of statements. After the whole Nazi love-child thing, maybe I'm seeing fascists everywhere, you know. Who hasn't seen *The Great Escape*? People get so excited when they see a Spitfire or a Lancaster Bomber. At least in my family they do, but then my grandad was in the RAF.'

'You seem a bit het up, mate,' Matt said, patting him on the shoulder. 'Amy, time for the big guns. Get out the camomile.'

'No,' Amy said. Matt stared at her, then Caius raised his eyebrows at her. 'Fine, but this is the last tea I make today.'

'Did you find out anything more about Charlie?' Matt said, turning back to Caius.

'Squires brewery belongs to Felix. And he was Charlie's first backer. Charlie has more than one company and Sienna said that they're tech, not property.'

'But he rents out office space?'

'Apparently, that's not what Charlie really does.'

## 29

## A Coffee Shop in Paddington Station

Rosie sat down in front of her mother. Josephine had already bought a latte for her, but it was cold now and had skimmed cow's milk rather than her preferred oat. Rosie was going to drink it anyway.

'Was the tube busy?' Josephine asked. Rosie was half an hour late.

'Yes, delays on the line,' Rosie said. It hadn't been. She'd just dawdled as she left Lucia's. She hadn't wanted to come.

'How are you?'

'As well as can be expected.'

'Yes. Of course.' Josephine shook her head. 'I can't believe what's happened.'

'Me neither.'

Mona's death was not mentioned again. They talked about the weather and then Sienna's children until both topics were exhausted. Josephine asked after her estranged son and Rosie denied speaking to him recently. Rosie asked about the village gossip. Something Josephine would usually relish sharing. Josephine looked uncomfortable. Rosie realised that they were the gossip this time, but then Josephine brightened when she recalled that their annoying neighbour Theresa's ratty dog had been put down that morning. A bowel obstruction did for the little shit. Rosie liked Millie the Jack Russell and was disheartened to hear of Theresa's loss, but Josephine reassured her that no one would miss Millie's yapping.

'Mummy, don't be cruel. Poor Theresa. She's all alone in that house.' Rosie shook her head. Her mother could be so cruel. Poor Millie barking occasionally was nothing compared to the companionship she had provided Theresa.

'Oh, Rosie, you are so sensitive.'

'No. No, I'm not.' Rosie picked up her coffee, determined not to rise at the jab. To move on. 'Have you spoken to Sienna recently?'

'Yes, why?' Josephine asked, sucking in her cheeks in anticipation of some sort of dig.

'I'm worried.'

'About Sienna?'

'About her views.'

'What do you mean?'

'She keeps hinting at things when I talk to her.'

'What things?'

'Well, she's a bit xenophobic.' Rosie fiddled with her necklace. 'Obviously because of what happened, which I don't want to talk about, it had been a while since I spoke to her properly but we've met up for coffee over the last few months and there's been a shift in her. I know she and Charlie always used to say funny things every now and then but since we've been on speaking terms I can't help but feel it's more than having slightly different opinions on how the economy is run. And that Johnny? He's awful.'

'I don't understand, Rosie. You think she's xenophobic?'

'Yes. Look, never mind.' Rosie realised her mother was never going to see Sienna as anything other than perfection, and looked at the time on her watch. 'I've got to get to the baby bank. I'll call you.'

★   ★   ★

## The Barnes Baby Bank

'I crocheted a few pram blankets and knitted a couple of cardigans in 3–6 months. We were low on those last time I checked. I've done them all in neutrals like you asked.' Rosie had started out by making lots of brightly coloured things and a handful of more muted colours, but the mothers all kept picking the neutrals instead. She'd switched entirely to balls of oatmeal, taupe and biscuit and they'd been much more popular. Rosie liked children in bright clothing – she figured they'd be easier to spot if they wandered off in the park – but she didn't want to impose her aesthetic sensibility onto other people.

'Oh, Rosie, those are lovely,' said Linda, the woman in charge of the baby bank. She picked up a clotted cream-coloured cardigan. 'How sweet.'

'What can I do today? I've got to go in an hour and a half, but I can have a good crack at something.'

'Oh, petal. Are you sure?'

'I need to keep busy.'

'I understand, sweetheart.' Linda gave Rosie's shoulders a squeeze. 'She was a lovely lady your gran.'

'She was.'

'Never saw anyone command a bric-a-brac table quite like her. She was like an admiral surveying the fleet.'

Rosie gave a painfully joyous laugh.

'We've just had a big donation of clothes come in. Do you want to sort through it all and see what's worth keeping and what's for rag?'

'Yeah of course.'

'I had a quick look through the bags and there were useful things like pram suits, but I also saw a vest that looked pretty stained. Honestly, people treat us like the tip.'

'I guess the person donating doesn't have a lot of time, little kids and all that, and maybe doesn't know what will be useful. People are funny about throwing things out too. Growing cotton uses a lot of water, after all. If it's got a bit of life in it still . . .'

'Oh, Rosie. Petal. You are charitable.'

★ ★ ★

## A Playground in Wandsworth

Rosie watched the twins climb up a slide at a park near Sienna's house. The same one she had brought them to yesterday. Grace had a dental appointment that afternoon, so Sienna had roped Rosie in at the last minute to collect the twins from their pre-prep. She didn't mind too much – the girls were delightful – but she needed to be careful not to get sucked too closely into Sienna's orbit though. She'd get Lucia to give her a pep talk about boundaries again later. The girls slid down the slide one after the other. Ottilie didn't wait for Flora to get out of the way and they crashed into a pile of giggles amongst the woodchips at the bottom. Rosie helped Ottilie up as Flora skipped around a climbing frame.

'Are you all right, Ottilie?' Rosie asked.

'I'm brilliant,' said Ottilie.

'Look, Auntie Rosie,' said Flora, pointing at a piece of graffiti.

'What is it, sweetheart?' Rosie asked, joining her next to the multicoloured play equipment.

'It's a swastika,' said Ottilie.

'Have you been doing the Second World War at school?' Rosie asked, wondering what they were teaching five-year-olds these days.

'Daddy has a book,' said Flora, climbing up the ladder.

'Does he?' Rosie asked.

'Daddy likes it when there's a big war,' Ottilie said, following her sister.

'That symbol is a bad symbol, used by naughty people.'

'OK, Auntie Rosie.' Flora slipped down the slide, scrambled up and stood in front of Rosie, crossing her arms.

Ottilie peered over the top of a primary-coloured turret. 'Auntie Rosie, can we have a chocolate bar?'

'Please, Auntie Rosie. We won't tell Mummy,' Flora said.

'Sure,' said Rosie, returning to the bench where she had left the girls' coats. It looked like rain again.

Rosie took the girls home via a corner shop for a bar of Kinder Chocolate. If Sienna complained that she was giving the girls sweets then she could at least say they were small and theoretically mostly milk. Rosie rang the doorbell and was surprised by Felix opening the door.

'Hello, girls,' he said, rubbing Ottilie and Flora on the head as they hugged him.

'Uncle Felix. Uncle Felix. Uncle Felix,' they said in a swirling cacophony as they swarmed past him and into the house.

Felix leaned in quietly, rolling his eyes as he said, 'I bought Sienna some flowers. I told her that we'd passed in the street and you asked me to pop them in for her.'

'That was kind of you. I suppose,' Rosie said, giving him a pointed look. She was a little confused as to why he felt the need to meddle in her relationship with her sister like that. 'No one ever buys me flowers.'

Felix shook his head.

Rosie walked into the house, finding Sienna sat on the sofa in the living room. Atticus was doing a wooden puzzle at her feet and Cosmo was in her arms. 'Thank you so much, darling. It really means so much to me. It really does.'

'What for?' she asked from the doorway. Rosie saw the vase of white lilies on the table. 'Oh, the flowers. We had a lovely time at the park didn't we, girls.'

Felix appeared at the door right behind Rosie. She could smell his cologne. 'I best be off, Sienna. Again, both of you. I'm so sorry for your loss.'

'So sweet of you to pop in. See you at dinner tomorrow, darling,' Sienna said over her shoulder, not bothering to get up and walk with him to the door.

Felix showed himself out, brushing along past Rosie as he went.

'He needs to stop "popping in". He only comes round to talk about money. He stresses Charlie out. I'll have to have a word with Charlie again. He's reluctant to say anything because he's known him for so long,' Sienna said, looking at the flowers. 'Thank you for the lovely flowers though. God, I'm tired. I need to hire a personal assistant. I've got so much work on what with the app and all the live events I'm planning.'

'You'll have to advertise.' Rosie could tell that Sienna was angling at whether she'd fancy the job.

'What are you wearing tomorrow?'

'Umm . . . Look, I've had a think and I'm—'

'Just as I thought. Everything's at Granny's house, isn't it? No matter, I have something for you. I'm sitting you next to Johnny.'

'I'm not up to a dinner party.'

'Of course you are. Granny would want us to keep going. Not let the bastards win.'

'Keep calm and carry on.'

'Well, yes . . .' A clanging could be heard from the kitchen. Sienna got up from the sofa and handed Cosmo to Rosie. She walked out to the hallway. 'Ottilie, put the lamp down. You're supposed to be a young lady not a hooligan.'

Once Sienna returned, Rosie made her excuses and left swiftly.

# 30

## The Police Station

'Amy, did you get Josephine's fingerprints?' Matt asked, glancing at the whiteboard with all the fingerprint maps stuck on them.

'Yeah. She wasn't pleased.'

The door to the incident room opened.

Caius stood up. 'Good afternoon, sir.'

'Good afternoon, Caius,' the Chief Superintendent said. 'I just wanted to check in with you as this is the first assignment under the official umbrella of the new special unit. Are the resource provisions substantial enough?'

'Yes, although we may need uniform to do some more canvassing of the area later in the week though.'

The Chief Superintendent liked this; he liked it a lot. He liked having the chance to speak to another precinct and remind them that it was his officers that had been chosen for this new initiative and to be at the forefront of advances in modern policing. Not that he knew much of what was going on in Caius's incident room – headlines only. It had come down from the Home Office itself that there was to be the minimal intervention in these 'special cases'. It had also been hinted that an invite for him and his wife would be in the post in the coming months for a garden party at the Palace as a little reward for his wife's decades of charitable works and sponsored fun running. That would be something to put in the annual Christmas round robin. 'Of course. I can liaise with Hammersmith and have the local lads,' he began before looking at Amy and trying to sprinkle a little sex equality in. 'And ladettes of course, at your disposal. It makes a difference if the officers on the ground know the terrain. As you were then,' the Chief Superintendent said before leaving.

Caius turned to Amy. 'Actually, Keith the Chief was vaguely useful then. What happened to canvassing for doorbell camera footage. Amy, go back again to Faisal and see where they've got to. I'm off tomorrow so if you guys could focus on that.'

'No problem.' Amy sat down at her computer and quickly bashed out a curt email. She preferred email to calling, partially because of her age – something about talking to a person directly like that made her deeply uneasy in a primal way – but then she also had a record of what had transpired. She was comforted by the time stamp, by the solidity of it, by the tangible proof that she'd done her job properly.

'I've been looking at the fingerprint maps,' Matt said, beckoning Caius and Amy over to a desk where he'd spread out six sheets, each had the same layout of the house but with the locations of where the six sets of prints were found marked. 'I'm waiting for confirmation of whether Josephine is one of the mystery fingerers. Fingerers? Person with fingers? Whether these are her prints.'

'You all right, muchacho?'

'No, I need a nap,' Matt said, eyeing up the time on his computer. 'This first map shows Mona's fingerprints and as you'd expect you find them everywhere. The second is Rosie's and likewise. The third has been confirmed as Zofia's, which you'll see seem to be concentrated on the bathroom and kitchen, which you would expect, but they are also pretty much everywhere.' She was also the second person to touch Manas's bedding.

'And these three are still a mystery,' Caius said, looking at the fourth map. 'This person's prints are only in the living room.'

'I reckon they probably popped in for an impromptu cup of tea,' Matt said, glancing at the timeline he had of Mona's week sans tea party.

'The fifth map is someone going up the stairs,' Amy said, looking at it and noticing that their prints appeared to be focused on the banister and the front door. 'Then into this bedroom here which is Rosie's, right?'

'So Rosie had a guest go to her room that week. Zofia said she polished the banister on Wednesday when she came. Was it Tristan?' Matt asked, raising an eyebrow.

'Was it lover boy indeed,' Caius said, remembering interviewing him. 'He was definitely a bit jumpy. Perhaps he popped in for a "euphemistic coffee"?'

'Is that one of those new low caffeine brands?' Matt asked.

'If you're going to make jokes like that then go home, Matt. I have no more need of you,' Caius said, shaking his head. 'That leaves our sixth and final fingerprint map.'

'The killer,' Amy said, moving towards the map, tracing a route through the house they may have taken with her finger. Their prints were on both murder weapons. Caius and Matt moved next to her. 'What are they doing in the house?'

'They've been touching picture frames and drawers,' Matt said, looking at the details of where the prints were found. 'They're on the front door and all over the kitchen too.'

'So the killer was searching the house then. That's what a burglar would do,' Amy said.

'It is. Not just any burglar either, that's a burglar looking for something pacific. Specific. I need a nap too. The burglar was looking for something specific. Amateur too; idiot left prints everywhere. Nothing was missing from the house though, well at least nothing that Rosie knew about. We should get her to do a walkthrough again.' Caius checked the time on his watch. 'All right, chaps and chapettes, have we crossed off our to-do lists today?'

'I've got one more thing to do,' Matt said, picking up his desk phone to call Zofia to double-check whether she did polish the banister on Wednesday.

'I've crossed everything off mine because I'm better than Matt,' Amy said.

'Is this the effect of your new netball team? Have they made you more feral?' Matt asked as he put the receiver down – he'd seen his opportunity and was going to take it. He could call Zofia later.

Amy stared at Matt.

'Who bit who? I can't take it any more,' Matt said, throwing his hands in the air.

'I can't tell you that, it was settled out of court.'

'Calm down, you two. I'm off tomorrow, being bossed about by my dad, so I need you to work together, go through that doorbell footage and speak to the other passengers from the train.' Caius, who had spent more energy thinking about what had happened to Amy at netball than he should have, pretended to be uninterested as he nonchalantly asked Amy the question to end this all. 'Oh, Amy, did you have to get an oral or an IV antibiotic?'

'Just oral, it got a bit infected. She had poor dental hygiene.' Amy rolled her eyes. 'Dammit. You can't tell anyone.'

'At least you didn't have to get a rabies injection,' Matt said. He'd lost £10 to Caius.

# 31

## Dotty and Georgie's House, Notting Hill

Dotty, Callie's faux bohemian friend from art school, had invited them over for supper, again. It was the third time this month. They had taken to Caius, but he was a little wary of them. Plus, while he liked to be social, he also really liked staying at home and eating Leerdammer straight from the packet on the sofa while he read whatever book he'd grabbed from the library in a frenzy when he remembered he'd paid his council tax and didn't have to buy it. He loved free books as much as he loved rolling up slices of mass-produced Dutch cheese and taking huge bites. A 'for sale' sign greeted them at the front of the house and Callie was itching to find it on the estate agent's website once they were safely within the confines of their own flat. Dotty hadn't mentioned any plans to move.

Dinner had been gorged upon. Roasted tomatoes with yoghurt on sourdough toast, then a preserved lemon, pea, potato and feta tray bake, finally followed by a passion fruit roly-poly with crème Anglaise ice cream. Callie was never going to mention it to Dotty – although she would absolutely get into it on the way home with Caius – but she was very sure that in the bin she'd seen a set of handwritten instructions sellotaped to the top of a piece of tin foil for each of the courses they'd just eaten. She wondered how long Dotty was going to continue pretending she could cook. Callie was also judging her for not recycling.

'We had such a lovely time visiting Georgie's family,' Dotty said, relaxing into her chair as Georgie removed the plates. Both Callie and Caius had valiantly offered to help with cleaning up, but their help was refused twice. 'It's so nice to not have to lift a finger.'

'Where does your family live, Georgie?' Caius asked. Callie had made him swear to ask them mildly probing questions that she had now known them too long to ask. Dotty and Georgie rarely spoke of their families. They were like epicurean goldfish – living in the fleeting moment and unable to recall much of what went on previously other than it had all been lovely. Callie had known them since 2009, a time in her life when it would've been mortifyingly uncool to ask about someone's parents. She had wanted to google them for years, but it felt a little grim. She'd be terribly embarrassed if they somehow saw her search history.

'Westmorland,' Georgie said as he bent over to load the dishwasher. 'Bloody cold up there this time of year still, but Mum has a marvellous cook. You can forget all the other shit, you know. All the adult crap you have to do to get by in London and just sit and draw.'

'That does sound lovely,' Callie said.

'Oh, it was. I had an amazing time at Christmas sat by the fire reading trashy novels,' Dotty said. Callie had seen her twitch at the mention of the cook. Dotty turned to look at Caius. 'How are your family settling in?'

'Fine. My parents are moved in now and my d— my father keeps messaging me about sheep.'

'Oh God, I keep getting livestock texts too,' Georgie said, sitting down. 'And bloody shooting party shit. We lived in Hackney for six years; I don't need to hear another thing said about guns.' Georgie had officially gone vegetarian – at Dotty's firm insistence. She had gone vegetarian last year for the sake of her microbiome and could not tolerate steaks in the fridge if she was not permitted to eat them. 'I'm very anti-violence.'

'You should come up to stay in the summer,' Caius said. He didn't think his family would have a problem with it. It wasn't as if they were short of bedrooms. Callie had gently floated the idea that it would be nice to socialise at Frithsden at some point in the near future and quite frankly, why not. It's what people did. They invited guests to spend weekends. Caius had been dealt this odd hand; he may as well make the best of it. 'It's only an hour or so outside of London if you set off early enough in the morning.'

'We'd be delighted,' Dotty said, wiggling in her seat. 'Especially as in the summer I'll be needing to escape the heat and relax somewhere charming.'

'We're expecting,' Georgie said loudly and with much enthusiasm. He'd heard Dotty do this odd euphemistic dance around the state of her uterus four times already that week and didn't care to let it drag on, so he overcompensated and threw his arms in the air.

'Congratulations,' said Caius and Callie in gleeful unison.

'Due in the early autumn,' Dotty said, clearly peeved that Georgie had taken the theatre out of her big announcement.

'What wonderful news,' Callie said.

'I thought you were probably wondering why I was off the vino.' Dotty laughed.

'I hadn't noticed,' Callie said. Of course she had – last year Dotty had 'discovered' natty wine and couldn't stop talking about it – she just wouldn't dream of commenting on it. She had assumed that this was why the house was on the market too.

'I feel fine, pretty tired and eating my weight in ginger biscuits.'

'How lovely,' Callie said.

'First one. One more. Maybe a third, but that's it then,'

Georgie said plainly. 'We're not those nutters who want eight children.'

'Eight children?' Caius asked. It wasn't the first time he'd heard people mentioning having that many children that week.

'Oh yeah, there was a piece doing the rounds on the internet recently about this tech bro and his wife literally breeding. Scary stuff. I'll send it to you.'

Callie started talking to Dotty about moving house.

'Caius,' Georgie said, turning to the man he had decided was going to be a good friend, partially because he seemed so normal, so like a regular person but was comfortingly not. 'Any good crimes recently, bruv?'

★  ★  ★

'I love Dotty to tiny tiny pieces but I do find it funny that she felt compelled to pretend that she cooked that whole meal,' Callie said, taking her umbrella out of her bag to shield herself from the sheets of rain.

'Didn't she?' Caius asked. His only defence against the deluge was an upturned collar. 'It tasted home-made.'

'It was home-made but just not in that home.' Callie gave up on her brolly, refolding it and shoving it into her bag before the gale could claim another broken spoke. 'I saw the instructions in the bin. Georgie's mum's cook must have sent them back with it.'

'Callie,' Caius said, holding her back and out of the splash zone caused by a supersized Range Rover driving straight through a puddle at 30 mph. He wasn't going to get drenched like that twice in one week. 'That's what happened to us on Sunday. We got sent home with a frozen Thai chicken curry and a ham hock pie by my parents' new cook.'

'Oh shit.'

'Yeah, shit. We're on a par with Georgie and Dotty.'

'Who the fuck are we?' Callie stopped at the top of the stairs to Notting Hill Gate station. She was used to her finances being more precarious than this. This new security had occurred at the same time as their relationship had begun, and while aware of Caius's change in fortunes – though she was loath to admit it this affected her too – she hadn't really considered hers. Her emotional ambivalence towards her father withstanding – even if it was beginning to warm – the hard realities of the financial help he offered were only now being recognised. The low, fog-like throb of anxiety that used to creep up on her at the end of the month had dissipated since he paid her mortgage off. 'I'm used to being the povo friend,' Callie said, pausing at the sub-terranean mouth of Notting Hill Gate station.

'Since we first met, I have acquired land, and you have acquired a manufacturing fortune.' Caius beckoned her down the steps and out of the rain. 'We are living in a nineteenth-century novel. Minus the infectious diseases, although I read in *The Guardian* that rickets is back in fashion.'

'What like heroin chic?'

'No, like malnourished children.'

'It's not supposed to be this bad.'

'And yet it is.'

'About that fortune.' Callie took her phone out to go through the tube barrier. She quickly pulled her messages up. 'My old man is really pushing for me to go for lunch tomorrow. It's all very formal sounding. I tried to wiggle out by saying I was too busy, but he's insisting.'

'How do you feel about that?' Caius asked as they got on the escalator down to the platform.

'I don't know.' Callie got on behind him and Caius turned around to gaze up at her. 'Dotty was asking me about Harriet earlier. She said that she'd requested to follow her on Instagram so she clearly is trying to work out what I'm up to. She's not contacted me or anything after Peter's solicitor sent that letter but still. I just feel awful about it. Inigo wants to catch up soon but I can't bear to. Jim said Inigo's happier now that he's called the wedding off and kicked Harriet out of the house in Richmond, but still. Dreadful. So dreadful.'

'I know,' Caius said, stepping off the escalator. 'But Harriet isn't your problem. You haven't done anything to her. Your father, on the other hand . . .'

'I'll go tomorrow. I don't think I know Peter well enough yet to decide what type of relationship I want with him. He wants a better relationship with me, so I suppose I need to try and meet him part of the way and see how it feels. I've never had a dad. I don't know how it's supposed to feel.'

'It's like having a mum but with fewer feelings.'

'That sounds nice. If anything, my mother has too many feelings.'

Caius held her hand. They walked down the tiled corridor to the platform.

Callie stared at a poster for Le Creuset pans. It was a raucous dinner party in a Parisian apartment attended by beautiful and yet odd-looking models. She should buy them a set. They lasted forever. She wouldn't have to go and buy non-stick pans that needed replacing all the time. It would probably work out cheaper in the end. They'd look chic eventually, once you'd had them for thirty years and they looked a bit battered. Or perhaps a set of those French copper pans.

'I nearly expired when Georgie called you "bruv",' Callie said.

'I'm taking it as an act of cultural appreciation of black and working-class London. He did live in Hackney, after all.'

'I fink he wants to be your fwend.'

They stepped onto the tube and were whisked away into the night and back into bed.

# FRIDAY

# 32

## Hampstead Heath

It was early. Caius jogged past the entrance to the men's bathing pond. There was no imminent threat of torrential rain and there were a few Londoners strolling about the park, grateful for the merely grey skies. Caius glanced at the app he used to track his runs: he was close enough to 5 km. He slowed down as he passed a woman pushing a pram. He took out his phone and dialled a number he hadn't thought he'd ever call.

'Georgie, bruv,' Caius said, walking now. He was going to embrace Georgie's class tourism as he embarked on his own in-depth study. 'I saw your message just now. Let's get a swift half. When are you free?'

'Tonight?' asked Georgie.

'Let me check with the missus,' Caius said. He had never said the word 'missus' like that before and he recoiled at his own usage of it. Did he think he was being ironic? He tried to focus on the real reason for the call. 'While I've got you, I just had a question to ask about something you said last night?'

'For work?' Georgie was thrilled that he could be useful in a murder inquiry. 'Really?'

'You said something about a tech guy who wanted to have eight children.'

'Oh that.' Georgie was a little disappointed it wasn't something intriguing. 'Just out of the sheer number of descendants you have, you become the basis of the human gene pool if it is repeated across so many generations. It's proper delulu San Fran thinking. I'll send the article over. It's very clearly white supremacy nonsense once you scratch the surface. They think their genes are superior and are worried about being outbred by this horde of inferior intellects.'

'And eight is the magic number?' Caius had a sinking feeling at the confirmation that he could no longer give Sienna's 'questionable' views the benefit of the doubt. And that meant he also had to think about Charlie's enthusiasm for WWII history books.

'Yup, it's maths, innit? Exponential growth. I'll send you the article I read. Look, bruv. I'm at my studio today in Hackney Wick. Meet me out that way if you can?'

'Sure.'

Caius jogged the short distance back to his flat, showered and changed. He was alone. Callie had gone to her studio for the morning before seeing her father. They both had balked about going to confession in the end. They felt like guilty hypocrites turning up and asking for forgiveness from a God neither of them really believed in any more.

Domesticity beckoned. Caius put a light wash on – he was down to one clean shirt for work. He made sure to cover the documents that Alan had given him with his running gear at the bottom of the basket. The kettle boiled. He let the water cool for a minute or two. He didn't want to scald his green tea. Caius downloaded an episode on 'The Great Replacement Theory' from a podcast called *Be the Man* to listen to in the car. It was hosted by a guy called Chad. He queued it to play before pausing to make his tea in his reusable cup for the drive to Hertfordshire to look at the damn almshouses. Just before getting in the car, his phone vibrated.

*Alan Gaffer*
*09.13*
*Any progress?*

*You*
*09.13*
*Not yet . . . I'm being bitten on the arse repetitively by my current case*

*I can get an interview with one of Crispin Beauchamp's two friends from the club easily enough, and I can get to Alethea's friends Fay and Penny too, but I'm a little reluctant to blow the case wide open yet. Alethea knew her murderer. She poured them a glass of wine . . .*

*Alan Gaffer*
*09.14*
*What are you going to do next then?*

*You*
*09.15*
*Nana Boateng, the mother's help, is the obvious place to start. She found the body. People let their guard down in front of the 'help'. She might know more than she let on at the time*

*Alan Gaffer*
*09.16*
*You've twisted my arm. Let me know when and where you need me to interview Nana. Nice girl if I remember*

*You*
*09.17*
*Are you up to it?*

*Alan Gaffer*
*09.17*
*No, you twat. I'm dying*
*(Smiling cat emoji)*
*Fucking picture things. I should've just called you*

*You*
*09.18*
*I'll call you later to arrange when and where*

*Alan Gaffer*
*09.20*
*You better or I'll haunt you, you bastard x*

Caius began the podcast. The intro was cringy rock music. He put his phone down on the empty passenger seat and set off for Frithsden Old Hall.

```
Interviewer:
OK, men, today I have the pleasure of
interviewing intellectual provocateur
Seth Robertson.

Seth Robertson:
What up, dude?

Interviewer:
Let's start off at the shallow end of
the pool. Can you explain The Great
Replacement Theory for our less-
enlightened listeners?
```

Seth Robertson:
Sure can, dude. Basically, white women
are having less babies than they should.
Abortions. College putting ideas in their
heads. The liberals brainwashing them.
The queers getting to them with their
agenda when they're children and making
them lesbians. It's a conspiracy by the
left to get rid of us. They've done this
to our women on purpose because it'll be
cheaper. Other ethnic groups are having
more of their kind which will lead to the
death of our culture and way of life.

Interviewer:
And by 'the death of our culture' you
mean what?

Seth Robertson:
The death of America. White, Christian
America. Free America. The America. Our
America. You better have your guns ready
coz the only way this can end is civil
war. You can already see it happening
in Europe. Paris, London and Berlin are
no-go areas. I wouldn't step foot in
Sweden. It is not safe for a white person
over there. The liberals over there
are shipping them in by the boatful to
replace native Swedes . . .

Caius pulled his car over somewhere in Hampstead Garden Suburb, turned the podcast off and dialled Abi's number.

'Caius, hello. I've been meaning to call you. We should go out for a drink soon.'

'That would be great, Abi.' Caius took a deep breath. Nineteen-year-old Caius would be dying right now. He pushed down a memory of her dressing up as a sexy witch on Halloween in 2007. 'I've got a favour to ask. Have you got any gossip on Johnny Bull?'

'That twat. Well, funny you should ask.'

'You're fishing around him?' Caius asked, frowning. That didn't bode well. Hampton may well be up to something after all.

'Are you?'

'Perhaps.' He didn't want to tell Abi too much but he couldn't see a way to avoid it – she'd be able to reverse engineer anything he asked her to see why he was interested. He didn't fancy his name popping up in print. 'Do you know much about his connection to Charlie Worthing and his wife Sienna?'

'The data wunderkind.'

'I thought it was a property company. Have I got that wrong?'
He remembered what Sienna had said but was playing dumb.

'He did the rounds in Westminster well over a decade ago with all this wonderful big data analysis on voters, but it was a bit too new, so no one took him up on it. He started the desk share as a side project while he hacked away at knowing our innermost desires from our browsing habits. Why?'

'Off the record.'

'All right.'

'Sienna Worthing's grandmother was murdered last week, looked like a burglary gone wrong, but it's not your average breaking and entering.'

'You think the Worthings are involved?'

'I don't know, but there's something really off with them.'

'I don't have anything on them specifically, but Felix Drake moves in their circle. On the downlow, *The Cutter* have got a junior reporter temping on the reception desk of the British Society for Rewilding. Drake seems clean, but Bull is on the board. We think Bull's planning on using the project as a way to find a network of environmentalists that have right-wing leanings. The environmentalist to far-right extremist pipeline is a thing. The two concepts sort of go hand in hand. You know, blood and soil. We got a tip-off that he keeps trying to gain access to their supporter database and influence the charity's messaging around the phrase 'native', although a lot of the staff are pushing back including Drake. We're waiting to see what Drake does but he seems a bit more decent than that.'

'Felix. Hmmm.'

'In all the footage I've seen of Felix Drake, he comes across as a puppyish and passionate environmentalist, quite sexy in a brisk country walk in wellies and zip-up jumper way, but you can't stomach a man like Bull for long if you don't agree with him at least a bit.'

'What's the actual deal with Bull? Not the pandering to the worst of us bit, but the actual aim is what?'

'Bull isn't just hard right. He's a full-on ultra-nationalist trying to look respectable. There's a rumour flying round Westminster that Bull is going to break away from the party. It may just be talk but we've heard from a couple of backbenchers on the hard right that he's begun making approaches. The PM is on his last legs, partly because he's been supporting Bull to hold the party together, but then bogrollgate has made him look utterly ridiculous. That presents opportunities to those ruthless enough to pursue them.'

Caius thought a new political party fronted by Johnny Bull with Charlie Worthing's data on the electorate could be a pretty hard proposition for the centre right to beat. That must be why Hampton was so interested. He wanted to remove his competition. It's what he does.

'But none of that has happened yet. At the moment Bull is just a fringe nutter with a sizable social media following.' Abi paused. 'Bull wants to be PM, but not yet. He couldn't pull it off. However, he can push public perceptions of key issues.'

'The Overton Window.' Caius felt proud of himself for remembering the term. He'd written a paper on it fifteen years ago.

'Exactly. Think tanks, charities, grassroot orgs. That's part of why Felix is so important to him.'

'Were you given a tip-off by a certain cabinet minister.'

'Perhaps.'

'You must have read the piece in *The Economist*.'

'I did.' Abi paused for a moment, wondering whether to share much with Caius but then he'd been the one to mention him. 'The thing I've come to realise about Hampton is that he isn't playing the game in the normal sense. He's not thinking about general election cycles and personal glory, he's thinking about the next century. About legacy.'

'He's up to something. Take him legalising drugs, for example. The increase in tourism has been huge in Liverpool following the "Riverhorse" trial run in the city. I read a piece in *The Guardian* about it. The Dutch are coming here. He's generating revenue to fund some grand scheme.'

'Can I ask about your investigation?'

'No, not really.'

'No problem. Caius, I've got to dash, I'm supposed to be in a meeting, but we have lots to discuss. Let's grab a vino sometime. Bring your girlfriend. We know lots of people in common.'

# 33

## The Police Station

'I bloody hate reviewing CCTV footage,' Amy said, dunking a digestive biscuit into her tea. Hammersmith had sent it over late last night.

'You need the right playlist,' Matt said, opening up his Spotify. 'Happy to send you one of mine. How do you feel about trance? Happy house? More of a jungle fan?'

'I'm going to break it up with little research deep dives.' Amy had had another look at Sienna's app *Freya* last night. She had sat on the floor of the living room trying and failing to do one of Sienna's meditation exercises while Fi made heaving sounds from the sofa. 'I want to get to the bottom of why *Freya* gives me such an ick.'

'I'm going to break it up with snacks,' Matt said. He'd got a share packet of Wotsits Giants, a banana, a large packet of salted pistachios and a packet of his beloved lavender shortbread. He'd gone out of his way to Waitrose to find them. 'If you're nice to me I'll share.'

'What qualifies as nice?'

'At least two cups of tea that you haven't made purposefully weak or left the teabag in for twenty minutes so that you can get out of making them.'

'As my tea-making services are being traded for goods then I accept this offer.'

They shook hands.

Matt looked at the video files that Amy had put into the folder. There were two recordings of doorbell cameras from Mona's road, one at each end and on opposite sides. Neither of them had footage of Mona's actual house. 'Between us we can see anyone entering or leaving the road. You take number 7 and I'll take number 26. Let's watch from 7 a.m. in case anyone is casing the place. We should be able to pinpoint when Philip, Rosie and Tristan arrive at least. Let's print out screenshots of everyone coming past on foot and in vehicles and then we can compare the street's comings and goings.'

★ ★ ★

'Can I have some Wotsits?' Amy asked.

'Can I have an Earl Grey? Black, please,' Matt replied, a slice of lemon was too much to ask from the police station's provisions.

'Yeah, sure.' Amy swiped the bag as she went towards the kitchen. She returned five minutes later with a perfectly brewed cup of tea and put the half-eaten packet back on Matt's desk. 'You find anything interesting yet?'

'Nope, I'm up to 3 p.m.'

## 34

## Frithsden Old Hall

Caius, having been on a tour of the almshouses in Frithsden Major, the village that his family owned much of, was back at the house with Paul. They were having a cup of tea in a small outbuilding that Caius's father had quickly turned into the new estate office. Paul was a smart man, who hid his cynicism behind controlled jolliness. He worked for the Beauchamp family's property company, had done so for twenty-three years and was finding it hard to adjust to the style of these new Beauchamps. Not that they were doing a bad job, the opposite in fact. Paul had just got used to laissez-faire Sir Edgar and absentee Rupert. Marcus Beauchamp on the other hand was much more present and far more demanding. It appeared his son was like that also.

'It's such a shame that the almshouses have been left empty for so long. Sir Edgar had intended to renovate them in 2002 but hadn't quite got round to it,' said Paul.

'Who were the intended,' Caius began, stumbling for the word. 'Tenants?'

'Recipients. Your ancestor Sir Roderick the 18th Baronet was a member of the East India Company.'

'Oh dear.'

'Yes, well, times have changed,' Paul said, bemused at Caius's reaction to something so long ago, something so pointlessly archaic to be embarrassed of. 'The original recipients were penniless widows of company men who died abroad.'

'I see.' Caius wondered how many men had died while

pillaging India and how many of their widows had lived here in blissful bucolic poverty.

'Your father has expressed a desire to continue part of that legacy and to charge struggling local families a social rent to live there.' Paul, who had until that point been a model of inviolable professionalism, twitched. He wondered what sort of mothers they would be and whether the residents of the sleepy little Chiltern village would appreciate a load of sweary toddlers running amok on the green smearing Asda value baked beans everywhere. 'As you saw, all eight almshouses have two bed-rooms each. The headmistress of the local primary school is delighted by the prospect. They'll have to close if they don't have an increase in pupil numbers in the next two years.'

'We better get cracking then,' Caius said. As glad as he was that his family were helping people, he'd much prefer a func-tioning welfare state over an ill-defined nineteenth-century agreement built on the largesse of the few.

'Your father has wisely used his contacts in the building trade to speed along the renovation process.'

'Are the almshouses going to be eco-friendly?'

'As much as a house of that age can be. They'll have new insulation and triple-glazed windows.'

'We need to future-proof. The best time to plant a tree . . .'

Caius and Paul shook hands as they concluded their business and Caius walked across the cobbled courtyard and into the house for lunch with his family.

'There you are,' his mother said as he stepped into the kitchen. They couldn't bear to eat in the dining room. Not yet. 'We were going to start without you. The cook. My God, I could marry her. Look at this quiche. She's a thing of beauty.'

'Don't stand on ceremony on my account,' Caius said, his

phone vibrating in his pocket. It was Callie. He left the kitchen and wandered down a corridor as he answered.

'Hello, my love,' Caius said. He could hear Callie crying. 'What's wrong?'

'He's bloody agreed . . .' She broke off into a sob.

'Who's agreed and to what?'

'My father, he's agreed that Jane can have my studio as part of the divorce settlement.'

'I'm so sorry. That's fucking awful.'

'He signed the papers this morning. He said that his lawyer thought Jane was using the studio as a bluff to get more but the hard-nosed bastard that he is took it. He didn't think I'd be upset because he's setting up a trust fund for me. I just said thank you and when I started to cry, I said I was on my period and just feeling sentimental.'

'Babe. It'll be all right. We'll work another arrangement out.'

'I should have yelled at him but then I was like, at least I'll have the money. I'm such a terrible person.'

'No, you're not.'

'Where are you?'

'I'm still at . . . the house.' Caius wasn't sure what to call this place.

'Have you finished with your meeting?'

'Yeah. I'll have some lunch with my family and then come home.'

'Don't speed back on my account. I don't fancy going out to the cinema tonight.'

'Sure. Georgie wanted to go for a drink tonight, but I can say no to that as well, and we can snuggle on the sofa.'

'No, you go out with Georgie. I'll eat cake and watch *Legally Blonde*.'

'Oh no, it's fine.' Caius quite liked *Legally Blonde*, more than he liked Georgie at least. He wasn't ready to admit yet that he was warming up to him.

'No really. Dotty's texted me about it already. He's really excited.'

They said their respective goodbyes and sweet nothings and Caius returned to the kitchen.

'The priest is coming over next week,' said Bridget as Caius sat down.

'Good.'

'Everything all right?' asked his grandfather.

'Not really.' Caius explained Callie's predicament to his family.

'Oh how cruel, the poor lamb has spent years building up her business,' said Bridget, who was so disgusted she put down her cutlery. 'Who could do that to their child. I've a mind to call him up and tell him what I think.'

'Hang on,' said Marcus, keen not to cause a scene with his potential new in-law. 'How much money are we talking here?'

'Dad,' Caius said, frowning. 'You mercenary.'

'With a face like hers she doesn't need money,' Bridget said, rising to Callie's defence in the most obvious way.

'I still don't know why she's letting you court her,' Caius's grandfather added. 'You do look less scruffy than before though. At least you know you need to make an effort to keep her.'

'If it's over seven figures then Callie can just get a new workroom. Hell, she can have one of the outbuildings on the estate. I'm planning on converting them into spaces I can rent to local businesses anyway.'

'That's a bit of a drive. It's at least twenty-five miles from mine,' Caius said, although timewise it wasn't that different from catching the Piccadilly line from one end to the other.

'You're going to want to move up here eventually when you quit your job. I can rent your flat out finally. There are houses on the estate that need renovating and will then be let. You two can have your pick.'

'You're quitting your job?' asked Caius's grandfather. 'What a mercy. I won't be embarrassed when people ask me what you do.'

'I'm not quitting my job.'

'You'll have to soon,' Marcus said.

Bridget, sensing that a stalemate had been reached, said, 'Caius, eat something, or you'll waste away.'

## 35

## The British Society for Rewilding, Clerkenwell

Rosie was sat in a meeting room with Felix and the boring but competent woman from HR, Candice, or Blandice as Felix referred to her when he was alone with Rosie. They'd been going through a plan for Rosie's return to work. Rosie was keen to get back at it and had turned up, much to Felix's delight, at the office unannounced that afternoon – she wasn't due in until Monday – to collect her laptop so she could clear her emails in advance.

'Candice, I really appreciate the compassion that you're showing me,' Rosie said, smiling with the utmost sincerity. 'But I think what I need now is to just get on with it. Find a little bit of normality. I know that's not really possible for me at the moment, but I need to try at least.'

Candice nodded; she really did feel appreciated. As soon as she heard of Rosie's family's misfortune, she'd set out to write the best return-to-work plan she could think of. 'Of course, Rosie. Whatever it takes. I'll support you in any way I can.' Candice left the room so Felix and Rosie could discuss the land acquisition they'd been working on. Candice left the meeting room ajar as she left.

'Just the last final bits now,' Felix said loudly, rubbing his hands. The land that the charity was trying to acquire included a lake and they were all excited at the prospect of dealing with wetlands.

'It's such an exciting project,' Rosie said. She was sincere. She found the ideals of the charity noble even if she was currently feeling a little bit mixed-up about its founder. She tried not to make eye contact with Felix but couldn't stop herself. Looking away at a picture of a Eurasian lynx on the meeting room wall. She blushed. 'I feel lucky to be a part of it.'

Maddy from marketing, who Rosie went for coffee with, walked past the meeting room and catching Rosie's eye gave her a sad-awkward smile and tiny wave of the hand that meant 'I'm so sorry for your loss'. Rosie crinkled her eyes as she sad-awkward smiled back in a way that said: 'Thank you for your concern. I'm doing OK.'

'Have you got your laptop?' Felix asked loudly, shutting the door in case anyone else walked past.

'Yes,' Rosie said, picking up her bag and swinging it over her shoulder. It was a beautiful leather one that Sienna had been gifted by some brand desperate to whore themselves on her channel and had made its way to her. 'I'll be online for a few hours today if anyone needs me.'

'Have the police had you in again?' Felix asked quietly.

'Not yet.' Rosie looked down at her shoes. 'They want me to do another walkthrough of the house to see if anything is missing again.'

'A burglary gone wrong, huh?'

'Yeah, that's what they're saying.'

'What was taken?'

'That's the weird thing. Nothing.'

'Oh?' Felix looked surprised.

'The silver was right there. The paintings in the hall aren't exactly Stubbs but they didn't come from IKEA either. There was cash in a drawer in the hallway. All still there.'

'What about those precious earrings that Sienna is always talking about?'

'Oh, I'm not sure they were even in the house. Mr Miller would know that.'

Felix furrowed his brow. 'What can I do? I don't think I've been supportive enough.'

'No. No. No, nothing. I'm fine. You don't need to do anything. I just want to get back to normal.' Rosie blushed.

'Are you still staying with Lucia?'

'Yes.' Rosie frowned.

'I can't believe Sisi didn't offer to put you up?'

'Oh she did, but I didn't fancy it.'

'I can understand that, but still . . .'

'Lucia is a wonderful friend to me.' Rosie straightened up. 'I don't get what you have against her. You couldn't pay me to live with Sienna.'

'How are things with her?' Felix raised an eyebrow.

'She's desperate to see Granny's will. She's after those bloody earrings. As if I have the time to think about that. I need to start arranging her funeral. Although my mother will have opinions and will take over organising it.'

'Those earrings . . .' Felix shook his head. 'I swear she'd kill for them.'

'I don't get it.'

'Do you not?'

'Huh?' Rosie looked at him funnily. Felix was peering down at her, expecting her to say something. He looked like he might interject but then he appeared to bottle it. 'I'm not really a jewellery person. I just wear this pair of gold hoops all the time.'

'Anyway, did Sienna mention anything about Charlie? He's being very evasive about this bloody IPO. I can't wait for it to be over, and I can get my money back. I still can't believe Charlie convinced me to invest half of my inheritance in his cockamamy schemes. He's so persuasive. At least I can make a packet at the IPO. Then I will disappear into the ether. I've found a farmhouse in Dartmoor. It comes with ten acres. I can homestead.' Felix had been staring expectantly at Rosie but when she didn't join in with his talk of self-sufficiency, started pacing up and down the meeting room. 'I'm sick of him. I'm sick of Johnny. I'm sick of them treating me like a cash machine. Johnny wants me to bankroll a whole brand-new, hideous political party now.'

'Just walk away. Lucia is forever telling me about boundaries.'

'It's not that simple. We've known each other for years. There's a lot of money involved. Professional entanglements. I'm going to kick them both off my boards.' Felix's phone rang. He took it out of his pocket ready to send the call to voicemail, but on seeing the caller he answered it quickly. 'Johnny mate, look can't chat.' There was a pleading quality to his voice that Rosie had never heard before. She wondered if for all Felix's bravado, he was scared of Johnny. 'I know but . . . No . . . Johnny, be reasonable. I can't talk right now. I'm at work. Yes, I will come this weekend, but it's the last time. I'm not interested in politics. I've said it before; I'll say it again: pollinators over politicians.' Felix hung up and shoved his phone swiftly into his pocket as if it had never left. 'Lord, give me strength.'

'Are you all right? You've clenched your fist into a ball.'

'Yeah. I'm fine. I've got a call with the brewery's advisory board in ten. The ducks are lining up. I hate having a day job. I'd love to be here all the time.' He stepped forward, closer to her. 'I want to be here with you making a real difference.'

Rosie's breath caught. She took a step back.

'I'm going to kick Johnny off the charity's board. I am this time. He wants to make it political. People are starting to complain. This change that's come over him the last year, the deepening of the hateful rhetoric. It's up to me to stop it.'

'I'm really sorry.'

'For what?'

'For not believing you about Sienna before. I can see it now.' Rosie looked down at her shoes. 'I'm so embarrassed that I dismissed what you said.'

'You hadn't been around them properly for a while. They've got much much worse recently. They feel more comfortable being arseholes now that people are ringing up daytime radio shows saying that they agree with Johnny. Don't get me wrong, I'm proud to be English but it's moved on now.'

'Granny saw through Charlie early on. Said he was a thug.'

'Look, I can fix this all. I can put an end to it all. I'm speaking to someone. It's going to be fine.' Felix stroked her face. 'You look really beautiful today.'

Rosie stepped back.

'Don't be mad with me, Rosie.'

She stared down at her shoes.

'Let me get you a car.'

'It's all right. I'll catch the tube.'

'No, I insist.' He booked her a car from Addison Lee on the corporate account.

'Thank you.'

'Not at all.' He stared at her.

She stared back. Rosie felt like the distance between who they had been and who they were now was perhaps too great.

'I guess I'll see you tonight.'

'Unfortunately. Sienna's bought me something to wear. I'm just a doll to her.'

'Lord, give us strength.' Felix held the door open and walked Rosie down the corridor to the reception area. He bade her goodbye in the most respectable way. As soon as Rosie left the building, he turned and smiled at the temp receptionist, a willowy blonde woman in her late twenties with pearl earrings and a navy pleated skirt, with every tooth in his mouth.

'You're new. I'm Felix, Chief Exec.'

'Nice to meet you. I'm Hannah,' said the temp.

'Great to have you on the team.' He smiled at her and left reception for his office.

'What's his deal?' Hannah the temporary receptionist, who was mildly bemused by his show of interest in her, asked Lori the office manager who happened to be passing through.

'That smoothie? Well,' said Lori, sitting on the reception desk. She checked quickly that no one was around to overhear as she indulged in office gossip. 'He's good-looking, isn't he? Don't tell HR I said that. I'm not sure what's going on there, but there was a rumour after the Christmas party . . .' Lori watched Rosie waiting patiently on the pavement. 'It was nothing really. They just got in the same taxi. I think he's friends with her family or something.' Lori saw a truck go past Rosie, drenching her with muddy rainwater when it dipped into a pothole. 'Poor girl!'

## 36

## The Police Station

Matt had nearly finished watching number 26's doorbell cam footage. He was coming up to midnight and there weren't many comings and goings at that time. He'd seen Philip jog past pretty nonchalantly in dark clothing at 9.08 p.m. Matt isolated the footage and emailed it to Caius to view tomorrow.

'Where are you up to?' Matt asked. Amy had been nearly silent for the last three hours. He was getting worried. She hadn't even bothered with the Wotsits.

'4.42 p.m.' Amy had rather got stuck down a rabbit hole and had sent Caius a whole library of links. 'The house opposite had a children's birthday party that afternoon so there were a lot of comings and goings down my end.'

Matt looked down at the printouts pile of people and the time they walked past the camera he'd collated. He was going to keep going until the police arrived after Rosie had called 999 after 3 a.m. 'Find anything interesting during your research breaks?'

'I ended up down a bit of a rabbit warren called *Freya*, Sienna's money-spinning meditation app. I've been writing a document detailing it all. I didn't realise I had to pay when I downloaded it, but I've been sent an email saying my week's free trial is ending and I need to start paying £19.99 a month to have access to the content.'

'That seems steep. Two hundred and forty pounds a year is a lot. Is it worth it?'

'I don't think so. Don't get me wrong it's very smooth. A lot of the app is actually an interactive journaling tool, but there are talks from Sienna you can listen to which are very much "having children completed me and will complete you too". It has some neat features. It saves your daily journal entry and indexes them using keywords so you can reread them by emotional state or people you mentioned. It has different sections that you can fill in with these cute emoji things, and it also lets you tick a set of boxes about how you're feeling that day. You can track your period too. I did it just to see what would happen and it sent a picture of a cute baby because I'm was ovulating.'

'Right?' Matt would have preferred her to have finished going through her assigned footage, but this sounded fascinating.

'I found the company that runs the app under the umbrella of a much larger political polling company that Charlie has owned for like fifteen years.'

'Caius said that Sienna was insistent that Charlie was a tech entrepreneur not a property guy.'

'He must know so much about the women who use the app. I don't know how legal that is; I need to trawl through the terms and conditions, but I think *Freya* is there to collect qualitative and quantitative data on young women. He knows when all of the users are ovulating.'

'Charlie knows when you're due?'

'That makes me so uncomfortable. What if anti-abortion weirdos got hold of information like that. Can you imagine what that could mean for women's reproductive rights?'

'Big Brother's fertility clinic. That's terrifying.'

'I had to enter my contact details when I downloaded it and I got an email about a festival of womanhood that's being organised in August by Sienna in the grounds of a country house.'

'OK, and what's dodgy about that?' Matt was waiting for the but.

'Most of it is holistic stuff. You know, sound baths, yoga sessions, a complimentary cold-pressed juice bar; there's a nutritionist running sessions about diet when you have PCOS, there's a talk by a former Olympic runner about how going through childbirth made her a better athlete. I don't have a problem with all that, very normal for a wellness retreat but it's just, the tone is off. Listen to this: "The highlight of the festival is Sienna Worthing herself talking about how important it is for YOU to have children." All of the women in the accompanying pictures are white. Matt, it says she's handing medals out to the women in attendance who've already had children.'

'Does it have the emphasis where you put it?' Matt stood over her shoulder and read the email. 'Oh shit, they've used capitals.'

Amy scrolled down the email and showed Matt the pictures attached to it. 'It's very . . .'

'White,' Matt said, looking at all the swishy pony-tailed women smiling serenely in their shades of neutral co-ord workout gear on yoga mats. 'She's talking about the importance of white women having lots and lots of children.'

'I think I filled in a form when I downloaded *Freya* with my demographic details.'

'Right.'

'I think I was invited because I ticked "White British".'

'That's fucking mental. Are you finished with your report?'

'Yep, just now.'

'Send it to Caius and me to look at and try and get through as much of this footage in the half an hour we have left.'

They returned to the tedium of grainy black-and-white comings and goings while the implications of Amy's discovery played at the back of their minds. The clock ticking away and the end of their shift tantalisingly close.

'Oh! Matt! Matt! It's Charlie, look.' Amy rewound by a few seconds as Charlie pushed a pram up Mona's road.

'That's not what Sienna told Caius that day.'

'Look, he crosses the street to Mona's house.'

'A little impromptu visit with their cute baby but minus Sienna. He wants something but doesn't want his wife to know.'

Amy sped up the footage showing Charlie and the pram leaving not too long after they'd arrived. She took stills of the images and printed them. Sticking them to the whiteboard they were using to track suspects.

'Charlie is in and out of there hours before Philip arrived,' Matt said, making a note of the times. 'Me and Caius will interview him tomorrow now. His businesses are fucked up but we have no reason to turn up there right now. I don't think he has motive for killing Mona and he's gone way before she dies. Sienna isn't going to inherit anything as it stands, and he's loaded as it is.'

'You doing anything tonight?' Amy asked. She felt like she'd dropped the ball today by doing too much of her own thing – not that the deep dive into Sienna was pointless – she just should have focused a bit more. Matt was being nice about it, which somehow made it worse.

'I'm sort of going on a date – but it's not a date, you know. Just a hang.'

'No, I don't know. I see a girl and I'm like, wifey. It's the main thing me and Caius have in common.'

'What are you doing?'

'A housewarming party in Camberwell.'

'Nice.'

'Sorry for not getting further on with the footage. We could've got Charlie in today if I'd found it quicker.'

'Don't worry about it. I'm pretty good at zoning out on those sorts of tasks and getting on with it.' Matt patted Amy on the shoulder and they both went on their merry way into the night.

# 37

## The Old Coniston Soap Factory, Hackney

Georgie's studio was in a converted old factory close to Victoria Park. The name of the former owners, 'Conistons', had been lovingly restored across the top of the building. From what Caius could tell the basement was all artists' ateliers while the ground floor held a community cafe and an art gallery. The rest of the building had been converted to flats, from studios to penthouses. Caius rang the buzzer for Georgie's studio. A crackled and yet still chipper Georgie came through the telecom system.

'Come in!' Georgie said, before a loud buzzing sound erupted from the speaker.

Caius opened the door and followed the arrow painted on the wall down a flight of stairs until he arrived at Studio 109. He knocked on the door.

'Hi hi hi. Just finishing up here,' Georgie said, opening the door as a woman got dressed behind a screen. Georgie went to wash his hands at the little kitchenette on the other side of the room. They were smudged with charcoal. He ignored the presence of both Caius and the model as he meticulously scrubbed under his nails with a brush.

Caius looked around the studio – it was cluttered with canvases and, to his surprise, a tremendous lump of marble. He was embarrassed to see that the art was good, better than good. He'd assumed it would be shit. Not that he was anything more than a dilettante in such matters – he knew that a once-a-year trip to Tate Britain did not qualify him to have an opinion beyond 'it moved me', but it did. He stopped in front of a landscape and was transported. Taken to the hills, the rolling green waiting for the soft impact of a weighty cloud, breathing in the air sharp and electric before a thunderstorm. He'd gained the impression from Callie that Georgie was a wealthy hobbyist-borderline-poseur who spent most of his time on holiday but here he was confronted by art, real art filled with an honest bravery. Caius remembered that the model was there. He felt prudish all of a sudden, embarrassed by the starkness of his adoration. He was also mildly scandalised by his proximity to the naked flesh of a woman that wasn't Callie – the process of transformation from real body to idealised nude did not lessen his embarrassment – but then Caius was not naive enough to separate artistic ideals from raw sexuality. God only knew how much trouble unwieldy lust caused and all the cases he'd worked because of it. He probably should've gone to confession after all.

'See you next week,' the woman said to Georgie, who glanced up from tidying away his materials and gave her a cheery goodbye.

Caius looked around the studio, taking it all in. On one wall was a collage of scavenged ideas: postcards, cut-outs from magazines, photographs. On the opposite side a few dozen sketches of bodies in various poses were stuck to the wall with drawing pins. Georgie, who had gone up tremendously in Caius's estimations for his blasé attitude to his own genius, grabbed his jacket from a coat stand near the door. 'You ready?'

'Yeah.'

'Shoreditch House? I know it's kind of lame but I have membership for tax purposes . . .' Georgie, who Caius had just about thoroughly changed his mind on, had suggested the blandest most mediocre expensive option. 'I take my accountant there for coffee.'

'Actually, there's this brewery that I sort of need to check out. It's not far from here.'

'Oh cool. Yeah, let's do that. I should jack my membership in. Have you been there in the day? The carpets are rank . . .' Georgie tailed off.

'I suppose as somewhere to take your accountant it's fine.' He was blagging it. Caius felt like a giddy teenager who the cool kids had started talking to. Suddenly he was some great arbiter of taste; despite being pretty unqualified. Georgie cared about his opinion. Caius began to wonder whether this was due to how Georgie felt about him or just how he looked. Was Caius supposed to be cool? Was Georgie projecting onto him some sort of cultural insecurity over his lack of authenticity? Did hanging out with the mixed-race guy solve that? White enough to be unthreatening but ethnic enough to make him feel edgy. Was Georgie the kid in halls from Wimbledon all over again? Or was it the baronetcy looming over his head? Caius had never been to Shoreditch House and now he never would.

They left the studio complex and walked the few roads over to the brewery.

'When's your next exhibition?' Caius asked.

'I don't know. I've not had one for a while. I sell paintings privately, mostly portrait commissions, and don't really have the need for spectacle. Funny really. As a creative you're both desperate to be seen in the vainest sense and desperate to not be truly seen. That little core of light that makes you exceptional is paradoxically both public and private. Each is painful and yet we can't stop ourselves.'

'Right.' Caius briefly considered the idea of art as a devotional act of service to one's own soul but then wondered if that was too pretentious and then he wondered whether what Georgie had really said was 'I make a lot of money and I don't want to be in the papers.' 'You're very talented.'

Georgie stopped and turned to look at Caius. He put his hand on his arm. 'Thank you.'

Caius smiled and they set off again. He was slightly taken aback. Georgie just said 'thank you'. There was no self-deprecation, no rejection of the compliment, he just took it gracefully. 'There can't be many people who work in marble any more.'

'No, it's not very fashionable.' Georgie smiled to himself. 'I source my marble from Naxos. I feel connected to all the other artists who came before me that way, like the medium speaks over thousands of years. I will never exhibit those though – the world shall know me as a passable portrait painter and an all right landscapist. The marbles have too much of me. My completed ones are in the wine cellar at my parents' house gathering dust.'

'You should show them. I think they'd really resonate with people. Art is to be seen, right? Like you said it speaks – so it means to be heard.' Caius said all this with force and without thinking. 'Sorry, I can be blunt to the point of social embarrassment.'

'Oh, no, you're probably right. Dotty is always trying to persuade me to submit to the Royal Academy Summer Show.' Georgie, who generally took quite well to being bossed about, had still resisted this. 'What I would really like is for Callie to sit for me, but she always waves me off.'

'Yes, she has the same paradox, but her art is worn. It's exceptionally personal. She wants you to see her work, but she doesn't always want you to see the person wearing it.'

'Apart from by you.'

'I hope so. You can never tell with women. They all hate themselves so much.'

265

'I don't know what we've done to them.'

They arrived at the brewery. It was in another red-brick Victorian former factory. There were benches outside with an awning and patio heaters in case the weather turned. They were filling up with men with little beanies in different colours. From above they must have looked like Skittles bobbing about. The sky looked threatening.

'You said you needed to check this place out,' Georgie said, lowering his voice. 'Is this for work?'

'No, no,' Caius said. He hadn't realised that Georgie would pick up on a slip-up of a verb – a 'need' not a 'want' – like that. He'd really got him wrong. Written him off as a toff with no sense.

Georgie was not convinced and walked with a spring in his step. They entered the brewery and were assaulted by the sheer amount of hay inside. People were sat on bales rather than seats. A woman leaving had even managed to get some in her hair.

'The country is reclaiming the land back from the city,' Georgie said. He seemed thrilled. The hay bales set against industrial revolution brickwork felt perverse. 'Look at all those brass horse tacks over the walls. Oh, and there's a display of Toby jugs. They're so ugly. I love them. Dotty would murder me if I brought one home.'

'I'll get the first ones in,' Caius said, wandering over to the bar. He was staring at a scythe hanging ominously above them as he waited for the barmaid to finish with another punter. If he'd have walked in here randomly he would've found it amusing, but now after all he knew about Felix's connection to the Worthings and Johnny Bull he was wondering whether hay bales could have another connotation.

'What can I get you?' asked the barmaid. She was rosy, apple-cheeked and healthy in a plump, rounded way.

Caius felt like sometimes he couldn't help but look, couldn't help but acknowledge it even to just himself. 'What would you recommend?'

'Jolly Yeoman is our pride and joy.'

'Two of those then, please,' he said.

'We have a hog roast pop-up on today? We're doing rolls with pork and apple with crackling on top.'

'Umm.'

'Do you not eat pork?' she asked rather pointedly.

'I do.' Caius should probably save himself for dinner. 'Go on then, two of those.'

She pulled the pints and Caius put a pound coin in the tip jar.

'She looks like she rolls around in the hay they have everywhere,' Georgie said, once Caius had returned to the table. 'There's another one. They all have wench uniforms.'

'Georgie!'

'I can look, but I won't ever touch or say it loud enough for Dotty to hear.' Georgie watched a redhead with freckles on her shoulder walk past with a tray of empties. 'I'm almost someone's father.'

Caius picked up his pint. 'Congratulations.'

'Cheers.' Georgie picked up his pint and took a sip. He looked a little nervous at the prospect of parenthood. 'Oh that's not bad actually. I can see why you wanted to come.'

'The decor hasn't made it taste off.'

'I love a corn dolly, what are you on about? Let's preserve the spirit of the harvest.'

'I feel weirded out by it.' Caius glanced over his shoulder, but no one was watching him.

'I know what you mean. It's so kitschy and English in a way that just doesn't seem to feature in modern life. But maybe that's just because so many places have been aesthetically diminished to one point of good taste that it's fucking boring. Any coffee shop could be on any continent. It's the internet, it's reduced the whole world into one flat visual language.' Georgie took another sip of his beer. 'It is a bit Wicker Man though, and very white. I always find that weird when you go somewhere in this bit of London. Did you see today that the government announced they are going to introduce an official English national dress? We've all got to wear ruffs and codpieces on St George's.'

'What? No, I missed that. They must be fucking desperate if they're appealing to people's sense of Englishness.'

'Yeah, they're fucked in the next election unless something crazy happens.' Georgie put his pint down. 'What's wrong with Englishness? Why are we so embarrassed by it? Why does a national costume feel so desperate? We're fine with kilts. Even the Germans get to wear their lederhosen.'

'There's no victim narrative to be had in being English. Worse than that. The English have never put their hands up and said, "Yeah, we're bastards – we're better at being bastards and getting away with it than the rest of you." But then the nice bits have been hollowed out. The maypoles and wassailing. Weird traditions attached to specific villages.'

Georgie nodded. 'My problem is with the codpieces.'

'I'd have gone Regency. Who doesn't love a good bonnet and a heaving bust.'

The conversation lulled as both men took the room in. 'Do you get people asking you your ethnicity a lot?'

'Yeah.' Caius wasn't expecting that, but in some ways it was easier if people did come out with it. 'I'm ambiguous. It's usually because they've been on holiday and think I look like their favourite waiter at the resort.'

'Nell, my friend Casper's fiancée, is also part-Jamaican but pretty pale and I've seen people start talking to her in Spanish and stuff.'

'Yeah, that's happened to me before.'

'Sorry, I'm not good at small talk. I've gone straight in there with the race chat but that's just because I'm avoiding the whole your grandfather is now a baronet thing.'

'You know what, I want to talk about it with you because you are probably the only other bloke I know that has half a clue about this whole having a fucking estate thing. I have no idea about your family. I just know that you're a bit posh and it doesn't seem to be a problem for you.'

'You're posher than me and Dotty is posher than the lot of us combined. My family are Quakers. "Cleanliness is next to god-liness" is our motto. We're manufacturing interlopers who secured all the right trappings over the last century. My mum is from Motherwell. She was modelling when she met my dad. Look, people make a thing about the schools you attend, or the university, whether you grew up doing this or that which "matter" but fundamentally if you have the lineage, you have the lineage.' Georgie left the subject alone and a bar wench arrived with a roast pork and apple sauce roll for each of them. 'Oh hello. What's this?'

'They had me at crackling.' Caius turned to the barmaid and said thank you. 'Oh shit, you don't eat meat any more.'

'I lasted three days. I've been eating ham sandwiches on the sly.' Georgie took a bite and melted. 'Look, these estates are basically small businesses. It's doable. You just have to deal with each problem as they arise.'

'Yeah.' Caius took a sip of his drink. 'I think fatherhood is probably the same.'

'There's no risk that you'll drop a farm on its head and give it brain damage.'

'You're not going to drop your baby.'

'I might do.' Georgie took another sip of his pint. 'It took a while for Dotty to get pregnant; we were sort of gearing up to go through IVF so it's a relief. My brother and his wife had to do it and it's just so gruelling. The poor woman. All those injections. I bloody hate needles.'

'You couldn't pay me to be a woman. Periods sound bad enough.'

'I know it's natural and everything, but why is nature so mean to them.'

Caius took out a piece of crackling and ate it. 'I want to be a vegan, but I just can't.'

'Dotty still thinks I am.'

'It's our secret, mate.'

'What did you think of the article I sent you?'

'It was terrifying.'

'It's so gross. So narcissistic to see your children as an extension of yourself in that way.'

'I listened to the manosphere podcast it referenced as well. I've been too busy to really care about anything like that, but we're starting to see the rhetoric creep in at work more and more. A colleague of mine had a case recently where the guy was spouting the worst shit you've ever heard in the holding cell justifying why he beat up his girlfriend so badly that she was hospitalised for three days.'

'Fuck! I heard some teenaged boys with bacne talking on the tube about "high-value" women the other day. They were so entitled.'

'There has to be a minority of women who agree with these

creeps otherwise the whole thing would collapse though, right?'
Caius thought about Sienna Worthing and some of her thinly
veiled quips. 'Enablers. Pandering to these men. Rolling around
in their gingham pinnies, constantly pregnant and claiming
they're choosing to do everything they're told.'

'Would the whole movement collapse without those women?
Or would creeps start kidnapping girls off the streets?'

'Mate, some of the things I've seen.' Caius didn't care to
elaborate.

'I guess. I don't know what to say. I know I said that I don't
know what we did to women, but I don't know what we've done
to men either.'

'It's more than that though, isn't it? Things are less shit for
women than they used to be, but still really shit, and things have
been getting shittier for men so they blame women rather than
the economy and wider society. It's all just shit.' Caius took a
bite out of his roll. 'I'm still on my first pint.'

The barmaid with the freckles appeared next to Georgie
holding an iPad. 'Would you like to join our mailing list?' she
asked him. Georgie was cool. He didn't do mailing lists.

'Can I sign up?' Caius asked.

'Sure, why not.' She cheerily handed him the iPad. For a
moment there, Caius had worried she was going to say no.

★ ★ ★

Caius opened the front door to their flat. He'd stopped off at the
pizzeria nearby that they both liked on his way back and picked
up a couple of pizzas and pistachio cannoli. The little snack at the
pub wasn't going to be mentioned. 'You're playing Joy Division.
Are you breaking up with me? That's dumping music.'

'The laundry basket.'

'Look—'

'One of the pictures fell out . . . I'm happy to sort of talk about your work a bit but nothing like that again, please. I don't want to see gruesome pictures like that when I'm doing the laundry.'

'I'm sorry. This isn't a work work case,' he said, pausing as he decided how much he was going to tell her. 'My old DCI is dying—'

'Dying?'

'Yes. He has terminal bowel cancer, Callie. He's asked me to look into an old case that disappeared as his dying wish.' Caius, aware that the room was heavy with mortal thoughts, lifted the boxes in his hand. 'I bought pizza.'

Callie nodded.

'Your dad's a shit.' He put *Legally Blonde* on. He kissed her on the forehead and went and got the pizza boxes.

'Have you solved the case? Your old boss's case?' she asked quietly.

'Not yet. I need to speak to a witness but I don't have time. I sort of don't want to solve it. It'll only bring trouble.' Caius opened the pizza box and took a slice of goat's cheese and caramelised red onion. 'Let's talk about something else.'

'Why don't you want to solve it? What sort of trouble?'

'Look, Callie.' Caius sighed.

'Is it a safety thing?'

'No, I don't think anyone's in danger.' Caius put his slice of pizza down. 'The victim was Alethea Beauchamp?'

'As in . . .'

'Rupert's mum.'

'Oh.'

'Yeah.'

'I thought that was an accident. Rupert talked about it as if it was.'

'Exactly.'

'So it wasn't an accident?'

'Definitely not.' Not unless Alethea's head fell into a cast-iron skillet, twice.

'Shit. Was it Hampton?'

'He has a solid alibi.'

'Wow. I can't imagine him taking you looking into this case well. I mean, he likes you. In a paternalistic way. I'd even say he was almost fond of you. But what will he think about this?'

Caius didn't have the headspace to think about Alethea's case. *Legally Blonde?*

'Yeah, go on then.'

# 38

## Sienna's House

The children were silent as Grace led Rosie up the stairs. The house was preternatural calm. Rosie wondered if Sienna had drugged them, then she chastised herself for such a dreadful thought. Rosie had arrived at 6.00 p.m. as explicitly instructed by Sienna. She'd washed her hair and put it in curlers – also as instructed. The door to Ottilie and Flora's bedroom opened, and a precocious little face popped out. Ottilie placed a finger to her lips and mimed a shush before slowly shutting her door again. Rosie winked at her as she carried on to Sienna's room. Rosie knocked on the door.

'Just me,' Rosie called as she opened the door to Sienna breast-feeding Cosmo while having her make-up done.

'Multi-tasking,' Sienna said, trying not to move her face as the make-up artist she had hired for the evening applied her base and a photographer took a picture.

'I'll just go and say goodnight to the little ones.'

'Atticus is down in his cot. Don't disturb him otherwise I'll have no peace, will I, Cosmo? No, I won't. Mummy won't get to enjoy herself, will she, even though she's worked so hard on tonight's launch.'

'Launch?'

'Oh drat, it's a surprise. Shh.'

'Mum's the word,' Rosie said, wondering whether her mother would be in attendance. 'Is she coming? If this is some sort of special event.'

'God no. Can you imagine. She'd be so pass-agg to everyone in her frumpy cardigan.'

'Yeah.' Sienna held their mother in contempt more often than Rosie had previously realised. She looked at Sienna, the make-up artist concentrating as she applied bronzer to her, and realised that Sienna treated everyone the way she treated Rosie. Even her mother. Perhaps it hadn't been Josephine who'd driven the whole house deposit debacle as Rosie had thought, or Charlie as Granny had suspected, but Sienna after all. Sienna was smart enough to manipulate the ambiguity over everyone's differing version of events that she didn't look like the 'bad guy' that she was. Rosie wanted to leave but knew she couldn't, not yet anyway, or Sienna would kick off. She needed to check on the children. Make sure they were all right. 'I'll just pop my head round and say goodnight to the girls.'

'Ten minutes and then it's your turn,' Sienna said, pointing with her free hand at the dress hanging up on the back of the wardrobe. 'Have you heard from Tristan?'

'No.'

'Oh, what a shame.'

'Is that for me?' Rosie said, staring at the dress. Sienna had said that she had something suitable for her to wear and she was expecting one of Sienna's beautiful cast-offs but this was a brand-new, full-length Sophia Wigginton gown in the same perfect shade of cornflower blue as Rosie's eyes.

'Of course, I couldn't have my baby sister letting the side down.' Sienna looked Rosie up and down. Yes, the dress was perfect. She'd win Rosie over this way with beautiful things and attention. Sienna turned back to the mirror, staring at her reflection and envisaging Rosie becoming her assistant.

Rosie almost crept out of the room once Sienna's attention returned to her own face and tiptoed into the girls' room. She gave them both a kiss on the cheek, tucked them up and did a quick read of *The Tiger Who Came to Tea*, before returning to Sienna's dressing room to be made to look 'acceptable'.

'What do you think?' Sienna asked. She'd changed into a bronze-coloured dress that made her look like a vase.

'You look like a goddess.'

'I know.' Sienna flicked her hair over her shoulder. 'Thank you. You're such a sweetie,' she said, giving her a wink. 'Breastfeeding makes my tits look huge.'

'Umm . . .' Rosie didn't want to comment.

'Grace has an exam or something tomorrow so she couldn't babysit tonight.' Sienna rolled her eyes. Grace had said yes initially but then she wanted treble pay so Sienna told her no. 'She's probably gone by now.'

'Oh.'

'I've seated you on the end, closest to the door. If you hear any movement, I'd be so grateful . . . You're so good with them.'

'Sure . . .' A glint caught Rosie's eye. 'Lovely earrings.'

'Thank you so much.' Sienna placed her hand over her heart then clasped Rosie's hands.

'Huh?'

'They mean so much to me. I was so happy when I saw them on my dressing table last night.'

'What do you mean?' Rosie was very confused. Sienna was acting like Rosie had given them to her as a gift. 'They aren't from me.'

'Exactly, sweetie.'

'Are those Granny's infamous earrings?' Rosie had never seen them but the way Sienna was acting could only mean they were.

'Divine, aren't they?'

'Where did you get them? Did Mummy have them? We've not even begun to sort out probate—'

'Darling,' came Charlie's voice at the door, interrupting Rosie. 'Are you decent?'

'When am I not,' Sienna said, ushering him in before Rosie could talk about anything tedious and legal.

'You look spectacular.' Charlie beamed at his wife from the doorway. 'Hi, Rosie. Johnny's arrived, Sienna.'

'I'll be down in a moment,' Sienna said, blowing Charlie a kiss. She didn't want to upset her make-up. He looked deeply disappointed, but made do with patting her firmly on the arse. 'Your turn.'

Rosie turned around to see the make-up artist looking at her expectantly. She sat down in the chair as Charlie trotted out of the room after Sienna, his hand reaching for her. This had been a mistake. She should've stayed at home.

'You've got this, babe,' Rosie heard Charlie say. 'We're all looking to you now. I believe in you and what you can do for the country.'

* * *

The kitchen extension had been transformed. The sofa that Rosie had chatted with Sienna on a few days ago had been removed as had all traces of the children. The dining table had a white and green patterned tablecloth. There were vases with delicate arrangements of magnolias in ceramic holders. The plates were shaped like cabbage leaves and all the glassware was various shades of pink. Everyone was milling around the room making small talk. Charlie clinked his knife against a pink champagne flute.

'Thank you so much for coming tonight to celebrate my supremely talented wife,' Charlie said to those gathered. 'She's worked exceptionally hard while being a phenomenal mother to our four beautiful children. My wife's work is vitally important; she's saying what needs to be said. Women used to be happy, didn't they? They used to listen to their bodies, to their biology. But now? Mothers are sidelined. They're disrespected when they deserve medals for what they do, raising the next generation of *British* youth. But my wife has taken on the challenge of restoring the natural order. Her social media outreach and her life-changing app *Freya* has already inspired hundreds of thousands of women to be real women. As we're here with friends, I'd like to soft launch the Worthing Foundation which aims to support policymakers with putting motherhood at the centre of the debate. History will look kindly at those of us gathered here today toasting the future. Hopefully, dare I say it, some of this will even end up as government policy.' He looked pointedly at Johnny. 'Everyone, raise your glass to my wonderful wife.'

'Sienna,' everyone chanted back, raising their pink flutes of English sparkling wine as Sienna basked in the praise.

A photographer discreetly took pictures of the guests as a hired waitress handed out canapés. Rosie took a miniscule piece of stilton and pear on sourdough and popped it into her mouth. Felix was stood next to a sideboard where the evening's wine was waiting, talking to an insipid woman who Sienna knew from university and had been her maid of honour. A couple of Charlie's colleagues and their suitably elegant wives were lingering by the French doors overlooking the garden. Not one of them seemed as uncomfortable as she was about Charlie's speech. Charlie looked like he was going to come over to her but she saw him pivot at the last moment.

'Rosie,' came a voice from behind her.

'Hello, Johnny.' She composed herself and turned around. 'It's been a while.'

'It has, and how are you? Still working with Felix?'

'Yes.'

'You poor thing. I've got to take him with me away on a work trip for the whole weekend and I'm dreading it. It's a big deal and you never know with Felix whether he'll follow through.'

'He's not so bad.' Rosie was also acutely aware that Felix was listening in on their conversation from the other side of the room. 'How's Parliament?'

'Same old. Frustrating. It's impossible to make any really positive change. We need something new, something fresh to really shake things up. I'm going to launch a new party. With the Worthing Foundation and my party it'll offer us all some hope at least.'

'Umm.' He was stood a little too close to her but she didn't feel able to step back. Rosie couldn't stand the man. He gave her a fight-or-flight response. He'd tried to shag her at Sienna's wedding a few years ago and she wished she had told him what she thought of him then.

'Did you enjoy the fundraiser a few months ago?'

'Yes. What a worthy cause.' Felix had invited her as a guest at Johnny's table and she had been sat between him and Felix – Sienna and Charlie hadn't attended because of Sienna's morning sickness – and Johnny had put his hand on her knee under the table. She discreetly removed it. Johnny had always been boorish, but now he seemed almost territorial as he stood in front of her, cutting her off from the rest of the room. She was disgusted by his politics. She kept thinking about the swastika in the park. How normal that had been to the girls. She looked up at Johnny who was blathering away at her unaware that she wasn't listening.

Rosie didn't want to be in Sienna's orbit any more. Rosie did not want to be an ornamental satellite to her sister's nasty ego.

'Where was he from?'

'I'm sorry. What?'

'The bastard who murdered your granny?'

'I don't know.'

'They should remove criminal elements in society, stop them from having children. It runs in families, you see,' Johnny said.

'You're a eugenicist now, are you?'

'Eugenics has a bad name.' Johnny shuffled about on his feet. 'Let me take you for a drink in the week, we can discuss things further then. I have a job coming up actually that I think you'd be great at. I know Sienna wants you to work for *Freya* but Parliament may be more your thing. You could have a stellar future with us, Rosie.'

Sienna appeared. 'Sorry to interrupt,' Sienna said, flashing Johnny a quick apologetic look. 'But little Atticus is crying for his auntie Rosie.'

'My poor little boy,' said Rosie, turning and fleeing the scene. She heard Sienna loudly say, 'She's so good with children.'

'Terrible bloody timing, Sienna,' Johnny hissed at her.

Rosie sat cuddling Atticus as he dropped off to sleep in a comfy armchair in his room. She stroked his head. The door slowly opened as light peeled in from the hallway. Felix popped his head round the door. 'Proceedings begineth,' he whispered.

Rosie nodded, stood up from the chair and gently put Atticus back down into his crib as Felix watched over them. They both slowly backed out of the room, softly closing the door behind them. They stood on the landing, neither of them desirous to rejoin the party.

'How do people as vulgar as Charlie and Sienna have such

sweet children?' Felix looked at Rosie in her tight cornflower-blue dress.

'The genes for sweetness are recessive?' Rosie smiled.

'Explains why you're not an evil cunt.'

'Shhh, don't wake the girls.'

'This foundation . . . Johnny's sodding political party . . . I'm spending my whole weekend with Johnny schmoozing . . . I've got to leave the house at 7 a.m. It's too much. It's a step too far.' Felix leaned against the wall. 'I hate them.'

'Felix, they really are far right, aren't they?'

'Yeah, I told you.'

'She said Lucia was too North London. I didn't get it at the time . . .'

'Yeah, she meant Jewish.'

Rosie shook her head. She didn't feel like she could breathe. 'Is that why you don't like Lucia?'

'What? No. I . . . Um . . . I just think she bosses you about too much.'

'I don't feel safe.'

'It's all right. Stay till pudding to be polite. Feign a migraine and I'll gallantly take you home to mine in a taxi.'

'To be polite.' Rosie pushed thoughts of the taxi ride she'd had with Tristan out of her head. She'd fucked it up. She knew that now.

Felix shook his head. 'Those earrings Sienna's wearing are really something.'

'Yes, the earrings. She thinks I gave them to her.'

'Are they the family heirloom ones?'

'She's acting like it. I don't know how she got hold of them. I've not even started the probate process yet. I've a right mind to say something.'

'No,' Felix said firmly. He gripped Rosie's arm. She looked down at where he was touching her and he relaxed. 'Not tonight. She's got guests. She'll be hideous to you.'

They heard Johnny calling Felix's name up the stairs.

'Fucking Johnny,' he whispered. He got his phone out and started booking a taxi for an hour and a half's time.

'If I get in this taxi with you after this is finished, it doesn't mean we're back together.'

'Come on, Rosie.' Felix stared at her. 'Johnny wants to take you to dinner, you know.'

'Oh God.'

'Don't you dare say yes.'

'Of course I won't.'

'Sienna will bully you into it like she always does.'

'No, she won't.' As much as Rosie thought Sienna treated her like a doll-turned-personal assistant that was a step too far even for her.

'She will.' Felix started making exaggerated hand movements. 'Sienna will invite you over and it'll be a trick or something and he'll be there. And then she'll bully you into going out to a restaurant with him, then again and again until she's bullying you into accepting whatever mediocre engagement ring appears in his sweaty palms in six months' time. Then she'll bully you into a hideous dress made of doilies because she can't bear the fact that you'd look far more beautiful on your wedding day than she ever did. Then you'd have dreadful child after dreadful child. One every year until your uterus collapses and slides out onto the kitchen floor.'

Rosie kissed him in defiance of her supposed future. 'Uterus is not a sexy word.'

'I am mad about you.' He kissed her again, harder, pushing

her into the wall on the landing, his hand gliding up her leg. 'I'm sorry if I've been a bit inconsistent. I just hope you see what I've been battling now. We'll go public once it's over, I promise.'

Rosie straightened herself up. Then smudged her lipstick off the side of his mouth. 'This dinner party is insane.'

'This isn't a dinner party, it's a set. They're laying out a step for their PR plan for world domination. It's a shared doc on Charlie's Google Drive. Right now, they're about to start phase 2 of their plan to get white people breeding again so we're not overrun with the genetically inferior progeny of Pakistani cousin marriages. Johnny's words not mine. Look, don't think about it. I'm speaking to someone who says he can stop all this. Hopefully I can claw back my money from the IPO before it all goes tits up. Rosie, it'll all be over soon.' He froze, thinking he could hear someone coming, then he stood up straight and fixed his bow tie. 'We'd better go back downstairs before anyone comes to find us.'

Rosie went down the stairs. She took two steps before turning back to look up at Felix.

'There you both are,' Sienna said, shaking her head at the two of them. 'Dinner's being served.'

# SATURDAY

# 39

## The Police Station

'Bambino, are you limping?' Matt asked.

'I threw my back out last night,' Caius said, gingerly sitting in his chair.

'Doing what?' Matt instantly regretted asking that.

'You're too young for me to explain that to.'

'Oh, mate. You could've lied and said moving furniture or even "your mum".'

'Honestly, I just slept funny, and my back has seized up. You're too young because you are in your early thirties not your mid-thirties. It comes at you hard. I didn't want to scare you with the horrors you've yet to experience.' Caius shook his head. 'I can't believe that you thought I would demean my serious relation-ship to get a cheap joke in.'

'Sorry, sir,' Matt said, pushing his tongue forward as he said it like a petulant schoolboy.

'Apology accepted.' That was indeed how Caius had thrown his back out, but for some unknown reason he told the truth like the lad he could've been in a different life and had had to style it out. 'Talking about serious relationships.'

'We publicly held hands last night,' Matt said as Caius looked at him expectantly. 'You want more info than that?'

'Well, yeah. You're holding hands now.'

'She's from Edinburgh. Her mum's Scottish and her dad is Japanese. She's studying for a PhD in Microbiology at Imperial. Do you need her blood type?'

'No, just her star sign?'

'I think she's an Aries.' Matt worked it out in his head. 'What does that mean?'

'Fucked if I know, mate.' Caius swivelled back round to his computer. 'I've seen that Amy went off-piste and has rammed my inbox full of stuff. What happened there?'

'There was a fairy-themed birthday party down her end in the afternoon – she got bogged down in tutus and sparkly wings and needed a break.'

'She should've listened to one of your playlists.'

'I did offer. She just ate most of my snacks instead.' Matt stood over his shoulder while he watched the clip that Amy had isolated of Charlie. 'Amy's instincts kicked in though, did do a deep dive on Sienna's business. She was handing out medals for motherhood.'

'Hitler did that.' Caius turned to look at Matt. 'I'm not reading something weird into this, am I?'

'Oh no, they've been beaten with fasc stick all right, just depends on how battered they are at this point.'

Caius opened the first email from Amy. 'Hello, Charlie.'

'I picked up Philip's entrance too.'

'Was Philip definitely on his own?'

'Yeah. We've been taking screenshots of everyone who walked past the houses from the camera footage.' Matt gestured to a new whiteboard he'd procured. 'We should stick them all up by time on two separate lines so we can see them going down the road effectively. I thought it might chuck up a witness or two who walked past the house between 9 p.m. and 11 p.m.'

'That's a spectacularly good idea,' Caius said.

'I know.' Matt was waiting for Caius to reward him with some form of healthy snack made of cattle feed, but it thankfully didn't materialise. He did get himself a green juice out of his bag, but another one didn't appear to be inflicted on Matt.

'Are you all right to finish up the CCTV footage while I get Charlie and Sienna in formally?'

'Yeah, it's a trance day.'

Caius read what Amy had written about Sienna's festival of lady parts and opened the email she'd forwarded him too. 'This family . . . I went to the brewery that Charlie is involved in yesterday.'

'Squires?'

'Yeah, that Jolly Yeoman is a bloody good pint, but I didn't feel welcome there.'

'How come?'

'The aesthetic for one thing. They had a hog roast on and the barmaid made a point of asking me whether I ate pork.' Caius swivelled on his chair. 'I need to call Hampton. The Worthings need to be reported to counter-terror, but I should give him a heads-up first. This Felix bloke . . . I have questions.'

'Have you heard from Hampton lately?'

'No. I haven't. I'm starting to feel nervous about his silence. Last time we dealt with him he checked in periodically. If Mona was Hitler's illegitimate daughter, then Sienna is his great-granddaughter. She's prancing around like a Nazi princess with a thuggish husband and his bezzie mate the dreaded politician who the bloody PM is still trying to defend for his awful views. Hampton has done it again. He's got us running circles to do his parliamentary dirty business. We've been taken for mugs a second time.'

# 40

*Tristan*
*09.36*
*Lu, are you free today? Just us. I need your advice*

*Lucia*
*09.37*
*Is it about Rosie?*
*(big eyes, lips, big eyes emojis)*

*Tristan*
*09.37*
*Sort of*

*Lucia*
*09.38*
*Look she's had a shitty week, but she does like you I can tell. You might just have to take it slow*

*Tristan*
*09.38*
*Lu, I think I've fucked up*

*Lucia*
*09.38*
*Harry bad?*

Tristan
09.39
Worse

Lucia
09.39
When do you want to meet? I can do this afternoon

Tristan
09.40
Great!
Do you know Rosie's boss?

Lucia
09.40
I've met him. Very full of himself. Handsome though

Tristan
09.41
I really need to talk to you
1 o'clock?

★   ★   ★

Rosie K
09.44
Hey Tristan! How are you?
Do you fancy grabbing a coffee soon?
I'm not normally this forward. Hahaha
(Read)

# 41

## The Police Station

'Thanks for coming in, Mrs Worthing. I just need to clarify a point with you,' Caius said to the bare-faced woman in front of him. She was wearing a floaty white shirt with a huge collar that Caius thought was vaguely infantilising and a giant pair of sunglasses. She looked more vulnerable than she did last time. She was rubbing her fingers together; she'd just had her prints taken.

'It's absolutely fine,' she said, smiling sweetly at Caius. 'Saturday is family time, and I did have to call Grace on an off day because Rosie didn't pick up, but if I can help with the investigation any way I can. We need to catch the burglar who did this. My mother said that you're probably concerned that someone is targeting family members of prominent people.'

'It's a possibility,' Caius said. That must have been a theory Amy chucked out. It was useful – he wanted her to think they were still treating it as a burglary. 'Do you have a key to your grandmother's house?'

'I do. I've not seen it in a while though. It'll be in a drawer somewhere.'

'When I spoke to you a couple of days ago you claimed that from the late afternoon onwards you were at home with your husband.'

'Yes, that's right.'

Caius checked his notes. 'So after going to buy vegetables at the market you all went home?'

'Yes.'

'Then what?'

'We made pizza for dinner.'

'Did anything else happen between shopping and pizza? All detail is useful here, no matter how mundane.'

'The children played in the garden. I fed the baby. I batch cooked some butternut squash and sage muffins as snacks for them. I fed the baby. I had a nap. I fed the baby. Then we started making the pizzas. I fed the baby. Then bedtime for the children. I fed the baby.'

'During your nap, did your husband look after the children?'

'Well, no, Grace swung by for an hour or two. I pay her double on the weekend.' Sienna started to cry.

Caius pushed the tissues towards her without comment. 'Are you all right?'

'Just a hormone dip.'

'No, I mean, is everything all right at home? This is a safe space.'

'Yes, of course. Everything at home is perfect.' Sienna frowned at the insinuation.

'Standard procedure,' Caius mumbled. 'Where was Charlie during your nap?'

'I think Charlie took Cosmo for a walk after I fed him. When I woke up he was stripping him out of his pram suit. Grace left not long after and we made pizzas.'

'Were you aware that Charlie called in on your grandmother that afternoon?'

'What? No.' She didn't look pleased that she was uninformed. 'Did he?'

'Yes, he did.' Caius thought she seemed genuinely surprised. He sat back as she composed herself. 'I had a look at your app.'

'Oh yes, the voucher. Did your girlfriend like it? She's quite a sought-after society milliner, isn't she?'

Caius had forgotten about the voucher she had given him. 'My colleague found it really interesting.'

'Did she, how lovely.'

'She said you do events.'

'Retreats.'

'Retreats.'

'Yes, a lot of healing happens there. A lot of the trauma around womanhood gets resolved. It really helps women move on to find their purpose.'

'She was wondering if she could come to your next one.'

'Oh of course,' Sienna said, taking a small notepad and pen out of her bag. 'What's her name?'

'Aqsa Shah.'

'Aq-sa.' She put her pen down. 'I'll have to check availability. We usually have a waiting list.'

'Sure,' Caius said. 'Thank you for your time, Mrs Worthing. I hope you enjoy your Saturday.'

'Not at all. Anything I can do to help. Going to go relieve the nanny now.' Sienna looked up at Caius through her lashes. 'Actually, detective, I wanted to ask you a question. Do your family rent out your house?'

'No.'

'Such a shame. It looks so beautiful in the pictures.'

'Oh, Mrs Worthing, before I forget.' Caius didn't want to imagine Sienna prancing around Frithsden like she owned it. It felt weird to be territorial about the place. 'Do you know what you're going to inherit from your grandmother? Or anything about her will at all really?'

'These piercing blue eyes.'

'No, I mean materially?'

'I don't know. She said the will was all sorted last time I saw her.' Sienna smiled to herself, then remembered where she was and looked theatrically sad. 'I don't care about the money. The only thing of hers I've ever wanted – and she knew this – was a pair of earrings. She was given them by her godmother. They're an heirloom. Rosie already gave them to me though; she understands that they should go to the eldest.'

'Her godmother?'

'Yes. Mary Stratford actually. One of the Stratfords. I'm sure you know. She was a childhood friend of my great-grandmother. I'm the eldest granddaughter. They're such a precious part of our history.'

★ ★ ★

Charlie was sat in the chair opposite Matt, his arms propped up on the table taking up as much space as he could. He stared at Matt, watching every move intently as he waited for him to begin his questioning. Matt pulled out the picture from the folder on the desk of Charlie walking down Mona's road pushing baby Cosmo in his pram and placed it in front of him.

'Why were you visiting your wife's grandmother without her?'

Charlie leaned over the picture, smirking at it before relaxing back into his chair. 'I went to apologise.' He shrugged. The answer was that simple.

'Apologise for what?'

He laughed, then he fixed his eyes on Matt, staring at him blankly for a moment before resuming his good-natured mask. 'Mona thought that I was the one who had pushed for the money from Josephine for part of the deposit for the house. It wasn't me. It was Josephine's idea. I kept telling Sienna that there was no need to ask but she gets anxious and spills how she's feeling everywhere. Women.' Charlie laughed again, but Matt thought his mirth was just him trying to hide how pissed off he was with the situation. 'We just needed to wait a little longer, just a couple of years for the business to really take off then I'd buy her a dream house and we could easily cope with one baby in our flat but then it was twins and Sienna panicked.'

'You were the scapegoat then?'

'Yes, and I did it gladly. The whole business has really weighed on Sienna so if relations could resume to normal, I'd gladly take the rap.'

'And you didn't tell Sienna this was what was happening?'

'No, no, she's stressed enough as it is. She keeps getting mastitis and hallucinating with a fever.'

'What happened when you got there?'

'We had a cup of tea. She held Cosmo. I apologised.'

'Was your apology accepted?'

'It was. Mona said she'd ring her solicitors on Monday and have her will changed back to include Sienna. Not that we need the money. It was symbolic. The whole nasty business was over finally. I could do without coming home from work and having to hear the latest instalment of the bloody saga. I'm a busy man. The house we're in now isn't even her dream house. She wants to relocate to country.'

'How long were you there for?' Matt asked. It was easily provable with doorbell cam footage, but he thought he'd ask anyway.

'Not long. Half an hour, forty-five minutes, something like that. I pushed Cosmo back and we all made pizza. Sienna insisted that hers was made from cauliflower. It looked very sad, but I cannot fault her commitment to her figure.'

'How is the IPO going?'

'Great.' Charlie stiffened in his seat.

'You own a few different businesses, don't you? A lot of big data.'

'In this day and age, it's a good idea to have your finger in many pies.'

'So what's next for you?'

'This and that?'

'Politics?'

'Maybe.'

'World domination?'

Charlie laughed, a little too hard.

Matt ended the interview.

★ ★ ★

'He was there for just under thirty-four minutes,' Matt said, looking at the time stamps on the screenshots of Charlie arriving and leaving. Yes, Charlie was there at the house but he had no motive to kill Mona.

'That's a quick cup of tea, an apology and a baby cuddle, isn't it?' Caius said, looking at the printed screenshot of Charlie and the pram going back past number 7. 'We can now safely assume that Zofia misremembered "boyfriend" for "husband". Easily done. I wouldn't describe Charlie as a likeable sort of chap.'

'So Zofia overhears Mona telling someone, probably her old friend Daphne, that she doesn't like Charlie.'

'Then gets him over to apologise for the whole debacle.'

'Probably easier for her to blame Charlie rather than accept that her daughter and granddaughter were awful to Rosie.'

Matt looked at the whiteboard. 'Everyone seems to think the will has been changed already.'

'Everyone apart from Charlie. He hadn't told Sienna he was going over. Charlie wouldn't murder Mona before the will had been changed. Sienna thinks it's already been changed. She's already loaded. All she needs to do is wait it out a bit longer for her frail grandmother to pop it.' Caius shook his head. 'Start from the top again.'

'All right. Josephine: disinherited. Limited contact. Money not an MO. Pride may be an MO – pretty weak. Amy checked her alibi – couldn't have got to London in time to commit murder.'

'Can't disagree with that,' Caius said, nodding along with everything Matt had said. 'Sienna: considers the mess about the house deposit over and done with. She only really wanted the earrings, which she now has. Lives close by but her husband has given her an alibi.'

'Those two . . . Would they commit murder?'

'If the circumstances were right.'

'He knows the will hasn't been changed and quite frankly she doesn't look like she has the iron count to take on a strapping bloke like Philip.'

'We've already discounted the brother Will. Not in the country.'

'So that leaves Rosie, who was set to lose a fortune on Monday when the will was changed.'

'I just can't see it. I know you think Rosie's unstable because she knits too much. She was a bit skittish at times when we interviewed her, but nah. It doesn't tally.'

'Don't forget there's the Nazi love-child thing on top of it all.'

Caius stared out the window for a moment. 'The timings of the murders just don't work. Mona was killed later. Is it a burglary that's gone wrong and the hoo-ha over the will is distracting us? Were we right in the first place? Did Philip have an accomplice?'

Matt stared at the whiteboard. 'I've only got to 7.40 p.m. on this set of footage. Philip walked past the other doorbell cam at 9.14 p.m. Other than all the tiny fairies going to a birthday party in the afternoon it's been pretty standard so far. Dog walkers, people carrying shopping bags and lots of joggers. There's been no one casing the houses.'

Caius's desk phone rang.

'Hello . . . Tristan Sowerby? Yes, he's connected to my current case. What? All right. Yes, we'll take it over. I'm on my way.'

## 42

## Glazed Over Pottery Studio, Chelsea Harbour

'Tristan hasn't texted me,' Rosie said as she painted a daisy onto a pot she'd thrown in the previous week's class. It had been getting to her all week – but then perhaps she'd been just distracting herself from the horror. Tristan had seemed so sweet and sincere at her door, but perhaps he'd been trying to take advantage of her. She thought she'd get an answer if she worked up the courage to message him first, but he'd left her on 'Read'. Rosie hadn't wanted to say anything to Lucia as she didn't want to put her in the middle and make it weird. She also hadn't said anything to Lucia about the limbo she was in with Felix – she knew Lucia couldn't stand him, so what was the point in bringing any of it up with her. She checked her phone again. Tristan couldn't even be bothered to fob her off.

'Oh, really?' Lucia asked, focusing a bit too intensely on the ivy she was painting down the handle of a mug. The handle was a little wonky. She hadn't quite got the hang of pottery yet. She thought a writhing dark green vine would distract from its lack of uniformity and perhaps even suggest artistic intention. 'He works a lot. And I mean a lot. His firm has an in-house dentist so you won't leave the building even if you need an urgent root canal.'

'Yeah?'

'I'm meeting up with him later this afternoon for coffee at that garden centre near Chelsea Town Hall. I'll see what's up and then buy another plant baby for my flat.' Rosie was still staying with Lucia and Lucia had begun to feel a little smothered. Lucia was used to her own space and now every time she came home she was greeted by more and more balls of wool. Rosie was trying to knit her grief away. Lucia was glad she was going back to work. It would give her something else to think about.

'Oh, you're seeing him?'

'Yeah.'

'I see.'

'He's probably just giving you space to grieve. He's considerate like that.' Lucia put her paintbrush down. 'Look, I'll find out what's happening.'

'Thanks.'

'He did message me about your boss actually.'

'My boss?'

'Yeah, weird I know.' Lucia raised an eyebrow. 'Considering you've always said there's nothing going on there.'

'There is nothing going on there.'

'Why are you blushing then?' Lucia peered at her sceptically. 'You were back late last night.'

'Took forever to get an Uber.'

'Was Felix there last night?'

'Yeah.'

'And? Come on, Rosie. Does he not feel the same way? Is that it? Well, he's a fool.'

Rosie put her paintbrush down. 'What did Tristan ask you?'

'Whether I'd met Felix.'

'He's in that new nature documentary about British wildlife on the BBC so . . .'

'He probably thinks he has competition.'

'From Felix? Don't be silly.' Rosie laughed a little too hard. 'It's not like that.'

'That's what I said.'

Lucia finished painting her mug and went to take it to be fired in the kiln while Rosie checked her phone. She had a friend request on Instagram from Grace, her sister's nanny, which she accepted.

*Sisi*
*10.43*
*Had to go to the police station for finger printing (sad emoji)*

*You*
*10.43*
*I had to do that. It feels weird. Like you're an old timey criminal*

*Sisi*
*10.44*
*Yes!!! That's it. I felt like a criminal and I haven't done a damn thing. Poor Charlie had to come too. He's worried the market will get word of him going down to the station and think that he's being investigated for a financial crime*

*You*
*10.44*
*Well, he's only helping with the investigation into what happened to poor Granny*

*Sisi*
*10.45*
*You're so right. He was being helpful. We'll have to go super public with what happened to Granny. I'll get his PR person on it*
*Any news from Tristan?*

*You*

*10.45*

*No . . .*

*Lucia is seeing him later this afternoon for coffee.*
*Apparently, he's on his way to the cinema right now . . .*
*Not that I'm watching his stories religiously . . .*


*Missed call from Sisi 10.48*


*Missed call from Sisi 10.49*


*Sisi*

*10.50*

*The girls were asking when you're coming round to play*
*fairies with them next??? Also are you free on Thursday?*
*I'm throwing this dinner at this private club for successful*
*and empowered women to celebrate two years of my app.*
*A select few influencers. Gorgeous girlies. Grace has just*
*handed her notice in and it's left me in a bind. It's a shame*
*otherwise I'd want you to come. Such a good networking*
*opportunity x*


*You*

*10.53*

*Can't take calls. At a pottery class*
*You need to get a new nanny ASAP*


*Sisi*

*10.53*

*Mummy's coming down on Friday to stay for a week which*
*is a godsend but I can't reschedule Thursday's dinner . . .*

*Did you have fun last night? Johnny thought you might be interested in a job working with him. I said you'd be much better suited to working with me on Freya, but I've given him your number x*

Lucia appeared next to Rosie. 'Are you finished with yours? The session's nearly over.'

'Just one more flower,' Rosie said, putting her phone down and adding the finishing touch. Lucia took it over to the kiln to be fired for her while Rosie started tidying up their workspace.

*Sisi*
*11.00*
*Just getting home now . . .*
*Grace is going to be mean to me (crying emoji)*

*You*
*11.02*
*I can swing by Thursday after work and babysit. I won't get to yours until after 6 though*

*Sisi*
*11.03*
*Amazing!!! Thank you. I'll pump so you can bottle feed Cosmo. Charlie will be there too so you'll have company at least*
*Can I have the contact deets of the woman that runs your baby bank? We've had a great idea for a brand partnership xxx*

*Just need to check, it's for British women isn't it? Can't be
too careful! Xxx*

*You*
*11.06*
*What do you mean?*

*Sisi*
*11.06*
*Just wanted to make sure they're the right sort*

*You*
*11.07*
*You mean white, don't you?*

*Sisi*
*11.08*
*Rosie, let's not get into this now*
*We can have a nice, civilised discussion later*
*See you Thursday!*

Lucia returned to the table and started gathering her things.
'The cafe next door had some delicious-looking cinnamon buns
in the window. Fancy one? They'd go great with a chai latte.'

Rosie looked up at her. She was trying to suppress tears.

'Oh, Rosie, you poor thing. Losing your granny must be so
hard.'

Rosie really started crying now. 'I wasn't even thinking of her.
God, I'm so selfish.'

'No, you're not selfish, Rosie. I know what selfish looks like, a
bit like your sister. Shit, I said that out loud.'

'You're not wrong. If anything, I've come to realise this week that you're underestimating how dreadful she is.'

'Did something happen at the party last night? Is that what upset you? Did Sienna say something?'

'No, I keep thinking about Tristan. I just want someone normal like him. Someone nothing like my horrible sister and her weird friends. Felix he . . . never mind.'

'Let's go to the cafe next door.' Lucia could see people eyeing up their workspace for the next session. 'My treat. I'll find out what's happening with Tristan. I'll kill him if he flakes out on you.'

# 43

## The King's Road

'Nasty accident,' Caius heard a passer-by say as he and Matt came up to the police cordon blocking the road.

'Can't have been an accident,' Caius said to Matt quietly. 'Too much of a coincidence.'

He flashed his warrant card, entering the crime scene. There wasn't much of Tristan left, his torso had been squished. Popped like a fat grape crushed under foot, bleeding sticky juice over the road. Paramedics had already taken his wallet out of his trouser pocket and it was now being handed to Matt by a uniformed officer on the scene. Matt, with gloves on, opened it up. There were a few bank cards, a driving licence, twenty pounds in cash and a cinema ticket for an eleven o'clock showing of a Hollywood film with sentient robot gods. Caius's card that he had given to him after his interview had been in his other pocket. Tristan was going to call him.

'Any witnesses?' Caius asked the uniformed officer in charge.

'The bus driver obviously. Poor bloke's shook up. He's saying that this guy just appeared out of nowhere. We're making our way through the passengers and there were people on the street, but it happened so quickly, apparently. A woman on the top deck said that she saw him being pushed but she's far too upset to get much sense out of at the moment.'

'Cheers, mate.'

'I'm going to see if any of the shops opposite have CCTV that caught the incident,' Matt said, walking determinedly towards a monochrome perfume shop.

Caius walked into the cinema. 'Excuse me,' he said to the young man on the box office and holding up Tristan's driver's licence. 'Did you see this guy come in a couple of hours ago?'

'Yeah. Oh no, was he the . . .' The young man gestured to the flashing lights outside the cinema.

'Yes. Was he alone?'

'Yeah, he was alone. I didn't see him with anyone else.'

'Do you have CCTV footage?'

'Only of the foyer.'

* ★ ★

The Police Station

Caius brought a nice cup of tea for Valerie and set it beside her.

'All right, Valerie, I know you've spoken to my colleagues already, but could you explain to me again what you saw.'

'The boy was stood near the road and then this man stopped behind him and then shoved him under the bus. It was fast and it wasn't a big movement, but I happened to be watching them as it happened. Over like that,' Valerie said, clicking her fingers. 'But I know what I saw. I'd been looking at the posters next to them, I've not been to the pictures in a while, when I saw the bigger bloke stand a bit too close and then move towards him quickly. I thought, that looks like trouble. Like he was going to start a fight. He got him with his elbow.'

'Can you describe what the bigger man looked like?'

'He was taller than him by a smidgeon. White. I can't tell you much about his face. I couldn't see it from where I was on the top deck. He had a cap on and sunglasses.'

* ★ ★

'Tristan's parents are in Bermuda. The consul is getting in touch with them to say there's been an accident,' Caius said, putting his desk phone down. 'I think we say it's an accident for a little while longer.'

'Look at him.' Matt had played back the footage of Tristan walking down past number 26, on his way home from dropping Rosie off. 'That's not the face of a guy who just got the phone number of the girl he's got a huge crush on. What did Tristan see?'

'He must have seen a person, not a cat,' Caius said, staring at Tristan's face on the screen. 'That interview we did with Tristan . . . I thought he got embarrassed about his feelings for Rosie but what if he saw something that night and didn't know what to think of it. Dismissed it as important maybe?'

'It looks more like it shocked him.'

'Yeah. OK, Tristan said he saw something as he left. It upset him, but he didn't quite get what the implication of it was. It couldn't have been a big thing because Tristan seemed like the type to help. What if the mystery sixth person saw him though? They could still have been in the house when Rosie arrived home. We know they'd been in the living room so they could have seen each other through the window. Did he see the murderer? But why would they kill him now? They must be recognisable and they can't risk him identifying them. I bet we can get access to some of his messages even if his phone is fucked.'

Matt's phone buzzed. 'I've had confirmation that Charlie was the fourth set of prints that entered the living room only. Sienna wasn't there.'

'We still have a mystery fifth set of prints: the banister person who went up to Rosie's room and the sixth set, our murderer.'

Caius rewound the footage. 'Tristan keeps looking over his shoulder, doesn't he?'

'When you interviewed him, he said there was a taxi, right?'

'Yeah, a cab. I pushed him on it and he said he didn't know who had got out.'

'He's really bugged by something.' Matt opened up the footage from number 26's doorbell. 'A black cab goes past number 7 at 23.32 and past number 26 at 23.35.'

'Tristan walks past number 26 at 23.38. He saw who got out of the cab and where they went. That's what shocked him.'

# 44

## The Police Station

Caius slid a screenshot of the cab driving down her road and then another of what they now knew was Tristan's reaction to it in front of Rosie. 'I'm guessing Tristan never called to set up that date?'

Rosie started to cry. 'I've blown it, haven't I? He's never going to talk to me again.'

'Listen, Rosie, you could get in a lot of trouble here if you're not totally straight with me. Do you understand?' Caius, who had gone into the interview a little more forcefully than he'd intended to, recoiled at her words. He had yet to tell Rosie that Tristan was dead. 'Rosie, do you understand? Rosie Krige has nodded her head.'

'Yes, I understand.' She glanced fretfully at her shiny-foreheaded solicitor who was ready to interject at any moment.

'All right, Rosie. Tell me everything. Don't spare me the details.'

'I just want someone nice. I want the silly things like flowers on my birthday that aren't from the whole office. I want to meet his parents. I want a big fat wedding. I want a house and a garden and children and a dog. I want old age together and a shared burial plot.'

'Rosie, who was in the taxi?'

'My boss.'

'Felix Drake?'

'Yes.'

'Start at the beginning, Rosie.'

Rosie took a gulp of stale air. 'My sister introduced us at a dinner party a couple of years ago, and he told me about the charity he'd set up. Charlie messaged me a week later saying that Felix had a junior position in the legal department and he thought I should apply because we hit it off, so I did.'

'And how long have you been seeing each other?'

'Nearly a year.'

'And you're not public?'

'We work together . . .'

'Lots of couples meet at work.'

'I don't think Sienna would like it.'

'What do you mean?' Caius could imagine Sienna being difficult.

'Felix asked Sienna out well over ten years ago, she said no and then Charlie went for it. Sienna sort of hates him but she likes to think that Felix still has a soft spot for her but actually he can't stand her and he just makes a bit of a fuss of her every now and then to make things easier for himself. He hates all of them. He just feels stuck in Charlie and Johnny's world. They're all over each other all the time. In and out of everything the others do. It's hard to break old patterns.'

'Johnny Bull?'

'Yeah, umm . . . I don't like him.' Rosie took a breath and looked about the dingy interviewing room. 'Is this connected to what happened to Granny and that man?'

'I think it is, yes.'

Rosie thought for a moment. She felt like she was betraying her sister, but then what sort of sister was Sienna really. 'They're all so intertwined. Not for much longer though. Felix is breaking away. He said he was talking to someone and it was going to solve it all.'

'Who was he talking to?'

'Some big wig. He wouldn't say more than that.'

'I see,' Caius said, sensing Arthur Hampton's hand. 'How would you describe your relationship with Felix?'

'Felix spent a long time saying that we weren't serious, but he texts me all the time. We have these conversations where he says things like if my pill fails then we should keep it. That's serious, right?'

'Did your granny know about Felix?'

'No. She knew that I'd sort of been seeing someone but that it had all gone a bit wrong. She wasn't keen on him though, she thought any man with honest intentions would be more forthright.'

'So you're broken up?'

'I don't really know. I broke up with him just before Bath – I didn't want to be a secret any more – but we're in a sort of in-between state now. He keeps trying to win me back and I can't bear to block his number. We've been messaging a lot since Granny died but I don't know what you'd call us. Then there's Tristan or the lack of Tristan looming over me.'

'And the night your granny died?'

'I texted him when I was drunk in the pub bathroom to come over to my house. I sort of forgot that he was coming until the taxi turned up. I was really drunk. I've been hoping that Tristan didn't see him arrive, but he must have done,' Rosie said, hoping she could sink into her chair and hide. She was embarrassed by her lack of spine.

'OK,' Caius said. He was really pissed off that she, and poor squished Tristan for that matter, hadn't told them this earlier. Tristan might still have been alive if he had. 'And what happened when he got to your house?'

'Felix came upstairs with me. We . . . well . . . we.'

'Sorry, Rosie, can you be clearer than that for the tape.'

'Is this necessary?' asked the solicitor.

'Yes,' said Caius apologetically.

Rosie stared at the table. 'We had sex and then he left not long after. Said he had a lot to do the next day. That he'd call.' Rosie turned to Caius, almost pleadingly. 'He's been nice the rest of the week though. He called me every day to make sure I was all right. Sent over some beautiful flowers, although they were technically from the whole office.'

'Did he go anywhere else in the house?'

'No. Not with me.' Rosie frowned. 'I don't know.'

'Didn't you walk him out to the door?'

'No. The door was on the latch. I thought he'd just pull it to. I'm sorry. I'm so sorry. I think he may have left it open by accident. I should've said but I wanted to keep his name out of it because well . . .'

'Why didn't you say anything?'

'Because I think I love him.' Rosie gulped.

That wasn't a good enough reason for Caius. 'Did he ask you to say that he wasn't there?'

Rosie stared down at her hands.

'Did he?'

'Yes.'

'Do you know where Felix is now?' Caius asked.

'He's with Johnny. I'm not sure where. Johnny kept insinuating about the trip being make or break, but it was hush-hush. I hope it's not something to do with his politics.'

'When did you hear Johnny say that?'

'Sienna had a dinner party yesterday.' Rosie shook her head and put it in her hands.

'What's wrong?'

'We've not even had Granny's funeral yet and she's out there posting these ridiculous pictures of the whole thing.' Rosie took her phone out and showed Caius Sienna's Instagram. 'Bloody black tie. Look, she's done up like she's off to the Oscars. There's a whole post about these bloody earrings.'

'Earrings?' Caius looked at the post. 'May I?'

Rosie handed over her phone.

'She has a thing about earrings, doesn't she?'

'About some pair of Granny's in particular.' Rosie pointed to her phone 'She did a post about how she inherited them from Granny, but I've not even thought about probate. I don't know where they came from.'

Caius read the caption to the image. Sienna claimed that they were her late grandmother's. 'Rosie, are you aware that your grandmother never changed her will back?'

'What?'

'Your grandmother's will gives a cash sum to your brother, and you inherit the rest.'

'I . . .'

'Were you aware that the post-reconciliation change to your grandmother's will had yet to happen?'

'No.'

'She didn't talk to you about it?'

'No. It's not my business. It's Granny's money. She can do as she likes.'

'Did you know that your brother-in-law Charlie visited her the afternoon she died?'

'No. I had no idea. Sienna never said and neither did Granny.'

'Is there anyone else you can think of who could have had access to the house that day?'

'No, I can't.'

'The thing is, Philip Campbell, the burglar, died two hours before your grandmother could possibly have done.'

'What?'

'There was someone else in the house before you returned from watching the Boat Race. They'd already killed him. Their fingerprints are also on the pillow that was used to smother your grandmother.'

'So they were there when I was?'

'Yes, and they left you alone. The thing is, Rosie, you've got a bloody good motive for murdering your grandmother.'

'No!'

'How does this sound? You're out for most of Saturday. There's a pub full of witnesses to say you were there all day, but you have an accomplice, say Felix. This accomplice breaks in to the house only to find that someone else has already broken in. They impulsively kill him. Another body is useful: we spent the beginning of the investigation looking for an additional burglar that did not exist. You then come home and tell them to finish the job, in between arranging your love life. We found an empty bottle of vodka in your room. Did you down some before you called 999 so we'd believe you? The Uber driver thought you might have been putting on a bit of an act in the back of his car.'

'That's insane. None of that is true.'

'It's not impossible though, is it?'

Rosie had started to cry. Something felt off to Caius still. 'Do you have anything to say to that?'

'I didn't do it.'

'Did Felix ask you to lie to us? Did he ask you to keep his name out of the investigation?'

Rosie didn't say anything, she just looked at her solicitor.

'Did he put pressure on you?'

Rosie still sat silent.

'Listen, Rosie. I've got some bad news.'

'More?'

'I regret to inform you that Tristan died today.'

'What?'

'He was pushed under a bus coming out of the cinema on the King's Road. We think it's linked to your grandmother's murder.'

'Oh my God.' Rosie's crying turned into a howl.

'Rosie, when asked previously on whether you were alone in the house the night your grandmother and Philip Campbell were murdered you responded that you were alone. It is an offence to purposefully give false information to a police officer during an investigation,' Caius said before reading her rights.

★   ★   ★

'Do we think Felix is Mr Banister? Goes up to her room, does his business and leaves,' Caius said. He had Rosie's phone in his hand. He'd seized it as evidence. She'd given him the code to unlock it. 'Or is he the murderer?'

'We need to fingerprint him.'

'Yeah,' Caius said, looking at the board of suspects. He took a printout of Felix's face from his charity's website and put it on the board. 'The lack of gloves is weird, right?'

'So weird. Philip caught them by surprise and the adrenaline kicked in. But why kill Mona? If the first attack didn't wake her . . .'

'No, we're still missing something here.' Caius put his head on the table.

Matt looked down at his crossed-off to-do list. 'I finished

317

watching the door cam footage. It doesn't look like anyone is on the prowl, just late-night joggers. I think it might be useful if tomorrow we compare screenshots from both houses just in case.'

'Yeah, that will be a good task for Amy.' Caius looked at the time on the clock; it was getting late. 'Has Tristan's phone been recovered from the scene?'

'The phone was more squished than he was. Tech are looking at it but they don't think there's much they can do as the sim card looks fucked. Once we've got his email et cetera when his parents return, we can see if we can access his WhatsApps that way.'

'I'll speak to tech. I need to go see them anyway to get all of Rosie's messages and whatnot downloaded.' Caius's phone rang. 'Not there. And his car's gone. Both residences. Cool. Let's put an alert out on both of their cars. Thanks.'

# 45

## Caius and Callie's Flat

'I called you earlier,' Callie said as Caius came through the door. She was sat on the sofa watching *Miss Congeniality* in one of his T-shirts. He could see that she'd been crying. 'But I think you were busy.'

'Sorry, I did see that you'd called. A lot happened at work today.' Caius sat down next to her and put his hand on her knee. 'What happened?'

'Jane and Harriet swung by the studio to evict me in person. Harriet's new wallpaper business is going to be based there.'

'Oh shit! I'm so sorry.'

'It's OK. It's not as if it was a life-or-death situation. It was creepy actually. Harriet just stood there grinning. Jane looked immaculate. She'd had her hair blown out for the occasion.'

'What did you do?'

'I just said, "All right." Then I went back inside, bolted the door and emailed Jane confirming what she had just said and that I agreed. I wanted it all in writing in case anyone tried anything.'

'When do you have to leave by?'

'I was given a month's notice.'

'We can get a van sorted easily.'

'I don't know what to do.'

'Can you work from here?'

'How do you mean?'

'Can you sit at the dining room table and work?'

'Yeah, although it'd get cramped with all my supplies.'

'We can store everything in a unit close by. You can pop in every few days for different materials.'

'I can't have clients here though.'

'Of course not, but you can have them at The Ritz.'

'What, like a trunk show?'

'Exactly.' He'd seen a documentary about a Savile Row tailor on BBC4 recently. Caius took his phone out and started checking the price of a room. 'Tell your clients that showrooms are tacky.'

'Naff, not tacky.'

'Tell them they're naff then. We'll book a suite and then you schedule them all over one day. I doubt anyone will say no to The Ritz and a glass of champagne.' The microwave pinged and the Thai chicken curry that they'd been given by the Beauchamps' cook was ready. 'We can make use of the bed once everyone else has gone home for the day.'

'You horny little genius.' Callie got up from the sofa and checked on the rice she'd been boiling. It was done and she started spooning it into large flat bowls for the two of them. 'Your grandfather called the landline earlier. He sounded a bit disappointed that you weren't coming to Frithsden for lunch tomorrow. He said there was something of his he wanted to give to you. He also said that I was still very welcome to come even if you can't.'

'He loves you more than I do.' His grandfather definitely liked Callie more than him at least. 'It might be good for you to leave London and get some fresh air.'

'I do like the air up there.'

'You can catch a train from Euston. I'm sure my dad will pick you up from Hemel Hempstead as long as the service is running.' Caius was hoping that Harriet would forget about Callie for a while now that she'd got her 'revenge' and that Callie could do the same.

'Caius,' Callie said, holding the microwave door open. 'I don't think I want to do this any more.'

Caius looked up. 'Do what?'

'Millinery.'

'Oh thank fuck. I thought you were dumping me.'

'That's the second time this week you've thought that.'

'Don't play Joy Division and don't say things like "I don't want to do this any more" without proper context. I'd go to pieces if you dumped me. I adore you.'

'God, you're so precious.' Callie removed the curry from the microwave and started serving it. 'I've been thinking about quitting for a while. Teaching that night class was me dipping my toe into something else, but this whole mess over the showroom has put my apathy into perspective. I've got orders to keep me going until the end of the summer and I'm doing that segment for the BBC coverage of the Chelsea Flower Show soon, but I think I'll stop trading in the autumn. I won't take anything else on. I just don't feel the same passion for millinery that I used to.'

'What will you do instead?' Caius got up off the sofa and filled two glasses with water.

'Well, that's the thing,' Callie said, setting dinner down. 'I called my dad about Jane. He pointed out that I'll be given a yearly allowance from the trust so I can afford to take a break while I work things out. I can do some volunteering. Pick up my sketchbook and go back to fine art.'

'You could sit for Georgie. He said he wants to paint you.'

'I could.'

'Callie, you're the idle rich now. You can do whatever you want.'

'I know and do you know what's worse? I like the sound of it.'

SUNDAY

# 46

## The Police Station

'Amy, I have a present for you,' Caius said to her as she settled in for the day at her desk.

'Caius, you remembered my birthday!'

'Yes, I did,' Caius said, looking at Matt who quietly got up out of his seat, grabbing his coat as he went. He had not remembered that it was Amy's birthday. 'We're having birthday cake for elevenses.'

'That's so lovely. The last team I worked with were so rubbish about things like this.'

'Yeah.'

'Where's my present?'

'Haha,' Caius said, revealing the packet of Blu-Tack that he'd stuck a leftover bow on. He'd found it at the bottom of his desk drawer. This was supposed to be a joke. 'It's not a real present. We'll do that with the cake later.'

Amy smiled at him with the sweetest, most sincere smile she had ever given him and Caius caught Amy up to speed with what had transpired the day before.

'I told you,' Amy said, lifting her arms out in benediction. 'Rosie is too fucking nice but not so nice that she wouldn't fuck a Nazi.'

'I'm not sure that Felix is a fascist. At the moment he just knows them. Albeit quite well. She did say that Felix is "talking to someone",' Caius said, not entirely sure why he felt the need to defend Felix. He supposed things weren't black and white, despite Johnny Bull and the Worthings seeing the world entirely through that lens.

'Is that someone Hampton?' Matt asked from the doorway.

'I think it's likely,' Caius said. That was a call he'd need to make today after putting it off. 'Amy, can you take the printouts of the screenshots that you and Matt took of every person and every car that went up Mona's road and arrange them chronologically in two parallel lines. One for each doorbell camera. I want to see people enter the road and then leave.'

'I'll pin them on the wall.'

'You can Blu-Tack them with your non-birthday present.'

★ ★ ★

'I've got a Spider-Man birthday cake, a card for us two to sign – I can't be arsed to trawl around the building looking for bland sentiments from people you pass in the lift – and five share-size packets of giant Wotsits,' Matt said, putting his supermarket sweep haul under his desk while Amy had popped out of the room for a wee.

'That's really impressive for a small Sainsbury's,' Caius said, peering over. 'Show me the cake.'

'She's a beauty.'

'She's got a yellow sticker.'

'There's no way I was paying full price for a fake birthday. You know Amy's birthday is in June, right?'

'Yeah, I put both of your birthdays in my work calendar. I checked it afterwards. I just want to see how far she's willing to take it.'

Amy came back into the incident room.

'I arrested Rosie at 6.49 p.m. last night so we have under ten hours before we either have to charge her or let her go. I've spoken to the CPS already to see if an obstruction charge would hold up and we're waiting for them to confirm either way. Even if we don't charge her, we have a good window where she's out of play. Amy is working on the Barnesyeux Tapestry,' Caius said, looking at the start she'd made at sticking the screenshots of the comings and goings on Mona's road around the room. 'Matt, can you look through Rosie's messages and pictures. IT have emailed over the files. We need to nail everything today. Review all our outstanding evidence before we interview Felix. Felix has to be Mr Banister – up to her room and back down again – but we're still missing our knife and pillow-wielding murderer.'

'Our final fingerer,' Matt said. He hadn't meant to say it especially considering the conversation. 'Sorry. It's stuck. That's the word now.'

'Matthew . . .' Caius tapped his head as if that would speed things along. 'You two, as you were. I'm going to watch the footage from the train passengers in fancy dress. Just ticking it off the list. It won't take long.'

'I think they'd be offended if you referred to their purposefully curated, antiquated aesthetic as a costume,' Amy said, resuming her work on the Barnesyeux Tapestry.

'Yell if you spot a murderer, folks,' Caius said, opening up the folder with the videos in. They looked short and Caius felt the need to cross something off his to-do list early.

★   ★   ★

Clip One: Opening shot of a London
Victoria sign on the platform panning
across to the train billowing steam.
Lauren and Lisa board the train. Emphasis
is placed on the seams of their stockings.

Clip Two: Lauren and Lisa sip their cups of tea, almost presenting the china, while looking theatrically nonchalant. Lisa leans over and whispers something into Lauren's ear. They laugh before turning to stare stonily at the camera.

Clip Three: A shot of brunch from above the table. Cutlery pierces the bright orange yolk of a perfectly poached egg.

Clip Four: Lauren and Lisa toast each other with their Bellinis.

Clip Five: Lisa reapplies her red lipstick while Lauren stares wistfully out of the window.

Clip Six: The camera follows Lauren and Lisa out of the train and onto Bath Spa platform.

Clip Seven: Lisa and Lauren start to walk down the platform and towards the stairs.

(Audio) Dan:
Girls, I don't think this shot is useable, there's too many muggles giving me evils.

★   ★   ★

'Matt.' Caius leaned back in his chair and yelled. 'Amy.'

'Yeah,' Matt yelled back.

'I'm yelling.'

'Why do you sound like a toddler?' Matt yelled back.

'I found something. Maybe.'

'Who is it?' Amy joined in.

'It's Grace.'

'Grace?' Amy came over. She couldn't be bothered to play his yelling game any more. 'Who's Grace?'

Caius played the video footage of Lauren and Lisa on the platform at Bath Spa. Grace was stood against a wall trying not to be noticed. She conspicuously peeped out from behind a fluorescent pink paperback in front of her face. 'Rosie had that book on her bedside table.'

'Sienna's nanny,' Matt said, coming over too.

'Grace followed Mona and Rosie to Bath,' Amy said.

'Grace quit yesterday. Sienna was messaging Rosie about it after we interviewed her and Charlie. Rosie was telling Sienna that she hadn't heard from Tristan, but Lucia was meeting up with him after he'd gone to the cinema to get the lowdown. If Grace was in the house when Rosie got back that Saturday night and is the person Tristan saw through the window, then she'd be watching him in case he identified her.'

'And Grace was where when this conversation between Rosie and Sienna happened? Could she have looked at Sienna's phone?' Amy asked.

'Grace was watching Sienna and Charlie's children.' Caius remembered Sienna making a joke about relieving the nanny. 'Sienna could have her WhatsApp on her laptop so Grace could've read the messages from Rosie and found Tristan?'

'How did she know which cinema though?' Matt asked, going

back to his desk and reading the downloaded messages. 'Rosie doesn't specify which cinema to Sienna.'

'She could be following him?' Amy suggested.

'What, like stalking?' Matt asked.

'No, on social media,' Amy said.

'Hang on,' Caius said. IT had given him Rosie's log ins. He went on her Instagram and looked at Tristan's profile and saw that Grace was indeed following him as she was Rosie. 'He took a picture on the way saying where he was going . . .'

'For fuck's sake. When will people learn it's a bad idea to broadcast the minutiae of their life to everyone all the time,' Amy said.

'All right, so Grace, the nanny, breaks in to Mona's house—' Matt began.

'No, she uses Sienna's key that she dumped in a drawer and forgot about,' Caius interrupted.

'Enters the house,' Matt continued. 'Murders Philip Campbell in the kitchen, roots around for a couple of hours. Rosie comes home, Tristan sort of spots her through the window, and then Felix turns up a hot minute later. She remains in the house while they're at it and eventually smothers Mona. Why? Did Sienna get her to break in for her and steal the infamous earrings that she mysteriously now has?'

'It feels weird,' Caius said, juggling imaginary balls with his hands. 'It can't be a coincidence that Grace, Rosie and Mona were all in Bath. She was there waiting on the platform. She must have taken a day off and caught an earlier train – I doubt she was on ours on a nanny's wage – just so she could follow them around the city. If that isn't the beginnings of a whole creepy, break-in to a house and maybe kill people in a stalkerish frenzy vibe, then what is?'

# 47

## Colliers Wood

Caius and Amy were stood on the doorstep of the average-looking 1930s semi-detached house that Grace shared with other students. The door opened and a young woman stared at them. Her hair was piled up on top of her head and she was wearing a T-shirt from a true crime podcast. Caius tried not to pull a face at her ghoulishness.

'DI Caius Beauchamp, is Grace Sanders here?' Caius and Amy both held up their warrant cards.

'Uh, yeah.'

'May we speak to her?'

'Is this about those murders? She won't shut up about them. She'll be in ecstasy. How thrilling,' she said, stepping out the way and pointing. 'Her room is the first door on the left.'

They climbed the stairs. Grace's housemate closed the door behind them and waited at the bottom expectantly. While she wasn't in ecstasy herself, she was going to savour any snippets that fell her way. Amy knocked on the door.

'Grace Sanders,' Amy said as Grace slowly swung the door to her bedroom open. 'I'm DC Amy Noakes. I think you've already met my colleague DI Caius Beauchamp. We have a few questions for you.'

'Hi, Grace,' Caius said as the harassed nanny stared back at them. 'May we come in.'

'Of course.'

Grace moved to allow Caius and Amy into her room. Caius walked into the space and stopped in front of the picture on the wall of the chimney breast. He'd seen some of these pictures before. 'You a Stratford fan?'

'Yes, I like Anne Stratford's books.'

'Is that why you took the job working for Sienna?' Caius asked, noticing a copy of the same pastel-coloured volume that he'd been sent by Hampton.

'I'm sorry. I don't understand.'

'Grace, you were recorded at Bath Spa station the day that Rosie and Mona were there.'

'I went on a day trip.'

'You like knitting, Grace?' Amy asked, noticing the balls of wool on the desk.

'It's a hobby.'

'It's Rosie's hobby,' Amy said. Matt had been vindicated – women who knitted were odd.

'Is it?' Grace asked, playfully feigning nonchalance.

'All right, Grace, you need to come clean with us. We know you're obsessed with the family—' Caius started before Grace interrupted him.

'With Rosie,' Grace said plainly. 'It's Rosie. She's my muse. Sienna can go to hell.'

'Grace, where were you on Saturday evening?'

'Ooo! She was with me,' piped up Grace's housemate who had slowly made her way up the stairs and to the action. 'It was my boyfriend's birthday so a load of us went out for tapas, he loves patatas bravas more than anything, and then we stayed at the pub round the corner until closing time at midnight. There were five of us by the end and then we walked back here. Me and Grace had a cup of camomile in the kitchen together before bed.'

'I can explain. I might have taken things a bit far,' Grace said, staring at the floor. The initial thrill of the police in her bedroom was beginning to be overshadowed by what her sensible parents would think. 'Look, I'm studying for an MFA and I'm writing a project riffing off Anne Stratford's novel *Romance in Frigid Temperatures*. I was trying to be all meta, I guess. I was deep deep in fan forums when I came across someone who claimed that Mary Stratford had had an illegitimate child. All it took was for me to look up her will on the probate registry—'

'Which alerted you to Mona Frogmorton and her daughter Josephine Krige,' Caius said.

'Yep. Mona's age is right and why else would the daughter of some random couple be included in Mary Stratford's will? Then I had a look on *The Times* archive and found a marriage announcement for Josephine and then subsequent ones on the births of her children. Sienna was super easy to find on social media. She posted that she wanted someone to do school pick-ups and drop-offs for six weeks. This was a month before Cosmo was born. I babysat a lot and have younger siblings so I applied not thinking she'd even take me seriously, but Sienna hired me. I was willing to work for less than professionals, I guess. I've got a DBS already – I volunteered at the youth centre where my mum worked. The school pick-ups morphed into holding Cosmo for twenty minutes so she could have a nap, to doing fucking everything. That woman knows how to take advantage of people. That's when I saw Rosie, she visited with Mona herself, and I knew she was going to be the star of my final piece.'

'What do you mean?'

'Charming wallflower and do-gooder who lives with the ailing grandmother. Slowly catching on to the fact that her sister is a monster. She's either going to be downtrodden her whole life or discover herself and set Sienna on fire.'

'Grace, have you ever been in Mona's house?'

'I'm going to get in trouble for this, aren't I?'

'Probably,' Amy said.

'I think it's best you come clean,' Caius said, shooting Amy a look. It was going to be easier if Grace just admitted it. 'We came over here expecting to arrest you under suspicion of murder.'

'A murder suspect? Me. Wow!'

'Please focus, Grace,' Caius said.

'Yes, I went to their house on the Thursday evening before the murders. I took Sienna's key from a sideboard and let myself in. I needed more material for my work.'

'Like what?' Amy asked.

'Smells, colours, textures. I don't know until I see it.'

'Did you take anything?' Amy asked.

'Like a keepsake?' Grace asked.

'Yeah, sure, like a keepsake,' Amy said, a little shocked at how brazen Grace was about admitting to burglary.

'I took a pair of knitting needles and some balls of this wool from a company that Rosie fetishises. It was hand-spun and dyed with bits of old leaves,' Grace said, picking up a ball. 'Rosie believes in simplicity.'

'These ones,' Amy asked, gesturing to the balls of wool on Grace's desk that she'd noticed when they entered her room.

'Yeah.' Amy took out an evidence bag and a pair of gloves from her back pocket and set to work. Grace shifted about uncomfortably, realising that she probably shouldn't have admitted to that.

'Where did you go in the house?' Caius asked.

'Just up the stairs and into Rosie's room. I wanted to know what cosmetics she uses. Her perfume. I needed to feel her clothes. See the wool collection that Sienna always took the piss out of her for. She was delighted with the things Rosie made for

334

Cosmo though. Did a whole fucking reel about the booties being pure wool, didn't she? What a bitch. She's jealous of Rosie. Rosie could be prettier than her if she put the effort in. And she could do so much better than that creep Felix.'

'Creep?'

'Yeah, I caught him going through Sienna's bedroom the other day. He was messing around with her dressing table. Sienna was delighted about it when I told her. She thinks she's still got it.' Grace rolled her eyes. 'They said you were all right because you had something called hybrid vigour, but I think she's just a snob really.'

'Me?' Caius asked.

'Yes, that went over my head I'm afraid. Something about breeding it out. Sienna and Charlie say weird shit when they don't think I'm listening. I'd already been picking up on a couple of phrases that she'd been using in her work which felt like dog whistles but the stuff they say about Jews and Muslims when they think they're alone, yikes.'

'They are modern eugenicists after all.'

'I tried to tell you,' Grace said, shrugging. 'The eight children thing.'

'You did,' Caius said, wishing that Grace had explicitly come forward earlier. 'Did you overhear anything else?'

'Charlie's worried about the IPO. They're putting pressure on Felix to dip into the last of his trust fund, but he refused him on Saturday morning before you called them in. Charlie was in full panic mode when you called. Charlie thinks the company is overvalued but he just wants to make a fast buck to pay for phase 2.'

'Phase 2?'

'The Worthing Foundation. They want to really expand into

politics. Charlie's going to run as an MP for Johnny's new party and Sienna's going to escalate the whole tradwife thing using this foundation as a motherhood think tank pressure group thingy. She hosted a dinner to celebrate it on Friday night. Their granny isn't even buried. Sienna has this whole wacky philosophy. A lot of it was about feminine nature. I don't know, it was weird. I only tolerated it for so long because I needed the material. I wrote a lot of it down. Sienna liked to use me as a "sounding board". I had to pretend to think that white people were superior and laugh at their horrible jokes.' Grace shook her head. 'And those earrings! She never stopped talking about them.'

'The earrings.'

'Yeah, but she has them now so she's ecstatic.'

'Where did they come from?'

'Sienna thinks Rosie left them in her room for her, but I'm not sure. I didn't see Rosie go upstairs.' Grace got down on the floor and pulled a clear plastic tub out from under her bed. She opened the tub and searched through a folder until she found a piece of paper. 'It's a copy of Mary Stratford's will. You can see here that she left Mona a pair of diamond earrings. They're supposed to be from Mona's birth father. From what I can gather Rosie doesn't know about the whole Mary Stratford thing. Josephine sat Sienna down once she'd turned eighteen and told her, but Rosie doesn't know.'

'Were you going to tell us this?' Caius asked.

'Oh yes. I was going to march into the police station tomorrow now that I've quit. I wasn't sure I could talk to you as Sienna made me sign an NDA, but fuck it.'

'Grace, we need you to come down to the station and take your fingerprints. It would be helpful if you brought your, ergh, material along too,' Amy said.

'Can I get a copy of my fingerprints afterwards? That would be such a good piece to include.'

'I don't know,' Caius said. He'd never been asked that. He was probably also going to arrest her for trespassing if not burglary, and issue her with a warning against contacting Rosie. Grace didn't seem to realise she was in as much trouble as she was. Caius could see her thinking about how she could turn this interview into material.

They took Grace to the car as her housemate photographed it. Grace smiled for the camera.

## 48

## The Police Station

Caius had Grace's fingerprints taken and then they arrested her for burglary. He was stood with her prints in the incident room and comparing them to the last two sets of unclaimed print maps.

'Grace is being processed,' Amy said as she entered the room. 'She's still bemused by the whole thing.'

'Grace is Ms Banister,' Caius said, matching her freshly taken fingerprints against the fifth map. 'Like she said, she went upstairs, she poked around Rosie's things and that was it.'

'So that leaves Felix,' Matt said. 'He's the killer.' He went to his computer and googled a picture of him. 'Do we have an idea of where he is yet?'

'No,' Caius said. He wasn't quite ready to start the manhunt as he had a feeling that one particular man would know. He picked up the notebook that Grace had been making notes in.

'Grace is nuts so I'm not sure how believable her account is,' Amy said, watching him flick through it.

'Oh yeah, she's batshit crazy but I don't know. She seems pretty astute when it comes to her observations of the Frogmorton clan. She's recorded all of Sienna's Stepford Wife plans for world domination in her stalker diary so I'm ever so slightly more well disposed towards her than I naturally would be.' Caius was looking at the website for the British Society for Rewilding again. He opened the corporate governance page. The advisory board was full of conservationists, as you'd expect, and then Johnny. It just kept leading back to him. Caius took out his phone and put it on speakerphone so Matt and Amy could hear.

'Hello,' Caius said rather abruptly. 'Where's Felix Drake?'

'Why?'

'I'm pretty sure he's a murderer.'

'Ah.' Caius heard a tone to Hampton's voice that he'd never heard before. He'd caught him making a mistake. 'He's here at Chequers with me, the PM, some of the richest men in Britain whom he's trying to convince to donate big to the party, and Johnny, unfortunately.'

'Felix Drake is pally with Johnny Bull from university. Johnny treats him like an ATM and he wants out. He bumps into you. You both see an opportunity to rid yourself of a problem called Johnny. Our "working relationship" would be much better if you were up front with me.'

'Where's the fun in that?' Hampton said dryly. He was trying to recover his infallibility. 'I operate on a need-to-know basis. It's better for everyone that way.'

'Rosie Krige is shagging Felix Drake, whose whole life seems very much entwined with Johnny Bull and Charlie Worthing. They are on the verge of launching a new hard right political party that would eat away at your party's votes.'

'My goodness, is she really sleeping with him? I didn't notice her pining after him over dinner.'

'You saw them together at the Colon Cancer UK fundraiser at the Dartford Hotel. Did Johnny have a table too? Trying to worm his way into your good books?'

'People on their way up, and down, like to pander to me. They know it's a personal cause and they try to endear themselves. Lickspittles. As if turning up to shmooze me at a fundraiser to cure the cancer that is eating my brother from the inside out would endear them to me. As if I didn't know what they were doing.'

Caius shook his head and paused for a moment to let Hampton's nascent grief fall away. 'Did you do a bit of digging on Felix?'

'Of course, he's the weak link in that gang. Doesn't really buy into the ideology but, Johnny is a snob, you see. Johnny needs Felix to make him look acceptable in society. The elocution lessons weren't enough. Felix speaks well, looks the part. Family are established. He had spare cash at some point – backed Charlie Worthing in the early days and is about to get a large payday if the IPO goes well. If.'

'So you are the person Felix is talking to about the Worthings being fascists.'

'I may have facilitated Felix's "come to Jesus" moment, but I'm not the one who is keeping tabs on that gang. The Worthings have been on counter terrorism's watchlist for a while now. A preliminary report on them just happened to pass over my desk at the same time that I connected with Felix at the fundraiser.'

Caius was furious now. He kept trying to remind himself that Hampton hadn't killed Mona or Philip for political point-scoring, but he was clearly going to use their murders to his advantage any way he could. 'You used the whole stupid Nazi love-child thing to manipulate me into embroiling a political rival in a murder case. Three people have died and you're only interested because you can use it to bring down the PM who's outlived his usefulness to you.' Caius didn't like the man, didn't vote for him and thought his election was one of the worst things to happen to civic dignity in the last century, but he still felt dirty.

'Last time we had dealings, you got an exceedingly charming girlfriend out of it so I wouldn't complain too much.' Hampton paused. He knew that Caius had a righteous streak. It was one of the qualities he liked about him, when it could be utilised to his own advantage, but perhaps he'd pushed it a little too far this time. 'All right. You've got me. I do think that Johnny Bull's removal from the public sphere and into a state facility is probably for the best, don't you?'

'Who's your contact at counter-terror?'

'I'll make a call.' Hampton paused. He felt that being a little candid with Caius would go down well at this point. 'Johnny Bull and Felix are here for crisis talks disguised as cocktail hour. The PM thinks if he can utilise Bull's support base then he can win another election. I'm about to go down for lunch. The food is passable. The company is not. Do not come down here. There's no need for you to be seen. Do keep me updated and I shall likewise let you know of any movements from Mr Drake.'

'All right.'

'We'll meet up face to face soon. I'm aware I owe you a case as per our agreement.'

'About that. Something else has fallen into my lap that you need to be aware of.'

'Next time.' Hampton ended the call abruptly.

'God, I hate Hampton,' Amy said. She had pinned up all the screenshots of people and cars going past number 7 and was about to start lining up the same for number 26 underneath.

'You know what, he's vaguely the hero this time round. The PM is a spineless shit and Johnny Bull is a threat to democracy,' Caius said.

'Is he though? The hero?' Matt asked.

'I did say "vaguely".' Caius checked his mobile phone. He'd had an email to his personal account inviting him to a St George's Day extravaganza complete with morris dancing, a hog roast and a joust outside the brewery. All well and good until he saw the picture of the morris dancers in what might be blackface. He definitely wasn't going to go.

'I've been reading through Rosie's messages with Felix,' Matt said. 'I've been updating the timeline.'

'Do tell,' Caius said as he went over to Matt's desk.

'She dumps him the day before you all went to Bath, but he isn't having it. Rosie doesn't respond after her last message at 11.53. He calls her on the Thursday evening, and she doesn't answer. Ignores him on Friday. He calls her a few times on Saturday, but we know she's at the pub. She looks like she's well away until . . .' Matt gestured at Amy.

'She calls him plastered. Rosie love,' Amy said, shaking her head.

'Rosie calls him at 22.32 for five minutes,' Matt said.

'Which is just before Lucia finds her in the loo and orders her the Uber which Tristan also hops in,' Caius said.

'Tristan says goodnight at the door and sees Felix being dropped off by a cab at Rosie's, realises she's seeing someone else and backs off,' Matt said.

'When I interviewed him he was embarrassed that he'd asked her, she'd said yes and then hopped into bed with another guy five minutes later,' Caius said.

'Poor Tristan,' Amy piped up. She needed a break from the Blu-Tack and came over to join in with story time.

'Everything seems to be back on with Rosie and Felix post-Saturday evening. He keeps sending her things about moving to Dartmoor, keeping chickens and dodging Sienna's multiple requests to watch her children. He really doesn't like Sienna. He made quite a big thing about Sienna not putting Rosie up for a while, saying what an awful sister she is,' Matt said, scrolling through. 'Saying that she shouldn't have to rely on Lucia like this.'

'I get that they're on and off, but why doesn't she stay with him?' Amy asked.

'He wants there to be distance between him and the case. Doesn't want us to suspect there's a connection,' Caius said, shrugging. 'He fucked up, after all, killed two people and touched half the house without gloves while he was at it. So Rosie stays at Lucia's instead. He doesn't like Lucia. What's her surname?' Caius asked.

'Green,' said Matt.

'Lucia's probably Jewish. I'd almost given Felix the benefit of the doubt that Charlie and Johnny just sharply turned far right and he was doing something about it, but no. Felix is a violent anti-Semite.' Caius put his head in his hands. He'd call Hampton in a moment and see what he could do about Lucia's safety. 'We need to get her some protection.'

'Remember at the beginning of this we were like "I don't want to have to think about dead Nazis" and now we're like they're alive and everywhere,' Matt said.

'Right, that's it. Amy, we know it's not your birthday. Matt, chuck me a pack of Wotsits. I need processed cheese powder to get me through this.'

'Dammit. I thought we'd get to lunchtime at least,' Amy said, getting a packet of Wotsits from Matt's desk and pretending to chuck them at Caius before opening them herself.

'The last message Felix sent to Rosie was that he won't be able to talk much because he's going away with Johnny this weekend, so I don't think he's missed her yet. We need to get to him quick,' Matt said.

'I've got Felix here,' Amy said, looking at the now completed Barnesyeux Tapestry printouts. 'He goes past number 7 at 20.48 and doesn't pass number 26.'

'What's he wearing?' Caius asked as he joined in the search.

'Jogging leggings. Fleece. Cap pulled down.'

'Valerie, the witness on the top deck, mentioned a baseball cap,' Caius said, looking at the picture. 'Matt, chase the stores you spoke to for the footage outside the cinema.'

'Here he is going past number 7 at 22.38,' Amy said.

'He kills Philip, searches the house. Gets a drunken booty call from Rosie so leaves. I bet he goes down the road and hails a black cab, timing it so that he arrives after Rosie,' Caius said.

'Then he kills Mona after they've had sex. Fuck, that's cold,' Matt said.

'He was searching the house for the earrings. He meant to frame Sienna. He must have woken Mona up, demanded she hand them over and then smothered her in her own bed with her pillow.'

★ ★ ★

Matt had been summoned by IT. He returned to the incident room as Caius put the phone down on one of Hampton's minions who had agreed to put Lucia up somewhere secure.

'IT wanted to show us the messages Rosie's been receiving for the last hour,' Matt said.

'Oh?' Caius said.

'Felix has been hitting her up like crazy.'

'He hasn't heard from her in over twelve hours.'

'It's worse than that, Rosie's phone is being tracked. An app had been installed remotely onto her iPhone which markets itself as the spyware app to use if you want to catch your partner cheating.'

'He can see that she hasn't left the police station, I guess,' Amy said.

'A spyware app. Felix knows that Rosie was still looking for a way out of their relationship and Tristan could be that knight in shining armour. He probably saw Tristan when he got out of the taxi.'

'So he shoves him under a bus,' Amy said, shaking her head. 'She must follow Tristan on Instagram.'

'I thought he was at Chequers when the murder happened?' Matt asked.

'Felix is at Chequers now. Hampton said so. He told Rosie he was there all weekend. Doesn't mean he was. He could have arrived yesterday afternoon.'

★   ★   ★

'Rosie, we have a few more questions to ask you about your relationship with Felix.'

Rosie looked at Caius. A dread that she'd been suppressing rose up her throat like bile. 'Why?'

'I want to be crystal clear on whether or not Felix pressured you into saying that he wasn't at your house that evening.'

'He asked me not to say. I called him after I spoke to the police initially. That wasn't a proper interview. It was short. They breathalysed me and asked me basic stuff. I called him straight after. He said that I shouldn't mention him or our relationship. He didn't want any press attention. I'm sorry, I've been an idiot.' Rosie started crying again.

'Do you need a moment?' Caius asked, nudging a box of tissues over towards her.

She took one from the box and went to dab her eyes. There were no tears so instead she began pulling the tissue to pieces. 'I can't stand Johnny. Never have been able to. He makes the hair on the back of my neck stand up. I never understood why Sienna adored him let alone tolerated him, until last week. I saw what she was. Felix was the one pushing me towards that conclusion. He kept on about how much he hated them. But . . . But . . . He must agree with them a bit, right? You can't be friendly with racists unless . . .'

'Did Felix ever get physical with you?'

Her eyes widened. 'Did he hit me?'

'Yeah, or push you, slap you, bite you?'

'No.'

'Did he do anything that made you alarmed?'

'He'd turn up where I was. It happened a few times when I was at the pub with my friends from uni or school and a couple of times when I went to a local coffee shop in the village. I was on my own. I like to read in there and get a latte. I love my granny but sometimes you need your own space. The first couple of times I put it down to having similar taste,' Rosie said, looking at her solicitor and then looking at the desk. 'He stopped doing that a while ago though.'

'Did you ask him about it?'

'Yeah, he got a bit mad with me. Said I was accusing him of being a psycho.'

'Had you been posting your locations online?'

'No, I don't like social media.' Rosie went rigid in her chair. 'What are you implying?'

'Did you know that your grandmother was adopted?'

'No. Was she?'

'Yes, she was the illegitimate daughter of the heiress, and potential Nazi sympathiser, the Hon. Mary Stratford. I think it's likely your sister is aware of this already.'

'What?'

'Rosie, do you know where your grandmother's infamous diamond earrings were kept? Are they at the house?'

'My mother used to joke that they were hidden in a shoe box, but that's just her calling Granny miserly. Hiding cash under a mattress.'

'They're kept in a vault at a secure facility,' said Rosie's solicitor, interrupting. 'Although I believe a replica pair is kept at Marigold House to be worn.'

Caius nodded. After all that Felix had tried to frame Sienna with a fake pair of earrings. 'We found a spyware app on your phone.'

'Oh my God.'

'We think Felix has been tracking what you say, where you go, who you interact with.'

'What?'

'Rosie, we think Felix broke in while you were out to steal the earrings. He was going to frame Sienna with them. She wouldn't inherit then. You'd get nearly everything. He was surprised by the burglar and killed him and then later killed your grandmother while you were sleeping once he'd found the fakes.'

* * *

Caius had called Hampton again. Too many times for one day. 'My team have found the photos from the Colon Cancer UK fundraiser. They were just up on their website. There's a picture with you in the background talking to one Felix Drake,' Caius said. Rupert was there of course, looking fucking dashing in black tie, the bastard.

'Well spotted. I'll get that taken care of. Don't want that

picture doing the rounds when he's convicted. Not good for the old image,' Hampton said. Caius regretted telling him. It wasn't the gotcha he thought it was going to be and all he'd really achieved was scrubbing a piece of evidence of Hampton's involvement in this whole mess. 'The moron let himself get preyed on by the likes of Charlie Worthing and Johnny Bull. God, what a name. His real one is much less emblematic.'

'When did Felix arrive at Chequers?' Caius asked.

'Yesterday afternoon. Why?' Hampton asked.

'He's murdered someone else. No probably about it. Matt's found him on the CCTV we have just received from a shop opposite the cinema where Tristan Sowerby was pushed to his death under a double-decker. Tristan saw him entering the crime scene and is a romantic rival.'

'Oh dear.'

'We've also come into possession of Sienna Worthing's nanny's diary recording their many conversations including their plans with Johnny Bull.'

'You are a gift, Caius.' Caius could almost hear the cogs whirring as Hampton thought of the best way to leak the diary to the press.

'Do you know where Felix is right now?'

'He was having cocktails with the party's largest donor and his long-suffering wife. It's hard to make small chat about disappearing insect life with a man devoid of concern for anyone but himself. He disappeared to make a series of calls. I shall have to make a few of my own now.'

'I'm sure you have other minions like me who can deal with the grubby end.'

'Are you jealous?'

'What?'

'You're my favourite muckraker; the only one who can get an arrest warrant.' Hampton paused. 'One moment.'

Caius heard muffled talking from the other end.

'Felix made his excuses ten minutes ago and has raced off to London on his own. Apparently, Johnny isn't too happy. Bully for him.'

# 49

## The Police Station

Caius was sat on a bench in a small park near to the station that he sometimes ate his lunch in when a torrential downpour of biblical proportions was less likely – although in England this was never a certainty. It was starting to get dark, the last rays of a chilly spring day hitting the empty children's playground before disappearing behind a row of houses. The clouds were sat precariously low and Caius felt the pressure drop. He put his hood up in anticipation of yet more rain. The phone in his hand started ringing. It was set to loud. A man with the concentrated demeanour of a stalking wolf entered the park. The call ended. He was tall and well built – but practically muscular, not vainly so. This was a man who'd done weekend survival bootcamps. His jaw was strong. He had the confidence of someone bred for power, for influence. He moved like he had a destiny. He looked around for someone. He failed to find them. He checked his phone for a moment, furrowing his brow, confirming that he hadn't made a mistake, and then began to call the phone again. He turned around and looked at Caius who'd decided on theatricality. Caius stayed sat on the bench with his legs splayed out, taking up as much of it as he could, refusing to take his eyes off Felix Drake.

'That's my girlfriend's phone. You stole it.' Felix stood in front of Caius, sizing him up. 'Filthy degenerate.'

'Everything all right, gentlemen,' a passing uniformed officer asked.

'This hooligan stole my girlfriend's phone.'

Caius took his hood off. The uniformed officer did a double take.

'Arrest him. He's holding it in his hand. I'll call her number. I can prove it.'

Caius stood up. 'Hello, Felix. I've been waiting for you.'

Felix had a surge of adrenaline and made a dash for the park's slender wrought-iron gates. Matt, who had been waiting patiently just outside, moved in front of Felix, ready to block the exit if needs be. There was a rustle from behind a laurel bush. Felix never saw Amy coming.

★  ★  ★

'All right, Felix. We can do this the hard way or the easy way. We've got your fingerprints now. They're all over the knife that you stabbed Philip Campbell to death with and the pillow you used to smother Mona Frogmorton.'

Felix was impassive.

'We know you've been "seeing" Rosie for a year, but you're messing her around. Maybe you just love her that much that it scares you, and you need to be in control of her to be in control of your own feelings. Treat her mean and all that blah blah negging blah blah high-value women blah.'

Felix laughed.

'You've realised you've taken it too far and Rosie's really close to dumping you for good. Meaning you'd lose any possibility of getting your hands on her inheritance. We've taken your phone into evidence. In between frog memes and racially abusing England footballers, we know that Charlie messaged you to tell you that he'd patched things up with Mona that Saturday after-noon and Sienna is going to be back in the will on Monday. That means Rosie's inheritance would be halved. But you need that money; Charlie's business is a piece of shit. It's a desk-sharing company masquerading as a tech firm, but it doesn't have any tech. It doesn't make anything. It doesn't help anyone. It's all marketing guff. He's probably confided in you that it's all about to go tits up, all it'll take is one in-depth article in the *Financial Times*, so you know that there may not be a magical payday on the horizon. Charlie and Johnny have burnt through your inheritance. You can't afford to keep buying patches of meadow. You're broke. So you decide to kill Mona. Tristan makes his move and you can't chance them going out for dinner, because then she'll definitely move on. Besides, you think he saw you going into the house and you can't risk that, so you kill him too. You were sloppy when you killed Philip and Mona. Not even wearing gloves. And we have CCTV footage of you approaching the cinema where Tristan was killed.'

Felix didn't say anything.

'Did you go and see that house in the countryside? The one you told Rosie she could keep chickens at.'

'Yes,' Felix said quietly.

'Is that your exit strategy? Flee to a smallholding and build a big fence.'

'Yes.'

'Are you actually scared of Johnny?'

'He, he . . . Johnny is taking things too far and Charlie and Sienna are swallowing it wholesale; they're all taking it too far. I'm not like them. I needed a way out.'

'You stole Mary Stratford's earrings, didn't you? You planned to kill Mona, fake a burglary, and Sienna would be charged when the earrings were discovered on her. And then you and Rosie could escape to the countryside with her money.'

'Don't bring Rosie into this.'

'Felix, I don't need a confession. You fucked up. We've got you.'

Felix put his head in his hands. There was no way to deny it.

Caius terminated the interview. 'There's a counter-terror unit scouring your flat. My only advice is to be the one who turns first. There's a nice officer called Kevin on the other side of that mirror. He's willing to listen to you. Tell him all about your nasty friends and their nasty plans. You're going down for murder, there's no doubt about it, but in my opinion that's an opportunity you can't afford to pass over right now. Do a little bit of a good.'

'I know someone. Someone important. I've been working with—'

'I know you have. He won't help you now. You are no longer useful.'

# MONDAY

## 50

## The Police Station

Amy streamed *BBC News at One* on her computer.

'Have we got popcorn?' Amy asked.

'There's more Spider-Man unbirthday cake,' Matt said, offering her a slice.

'Or giant Wotsits,' Caius said, chucking her a packet.

Matt checked his phone. 'Yesss, my mortgage has been approved.'

'Look at you. You grown-up,' Caius said.

```
Presenter:
Breaking news this lunchtime. We are
going live to Downing Street where the
Prime Minister is making an address to
the nation.


The Prime Minister:
Today is the right day for me to step aside
as Prime Minister. I would like to take
this opportunity to thank my colleagues who
have worked tirelessly to help achieve what
we have achieved. I am looking forward to
spending more time with my children.


Presenter:
The leader of the opposition has called
for a general election. The Deputy
```

Prime Minister has said that a general
election will be called in good time
once a new party leader is elected. The
PM's resignation is said to have been
caused by Cabinet Minister Lord Arthur
Hampton's defection to the opposition
late last night, in protest at the PM's
continued support of MP for South-East
Gloucestershire Johnny Bull, who has
been subsequently arrested this morning
under terror charges along with his long-
standing friend Charlie Worthing, CEO
of tech company YouRent, and his wife,
the influencer Sienna Worthing. The IPO
of YouRent has been postponed. More to
follow on that story as information
becomes available.

Amy closed the tab. They'd spent the morning filing
paperwork and they'd likely spend the rest of the week doing
it too.

'Felix was working with Hampton all along. We saw the photo
from the fundraiser. He told Rosie he was talking to someone.
He always was going to shop them to counter-terror. Felix didn't
need to kill anyone. He just wanted to get back at Sienna and
take control of Rosie and her money.' Caius thought there was a
chance Felix would get a reduced sentence with a deal exchang-
ing info on Johnny Bull and the Worthings.

'Don't think about it,' Amy said.

'I think we deserve something exciting for lunch today,'
Matt said. He needed something to motivate himself through

all the paperwork they had yet to do. 'We've not had bánh mì in a while.'

'It's a god-tier sandwich,' Caius said.

'Oh good, I thought you were going to suggest pizza,' Amy said.

'We get it, Amy; you don't like pizza. It can't be your whole personality,' Matt said.

'Of course not, that's rugby tackling creeps. There's no room for any other facets of human nature once that's factored in.'

'Bánh mì it is then,' Caius said, opening his email. 'CPS have decided not to charge Rosie as there was coercion from Felix. I think the spyware did it.'

Caius's personal mobile phone went off. It was Hampton calling him. He ignored it. He didn't want to talk to him just yet.

His desk phone rang.

'Hello, is that Detective Beauchamp,' a woman asked.

'Yes, speaking.'

'This is Josephine Krige.'

'Hello, Josephine.'

'I wanted to thank you for solving it. The case. My mother's murder.' Caius could hear her grandchildren in the background.

'Not at all.'

'I also wanted to say that I knew who my grandfather was. And it wasn't Hitler or Himmler or any other member of that grim gang of death merchants. My grandfather was a British diplomat based in Berlin. He was married and his wife was devoutly religious and refused a divorce, that's why it was scandalous. His wife died two years later but they'd fallen out of love by that point.'

'Right.'

'I just assumed you were wondering about it. I can't bear the idea . . . I told Sienna the truth and I also told her what people had said at the time. I can't bear the idea that my daughter got so taken in by a nasty piece of gossip that she glamorised it and made it her life's work.' Josephine paused. Caius could hear the baby crying. 'I'm a terrible mother.'

Caius didn't say anything.

'Thank you again, detective.' She hung up the phone.

# 51

## Caius and Callie's Flat

'You need a holiday,' Callie said, watching Caius staring at his dinner in silence.

'Sorry, I always feel like a zombie at the end of a case. Especially if Arthur Hampton is involved.'

'He's not coming over again, is he?'

'No,' Caius said, taking a bite of ham hock pie. 'Having a professional cook is absolutely crazy.'

'Yeah, but this is so good.' Callie took a sip of water. 'I suppose it's like having a cleaner, right. You're buying your time back, so if the cook comes for an eight-hour stretch, batch cooks and makes two weeks' worth of food, then that couple of hundred quid has probably bought you a day back in time.'

'You're not wrong, but that's bougienomics.'

'What can I say, that's who I am now.'

'Where do you want to go on holiday?'

'Let's go to Florence for a few days. We can stay at the Pensione Bertolini and I can crack out a Baedeker and wander around churches. Someone might kiss me and I will repress how I feel about it.'

'I'll have a look at a hotel booking website,' Caius said, laughing. 'Do Baedeker guides still exist?'

'I doubt it. It's not even Lonely Planet any more. It's all fifteen-second videos. God, I sound old.' Callie put her knife and fork down. 'Your dad had a business proposition for me yesterday and I'm tempted by it.'

'Oh really,' Caius said. His father was determined to get him to move out there.

'So apparently your family has quite a lot of sheep.'

'Oh God. I don't like sheep. It's their eyes.'

'A whole flock of sheep and their fleeces are practically worthless.'

'But I'd pay more for real wool.'

'Exactly, so he was wondering with my degree and connections whether I could work out what to do with it to turn it into a profit. He's got all these outbuildings and a bit of cash to invest in machinery if the idea is solid.'

'I came across a brand of wool the other day that's hand-spun and dyed with foraged plants.'

'Hand spinning is too much work. I admire stuff like that but sometimes you need to accept that the Industrial Revolution happened.' Callie was imagining it all. 'I bet we could make dye from plants foraged from the parkland. That could work. Great marketing. It would be seasonal though. We could start by just selling balls to home knitters but if you could get enough wool and a consistent enough dye then I guess we could sell to luxury brands.'

'You know who's an expert in woollens?'

'Who?'

'Your dad.'

'Oh yeah, of course he is.' Callie frowned. She wasn't sure she wanted business advice from him. His expertise in fast fashion had made him a disgusting amount of money – her money – but she wanted something more simple, morally and aesthetically speaking. Artisanal, hand-dyed balls of English wool somehow felt like an act of atonement for the dirty money she wasn't turning down. 'He's invited himself to dinner with us next week, by the way.'

'All right.'

'I've booked a removal van for my workshop to move everything into a storage unit.'

'What day? I'll see if I can switch my shifts about.'

'Friday. I want to get out as quick as I can, and I've booked a suite at the Stafford Hotel in three weeks' time. A bit more understated than The Ritz.'

'I'll take the day off for that.'

# TUESDAY

# 52

## Heathrow Airport

'Here we are: Terminal 3,' Caius said, pulling his car over to the drop-off bay. It was still dark out.

'Dad, we're here,' said Marcus, turning around in his seat. 'Dad.'

Caius's grandfather woke with a start.

'Oh my God,' Caius said.

'He sleeps like the dead and wakes like the undead,' Marcus said.

'Who died?' asked Caius's grandfather.

'No one, Dad, we're at the airport. Caius, get the cases out and I'll see if they've got a wheelchair we can use.'

'Sure.' Caius got out the car and opened the boot. Took out the cases and put them on the side of the drop-off bay. He then opened the car door on his grandfather's side and helped him out. His father was on his way back with a porter pushing a wheelchair.

'I'm proud of you,' Caius's grandfather said, while holding on to his arm.

'I'm proud of you too.'

'I want you to have these.' Caius's grandfather gave him a small box. 'Open it later.'

'Thank you.'

'You ready, Dad?' Marcus asked.

'Yes,' he said, getting into the wheelchair.

'Don't forget your hat,' Caius said, reaching into the back of the car and taking out the panama that had been on the seat next to his grandfather. Callie had replaced the band especially for the trip.

'I've never left the house without a hat,' Caius's grandfather said as the porter wheeled him off towards check-in.

'Bon voyage,' Caius called after him.

'See you later, kid,' Marcus said, patting Caius on the arm.

'Are you all right?' Caius asked his father, who for a sturdy no-nonsense builder looked like he might cry.

'Fine, thanks,' Marcus blinked the emotion away. 'Did he just give you his medals?'

'I don't know what's in the box. I've not opened it yet.'

'He always said he wanted you to have them when he died,' Marcus said, following his father with his eyes. 'You need to get moving or they'll charge you.'

Marcus headed into the terminal and Caius drove away.

# 53

## Clapham Junction

Caius waited outside McDonald's. That very particular stink didn't sit well with him so early in the morning. He'd grabbed a decent coffee from an Italian cafe further down the road and took a sip from his reusable cup as he perched opposite Nana Boateng's office above a bespoke lampshade consultancy. Caius had worn his Barbour that brisk spring morning and he almost blended in perfectly with the signet-ringed Henrys and pearl-earringed Carolines trotting off to the Northern line and their inconceivably well-paid and yet indescribable jobs in the City. Almost. He watched as a smartly dressed woman arrived and opened the shiny black door. It had a gleaming brass plaque:

Boateng & Smith
Chartered Accountants
Established 2012

Caius finished his coffee and put his cup away in his bag. Alan appeared beside him.

'Sorry about the early start. I've been up since 4 a.m. so thought we may as well push through,' Caius said.

'That's all right. I've never felt more alive than on a packed commuter train,' Alan responded. Caius thought he looked gaunter than the other week. 'Shall we?' Alan asked as he crossed the road.

Caius rang the intercom. Nana Boateng buzzed them in. They

traipsed up the recently vacuumed stairs to her equally tidy office.

'How may I help you?' Nana asked. She had the faintest hint of a Ghanaian accent.

'Hello again, Nana,' Alan said.

A short burst of air leapt from her mouth as she struggled to compose herself before a look of quiet resolution settled on her face.

'I thought I might hear from you again. Little Rupert has been in the papers.'

'He has indeed,' Alan said.

'Little Rupert?' Caius asked himself out loud. He tried to imagine him as a cherubic child but failed, seeing only a smug, cretinous lump of snot. Alan looked at him pointedly.

Alan took the seat opposite her. 'I, we, just have some questions about what happened, Nana. You're a good person, I know you are, and if you're anything like me this nasty business has been eating away at you for the last twenty-odd years too. They closed the case, put money in my bank account and threatened to frame me for corruption if I spoke out.' Alan settled back into his chair and fell silent for a moment. The office's strip lighting made him look greyer. 'I'm an old man now, Nana, I've not got long. I need to know the truth even if it's too late to do anything about it.'

'Poor Alethea, she was a nice woman,' Nana said, fiddling with the cross on the gold chain round her neck. 'Who knew the British were so violent? Towards each other . . .'

'I know you've said all this before,' Caius began, he looked over at Alan who nodded at him to continue, 'but what exactly did you do for Alethea Beauchamp?'

'I was what they call a mother's help. I cleaned for her. I would pick little Rupert up from nursery and occasionally babysit in the evenings. She was lovely. Very clever. Always doing puzzles. I was studying in the day and my work fitted around my classes. My uncle was heavily involved in the church back home and her uncle was an Anglican bishop. That's how they knew each other and how I got the job.'

'Did you know why she was getting a divorce?'

'I, um, well . . .'

'Please, Nana, it's important.'

'I think she had a boyfriend. There was a box of condoms in the bathroom. I think they used to meet there, at the mews where she died. I never saw him. I used to clean that house once a week, but no one had properly lived there for a while. She rented it out sometimes. I cleaned the house off the King's Road with the pretty garden.'

'Thurstone?' Caius asked. It had of course now fallen into his grandfather's possession.

'Yes, that's it. She usually lived there with her husband, but Alethea and little Rupert had moved into the mews house on the day she died. I don't think Mr Beauchamp knew anything was wrong. I thought he really loved her.'

'I read your statement, Nana. It was extremely matter-of-fact.' Caius watched her shift her weight about in the seat. 'Did someone tell you what to say?'

She paused. Took a deep breath and made the decision to tell the truth after all these years. 'Yes.'

'What really happened that morning?'

'I turned up to clean as I normally would.' She looked relieved to be telling them. 'Alethea was very neat, very particular. She liked me to come in early. I got to the mews and there was a blond man stood outside cradling little Rupert. He was still asleep in his little pyjamas. The blond man told me not to go inside. Another man appeared in a big fancy car moments later and they talked to each other in a language I didn't understand. They had an argument I think, the first man was distraught; the second man asked me to come with him into the house. He was very polite, but I was scared to say no to him. He wiped the door handle with his jacket sleeve and told me to touch the doorknob into the kitchen. That I had to say that I was the one who found her like that. He wouldn't let me go into the kitchen and see her, but he asked me to call the police to say that I'd found her dead. He stood next to me to make sure I said the right things. Then he took me outside again and made the first man give me Rupert to hold. He didn't want to hand him over. He wanted to take him with him, but the other man started talking in the foreign language again. The second man told me what to say to you, to say that they weren't there, that they'd look after me if I did what they said. They got in the car and drove away as if nothing had happened just before you arrived, detective.'

'What did the two men look like?'

'English-looking. Blond. In their twenties maybe thirties. They were wearing tuxedos. I can't remember any more, it was so long ago. They looked alike, but so do all the English.'

Caius took out his phone and showed her a picture of Arthur Hampton to which she nodded. 'That's the first man, the one who was there with Rupert when I arrived.'

'And did they look after you?' Alan asked.

Nana nodded. She looked ashamed. 'They gave me £5,000 in cash.'

'I see. Nana, did you get a phone call from anyone about the money?'

'No. The second man turned up at my flat the next week with it, thanked me for what I had done, apologised for any inconvenience they may have caused, and told me not to speak to anyone about what I had seen.' Nana bit her lip. 'I'm not in trouble, am I?'

'Of course not,' Alan said, slowly rising from his chair. 'How's business? You've got a very nice office here.'

'It's good.'

'Excellent. Don't worry, Nana. No one will ever know that we were here.'

Caius and Alan left Nana's offices and headed to a cafe. They took a seat and ordered tea. Alan ordered a bacon sandwich too; Caius declined.

'Did we learn anything useful?' Alan asked.

'I think so,' Caius said, nodding. 'You were threatened, and she wasn't. I think you and Nana dealt with different people with different motivations.'

'Nana spoke to that Arthur Hampton chap who designated Rupert his heir as his biological dad.'

'Alethea left her husband for him. The brothers Hampton took poor Crispin Beauchamp to their club, broke the news to him that his marriage was over and that he wasn't Rupert's father. Poor Cousin Crispin is distraught and probably a bit wet behind the ears, gets drunk before being carted off to bed. Arthur Hampton arrives back at his and Alethea's love nest to find her murdered. He takes Rupert and calls his big brother from a nearby payphone. His brother turns up, sorts it all out. Makes him give Rupert to Nana so no one knows they're connected, and they disappear. His brother has colon cancer and is the bloke I think you saw in hospital. Nana was paid off not to mention that the Hamptons were there at all or even connected to it. You were paid off to stop the investigation.'

'What are you going to do next?'

373

'Go through your papers again and try and work out who had a motive.'

★  ★  ★

Caius had returned home to the flat and the chores he'd been neglecting. He did the washing-up, swept the kitchen floor and ironed his work shirts. He sometimes found that doing menial tasks freed a bit of his brain up so that whatever was bothering him would resolve itself. It hadn't worked this time. He'd tried tidying up, but Callie's work materials had started to make their way to the flat and he didn't want to disturb the pile of netting on the dining room table. He flopped onto the sofa, but he didn't feel like watching anything. He'd read the first two thirds of *Romance in Frigid Temperatures* but couldn't bring himself to finish it. Truly bored, and only ready for the most brain-rotting material, he suddenly felt compelled to reach under the coffee table and picked up the copy of *Tatler* that had caused him so much bother and flicked to the offending article.

> Tragic heart-throb, and one of London's most eligible bachelors, Sir Rupert Beauchamp is a Beauchamp no more. The former baronet, whose ex-girlfriend Clemency O'Hara was killed last summer in what has been ruled as a case of misadventure, was officially designated the heir of Lord Arthur Hampton MP, the younger son of the 16th Duke of Shropshire, after a DNA test confirmed his parentage. Following recent modernisation of the laws around the inheritance of aristocratic titles it was revealed that Rupert is the son of Lord Arthur and the

late Alethea Beauchamp, née de Courcy. Lord Arthur has been married since 2014 to his long-term partner Gideon Jeremy Stark-Howe. Rupert commenting on his change of name said, 'I'm delighted to make my parentage official. My father has always been an important part of my life and we have a very close relationship.'

The Beauchamp baronetcy has now passed to Sir Caius Beauchamp, a gallant British-Jamaican RAF veteran who flew Hurricanes during the Battle of Britain. His son Marcus is a property developer and his grandson, also Caius, a detective in the Metropolitan Police, is rumoured to be connected with celebrated society milliner Calliope Foster, the daughter of former MP Peter Simpson.


'Did you know that Hampton's husband Jeremy's first name is actually Gideon?' Caius asked Callie, who'd just stepped through the door holding a missed package she'd gone to collect from the Royal Mail depot.

'I quite like Gideon as a name. More bullyable than Jeremy though,' she said.

'What's in your package?'

'I don't know, but the box smells divine.' Callie started opening the box, revealing a scented terracotta pomegranate.

'Oh, I forgot I'd ordered that.' Caius felt funny. He'd ordered it from Italy after interviewing Sienna for the first time. 'Do you like it?'

'I love it.' Callie took a ceramic dish out from under the sink. She'd bought it on eBay a few weeks ago and had been desperate for it to have a purpose. 'It's heavenly.'

'Gideon. G-I-D-E-O-N. Fuck.' Caius went into the bedroom and took out Alan's folder. He flipped through until he found a crime scene picture. It was of the blood-smeared document from Alethea's solicitor writing to Crispin about the divorce. He took his phone out. 'Hello, Arthur . . .'

# 54

## Caius and Callie's Flat

Caius's doorbell rang. He went to open it and Arthur and Rupert Hampton were standing on the doorstep. The sun had set and the street lamps had come on. Caius locked eyes with Rupert who couldn't understand why the fuck he had to be there. Caius suppressed the need to punch Rupert in the face. Matt and Amy were discreetly waiting outside in case anything went down.

'Please come in,' Caius said, leading them into the living space.

'Good evening, Caius,' Hampton said, moving down the hallway. He shot Rupert a final warning to behave.

'You have one drink with this cretin and now you're on first-name terms. Why are we even here?'

'Rupert!' Hampton said. He looked a bit peeved to be there too, but he thought that if Caius was telling him it was important then he would be wise to listen. 'You said it was urgent.'

'And that we both needed to be here,' Rupert said, flopping onto one of Caius's armchairs. He took out a small jewellery box from his jacket pocket and conspicuously placed it on the coffee table. He surveyed the room, languishing as he thought of something awful to say. 'This is less of a damp-riddled hovel than I expected.'

'Rupert!' Hampton scowled at him. They'd had a chat in the car about not saying things precisely like this.

'Well, my grandfather is a baronet, after all.' Caius sat on the sofa. 'Most of the decorating choices were Callie. She has a wonderful eye.'

Rupert didn't respond. He was short of missiles to throw at

Caius after his change in status, and more than a little pissed off that Callie had chosen Caius over him. He'd spent a whole session with his psychotherapist trying to work out where he'd gone wrong with her and was deeply uncomfortable sitting amongst the domesticity that she had denied him. He took his phone out and drafted a message to Callie asking her out for a drink 'as friends'. It remained on one tick. He knew she'd blocked him, and he knew there was now going to be a whole other session devoted to why no one would love him.

'My brother has taken a turn so we're all heading over there now. Jeremy is in the car waiting. We can't stay for long.'

'I'm sorry. My timing is appalling.' Caius picked up the file that Alan had given him from the coffee table and held it close. 'Call me in the week and we can arrange something.'

'What's in the folder? Is this your bonus crime?' Hampton held his hand out expectantly. He was here so he may as well find out. Caius reluctantly handed it to Hampton. The colour drained from Hampton's cheeks as he read it. 'Rupert, go wait in the car.'

'What is it?' Rupert asked.

'With all respect, I think Rupert should hear this.'

'No—' Hampton began to shout before taking a deep breath and calmly turning to Rupert. 'Please wait outside.'

'All right. I'll go sit in the car with Jeremy like a child.' Rupert got up and sulked out of the room like a dog and left down the hallway. The door slammed shut.

'Rupert doesn't know what happened, and you aren't to tell him. You understand that, don't you? He isn't stable enough, not yet. He regressed when Nell got engaged. It's been tough. He still thinks his mother died in a car crash.' Caius went to take the folder back, but Hampton kept hold of it. 'Where did you get this? There was no investigation.'

'My old DCI worked on it when he was younger. He's dying too and wanted me to see if I could do anything. I wanted to tell you both before I make the arrest.'

Hampton stopped breathing and stared at him. Taking a minute of pure silence to comprehend. 'You know who did it?'

'Yes, but I just want to be sure of some of the details.'

'Let's go into it now, quickly.' Hampton, who Caius had only ever observed to be calm and collected, was almost frantic. 'You can arrest them while we're visiting my brother at the hospice.'

'Well, that's it . . .'

'What do you mean?'

'I'll go from the top. You were wearing black tie, so you were with Crispin Beauchamp that evening.'

'Some things have to be settled like gentlemen.'

'Alethea was murdered when she was entertaining. You must have realised that you would have known who did it. Alethea let the killer in and poured them a glass of wine. She was friends with them, she knew them well, as must you.'

'Actually, we should probably leave it there for today,' Hampton said, getting up from the armchair with his arm outstretched. 'We'll talk in a few days.'

'Why were you late back to the mews?' Caius asked Hampton. He needed to tell him now that he'd started. 'Blind drunk, Crispin Beauchamp was put to bed at 11 p.m. Yet you didn't turn up until early the next morning.'

Hampton sat back down perched on the edge of the seat. 'My brother and I kept drinking until 3 a.m., then we sat in an all-night greasy spoon off the Strand eating egg and chips trying to sober up.' Hampton acquiesced and crumpled into the chair. He'd buried it for so long. The pain bubbling upwards. 'I got a taxi about 5 a.m. My brother is more abstemious than me and he drove back to his flat. It was the early nineties, no one gave a fuck about drink driving then. I rang him from a payphone after I um . . .'

'Did you stop the investigation?'

'No, I didn't. Of course I didn't. I couldn't have even if I wanted to. I was just a solicitor back then. Do you really think that this hasn't plagued me for the last twenty-five years? That I don't wake up in the middle of the night haunted by the idea that if I'd had fewer glasses of port and more coffee and gone back at 11 p.m., then it wouldn't have happened?'

'This is your chance to rectify that.' Caius shook his head in despair. 'Why was she drinking water, Arthur? And why was the investigation stopped before the autopsy? They didn't want it coming out that Alethea was pregnant. I think they specifically didn't want you to know that. They didn't want to hurt you even more. That was why she was killed. You wouldn't leave her if she was pregnant with your child, again.'

Hampton took a deep breath.

'Did Alethea like word games. Puzzles?'

'She loved crosswords. She tried to teach me how to do the cryptic ones, but I don't think that way,' Hampton said.

Caius took a picture from the file. 'The last thing Alethea did was to try to tell you who killed her. She touched certain letters with her own blood to tell you. Look at the letters she smeared in blood from "Proceedings": o-e-d-i-n-g. Gideon.'

Hampton could not cry. It had been successfully brutalised out of him. 'She refused to call him Jeremy. She'd known him for so long, since they were children.' Hampton put his hand to his mouth as he pushed his feelings down. 'We'd had a casual thing on and off for years, but I broke up with him for good once Alethea had made her mind up to finally leave Crispin.' He looked down at his wedding ring. 'Did I always know?'

The front door opened and slammed in quick succession. Caius shot up and after Rupert, who had been listening from the hallway this whole time. He opened the door to find Amy running up the path, trying to stop Rupert who dodged her and sprinted towards the parked Land Rover they'd arrived in. 'Jeremy's sat in the car. Matt's trying to get him to come out.'

'Rupert, Rupert!' Caius called, and grabbed hold of his arm, trying to tear him away. 'Hold on! Calm down. I'm going to arrest him.'

'Get out of the fucking car, Jeremy,' Rupert yelled as he yanked Caius backwards. Surprised, Caius fell back over the kerb, and landed awkwardly on his wrist.

'Jesus Christ,' Caius cursed as Amy helped him up from the pavement.

Arthur and Jeremy looked at each other and in that moment Jeremy knew that Arthur knew what he'd done to keep him.

'Jeremy, get out of the car,' Matt shouted as he tried to stop Rupert from yanking the car door off.

'Open the door,' Rupert demanded, rushing forward again and out of Matt's grasp. He started clawing at the handle as Jeremy turned the key in the ignition.

Jeremy slowly pulled away from the kerb. Rupert dashed in front of the car and stood in the middle of the road like an unconvincing messiah with his arms outstretched. They stared at each other.

Jeremy accelerated.

# 55

## Royal Hampstead Free Hospital

Callie had vacated the flat as Caius had asked and gone to the pub at the bottom of their road. She'd taken a novel that she'd seen practically everyone reading on the tube – it had a fluorescent pink cover, terminally morose heroine and a glorious amount of painful introspection – and ordered a glass of Merlot while she waited for Caius to give the all-clear. Callie put her book down to tell a man at the bar who was waiting to interrupt her that she didn't care what he thought of the writer and that she'd never read *Infinite Jest* when a blaze of blue lights flashed past the pub. She left her wine and her book and the awful man and his unsolicited opinions and dashed out of the pub, horrified to see that the blue lights had stopped outside their flat. She ran over to Caius and sat on the kerb with him until the ambulance came. At the hospital, she handed him a Snickers that she'd just bought him from a vending machine.

'You'd think hospital vending machines would sell fruit, wouldn't you?' Caius said, passing the Snickers back to Callie who opened it for him. He'd just got off the phone with Alan and told him what had happened. Alan then invited him to his funeral. He reckoned it would be in a few short months from now.

'Do you think Rupert's going to make it?' Callie asked, watching a distressed small child with a broken leg go to be X-rayed.

'I don't know,' Caius said. He didn't, but he didn't want to say it out loud. They'd scraped him off the road and into an ambulance as a formality. 'Talk to me.'

'What about?'

'Anything. Absolutely anything?'

'I'm not taking my dad's money. It's filthy. I saw a thing today about the conditions in those factories.'

'Fair enough. I've got dirty money enough for the both of us.'

'I'm going to ask him to give it back.'

'Who to?'

'The workers.'

'I like that you're blossoming into your communist era. You look lovely in red.'

Caius's phone began to ring.

'Hello. No, I'm with Callie. I've hurt my wrist and I'm getting an X-ray. Oh . . .' He fell silent. After a minute he said goodbye.

'Everything all right?'

'He's dead.'

'Rupert?' Callie, despite disliking him in life, now felt sorry for Rupert in death.

'My grandfather. He got off the plane, refused a wheelchair because he wanted to step foot on Jamaican soil one last time and collapsed.'

'Oh, Caius. I'm so sorry.' She stroked his hair.

'He had a good innings.'

'He was one hell of a batsman.'

'He knocked us all for six.'

Matt appeared. Caius looked up at him. Matt gave him the look that said they'd declared Rupert dead. Matt sat down next to them.

'Well . . .'

'Oh my God,' Callie exclaimed. She started to cry.

Caius looked up at the door to the waiting room and saw Arthur Hampton looking at him from the corridor. He stood up and faced him. Hampton seemed empty as he watched the three of them. Callie looked up and saw him. Rising as if to hug him. He turned and left.

'I swore on the River Styx I'd get him, and I did,' Caius said.

# TWO WEEKS LATER

## 56

## St Clement Danes Church, the Strand

More of a fuss was made for Caius's grandfather's funeral than he would have probably liked. There was even an article on the *MailOnline*. However, his grandfather would very much have liked that the Jamaican High Commissioner had turned up. It turned out that Caius senior had been the last surviving pilot from his squadron so the service was being held at the RAF church St Clement Danes at the bottom of the Strand. It was a curious mixture of moments of stoical English establishment reflection and a hurricane of Caribbean grief. One of Marcus's cousins on his mum's side sang 'Amazing Grace' and nearly lifted the pews off the ground. Marcus was too distraught to really say anything to a crowd of mourners, so Caius did it instead. He'd made reference to his grandfather's wartime record, 'a teenager in a tin can fighting the greatest tyranny we have ever faced', and his life in Britain, a country that he'd been willing to give everything to but wouldn't always do the same for him.

★   ★   ★

The wake was held in a private room at The Savoy. Marcus said he didn't care about the expense and that his dad would've got a kick out of it. Waiters carried canapés and bowl food as well as flutes of champagne around on trays. Caius senior wouldn't like anyone to have had a dry mouth. The Jamaicans had turned out in force, as had Bridget's extended family. The consensus between both island nations was that it was a shame there was no music, not much of a party atmosphere, but they understood: the Beauchamps were English now. Caius saw a man trying to make eye contact with him. He was tall and thin, with grey hair and green eyes. His suit fit him perfectly. Caius smiled at him, and he came over. Caius broke away.

'I'm so sorry for your loss,' said the man.

'Thank you.'

'I saw the announcement in *The Times* this morning that your family are donating a Turner painting to the nation in your grandfather's honour.'

'Yes, he was keen to share his good fortune.'

'Hunderby,' he said, stretching out his hand. 'I work with Arthur. He sends his regards. He would've liked to come today, only his brother . . .'

'Of course. I've been meaning to call.' Caius had truly meant to. As much as he hated Rupert, he felt responsible for his death. He'd cursed him to Hades, after all. Matt kept reassuring him that he didn't make Rupert do anything, but Caius regretted not seeing Hampton privately. He knew that Rupert was a loose cannon.

'He doesn't blame you, you know. Rupert was also going to be Rupert right to the end.' Hunderby took out a business card. 'You should call me next week.'

Caius took the card from him and Hunderby graciously bade farewell.

'Who was that?' Callie asked, appearing at his side.

'One of Hampton's associates.' He turned the card over before putting it away in his pocket. He hated himself for it, but he knew he would call when his curiosity got the better of him. 'Rupert gave me his old Beauchamp signet ring. He left it that night on the coffee table. I'd seen him playing with it the first time I met him.'

Callie squeezed his good arm. 'The Sunday I went round to Frithsden before the flight . . . your grandfather pulled me aside and told me that I needed to look after you.'

'Yeah, I'm fairly useless.'

'No, that wasn't what he meant.'

'You want me to come spin yarn on the farm, don't you?'

'I don't want you to get hurt.'

'Me neither.' Caius looked down at the cast on his wrist.

# Acknowledgements

Tremendous thanks to my wonderful family and dear friends. Thank you to the wonderful team at Faber. Thank you Libby Marshall, Aisling Brennan, Phoebe Williams, Hannah Turner and Rachael Williamson for your continued support. Thank you to my brilliant agent Jon Wood and everyone at RCW.